WILL SAVE THE GALAXY FOR FOOD

PRAISE FOR
YAHTZEE CROSHAW

"Hilariously insightful."
—Slashdot

"The first legitimate breakout hit from the
gaming community in recent memory."
—Boing Boing

"Yahtzee consistently makes me laugh, and even though I dig computer and
electronic games, he has cross-genre appeal to anyone who enjoys a sharp wit,
unique sense of humor and plenty of originality—not purely gaming fans."
—The Future Buzz

"*Jam* is as gruesome as it is ridiculous, but man is it ever an enjoyable read."
—The Fandom Post

"[Croshaw] knows exactly how to make characters that are utterly believable
and furiously compelling—often in the worst kind of ways."
—Destructoid

"*Mogworld* is a huge success, and a fantastic debut . . .
[Croshaw has] used his knowledge of video games to make a novel that
perfectly satirizes video game fantasy-lore and culture, while providing some
refreshingly original and interesting characters, a fully-developed mythology,
all wrapped up in Yahtzee's trademark humor. Any gamer who has wasted
hours, days, weeks, months, possibly even years on *World of Warcraft*
should feel right at home with *Mogworld*'s excellent satire."
—Game Informer

"*Mogworld* is a triumph of storytelling and humor that just
so happens to be perfectly keyed in to the wild world of video games.
I cannot stress enough, however, that it can also be enjoyed by those
who have never logged in or picked up a controller in their life."
—Joystick Division

WILL SAVE THE GALAXY FOR FOOD

YAHTZEE CROSHAW

Dark Horse Books
Milwaukie, OR

Cover design by David Nestelle
Cover illustration by E. M. Gist

Published by Dark Horse Books
A division of Dark Horse Comics, Inc.
10956 SE Main Street
Milwaukie, OR 97222

DarkHorse.com
International Licensing: (503) 905-2377

Library of Congress Cataloging-in-Publication Data

Names: Croshaw, Yahtzee, author. | Gist, E. M., illustrator.
Title: Will save the galaxy for food / Yahtzee Croshaw ; illustrated by EM
  Gist.
Description: Milwaukie, OR : Dark Horse Books, 2017.
Identifiers: LCCN 2016045698 | ISBN 9781506701653 (paperback)
Subjects: LCSH: Science fiction. | Humorous fiction. | BISAC: FICTION /
  Science Fiction / Adventure. | FICTION / Science Fiction / General.
Classification: LCC PR9619.4.C735 W55 2017 | DDC 823/.92—dc23
LC record available at https://lccn.loc.gov/2016045698

Special thanks to Daniel Chabon, Cardner Clark, and Annie Gullion

First edition: February 2017
ISBN 978-1-50670-165-3

Printed in the United States of America

10 9 8 7 6 5 4 3 2 1

Mike Richardson President and Publisher • Neil Hankerson Executive Vice President • Tom Weddle Chief Financial Officer • Randy Stradley Vice President of Publishing • Matt Parkinson Vice President of Marketing • David Scroggy Vice President of Product Development • Dale LaFountain Vice President of Information Technology • Cara Niece Vice President of Production and Scheduling • Nick McWhorter Vice President of Media Licensing • Mark Bernardi Vice President of Digital and Book Trade Sales • Ken Lizzi General Counsel • Dave Marshall Editor in Chief • Davey Estrada Editorial Director • Scott Allie Executive Senior Editor • Chris Warner Senior Books Editor • Cary Grazzini Director of Specialty Projects • Lia Ribacchi Art Director • Vanessa Todd Director of Print Purchasing • Matt Dryer Director of Digital Art and Prepress • Sarah Robertson Director of Product Sales • Michael Gombos Director of International Publishing and Licensing

CHAPTER I

I MASHED THE button to open the port-side observation shutters just as day broke on the planet below. An orange crescent slashed brilliantly across the blackness, and the sleeping world was gradually unveiled, the rising sunlight spreading like glittering marmalade across the toast of God.

"The planet Cantrabargid," I announced. "Homeworld of the Zuviron people. A proud and noble warrior race. When I aided their struggle against the enslaved cyborg army of the Malmind, I watched their fighting men sweep across the plains like a rolling storm cloud. The clash of sword on cybernetic implant was deafening, all night and into morning, until the fields were ankle deep in blood and transmission fluid. For it was their very future that they were fighting for that day."

"Bor-ing," said the cabin intercom, in a voice several years shy of doing descent. All the remaining air in my lungs left in an irritated blast.

"Ronald!" continued the intercom, in an older voice. "It is not boring! Sit up straight!"

"I'm boooooored," said young Ronald. I could faintly hear expensive trainers rhythmically kicking part of my ship's interior. "I wanna go back to Luny Land."

"Come on, Ronald," said a new, tired, female voice. "We've had your holiday; it's our turn now. Don't spoil it for your father."

"Yes, stop spoiling it for your mother!" said the father. "Look! Just think of all the millions of years of history below you."

"It's just a planeeet," whined Ronald. "It's just an orange planet in lots of space. I've seen space."

"It's . . . not terribly interesting, is it, dear," said the mother.

"You haven't seen space! Not real space!" said the intercom's increasingly flustered adult male voice. "This is space from the Golden Age of star piloting, you know. You won't see any of this if you only ever use those bloody teleport holes."

"It's just blaaack," said Ronald.

"But we could have seen it just as well from the observatory, dear," said the mother. "And we wouldn't be paying fifty euroyen an hour to someone who, frankly, I find very suspect."

I'd had enough. "This is your captain speaking," I said, in my bored-professional voice. "All passengers, please be informed that the cabin intercom is two-way if you haven't pressed the Disable Speaker button."

Promptly, the speaker made a scratchy little thumping noise. "Oh, well done, Janice," said the father's voice. "What on earth must he think of us now?"

"I do find it very suspect that he didn't mention that earlier," sniffed Janice.

"Give him a break. You know it's been tough for star pilots since quantum tunneling. Leave the rest of your sandwich under the seat. He'll probably still eat that."

"This is your captain speaking again," I added. "All passengers, please be informed that the button is a bit sticky and you need to press it quite hard."

The following silence was eventually broken by a cry of "I'M BOOOR—," cut off by another, louder thump.

I swung my feet up onto the control panel and leaned back. The heel of my shoe knocked the self-destruct lever. Not that it mattered; it hadn't been working since at least last year, when I'd been in a rather dark mood and given it a try.

I stared sullenly at the now fully illuminated Cantrabargid through the forward viewing port, a strong taste of bitterness pooling in the back of my mouth. Doints, I thought. Plying tourist doints. And Prince Ronald, the tracciest little bracket of Dointland. Him I hated most of all, because he'd realized in five seconds what had taken me a month of post-war R&R: that Cantrabargid was a very boring planet. Yeah, it livened up when you were fighting alongside the spearhead of a major battle for the freedom of the people, but once freed, those people were awful conversationalists. If it wasn't about swords, they just didn't want to know.

After a token orbit around the planet—long enough to milk my hourly rate as much as I could—I set a return course for the trebuchet gate that led back to the solar system. I took my usual route back through the asteroid belt, in the hopes that a bit of close dodging and weaving would give my passengers the excitement they craved, or at least shut them up. The autonav would prevent any actual collision. Ostensibly. It was past warranty, and I had resolved not to think about it.

We turned, placing the light of Cantrabargid's larger sun behind us. It was then, as I did a close sweep across a large asteroid, that I noticed that my ship appeared to have two shadows. I gave my sensor unit a kick, causing it to briefly whir into life and display a blip on the screen. The atmosphere in the cockpit became a lot less boring very fast. The blip had a pirate signature. And it was closing in.

I threw myself upright, took the control stick in one hand, and palmed the intercom button with the other. "Attention passengers!" I said urgently. "We are being engaged by a pirate vessel. There is no need to panic. The doors to the passenger cabin have been sealed. Remain inside and brace yourselves for evasive action."

After about a quarter second of bracing time I slammed the control stick to the left, banking toward the asteroid, and took momentary pleasure in the distant sound of a ten-year-old body being thrown from a seat. The pirate ship was prepared for this, and its boosters came on.

I could see it in the rear view. A smaller vessel, a standard sort of interstellar clipper modified for aggression and spray-painted with colorful imagery like a biker's sleeve tattoo. Along with the usual assortment of highly illegal weaponry, the pirates had attached a great many cosmetic spikes and fins that didn't do much more than give me a slight aerodynamic advantage.

I'd have to make the most of it. I sped toward the asteroid with the front thrusters simmering, firing them at the last second before impact and making a hard ninety-degree turn. But the pirates weren't falling for that old trick, and pursued me across the rocky surface.

They hadn't fired. Not even a warning shot. Even bullets have value, and you might not need to waste one if your target is on full thrusters ten feet away from uneven terrain. The pirate ship made little feints in my direction, trying to make me flinch myself to death. But I knew they wouldn't risk an actual collision.

So I feinted back, to call their bluff, and they withdrew just far enough for me to make my move. I pitched my ship until her left nacelle was practically scraping the ground, then reached up and pulled the special lever on the autonav. The one set up to fire off a complicated series of programmed movements designed to closely resemble a ship careening out of control.

I clung to the seat of the control chair with all my available limbs as the ship pitched and barrel rolled. Something large and fleshy thudded against the wall dividing the cockpit from the passenger cabin. Red lights flickered across every readout, and the tortured engines were making every loose panel on the ship vibrate with a rattling scream. The ship's movement described a wide arc, almost completing half an orbit around the asteroid, until I broke line of sight with the pirates.

I shoved the second lever, and a colossal bang rang out from the ship's rear as the luggage compartment depressurized at the exact same moment that the rear thrusters belched a cosmetic ball of fire.

A credulous person, which thankfully most pirates are, would assume that my ship had crashed into the rock and been destroyed. They would be surprised, probably exchange a high-five, then leisurely come around to loot the wreckage. That would buy me enough time to quietly move out of sight. They'd notice my absence, realize my ruse and assume that I'd escaped, angrily leaving the scene with half-hearted ideas of pursuit. Meanwhile, I'd be in silent mode, hugging the far side of the asteroid and waiting for the engine to cool.

I let myself relax, and hit the cabin intercom again. "Crisis averted, everyone," I reported. "I managed to shake them off with some fancy flying. Not, I'm afraid, without loss, because I did have to jettison the luggage compartment to make a quicker escape. I'll put you in touch with my insurance company, but you should just be glad we weren't captured. Seriously, these pirates . . . I'd tell you some stories, but kids are present. Anyway, we'll wait a few minutes for the engines to cool, then head back to Ritsuko. Hope it'll be a tour to remember."

I'd made the speech plenty of times, but it was always exhausting. I counted a full minute, enjoying a silent moment to myself before the inevitable next step. Then I leaned toward the external communicator, which was quietly chirping the reedy electronic version of "La Cucaracha" I'd chosen for a ringtone, and hit Receive Call.

"Heeeey, English!" came a heavily accented voice.

"Mark," I identified aloud. "Where's your brother?"

"I'm here too English!" came a virtually identical voice from slightly farther away. "Nice performance. Greatest show off Earth, yah?"

Den and Mark. Not actually brothers, and those weren't their real names; they were just inordinately proud of having been born in the minuscule Danish immigrant community in Ritsuko City. I say *community;* it was one maisonette above a bakery.

"What the hell, guys?" I said. "You did me two weeks ago. I'm going to get a reputation."

"Not our fault you're keeping using the same routes, English."

"Whatever. You pick up the luggage?"

"Yah. She's a slim picker, though. How much they paying you?"

"Two licorice allsorts and a kick in the doints. 'Cos I'm obviously going to just tell you that, aren't I, you grabby brackets."

"Calm down, English. You could just take them hostage, yah? Cross the Black. Make the smart career change."

"Oh, sure. 'Cos life's so much better now you've crossed the Black, isn't it? Living off scavenge and straight to jail if you ever touch down. How's the dog-food diet?"

"As we are keeping saying, English, the labels fell off the cans. And we only ate five or six. Tasted better than the bumholes of tourists, which are the staple of your diet is my point. Ciaoing for now."

"Wait." I rubbed my eyes. "Seriously, guys, could you please just lay off me for a while? I can't afford trac like this every plying fortnight."

"Hey! We're making it more exciting for your cash cows in there. If you finding us such repellant company you could find some other planets to be reminiscing about. We don't have to be performing these little skits for you, you know. There's other work out here we can be getting it on with."

I wasn't sure what they meant by *other work,* but I didn't care enough. "Yeah, whatever. Denmark wasn't even a real country, you plystains. It was just Germany's little hat."

They'd already hung up. I slumped back, basking in that familiar defeated feeling. Finding different locations to reminisce about was easier said than done. Like most star pilots, I had more than a couple, but Cantrabargid's system was in convenient flying range and my fuel budget couldn't—

"Captain?" said the cabin intercom.

My gaze flew to the speaker. The light was on. It had been on for some time. My blood froze over. Jagged chunks of ice dug into the walls of my heart.

"Remember?" said the voice of Ronald's mother nastily. "The button gets a little bit sticky?"

CHAPTER 2

THE USUAL ROUTINE upon touching down in Ritsuko City Spaceport was to go out into the cabin, open the airlock, walk the passengers to the exit ramp, bow and scrape, try not to cringe too much, maybe recommend a few other star pilots to spread some of the good fortune around and hopefully earn a favor. On this occasion, that didn't feel like a good idea.

Instead, I stayed in the cockpit, hugging myself and staring at the ceiling, only remembering to remotely open the airlock after someone thumped the passenger-cabin wall and made an angry promise of legal action.

I waited an amount of time long enough for the tourists to disembark and exit the landing bay, waited it a second time just in case, then recovered my frayed cardboard sign from the gap between my chair and the wall. I left the shuttle by the cockpit escape pod hatch, which led directly outside. The escape pod itself had been sold some time ago to pay off the safety inspector, which was probably ironic in some way.

Halfway across the large and near-deserted landing bay I looked back at my ship, the *Neverdie*. At the sleek, streamlined chassis that had been beaten back into shape after a thousand close calls. At the weathered paint job, once brilliant red, now a dismal maroon. At the name that was probably also going to become ironic soon enough.

Because even the best-case scenario was coming out of this looking rather toxic and threadbare. At worst, this was jail time. This was collaborating with pirates. Ritsuko City had a zero-tolerance policy on piracy. A law that had been put in place for the benefit of the city's population of poor, victimized star pilots. More irony.

As I passed through the old concourse, flanked by rows of abandoned stalls and restaurants, I formulated a courtroom defense under my breath. "No, you could hardly say I was collaborating with those two brackets who aren't even sure what a Danish accent is supposed to sound like. It's not like I told them I was going to be there. Most pirate shakedowns go like that. If they're happy just to take the luggage, then a protracted fight doesn't make sense to anyone. Pirates are reasonable people. Most of them used to be . . ."

I stopped in my tracks as the thought came, and almost immediately despised myself for thinking it. Yes, most pirates used to be pilots. That fact forms the center of a slightly racist joke referencing Ritsuko City's large population of Japanese speakers. And I could certainly have escaped justice indefinitely by crossing the Black. But I'd have to lose my last scrap of self-respect, and in that case I would take up transvestite hooking before piracy. At least that would make for a less awkward conversation with Dad.

The hum of distant crowds transitioned into the roar of close-by ones when I reached the checkin plaza, ducking under the velvet rope and Wrong Way sign. Out of ingrained habit I made for the newer wing of the spaceport, holding my cardboard sign tucked firmly under one arm.

The newer concourse was crowded with more shops and businesses than the old one had ever enjoyed in its heyday and was illuminated at this time of the lunar day by the majestic display of the Earth, hovering in the sky directly above the magnificent curved glass ceiling. Directly in the middle of the floor was the statue of Ritsuko Saito, very deliberately placed to be the first sight of Ritsuko City, greeting its visitors with her cheerful permanent V sign. I took up my usual position leaning companionably on her pedestal.

Style over function; that was the entire philosophy of the new concourse. The only part of it that served any practical purpose was at the far end, where the huge hallway terminated in a wide circular chamber with an ornate archway in the middle of the floor. A control booth was discreetly tucked away in the upper region of the far wall to distract as little as possible from the splendid artistry of the place.

Absolutely none of which was being appreciated by the hefty number of star pilots present, leaning impatiently against every solid object. They were clad in the widest variety of jumpsuits, flight jackets, and metallic fabrics imaginable, in every color on the tarnished spectrum, and all held cardboard signs similar to my own. Most were human—the extrasolars almost all went back to their home systems after the Golden Age ended—but there was the occasional glimpse of green skin or tentacles among the crowd, the ones with no home to go back to.

We all knew each other; I'd fought against and alongside half the room in some galactic battle or another, back in the Golden Age. But there was no chatting. Camaraderie might return later, when we were all back in the Brandied Bracket swapping war stories, but here on the concourse, there were no friends. There was only competition.

As I was waiting for the action to start, my phone buzzed briefly in my back pocket. I fully inflated my lungs, closed my eyes, brought the device up to my face, exhaled, then looked.

Aaaand there it was. Court summons, first thing Friday morning. It was going to be civil action rather than criminal, but it hardly mattered. It was over. I was definitely going to have to sell the *Neverdie*, and that'd only cover legal fees. I made a mental note to look into options re: transvestite hooking.

I noticed faces all over the concourse looking in my direction, some sympathetic, mostly gloating. Even without open conversation, gossip had a way of getting around fast. I nonchalantly fixed my gaze upward, trying not to look like I was about ready to burst into tears. Now I merely looked like I was trying to look up Ritsuko's marble miniskirt.

A ripple of excitement ran through the crowd, not because of the miniskirt thing (whose contents were frankly underwhelming) but because the red light had come on at the top of the grand archway. The star pilots wobbled into a pair of haphazard straight lines to either side of the main walkway, straightening signs and smoothing velour. Shortly there was a rustle of thin metal sheeting, and massive shutters came down over both sides of the archway, leaving a space of about six inches between them.

Someone had told me once that the shutters weren't there for safety purposes, but rather because quantum tunneling refuses to work when anyone's observing it, and no one really knows why. Which doesn't sound to me like technology one should trust, least of all base an entire transport revolution around.

And for all that it was always rather underwhelming to witness. A science-fiction blue glow or some whooshy noises wouldn't have gone amiss, but there was only about a minute of silence—save a few uneven clangs from the metal shutters being momentarily exposed to vacuum—before the nearer shutter noisily rolled back up.

But instead of the same six inches of empty space and backside of rear shutter that would be expected by a sensible person, the archway now led into the concourse of the main spaceport in New Dubai, the human colony on the desert moon Sigma 14-D. A destination that would have taken me and my ship an eight-day journey to reach, assuming nothing along the way tried to molest us, or eat us, or any combination of the two.

A semi-orderly queue of visitors, migrants, and tourists were belched into Ritsuko City, crossing the light years of distance in the thickness of a shadow. The seasoned travelers did so without thought, some holding phones to whatever they used for ears with whatever they used for hands. The newbies did things with a little more ceremony, pausing at the point where the ornate carpet met the shiny white tiles to take a big, nervous stride. I noticed a family of four Slignns close their eyes and interlock their tentacles as they did so.

"Ritsuko City Spaceport welcomes visitors to Luna, the cradle of human spacegoing," droned a prerecorded announcement over a loudspeaker. "All visitors are reminded that they are under no obligation to charter unemployed star pilots."

By then all the star pilots were fully animated and selling their services as loudly as they could to drown out the loudspeaker. I shook my sign and joined in. No reason I couldn't get lucky and reel in two tourists in one day. I was aiming to make as much income as possible before Friday. I could at least cover the rickshaw fare to the courthouse.

"Luxury tours!" I called. I picked out a family in matching "I'm Luny For Luna" T-shirts and tried to catch the parents' eyes. "Just fifty euroyen per hour! Stories from the Golden Age of star piloting! Space as it was meant to be seen! For a little extra I'll do a little dance and then you can kick me in the doints! You're not even paying attention to me, are you, you bunch of brackets. Oh, don't go over to him! I'm much better looking!"

My attempt at banter died when I noticed that the pilot who had caught the family's attention appeared to be pointing at me as he spoke. Looking around, I saw a few other pilots who'd reeled in clients doing the same thing. My arms fell listlessly by my sides as I realized what they were doing.

I was no lip reader, but I could get the gist. "Hello sirs or madams, you're so lucky to have come to me. There are some very dishonest people around here. That shady character over there—this very morning he was hired by some tourists just like yourself and he sold them out to pirates! Of all the things to do! People like that just let us all down, don't you think?" And I just knew they were planning to fly straight into the Black and into sniffing range of whatever pirate families they had loose arrangements with.

Plying, trac-eating divs, doints, and brackets.* I couldn't stomach it any-more, rickshaw fare be damned. I hung my head and made for the food court, letting the edge of my cardboard sign scrape along the ground.

---

* The reader probably deserves an explanation at this point. Ritsuko City Spaceport, in an effort to mitigate the image problems caused by being infested with unemployed star pilots, had taken the step of banning all swearing. This led to pilots like our narrator taking up the practice of using mathematical terms as swear words, on the vague understanding that the hated quantum tunneling technology was in some way related to applied mathematics.

In "Pilot Math", the word *multiply* (shortened to *ply*) replaces the most popular swear word, with *subtraction* (or *trac*) filling in as an all-purpose noun with scatological leanings. *Bracket* became a common insult, as did *decimal point* (or *doint*) and *division* (*div*), which also came to mean male and female genitalia, respectively.

The origin of Pilot Math lay in a televised interview between Dr. Terence Dawkins, inventor of quantum tunneling, and David Blanche, noted star pilot and interplanetary war veteran. Dr. Dawkins expressed wonderment that such a massive technological and cultural leap had been achieved with "just a little addition and subtraction." A surly Blanche replied, "I'll give you subtraction in a minute."

CHAPTER 3

I WAS IN the food court, waiting in line for a sushi sandwich, and I found myself staring at the wall, which was decorated with a collage illustrating the history of Ritsuko City. Great prominence had been given to one of the famous photos from around the time of independence. It showed a Japanese soldier in an environment suit, standing on the lunar surface just outside Ritsuko's containment bubble, staring in stunned disbelief at a huge pile of nearby shipping crates.

The moment requires context. Ritsuko City, humanity's first permanent off-world colony, had been established on the moon by the Japanese government. Overcrowding on Earth had been widespread, and the Japanese had plans to establish a haven to which a selected slice of their populace could move. But the man they put in charge of the project, Kaito Ayakama, believed that the new colony should be a free state, without obligations to any Earth nation and open to refugees from all countries.

When he made the now-famous broadcast declaring autonomy to the world, his superiors in Tokyo were not pleased. They immediately ceased all supply drops and sent a platoon of soldiers to retake the colony. They were expecting to deal with a bunch of half-starved settlers in a flimsy huddle of inflatable habitats.

What they didn't know was that Kaito had secretly been corresponding with a wide range of like-minded associates on Earth. Mainly independently wealthy visionary types who had seen the same writing on the wall. Between them, they had bankrolled a lengthy series of "scientific" rocket launches, all of which had been secretly dropping crates onto the dark side of Luna where

Japan couldn't see. Kaito had been bringing up food, people, and building supplies behind his government's collective back for almost as long as he'd been on the moon.

So what those soldiers found when they landed was a plexiglass bubble the size of Manhattan, strong enough to withstand a meteorite strike and populated by a thriving, self-sufficient community. And when he saw that pile of crates, the soldier in the photograph knew exactly what they were and what message they were intended to send.

They were the full and complete inventory of every single supply drop Japan had sent to the moon over the previous three years. Unused. Unopened.

We don't need you anymore, Kaito was saying. You are obsolete. Join us or get out of the way. I stared at the expression on the soldier's face and felt a gloomy kinship for the poor dumbfounded bracket.

"Are you a star pilot?"

One of the new arrivals was in the queue behind me. He was young and pudgy, with overgrown, greasy hair and thick spectacles, like a car with massive headlights wrapped around a weeping willow.

I turned away for a moment to flick the little imaginary switch I have, and the transformation washed over me. Warm smile. Interested eyes. Hands open and welcoming without making motions that could be interpreted as grasping. Then I turned back. "Certainly am!" I announced. "Fifteen years in the Black. I've got stories that'll make your pube stand on end. And you'll be hard pressed to find more reasonable rates—"

"Do you know Jacques McKeown?"

I noticed the paperback book he was fidgeting with, and my internal switch snapped back like a kick to the doints. Jacques Mc-plying-Keown. Every single time he had a new book out, the spaceport was full of his plying fans. And then the media speculation on Jacques McKeown's true identity would flare up again, because he was almost certainly a pilot or an ex-pilot, and half the plying potential clients in the spaceport would turn out to be journalist doints with no intention of hiring anyone.

It was the newest book this kid was holding, and the cover was a typical one. A square-jawed pilot, his flight jacket barely containing chest muscles like those of a sweaty horse, was fighting off a horde of insectival monsters with a gun in each hand. And there was the usual beautiful woman in a torn kimono clinging to the hero's leg. Classy as ever.

"Was it really like he says it was?" asked the kid.

I was still too far back in the queue to pretend I had better things to do than talk to this doint. "Oh, yeah. Twenty-four-seven. Non-stop excitement up there. Tell your parents, and maybe they could charter my ship and learn all about—"

"Have you ever had to fight off aliens with a gun in each hand?" he pressed.

I pointed to the cover art. "Yeah. That was an average Monday morning. The only thing he forgot is that usually everything would be on fire at that point."

He looked furtively left and right, as if we were exchanging classified information in a darkened car park, then leaned closer. "Is it true about Jacques McKeown?"

I leaned in too. "It is. He really does rape dogs. He can't help it; it's an impulse. I've never seen one get away from him in time."

He shook his head earnestly. "I mean, is it true that all the pilots secretly know who he is but they've made a pact not to tell?"

I was bored with this. I blew out my cheeks. "Kid, if that was true, Jacques McKeown wouldn't be writing books. Because I and all my colleagues would be shoving them all up his arse with the rest of his trac. Now do me a favor: go forth and multiply."

He did so, scampering off to the nearby bookshop to join a small huddle of scene kids in designer distressed flight jackets. Above them, a large poster depicted the cover art for some other, equally traccy McKeown book.

Every star pilot had stories from the Golden Age. You couldn't have avoided it even if you tried; you could attempt to stick to transporting cargo or passengers across the Black, but the Black was the new wild frontier, and adventure would find you nevertheless. If you hadn't saved at least one planet by the end of your first year, then you weren't considered to be taking it seriously. We all had stories, but only one of us had had the idea to take everyone's stories, rewrite them to be about himself, and sell millions of copies.

My own exploits on Cantrabargid had "inspired" the bulk of book 12: *Jacques McKeown and the Malmind Menace*. And every time a tourist accused me of ripping it off, I envisioned another six-inch nail being shoved down Jacques McKeown's organ of generation. In my mind's eye, it was starting to look like some kind of S & M wedding bouquet. You'd be hard pressed to find a star pilot who didn't have similar fantasies. All in all, keeping his true identity secret was a surprisingly smart move, for a man apparently incapable of original ideas.

I couldn't enjoy my unagi sandwich after that, sitting in a booth intended for nine, bitterly picking off bits of bread and rice. I wondered if it had been like this for cowboys: lionized by popular culture, while at the same time, everyone was buying cars instead of horses and tutting about the death of the Old West.

There'd been a lot of that sort of talk when quantum tunnels first came about. A lot of people had gone on about how it would kill the adventurous soul of space travel. Which would have been gratifying, but very few of those people continued paying for arduous passage through untamed star systems when the journey could be made instantaneously, for a fraction of the cost and with no risk of being eaten by crystal crabs.

"Excuse me. Are you a star pilot?"

I slammed my hands onto the tabletop, flipping my sandwich messily, and was prepared to yell another thing relating to Jacques McKeown's arse before I took in the person addressing me. The words died in my throat.

This was new. At first I thought she was one of the newly-arrived business travelers, going by her outfit: dark gray pant suit, severely straightened hair. But then I noticed the understated gold cufflinks and leather-bound, top-of-the-range datapad inserted under one arm. There was serious money here. The kind that normally travels first class. Quantum tunneling being what it is, first class is basically the same as economy class, except star pilots aren't allowed on the concourse and they put a red carpet down.

Both of us were staring and things were starting to get weird, so I felt moved to respond. "Yes, I am." I adjusted my flight jacket to give a better view of the words "Star Pilot" emblazoned across my T-shirt.

Her eyes shifted around, and she hugged her datapad. "Are you ... available for hire?" she said, her mouth curled slightly in distaste at her own words.

My mind's hand was hovering over the little switch, but something felt off. I momentarily went against all my instincts and nodded toward the concourse behind her, still rumbling with full-volume sales pitches. "That's the usual hiring place over there," I said. I prodded my distressed sandwich. "This is the lunch place."

She looked around again. Bits of her were vibrating nervously. Her cufflinks were tapping a little drum-beat on her datapad. "I need to make an arrangement as discreetly as possible."

"Ohhhh," I said, nodding slowly. I was starting to feel like a school counselor attempting to extract information from a crying child. "Would you like to go somewhere private?"

"Yes," she said quickly. "Yes, that would probably be for the best."

I stood up, leaving the tormented remains of my sushi sandwich to brighten up the day of one of my peers. "Right," I said. "We can go and talk in my ship."

"Er, no," she said, wrinkling her nose. "I don't think I would be comfortable actually going onto a . . . onto your . . . thing. Is there somewhere private that's . . . not as private?"

I came to the decision that this was one of the many tests life presents us with to separate the fast of thought from the roadkill. I glanced searchingly around, and my gaze fell upon the bright pink photo booth beside the pharmacist. "All right then," I said, gesturing toward it with an open palm. "Step into my office."

Once the two of us had squeezed around the stool, our shoulders rubbing up against the ceiling of the booth and the tops of our heads pressed together, the little door could finally be persuaded to close.

"Okay," I whispered, after ensuring secrecy by hanging my jacket over the camera screen. "You were saying?"

She looked at me uncertainly over her brow. "I need absolute assurance that you are a star pilot and that you are available for immediate hire before this goes any further. I cannot risk any spread of sensitive information."

I attempted to nod, but our scalps scraping together felt very unpleasant. I drew her attention to my hanging flight jacket so I could show her the parking permit I kept clipped to the inside pocket. "I guarantee absolute confidentiality for all clients. I completely understand your situation. Can I start by asking what, exactly, you did, and which organizations are hunting you for it?"

"You . . . what?"

I displayed my palms. "It's fine if you don't want to say, but I do have to charge extra for the no-questions-asked package. It's just a risk assessment th—"

"I am not a fugitive!" snapped the woman, stopping just short of straightening up with offended dignity and consequently knocking herself unconscious on the ceiling. "I just require someone who can pilot a ship."

"Oh. Right. Good." I bit my lip. "That's good, because . . . if you were a fugitive . . . I would of course have immediately notified . . . Actually, could you just forget this entire conversation up to now?"

"I'm sorry, this was a bad idea," she muttered, groping for the door handle behind her back.

"No, no, no, it's fine," I was about to grab her arm, but stopped myself, as any violent movement in these close quarters might have led to me being the one on the run from the law. "You've obviously got a problem, and I want to help you with it. Really. I'm basically as trustworthy as any other pilot you'll find here, and my hygiene is better than average. Just tell me what you need."

She exhaled at length, through gritted teeth. "My employer believes that I have hired a pilot for a private vessel. That pilot has not appeared. I am supposed to introduce this pilot at a dinner this evening."

A private gig. A private plying gig. I hit my internal switch so hard that it also illuminated strings of imaginary Christmas lights in my head. "You need a last-minute replacement? Look no further. I can fly anything with at least one wing."

"The other matter," continued the woman, "is that my employer may have already signed a check for the previous pilot's advance. I believe I may have been the victim of a scam."

"How exactly did you meet this pilot?"

"I . . . used an online search engine."

"Oof." I winced.

She scowled at me. "The point is, I cannot allow my employer to know that I, he, both of us, have been . . . dishonored in this way. That could be very damaging in every sense of the word."

At this point my potential client's uneasy use of the word 'dishonored' made me realize that she had a Terran accent she had been attempting to conceal. "Right," I said.

"So I need you to pretend that you are this pilot. I'll introduce you under his name, and you must keep up the identity for the entire length of your association with us. It is vitally important that my employer not realize that a mistake has been made."

"By you," I said, nodding.

She made a brief, irritated sigh. "Broadly speaking."

"Well, I don't see any problem at all. I mean, star pilots, right? We're all pretty interchangeable. Smell weird, talk about the old days a lot. Where is this dinner?"

Her datapad was suddenly open and taking up most of the tiny space between us. A spot was indicated on a map of the city, just off Ritsuko's Heart at the corner of Ritsuko's Leg. "It's a place called La Vache in the city center. You'll need to be there at eight. I can't offer you the same advance that my employer already paid, but I can offer half the sum from my personal finances." She switched to some kind of database app and indicated a box containing a figure. "Would this be sufficient?"

Being very careful to keep my face straight, I brushed at the number, wanting to make sure there weren't any stains on the surface that I was mistaking for zeros. "I think that will be satisfactory," I said, after swallowing hard.

I let her scan the ID chip in the back of my hand, and with a few quick swipes, the balance on my credit account was replaced by a much more encouraging one. She swiftly exited the photo booth and was already speed walking away by the time I'd squeezed myself out and rubbed the ache out of my spine.

"Hey," I called after her. She stopped, but didn't turn. "Relax. You can relax now. Problem solved, right?"

"I will make that particular status update only after this day is over," she replied, over her shoulder. "In the meantime, do not mention this to anyone."

"Absolutely."

CHAPTER 4

"YEAH, SO SHE'S paying me half a plying continent to fly some rich doint's cruising yacht or something," I said, standing at the ironing counter in my T-shirt and underpants.

"Right," said Frobisher, not looking up from working a crease out of my jeans. "So now we're just waiting for the part when this all blows up in your face, aren't we."

Flat-Earth Frobisher had been a fellow star pilot and occasional friend back in the day. After quantum tunneling he'd seen the writing on the wall earlier than most, and had sold his ship to start his own laundry business. A pettier man than I might have resented this, but I appreciated having one person to talk to who wasn't also competition. "Not everything blows up in my face."

He smiled that little patronizing smile of his that made his face so very punchable. "No, fair enough—just all your business decisions lately. You were talking exactly like this when you got that nuclear waste dumping contract."

"We do not talk about the nuclear waste dumping contract," I said, in a jovial but very clearly threatening kind of way. "Are you done with those trousers?"

He slid them over and moved on to my flight jacket, reaching for the deodorant. "I like that this is your idea of formal dress, by the way. The same clothes as always, but recently laundered. Do you even know what level of swank La Vache is?"

"I wasn't aware that swank operates on a tiered system," I said, pulling my luxuriously warm jeans back on. "They want a star pilot; I'm giving them what they expect. If you were hiring a mime artist, you wouldn't expect them to show up in business casual, would you."

He laughed his little patronizing laugh that often went with the smile. "I hope you haven't been going around crowing about this. 'Cos if you'll do as a last-minute replacement then pretty much any other pilot would, you realize" — the bell on the entrance door rang — "is what I said to the guy this morning who was crowing about his new client."

I turned to see a man standing in the doorway, with a significant emphasis on the word *man*. He was well over six feet and packed head-to-foot with rippling, tanned musculature. This was extremely obvious, because he was covering his physique with nothing more than a chain mail loincloth and a pair of leather bandoliers criss-crossing his chest.

"Ho, fellows," he boomed, tossing his mane of black hair.

"Hi, Angelo," said Frobisher and I.

Back in the good old days, when a star pilot saved a planet, there was sometimes the temptation to stay there. For a while, it had even been something of a fashion trend among extrasolar queens and princesses to be seen with a space-hero paramour on one's arm. The trend was fleeting, as they so often are, and a lot of spurned lovers had drifted back to Ritsuko.

Angelo had apparently proved himself to some kind of warrior race, not dissimilar to the Zuvirons, and had lived as the queen's consort for long enough to go a bit native. Until some other brick trac-house had caught Her Majesty's fickle eye and he'd been out on his ear. He stomped up beside me and held up a bulging laundry sack that clattered metallically when he dropped it on the counter.

"Why yes, I'd be happy to polish your armor, Angelo, thank you for asking so politely as always," said Frobisher quietly, busying himself with the sack's contents.

Angelo glanced at me over his ridiculously square jaw. "Am I correct in hearing that congratulations be in order?"

I met Frobisher's urgent look for a split second. "Er, what?" I said innocently.

"I hath heard that Den and Mark and thee are pledged to be gay married."

I'd forgotten about that. Before I could stop myself I'd started a sigh of relief, but was able to translate it into one of weary good humor. "Oh.

Yeah. Nice one. Look at me rolling with your expert punches. Oof. Ooh. A well-landed blow, sir."

"'Tis well," said Angelo, instantly bored by the topic. "Hast thou heard the news of Jacques McKeown?"

I paused momentarily in the act of shaking my sleeves into my now-laundered flight jacket. "The dog-raping thing? Yeah, I think someone mentioned it. Frobisher, I gotta go. See you later."

"Nay," said Angelo, turning to Frobisher as I made for the exit. "There hath been rumor that he intends to break cover. There is talk of a public appearance."

I paused at the door, slinging one ear over my shoulder.

"Where did you hear that?" asked Frobisher. "'Cos if it was Fat Matt, he was the one who said that Deirdre's was giving away free banana splits, and now Deirdre's has been closed down, hasn't it."

"'Tis but a rumor, but I pray to Mighty Bolor that it be true," said Angelo. He reached behind his back and drew a massive knobbly sword as long as my leg, which he held aloft and stared at as he spoke as if reading off the blade. "My sword Slaybracket thirsts for the blood of the traitor. When he scuttles from his hole, I shall gather our brothers in betrayal, and together we shall tear him to morsels fit for the gullets of Ulunian swamp maggots."

"Yeah, well, save me a nibble," I said, leaving. It wasn't my finest parting shot, but I had better things to devote brain cells to. I had to look for a Quantunnel booth, for one. And I had to have a little panic, for another.

I'd been so chuffed by this new gig that I'd forgotten I was due for a scheduled court appearance in a few days, and missing it wouldn't be one of those things that the justice system could be easygoing about. But that was only if the gig went on that long. And even then, the client might be fine with me taking a morning off. If not, well . . . I wasn't going to be me for a while, was I? I was going to be this other, non-existent, scam-artist pilot. I could certainly manufacture an excuse for being out of contact. Worst case, I could just mangle my leg in the gearbox. Again.

Yeah, this was probably all going to work out fine. And there was a vacant Quantunnel booth near the spaceport that hadn't been vandalized, so plying miracles were on my side that evening. I had a lot of colleagues who flatly refused to use the things out of principle, but I had a pragmatic attitude, and more importantly, an advance.

I thumbed the topmost option on the touchscreen and passed my chip under the scanner. The machine deducted an amount that would have been much more significant a day ago. One rattle of shutters later, the white plastic doorway opened up into the middle of Ritsuko's Heart, two miles away, in defiance of old-fashioned physics.

The city's main square was at maximum bustle. It was that lively time of the evening when the businessmen were on their way home and the nightlife crowd were out looking for somewhere to be seen. The two were trying to plow through in opposite directions like a pair of combs jammed together. I did a little hop, took a deep breath, then broke into a sprint toward the junction of Ritsuko's Leg, hoping momentum would carry me through the mass.

History tells us that Kaito Ayakama was serious when he suggested naming the central plaza Ritsuko's Heart. Ritsuko was his girlfriend at the time, and very dear to him. His wife, Naomi, wasn't too happy about it, but she was stuck back on Earth and he didn't care. History is pretty sure he was joking when he suggested naming the main street Ritsuko's Leg, though. It stuck because no one could think of anything better and Kaito was having to spend a lot of time on the phone to his divorce lawyer.

For a short while my world was a confusing maelstrom of expensive suits and shameful clubbing gear before I burst out into the open and was very nearly hit by a cyclist crossing the top of the Leg.

I could see La Vache, now. I'd passed this area many times before but I'd never noticed it, for the same reason I never noticed gynecologists' offices, or places that sold insurance: they just weren't part of my world. Now having to contemplate going inside the place, I could see that if swank really did operate on a tiered system, then this was pretty much as high as it went.

It was the kind of rich that's so rich it doesn't have to prove it. No flashy architecture on the exterior, no giant, lit-up signs. Just a set of huge, plain glass windows with perfectly straight beige curtains, and the name of the place was embossed in barely visible serifed letters on a brass plaque above the door.

I was contemplating the best swagger to put on as I entered when I picked up a familiar scent of wealth and noticed my mysterious client, now wearing a pastel dress that acknowledged the wearer's bodily characteristics as begrudgingly as possible, standing at the entrance to the alleyway that ran behind the restaurant.

Her back was to me as I approached. "Boo," I said, in a perfectly level tone of voice, but she jumped anyway.

"Ah," she said, tucking an errant strand of hair behind one ear. "You may wait inside for us at the table. Give my name to the doorman."

"You haven't told me your name yet."

She was ever so subtly inching to the side in order to get firmly between me and the alleyway entrance. "You can call me Ms. Warden," she said. From behind her came a sound like a deck chair being attacked with a side of beef. She loudly feigned a cough.

"Riiight," I said, attempting to subtly peer around her.

"And you are?" she asked, pretending to lean comfortably on the nearby wall, slightly misjudging the distance, and stumbling in her heels.

"That's another thing you're supposed to tell me," I pointed out.

"Now then," came a male voice from the alleyway. "What was that you were saying about dress code?" The voice possessed the same Terran accent Ms. Warden had attempted to suppress in her own voice. "Black tie, or . . ."

Somebody spat, and there was the plink of teeth settling on wet concrete. "Phwuh?"

"The options, I believe, were black tie, or something else?"

The second voice sounded more local, and considerably more pained. "Black tie or . . . reindeer sweaters?"

"Yes! Black tie, or a sweater that I find very comfortable. You're a bright one, aren't you. Let him go, Carlos."

Something clattered to the ground, and a second later, a middle-aged man in the garb of a maitre d' limped around the corner. His pencil-thin mustache was caked in blood from a nose in severe disarray. He looked like he was going to try to maintain his dignity, until he saw me. His gaze tracked up and down my outfit, then he burst into tears and slunk, dejected, into the restaurant.

From the alley came a jaunty whistling, followed closely by its originator. He was a middle-aged man with thick black hair graying at the temples, and he had a tanning bed complexion that was close to that of a tangerine. Perhaps as an attempt to offset this, he was wearing a vibrantly colored reindeer sweater over a collar and tie.

Behind him was what looked at first glance to be an enormous red capital M in a tuxedo. It was, very broadly speaking, humanoid, but the tops of its massive shoulders were about ten inches higher than the top of its head. Its tree-trunk arms reached to the floor, making its somewhat sensibly proportioned legs almost redundant. What I could see of its flesh was hairless, but for a black thatch on the front of its "face," artfully combed into the shape of a fat handlebar mustache. I didn't recognize the species, but I could say for sure that its home planet's ecosystem had valued grip strength a lot higher than it had aesthetics.

"Oh, hi there," said the man in the reindeer sweater, noticing me. "You must be the pilot. I hope you don't smell as bad as they all did in the spaceport."

"If I might introduce my employer, Mr. Henderson—" began Ms. Warden, not meeting my gaze.

She was interrupted by Mr. Henderson loudly clapping his hands and rubbing them together. "You know what, let's save introductions for when we're all comfy inside. The air in these bubble cities makes me want to have a great big spew sometimes."

I attempted to follow directly behind him into the restaurant, but a hand like a leather armchair wrapped itself around my shoulder and held me in place until the hulking mass named Carlos could get between me and Mr. Henderson. I followed meekly, my eyes about level with Carlos's buttocks. Ms. Warden brought up the rear, and I heard her sigh for longer than I'd have thought possible for a normal pair of lungs.

My entire view consisted of a featureless plain of black silk until we were inside the restaurant. It was obvious which table was Mr. Henderson's: it was the one surrounded by wait staff making big earnest smiles and the occasional worried glance toward the maitre d'. He was holding a tissue to his face and bowing in a regular rhythm like one of those drinking-bird toys. Most of the other guests were either already leaving or attempting to wolf down their meals.

Already sitting at the table was a skinny boy of about fifteen, wearing a T-shirt in designer disarray and an unnatural red streak in his unruly black hair. He folded his arms and scowled as Mr. Henderson took a seat opposite him. "Have you gotten your way, then?" he said, spitefully.

"Oh yes," chuckled Henderson as he took a seat at the head of the table. "We all love coming to places where the Henderson name hasn't gotten around yet, don't we?"

"No, I don't," insisted the boy. "You always use violence to get your way and no one's impressed. Everyone just thinks you're a big thug."

Henderson laughed again. "Danny's got big ideas for the organization. Just can't wait to step into his old man's shoes, can you."

"DON'T CALL ME DANNY," snapped Danny, a prepubescent squeak entering his voice. "You're always trying to embarrass me! I'm not taking over your company! I'm going to be a star pilot!"

Henderson chuckled. "Yes, of course you are. And what were you going to be last year? VR game designer, wasn't it? Poetry the year before that."

"URGH," grunted Danny, letting his hands drop onto the table hard enough to make all the plates rattle. "I HATE you."

Henderson winked at me. "Kids. They're great at this age, aren't they? Danny's going to do great things with the family business one day, you just watch."

Right, I thought. With every second that passed, more things about this situation seemed to be completely bananas, but these were clients, and rich ones at that, and I was willing to take a banana in every available hole for a private gig. Warden had already taken a seat beside Danny, so I flicked my internal switch and pulled out the chair next to hers with a confident flourish. "And what is your line of business, Mr. Henderson?" I asked conversationally.

Henderson's smile froze, and his offended glare pinned me in place half in and half out of the seat. Then he laughed with seemingly genuine warmth, although his eyes didn't change. "You're a nosy one, aren't you?" I had no idea how to interpret his tone of voice. "How about those introductions?"

I glanced with slight desperation at Ms. Warden, who was sitting to my right. She appeared to be staring into space, clutching her datapad with white-knuckled hands, but snapped into alertness when Henderson addressed her. "Yes," she said smartly. "Mr. Henderson, Daniel, may I introduce Mr. Jacques McKeown."

CHAPTER 5

THE CONFIDENT, EMPLOYABLE smile I'd been wearing suddenly felt like it was being held in place with two six-inch nails. About twelve sweats broke out simultaneously throughout my body.

"Ah yes," said Mr. Henderson, clapping his hands. "Danny's been so looking forward to meeting you. He's been jumping up and down all week."

"YOU'RE EMBARRASSING ME," wailed Daniel.

"Daniel," said Warden suddenly. "Indoor voice."

"BUT HE—but he is!"

Mr. Henderson leaned toward me conspiratorially, and then spoke in an exaggerated hushed tone, clearly audible to the entire room. "He's worried his old dad's going to show him up in front of his big hero." He leaned back, chuckling. "But to answer your question, Mr. McKeown, the family business serves a number of functions. I like to think of us as problem solvers, don't I, Carlos?" He elbowed the massive bodyguard creature in the ribs, not provoking the slightest reaction.

Wait staff were circling the table, carefully laying crusty rolls before us. Still smiling, I reached out and tipped both my and Ms. Warden's plates toward me, sending both our rolls under the table. "Oh, how clumsy of me," I barked. "Help me look for our rolls, Ms. Warden." I grabbed her arm and ducked under the tablecloth, pulling her with me.

"Take your hands off!" she hissed.

"Three things," I hissed back, displaying the appropriate number of fingers. "First, I think Mr. Henderson is some kind of crime-lord-leader-boss thing. Second, you never said anything about having to pretend to be Jacques Mc-plying-Keown. Third"—I gestured wildly— "aaaaaaaaah!"

"Keep it down," she whispered. "You took the money. You agreed to be whoever I said you were."

"But Jacques McKeown! If any other pilots even suspect that I might be Jacques McKeown, they will use me as an exhaust muffler. I know they will because I would."

"What? Why would pilots hate Jacques McKeown? The books have made them into icons."

I made a little frustrated sound into my cupped palms. "I wouldn't expect someone of your tax bracket to understand. You're just going to have to tell them I'm not Jacques McKeown. Tell them Jacques McKeown is actually a book-writing computer program or something."

She grabbed me around the back of the neck with one hand and squeezed just hard enough to make my brain start feeling weird. "I know you are not from Earth, so I will explain this to you," she said softly, her lips right next to my ear. "Mr. Henderson gets whatever he wants, and what Mr. Henderson wants is Jacques McKeown. So you will be Jacques McKeown, or I will kill you, and Mr. Henderson will kill me. You will be my first. I will not be Mr. Henderson's first. Do you understand me?"

"Yech," I said, through a slightly distorted windpipe.

"What are you two whispering about down there?" asked Mr. Henderson. "I know it was a big advance, but you can't have gotten married on it already."

We rose back up from under the table. I kept my head bowed, rubbing my aching neck. Ms. Warden had her nose held high, and placed her roll back on her plate with offended dignity.

"Hello, I am Jacques McKeown," I murmured. I reached for my own roll and was about to take a sulky bite when I caught the gaze of Daniel, seated across from me. He instantly looked away furtively, as if he were afraid of being caught peering through his neighbor's bathroom window.

"I really like your books," he managed to say, already the color of a beet sandwich.

"He's going through that phase of looking for any father figure less embarrassing than me," said Mr. Henderson, as happily as ever. Daniel made blustering noises that didn't quite make it all the way to becoming coherent words. "So I promised that for his sixteenth I'd get him his very own ship and pilot. And of course, I didn't want to leave him with any of those horrible freaks you see at the spaceport—they'd probably eat him. So who better than the most famous pilot in known space?"

The waiters were doing the rounds again, this time filling our glasses with red wine. Ms. Warden and I both picked ours up and took huge gulps in almost perfect unison.

"Well, you've definitely come to the right man," I said, the instant my empty glass touched the tablecloth. "I can fly any ship with at least one wing. The thing is, though, I will need to keep a low profile. My identity and appearance are currently a secret because other pilots can be a little jealous of my success."

"Oh, I shouldn't think you'll need to worry," said Henderson, waving his wineglass. "They're only pilots. You can distract most of their sort with a dog biscuit. Besides, you can't deny Danny his chance to show off his new best friend, can you?"

I tore another piece off my roll, feeling sick. "Well. I suppose not."

"Actually, I've been wondering," said Henderson, still smiling. "How did you first get in touch with Mr. McKeown, Penny?"

"Email," she replied instantly.

Henderson kept smiling, but his brow furrowed. "As simple as that? Everyone I spoke to back on Earth told me that Jacques McKeown has never responded to email. Some of them swore that he doesn't exist."

She seemed to have frozen, the rim of her wineglass pinned to her lip, so I took over. "Well," I said, "obviously I get a lot of email, but it was the sheer number of emails Ms. Warden sent that made me take notice. There must have been hundreds. She was like some kind of psychotic ex."

"Really?" asked Henderson.

"In the end, I told her the only way I would consider it would be if she posted a video of herself dancing around in her underpants." A rather strangled choking noise burst out from between Ms. Warden's mouth and her glass. "I meant it as a joke, obviously; I didn't expect her to actually do it. Well, that's when I knew that this had to be an important cause, if someone was willing to completely humiliate themselves for it."

Henderson sat with elbows on table, his chin resting on the backs of his hands, mouth agape. "That is thrilling. Is that true, Penny?"

"Yes," she said, squeezing out the word like the last bit of toothpaste in the tube.

"You should employ her for as long as possible, Mr. Henderson," I said, patting her shoulder. "This is something you need to hang on to."

"Oh, I agree, Mr. McKeown," said Henderson, eyebrows waggling. "And did you know, in less than a year she's worked more miracles than my last PA ever did." I picked up on a faint edge in Henderson's voice, and there was a brief exchange of glances between him and Warden that froze her solid.

Then she unthawed and turned her gaze to the menu in front of her. "Yes, Mr. McKeown and I undertook quite an intimate exchange of emails," she said, conversationally. "He was very forthcoming after I sent him a video of me dancing around in my underwear, and I learned many details about his life. I had no idea how little money novelists actually make in today's market."

"Mm, so I've heard," said Henderson, nodding eagerly. "I suppose that explains why you still have to do the . . . prosti-piloting, I think I've heard it called."

"Under the circumstances, I'd like to recommend offering Mr. McKeown an indefinite contract," she continued, looking at me with no readable expression. "He would have the opportunity to write books in his spare time. Perhaps Daniel could even watch."

Daniel gave her an urgent "don't ruin this for me" look, then turned to me, clasping his hands under his chin. "Oh you don't have to do that but it would be so completely awesome," he said, almost as all one breathless word.

Henderson clapped his hands joyfully. "Excellent! Perhaps Danny could be written in, yeah? A whole new character! Although you'll probably have to tone down his good looks, or no one would believe it."

"URRRGGGH," added Daniel, slapping himself in the face with both hands.

I kept smiling, but I moved close to Ms. Warden's ear and whispered "one-all" through my teeth. She smiled right back.

Our party emerged from the restaurant at around midnight, the wait staff waving and smiling with naked relief from the door. I was first out, not entirely confident that I wasn't going to throw up at the first taste of Ritsuko's recycled air. I was feeling a new sensation: nausea from two different directions. Rich food on an empty stomach from the left and staring mortal terror from the right.

Henderson came up behind me. The hand he placed on my shoulder felt like a warm tarantula. "Jacques," he said. He'd had quite a lot of wine. "You're my kind of guy, Jacques. You're a success story. Space hero turned storyteller.

When Quantunneling came along you didn't just squat in a spaceport begging for clients like most of those visionless losers—you damn well adapted. Penny! Sort out Mr. McKeown. I'm going to piss in an alleyway."

"UGHHH," added a frustrated Daniel.

Mr. Henderson went off to reminisce in the alley where he'd beaten up the maitre d', and Ms. Warden stepped up, datapad at the ready like a flag at half-mast. "Here is the address of Mr. Henderson's private landing pad," she said, handing me a card. "Be there tomorrow at ten a.m., sharp."

I pocketed it. "Just to be safe," I said quietly, "you should get that video made. In case he asks to see it, y'know."

"I will probably have to do that, yes," she replied, stonily. "I need to scan your chip again to make the payment."

"I thought you already made the payment?"

"That was the advance. Your kind are paid by the hour, yes? Tonight counted as work. It certainly felt like it for me."

I offered my hand, and she moved a few windows on the touchscreen around with angry little jabs of her fingertips. I tried to peer around at what she was doing, but she deftly angled the pad away.

"I'm also sending you my personal contact number," she admitted, still tapping and dragging away. "If anything prevents you from arriving tomorrow, inform me. Bear in mind that it will need to be nothing less serious than a lost limb."

A sleek black town car the width of two normal-sized cars pressed together pulled up at the curb and Carlos unfolded from the driver's seat, moving around the car swiftly to open the rear passenger door.

"See you later, Mr. McKeown!" called Daniel, loud enough to make me glance fearfully around for passing star pilots, before boarding the vehicle. Warden gave me one last meaningful glance, then followed, taking the rear seat beside him.

The tarantula settled on my shoulder again. "Right, that'll increase the average property value of this district," said Henderson, still doing his fly back up. "One more thing, Mr. McKeown, man to man."

He gently but firmly spun me around until we were practically nose to orange nose, keeping one hand on my shoulder. "Boss?" I said.

He grinned at my use of the word. He had rather unsettlingly white teeth. "Jacques. I'm not a stupid man. I can see you've been, shall we say, ill at ease tonight."

"No, Mr. Henderson, really—"

Carlos's hand came down upon my free shoulder and all the air blasted from my lungs, as if I'd suddenly been burdened with a rucksack full of bricks. My knees almost buckled.

"Don't call me a liar, Jacques," said Henderson, pressing down with his hand. A sharp pain blossomed out from my shoulder. "You're nervous. I can tell. It's completely understandable. Really."

"Ughnk?" That wasn't what I'd intended to say, but the pain was making it hard to think.

"I'm asking you to take responsibility for my son's happiness and well-being, and it's completely understandable that you'd be nervous. Do you know what a cassowary is, Jacques?"

"Murngle?"

"It's something we have on Earth; you can look it up. I have a talon from a cassowary on my signet ring. Feel it?"

It wasn't breaking the skin, but it was less than a stone's throw from the threshold. Carlos's fingers flexed one by one, signaling me to respond. All I could do was nod.

"One, two more pounds of pressure," he said, leaning his face in closer. "And then all I'd have to do is move my hand diagonally down to about belt level." He placed his free hand on my waist like a dance partner, then blew a short raspberry. "And there you are. You're on the floor. Well. Bits of you are, anyway."

The pain had spread all the way to the fingertips of my left arm. I could feel them shaking. Carlos's hushed, hoarse breathing filled my ears. Henderson's face was like a little orange sun invading my personal space and pleasantly blasting the flesh from my bones.

Then he stepped back, displaying his hands as if expecting a hug. The weight of Carlos's hand vanished so suddenly that my feet left the floor for a moment. "And it's so good to know I won't have to do that, isn't it? Because Daniel and I are going to be very, very happy with the work you do for us."

He sauntered past me and took the front passenger seat as Carlos poured himself back through the driver's-side window. Moments later the car roared with unnecessary volume and sped off down Ritsuko's Leg, scattering cyclists.

I watched it go, waving like a theme park mannequin, dreamily rotating my forearm until the car was out of sight. Then I turned and ran.

CHAPTER 6

I ARRIVED BACK in the spaceport district—or Ritsuko's Arse, as it was colloquially known—at a full sprint, scattering a small queue of late-night drunks
who were waiting to use the Quantunnel booth. I wasn't even sure what I
was in such a hurry for. I just knew that I had to be somewhere familiar and
safe, a comfortably long distance from Ritsuko's plying Leg.

The spaceport was still open, of course; the day-and-night cycle from
planet to planet would take a far better brain than mine to comprehend.
And there were still a lot of pilots around. The night shift bunch were the
ones who were convinced that there was more money in the drunken bach-
elor-party crowd than the daytime tourists, but I'd never been convinced of
that. And cleaning the cabin afterward was a nightmare.

I paused in the receiving area where the old concourse connected to the
new one. My first instinct was to head for the old spaceport, get aboard my
ship, set a course for the nearest pirate hangout, and sign up, completing
whatever admission procedure was necessary with a slightly pained smile
on my face.

Alternatively, I could calm down and think for five seconds. Just because
I had been tacitly threatened with disembowelment by a very orange man,
that didn't mean I had to abandon the Solar System altogether. I had ten
hours and a generous advance with which to make a decision. Some research
was in order.

There was an Internet café on the new concourse, opposite the Sushi Station where I'd made that first fateful encounter with Ms. Warden. I headed
there briskly, exchanging the briefest of nods with the pilots I passed along

the way. Few of the faces were familiar, since I was strictly one of the day crowd. No one has much of a tan on Luna, but the night brackets were pasty even by Ritsuko standards. Walking through the place was like coming to your high-school reunion to find it haunted by the ghosts of all your life's ambitions.

I chose a nondescript booth with a working terminal and sat down, leaning close to the screen. I waved my chipped hand over the sensor on my right, and a paper cup dropped into the hopper underneath, filled a moment later with watery black coffee. This formality over with, the terminal unlocked access to the Internet.

I'd gathered from school history that the big push for space colonization began in earnest after pollution was left unchecked for too long, and it was begrudgingly realized that snot yellow was not a healthy look for what was ostensibly blue sky. After everyone with any sense cleared out, the only people left on Earth were the planetary equivalent of rabid nationalists, whose best argument for staying was "It's EARTH." They'd only gotten more insular and paranoid over time, so now most off-world traffic wasn't permitted to land, off-world quantum tunnels were illegal, and there was little diplomatic communication. This rather underlined Jacques McKeown's popularity if his books had managed to make it down there, but the point was, Henderson could have been the god-emperor of the entire Northern Hemisphere and most non-Terrans wouldn't know.

A quick search for "Henderson" produced results almost immediately, and I read with one finger to my lips, my concerns swelling and growing like tulip bulbs. A cursory glance at the suggested-words list would have raised eyebrows enough: the top three were "awful," "bastard," and "aaargh." On the first page of results alone the name was being linked to everything from food-rationing scams to assassination syndicates, that grinning orange face beaming forth from the attached news stories like some kind of overseeing satsuma.

I knew this much about Earth's politics: the walled-off United Republic was the only remaining government, which spent half its time diligently maintaining order through judicious use of secret holding camps and the other half accusing a token and ineffectual opposition party of being less than mouth-foamingly patriotic at all times. Everywhere else was a near-lawless swarm of former countries, wiping more and more of each other off the map with every water war.

I'd assumed that Henderson operated from one of the latter, but the surprise was that all the stories were coming out of the UR. My understanding was that you couldn't wipe a bogey off on your bathroom mirror there without being arrested for obstructing a surveillance camera. Maintaining a crime syndicate there would require a terrifying amount of power and influence. And sure enough, I found a photo of Henderson smiling and shaking hands with one of the previous puppet presidents, who looked rather pale and nervous. But then, next to Henderson, everybody did.

I leaned back. Crossing the Black was seeming more and more like an option. I sighed. I'd hate myself for it, but frankly, I'd entertained the notion often enough that the plan was already fully formed in my head. Step one, cash out my entire account and invest in enough food and shiny objects to impress one of the less psychotic pirate families. Step two, cut out my identity chip with a staple remover. Step three, clutch my hand and swear a lot.

Alternatively, there was always Cantrabargid, or one of the other primitive extrasolar worlds I'd saved. But the problem with living somewhere that knows you as a war hero is that that's kind of what you have to continue being. I'd be safe from my current enemy list among the Zuvirons, but not so much from their endless plying tournaments . . .

My thoughts stopped with a jarring clang when my eye caught the bar running along the top of the terminal screen. "Current User: Jacques McKeown," it read.

I'd been hearing that bracket's name so often in the last few days I'd barely noticed it at first, but now it had finally sunk in that this was a context where the name did not belong.

I glanced at the scanner above the coffee-maker, my guts still on the fence over whether to start churning or not. I passed my chip over it again.

A second cup plopped into the one that was already there, spraying unpleasant pseudo-coffee. I glanced at the screen again. "New User: Jacques McKeown."

I swiped my chip back and forth a few more times, and the same message dutifully flickered across the screen again and again. The hopper vomited a small avalanche of paper cups, scalding my thigh with coffee routinely kept at bacteria-killing temperatures, but I was only half-aware of it. Something in my gut was now decisively going at it with a pneumatic churning device.

"Excuse me, sir?" said a pretty young barista, uneasily appearing behind me with hands clasped behind back. "You are actually required to drink that coffee. The company signed an agreement with the city's waste processing . . ."

She was about college age, with her black hair tied back in a ponytail. I stared at her, momentarily unable to speak, some coherent part of my mind silently praying that she wouldn't notice the thing she, of course, noticed immediately.

Her words died in her throat as she looked past me at the computer screen, and the two of us goggled together for a second. "Oh my god," she said in a dangerously flat tone.

I noticed a Power Off button on the monitor and none too subtly tried to slap it as I stood and turned around. "Yes, I did make quite a mess, didn't I. I'll find a towel immediately." I made an attempt to leave that she stepped in the way of with no apparent conscious thought.

"Jacques McKeown?" she squeaked.

I pantomimed looking behind me, over the wall of the booth, briefly noticing that a few star pilots' heads were already staring in my direction. "Where? Was he over there?" I said loudly, enunciating as clearly as I could manage. "I'll go over and have a look for you."

"You're Jacques McKeown! The computer said your name's Jacques McKeown!"

I ducked out of sight of the other star pilots. I was definitely hearing some interested muttering from over there. My current approach wasn't paying off, so I decided to try working with rather than through. "I'd really appreciate it if you kept your voice down about it," I said, holding my hands out. "It's like a secret-identity thing, right?"

She nodded rapidly. Her face had gone very red. "Of course! Of course. Listen, I know this must be annoying, but my friend Kimmy, she's over there, she is such a huge fan of your books. Could I just quickly bring her over? This will make her completely freak."

I made another abortive effort to leave. "Look, I . . . I don't want to cause a complete freak. I'm not sure how I could live with the guilt."

"No no no, it's fine, I won't give you away. KIIIM!" She called over to another female employee on the other side of the café, who seemed to be functionally identical to her. "THERE'S SOMEONE HERE YOU WILL JUST FREAK OUT WHEN YOU MEET!"

"IS IT JACQUES McKEOWN?!" replied Kim, easily matching the first girl's volume.

"ER . . . HE DOESN'T WANT ME TO SAY," bellowed the first girl.

I didn't pay attention to the rest of the exchange, because by then I was speed walking out of the concourse, having slipped away the moment the first girl's back had turned. The important thing was to not look like I was fleeing for what could very well be my life. I kept my head down, my hands in my jacket pockets, and concentrated on putting distance between me and the food court.

I was half-certain that an uncouth, pilotesque voice shouted something, but I didn't dare stop or turn around. Fortunately I was not the kind of star pilot who did business in a cape or a silver jumpsuit; a flight jacket and peaked pilot's cap could disappear into any spaceport crowd, as long as I serpentined a bit and broke line of sight a few times.

When I'd reached the central plaza where the old and new concourses met, I hadn't yet felt an angry hand clamp around my shoulder, so I ducked into the gap between two vending machines and pretended to be checking my phone. Out of the corner of my eye, I saw somebody run into the middle of the circular floor, then falter, glancing around. I could feel sweat gathering hotly about my nose and forehead, until my pursuer made a frustrated noise and kept running in a randomly chosen direction.

I took stock. I thought back to the strangely elaborate motions Ms. Warden had been making with her tablet while paying me. She must have done something to have my name changed on the chip-ID register. Rather an impish prank for a woman who smiled as comfortably as a camel break danced.

If I could just get to my ship, I could be out of danger within the hour. Once I was through the trebuchet gate and hooked up with a pirate clan, or on Cantrabargid, I could forget about my current array of problems and concentrate on the inevitable new ones.

Resuming my head-down, hands-pocketed walk, I made my way through the old concourse, to the bay where the *Neverdie* was parked. I wasn't as worried about being spotted—no tourists came through here, and therefore, no star pilots loitered, only ever passing quickly back and forth between their ships and the Quantunnel arrivals area. Nevertheless, I kept to the shadows formed by piled-up crates and landing legs, and the *Neverdie* was soon in sight.

I tried to think about what I would do if I were any other pilot with reason to believe that Jacques McKeown was in the spaceport. I'd probably start by punching my open palm a few times. Not too much to worry about.

Then what? Without more concrete details I, personally, probably wouldn't go out of my way to act on it, not if it meant leaving my spot. That running person in the entrance plaza might not even have been after me. I was probably worrying over nothing.

I fingered my key ring remote, in the vain hope that maybe for once I wouldn't have to manually pull the airlock door open, but no such luck. The door didn't budge, although the boarding steps unfolded wonkily from underneath, clattering heavily onto the concrete. Of course, there was one thing that I might consider trying, just to appease my curiosity . . .

"That your ship, mate?"

. . . and that would be to check the parking registry, and see if any docked ships were registered to Jacques McKeown. Frozen, with one foot on the first boarding step, I wondered exasperatedly why the chip-ID system had to be integrated with plying everything.

Behind me was a group of around five or six star pilots, none of whom I recognized; they were all part of the night shift crew. As one, they stepped out from the shadow of the ship next to mine, watching me with varying degrees of neutrality in their facial expressions.

"Yeeees," I said, prolonging the word as my mind raced. I was still holding the door remote, so a denial would have immediately lost me credibility. They hadn't immediately set upon me, so there was still room for doubt.

The man who'd spoken was a completely bald, craggy-faced star pilot in a cap and flight jacket virtually identical to mine. He was holding a crowbar, and making a halfhearted effort to keep it concealed behind his leg. "It's nice," he said, nodding slowly. "Cost you much?"

"Er, well, it did when I bought it," I said, trying to look more bemused than terrified. "About ten years ago."

"Ten years ago," parroted a taller star pilot to the speaker's left, wearing a red tunic with faded gold trim. Someone else in the throng made a sarcastic appreciative-whistling noise.

"Must be hard to pay upkeep on a ship that old," said the first speaker. He had his face thrust forward toward me, wearing the kind of confrontational expression that makes you look like you're trying to dislodge a stubborn toffee from the roof of your mouth. "Got a lot of money coming in, then?"

I didn't like the direction things were taking. The situation called for a de-railing. I closed my eyes, flicked my imaginary switch, and felt my confident persona flush through my body, right to the tips of my fingers, which immediately flew to my face. "Oh my god. I'm so sorry. Is this your space?"

The spokesman's brow furrowed, making him lose his confrontational-toffee aspect. "You what?"

I allowed myself to look convincingly frightened, which was not difficult. "Look, I don't want any trouble. Just . . . hear me out. I couldn't afford to cover bay rental this week, and I had to make a landing, and I saw the empty space and I thought I could just drop in and out before—"

"Wait, wait," interrupted the spokesman. "You aren't the one registered for this bay?"

Some members of the throng were starting to look reassuringly disappointed, but I couldn't let it slip, even for a moment. "No," I said, bemused. "Isn't that . . . what this is about?"

"He's not McKeown," said the tall bracket.

If I had let it lie there, turned around, laboriously yanked the airlock door open, and boarded the *Neverdie*, things would have turned out so very differently. But I was afraid of dropping the innocent, unconnected star pilot act. And I knew that any star pilot, even an innocent and unconnected one, would have been intrigued by the sound of that bracket's name. "McKeown? Why would you think I was McKeown?"

The spokesman stopped half concealing the crowbar and started fondling it inoffensively, which was encouraging. "Some doint online has been bragging about how he's gonna meet Jacques McKeown in person," he said. "And someone said they saw him in the spaceport tonight, and his name's on this bay."

I looked down at the square region of concrete that the *Neverdie* occupied. "Serious? Why would he do that? He'd be lynched."

Nobody had moved from their spots, but some of them turned and relaxed their shoulders in ways that changed the situation from a confrontation with a mob to a relaxed discussion between friends. "Yeah, that's what I said," said the tall pilot, looking pointedly at a small chap off to the side.

"He was in the café, I swear!" said the small chap. "He was still logged in! And you know what that rich bracket did? He bought, like, six coffees. Just to rub our noses in how much coffee he can buy. Didn't even drink the plying things. Just spilled them all down his . . . front . . ."

His sentence slipped away from him as he glanced down at my crotch. One by one, the pilots' heads tilted downward like a row of switches on an old-fashioned control panel. I followed their gaze and saw a large coffee stain on the front of my jeans, still wet and glistening.

"Ah," I began.

The body language of a mob came back, along with the crowbar. "I told you!" said the small pilot excitedly. "I knew he had to be one of the plying daytime mob!"

There were any number of logical arguments I could have made. I could have reminded them of what we'd just discussed, that it made absolutely no logical sense for the real Jacques McKeown to use that name in his personal dealings, least of all in a place full of people who fantasized nightly about force-feeding him his own books. I could even have come clean and explained that someone had changed my name on the chip-ID database in aid of a long con at a wealthy Terran's expense. It was the kind of classic fable that may have appealed to their mindset.

But show me a man who thinks that reason will work on an angry mob and I'll show you a man who could be carried away in several standard business-sized envelopes. Instead, I held my hands up in a placatory kind of way and made myself look unconcerned. "Maybe you guys should back off before you do something you regret," I said. Then I focused my gaze on something behind them and injected just the right amount of satisfied relief into my voice. "Wouldn't you agree, officer?"

The pilots collectively spun around. Security at the spaceport was no joke, since they had very little tolerance for anything that might spoil a visitor's first impressions of Ritsuko City and had to be capable of dealing with people like Angelo. The smallest of the rookie night watchmen looked like he could bench-press a Pestulon desert cow.

Fortunately for the belligerent pilots, he wasn't there. And by the time they turned back around, neither was I.

CHAPTER 7

THIS TIME, I just ran. Looking innocent was no longer as viable as simply putting distance between me and my colleagues as quickly as possible. There was shouting behind me, but I didn't dare glance back. I wove between the forest of landing legs and stacks of cargo crates, to use the word *wove* generously; obstacles slammed my shoulders repeatedly and sent me careening in a vaguely consistent direction like a pinball.

With every muscle pulsating with pain, I glanced rapidly around, seeking a security guard to hide behind. But in accordance with my current run of luck, the guards that appeared with such reliability every time I was looking for a place to stick my used chewing gum were nowhere to be seen.

I reached the entrance plaza, neatly hopping the Wrong Way sign without slowing. There were no guards here, either, just some startled visitors waiting for a late-night rickshaw. Why the hell weren't there guards at the entrance plaza? It was literally the first plying place a terrorist would be.

Surely they hadn't been paid off to look the other way for the night. They took pride in being incorruptible, which just meant that their prices were very high, way too high for a group of star pilots with strict budgets for hydrogen fuel.

I hadn't stopped at any point while thinking this, but my speed had faltered, and the sound of several pairs of running feet and shouted mathematical terms was getting louder. I put my mind back to sprinting in the direction I was already facing, which happened to be toward one of the sets of glass entrance doors.

When I had hurled myself toward them and was about six inches from impact, it occurred to me that these doors might have been locked. They did lock some of the doors at night, to reduce the foot traffic they needed to monitor when less staff were around. So the best scenario in that case would be me occupying the same general space as hundreds of shards of broken glass. Or, more likely, bouncing off and falling straight back into the same general space as several fast-moving fists and boots.

I made what effort I could to slow down in the six inches remaining, but the doors swung open under my forearms, unlocked. Disoriented, I stumbled right out into the street, was narrowly missed by one cyclist and was sent spinning on my heel by another.

(Very few residents drive cars in Ritsuko City, or in off-world colonies generally. In a bubble city's enclosed atmosphere, air pollution from vehicle emissions couldn't be written off as the next generation's problem.)

I strung together whatever parts of my conscious mind were still function-ing and managed to dodge my way to the far side of the road. Once there, I dropped to my knees in a convenient patch of grass. I didn't think the other pilots would follow me out into the open. There was no dignity in public scuffling, and we had precious little of that left. I looked behind me anyway.

Unbe-plying-lievable. They were still there. Not only that, but they'd picked up a few more faces along the way, still spilling out of the spaceport's main entrance. Most of them were hopping from foot to foot on the road-side, waiting for a break in bicycle traffic.

Something that looked very much like a beer bottle was hurled toward me and bounced jarringly off the helmet of a random cyclist. I slammed the rough ground with the palms of my hands, just because I wasn't in quite enough pain yet, and shakily resumed running.

I realized that, perhaps unconsciously, I was running for the functioning Quantunnel booth I'd used before, in the middle of the pleasant pedestrian precinct opposite the spaceport. That made sense. I could transport myself to any other location on Luna, literally any of which would be an improvement, as long as I closed the door behind me.

The booth was in sight now, mercifully unattended, and I put whatever energy I had left into the sprint. Wait, I thought. Keying in a destination would take time. Time that, judging by the sound of distressed grass coming from be-hind me, I did not have. The Quantunnel booth only represented an upright, solid object into which I would soon be stomped by a hundred angry feet.

Unless . . .

Still running, I fumbled with my key ring until I had separated my keys and spaceship remote from a narrow plastic tag, printed with the words *U-Stor Storage Solutions*. I had no idea if it would even still work, but since my chances weren't going to get much slimmer, I spun it a few times and flung it toward the booth.

My aim was dead on. The tag, along with the rest of my key ring, bounced off the large metal plate on the lower part of the booth's control panel. In that moment, a green light blinked on, registering the ID number encoded in the tag, and the booth connected conveniently to a preset destination.

I rolled as I reached the booth, neatly recovering my key ring from the ground as I did so, and passed under the shutters as they opened, scraping my back on the two sheets of metal. Then, in two quick, smooth movements, I turned myself around, grabbed the inner shutter, and pulled it down to the ground. An angry fist banged upon the other side as I leaned on the shutter with all my strength, keeping it pinned in place.

It took me a few moments of panting adrenaline comedown to notice that I was in pitch blackness. Keeping one foot holding the shutter down, I fumbled at the smooth rock walls to either side of me and found the light switch. The ceiling was so low that the lightbulb immediately started warming my shoulder. My amazement that the light battery hadn't run out was swiftly replaced by my amazement that my card had still been valid.

For some time after quantum tunneling became part of the public sector, innovators in every field of business (with the obvious exception of mine) were finding new uses for it daily. It was the U-Stor Storage company that first came up with the idea of firing small Quantunnel gates below the surface of Luna, carving out five-foot cubes of rock far underground, selling the stone to building suppliers, and renting out the resulting cube-shaped spaces for storage.

Like virtually everyone else on Ritsuko, I'd rented one. They gave you a plastic tag encoded with the location of your space, and then you could access your possessions from any commercial Quantunnel booth in the universe.

I was surprised that my tag still worked, because I hadn't paid the rental fees in months. They'd even stopped sending me threatening email. I'd assumed they'd given up, canceled the tag and auctioned off all my stuff.

I glanced around the tiny space. Nope, it was all still here: a few cardboard boxes and an ancient bar fridge from my flight school days that my former housemates had insisted I take away. Maybe they hadn't gotten around to the auction. Or maybe they had simply forgotten about me after I stopped drawing attention to myself with late payments.

More angry fists were hitting the shutter behind me. Someone made an effort to pull it open, so I stomped it down hard with both heels. My mind raced for a solution. Then it hit me that if all my stuff was still here, then that would include . . .

Feet still keeping the shutter down, I leaned over and tore the parcel tape from the topmost box, then feverishly opened the flaps. There it was, beside the medal I received for saving the Skurobo people, and cushioned by several crumpled letters from individual Skurobos inviting me to visit (they were a needy bunch): my old blaster pistol.

I weighed it in my hand, reminiscing. Back when I had spent my days adventuring through the galaxy, it had been a constant, reassuring weight on my hip, like a clingy child in a crowded shopping mall. I'd had to put it in storage when I started spending all my time in the spaceport. Security wasn't exactly over the moon (ha ha) about putting up with hordes of destitute star pilots; they took an even dimmer view of us exercising the right to open carry.

And they doubly wouldn't be big on the illegal modification my gun had. Originally it had had two settings: Stun and Kill. These had proved inadequate against the ridiculously well-armored skin of monsters from particularly rough planets, so I'd found a way to tinker with the built-in limitations. The dial now had a third setting, labeled with the handwritten words "Solve All Immediate Problems."

The important thing was that there was still charge in the ammunition cell. Not much, but enough to change the dynamic of the situation. Those pilots out there had come straight from the spaceport's secure area, and therefore wouldn't have been carrying any guns.

I checked that all the blaster's parts were in order and held it close to my face as I crouched and prepared to open the latch. All was silence out there, but I doubted my lynch mob had given up. They must have seen me use the U-Stor tag, so they knew I had no other way out and were almost certainly lying in wait. I didn't have the charge to shoot all of them, but ideally, I wouldn't fire it at all. I'd just step out, make it clear who did and who didn't have a gun, and we'd all discuss things like sensible people.

I puffed out my cheeks and tightened my grip on the gun. Open shutter. Step out. Wave gun. Talk sensibly. Easy.

I closed my eyes, opened the shutter, took a step forward, and then my face bounced painfully off a solid wall of moon rock.

Okay. This? This was smart. The interior of U-Stor Storage spaces didn't have control panels, so users couldn't do something incredibly stupid, like deactivate the tunnel while inside the space and become trapped forever in a ready-made tomb hundreds of feet below the lunar surface. But there were ways that a spiteful person could deactivate it from the outside, thanks to a design flaw now removed from the newest booths. Quite a hellish way to die— and an effective revenge. I wondered which one of them had thought of it.

I bit my lip as hard as I could to stop myself from going immediately into jumping-up-and-down hysterics, which in this space would probably have resulted in brain damage. I sat down heavily on the nearest box and was only half-aware of the hard-earned awards for heroism from a hundred different cultures being squashed, snapped, and broken.

In sitting down, I felt my phone pressing against my hip. I couldn't remember the last time I'd charged it, but to my relief, there was a good 10 percent of battery life. So I wasn't going to die. Or at least, not here, alone and forgotten, entombed with a hundred broken treasures of no worth to anyone but myself. Shame; it would've been a fitting end.

Quantum tunneling had left its pernicious influence on the telecommunications industry as well, so I could now call anyone in the universe. Except my parents, or any other stubborn elderly bracket who just could not be persuaded to upgrade to a QT-supported phone.

The next matter was thinking of someone to call who would not be waiting for me on the other side of the shutter with a baseball bat. That meant I couldn't call any star pilots. I couldn't be sure that any of my fellows would completely dismiss the idea that I was Jacques McKeown.

And that was when I started worrying again, because my phone pretty much only held contact numbers for star pilots. None of my old friends among people I'd saved on extrasolar planets were sophisticated enough to have phones, let alone Quantunnel booths. That's why someone like me could impress them with nothing but an aging ship and a modified blaster pistol.

I started frantically scrolling down my contacts list. Pilot. Pilot. Pilot. Dead. Pilot. In prison. Pilot. Pilot. Gone native. Frobisher.

There was a thought. Frobisher was more of a friend than most, and no longer a pilot. What's more, hadn't I told him that I was being asked to impersonate someone, before anyone had even started throwing names like Jacques McKeown about? I called his number, mindful that, were I not planning to flee the Solar System, he would never let me hear the end of this.

No answer. Of course, it was quite late, and as one of my few sensible friends, Frobisher would be asleep, not out looking for clients, drinking, or getting locked in storage units. I called again, in the hope that maybe the last ring had woken him up and he needed further prompting. Nothing.

I checked my phone's charge. Six percent left. Did I really want to use it all up putting all my eggs in this basket? I could have left a voicemail, but it hardly seemed like a solution, since I would suffocate to death before he heard it.

I kept scrolling. I was reaching the end of the alphabet and starting to sweat, when I saw an entry that had been highlighted, to indicate that it was newly added. It simply said "Warden."

Not only did she know full well that I was not really Jacques McKeown, but this entire situation was directly her fault. It would practically be her duty to rescue me. The problem, though, was that this would go against my original plan, which was to get the trac away from the entire Henderson situation.

I tapped my phone against my knee, thinking. Perhaps succumbing to death was the way to go after all. It's not like I hadn't lived a full life—the box of objects currently disintegrating beneath my arse attested to that. Maybe it was time to lie down and let this brave new Quantunneling universe go on without my burden.

Doints to that. Thirty-seven is not the right sort of age for embracing euthanasia. There were still hours before I had to report to Henderson; I'd just get rescued by Warden, then excuse myself and pick the right moment to attempt legging it again. I called her number.

"Warden," came her impatient voice, after four rings.

"Hello—"

"Please spare me the chatter. State your reason for contacting me."

I only hesitated for a moment. "A bunch of star pilots chased me into a U-Stor booth and shut off the tunnel. I am currently trapped underground and I need rescuing."

"Why did they do this?"

"Because they think I'm Jacques McKeown." The words triggered something in my head. "And why did you change my name to Jacques McKeown, you crazy div?"

"Henderson took your wineglass from the restaurant," she said, keeping her voice as flat as possible. "He intended to fingerprint you to confirm your identity. You are very lucky that I was able to get the change made in time. I have had to exert influence over some people at the ID network's administrative facility."

It was a maddeningly sensible reason, but she could easily have been lying to cover up her psycho-div control-freak head games. "I think you mean that we're *both* very lucky," I pointed out. "Considering what Henderson would do to you if I get found out."

"Do not think that that gives you power, Mr. McKeown."

This, I decided, was one of those "pick your battles" situations. I dropped the matter. "I'm sending you the access code for my U-Stor space. Can you open it from a Quantunnel booth away from the spaceport and let me out?"

"How long have you been in there?"

"What? I dunno. Ten minutes?"

"But you said you were chased inside, so I assume you had an elevated heart rate for a while. Has that come down to a normal level?"

I frowned, confused. "Yeah. Er. Physically, I'm fine; I'm just trapped."

I could hear paper rustling in the background. "Those U-Stor spaces average about five feet cubed, correct?"

"Yeah, they're all pretty standard . . ."

"And the contents? Besides yourself? How much of the space has been filled?"

"A third? Maybe? Why the trac are you asking me that?"

I heard the faint sound of scribbling, and then of a stylus clattering triumphantly onto a datapad. "I'd say, on the low end, that you have around four hours and thirty minutes of oxygen left."

"Right, so . . ."

"In which case, you can expect rescue in four hours and twenty-five minutes."

Before replying, I clenched my fists as hard as I could and counted slowly to five. "I would really appreciate it if you could drop the psycho-div revenge one-upmanship for one second. I am asking you to rescue me from a deadly situation that you got me into."

"Don't misunderstand me. My time is very tightly scheduled, and several equally urgent matters currently require my attention."

"Like what?!"

"Firstly, I have to spend the night faking a lengthy correspondence of emails between us, in case Henderson checks into it. Secondly, I am currently only wearing my underwear. You called in the middle of the shoot. And it was extremely difficult to hire a cameraman and a lighting engineer at this time of night."

I blinked a few times. "You know, most people would have just recorded it by themselves," I suggested. "With a phone camera or something."

"That attitude, Mr. McKeown, is why I am the personal assistant to the richest and most powerful man in the Solar System, and you are going to be spending the rest of the night trapped in a U-Stor facility."

CHAPTER 8

THE CEILING LIGHT was programmed to wink out every few minutes, making the assumption that the user had enough sense to not be inside after the tunnel connection was closed, and I made a conscious decision not to keep turning it back on. It would be wiser not to exert myself, and it decreased the chances of me smashing my head against the ceiling.

My phone's battery lasted to about halfway through the first word of my voicemail message to Frobisher. Then the screen died and I was alone, on an uncomfortable box, in pitch blackness and silence, with one solitary psycho-div the only person in the universe aware of my plight.

With no means of telling the time, paranoia set in. After what, in retrospect, was probably only the first hour, I became convinced that my remaining three and a half hours had been and gone. As even more time passed, I grew more and more certain that Warden was not going to keep her promise and rescue me.

It was like Frobisher said: if I would do for a last-minute replacement, anyone would. Oh sure, she'd introduced me to the Hendersons as McKeown, but they were Terrans, and Terrans were all self-absorbed trac-heads who couldn't tell one Lunarian from another. It was all that high gravity they had down there squashing their brains in. She'd probably finished her shoot and gone straight down to the spaceport again to grab the closest vaguely similar bracket in a flight jacket. There was absolutely no shortage.

Leaving me here. To die. And as the air grew thin and death became a tangible reality, the philosophical attitude I had displayed earlier disappeared in an impotent, childish rage. I didn't want to die. Not in an inescapable five-foot cube. I wanted to be in my cockpit again, with infinity stretching off in all directions beyond one slim layer of plexiglass.

Here, now, my frustrated mind seeking desperately for exits that did not exist, I was thinking clearly for the first time in years. If I could have been allowed to live just a little longer, I wouldn't have gone back to the spaceport, struggling every day to make money because I couldn't move on from the past. I was going to find a new Golden Age for myself.

I leapt to my feet, then sat suddenly back down again after nearly braining myself on the ceiling. Ply tourists, ply Mr. Henderson, ply Jacques McKeown, and ply piracy, for that matter—I'd forge my own path. Set out into the Black. Do what I used to do—help people less fortunate than myself. Make a difference. I'd work to make the universe better if I could only have just a little bit more life . . .

At that point I think I must have been throwing myself around the room, because the next thing I remember is flying toward the shutters, and them rattling open just as I did so. I stumbled and landed on my back, sliding across a tiled floor before coming to rest with my head against what felt like a high-heeled shoe.

I blinked until my blurred vision had cleared up, and I could see the disapproving face of Ms. Warden, silhouetted against a bright fluorescent ceiling light. She was back in the pantsuit she had worn when we'd first met, unless she had several identical ones, which would not have surprised me in the least.

"Your first day at work has begun, Mr. McKeown," she said, looking at me over her omnipresent datapad.

"Urgh." I sat up a little too quickly, and it didn't feel like all of my brain had come for the ride. "I am not ready for this."

"Nevertheless," said Warden primly.

"You know what, I think I forgot something in there." I made an attempt to scuttle back through the shutters, but Warden stepped smartly over me and pulled something out of the Quantunnel booth's console, causing the shutters to slam down. I pawed uselessly at the ridged metal.

"This way," she said, trotting along the corridor without looking to see if I was following.

I took a moment's pause to lean on the side of the Quantunnel booth and pinch my eyes a few times, then jogged after her to catch up. "Don't suppose it matters to you that I genuinely thought I was going to die in there?" I said.

She gave me a cold look. "Then consider yourself inducted into the Henderson organization."

I followed her through a set of double doors into a bare corridor painted in beige, with visible pipes and cables running along the walls. More a transition between places than a place in itself, like the behind-the-scenes parts of a cruise liner, or . . .

"The spaceport," I slurred aloud. "Tell me this isn't the spaceport."

"Calm yourself," she sniffed, bobbing along on her high heels. "This is Mr. Henderson's private spaceport, on the north side of Ritsuko City."

"There's only one private spaceport in Ritsuko City. It's on top of the Ubatsu building."

"And the Ubatsu building is the new headquarters of Henderson Lunar and Extrasolar Enterprises."

We passed through a set of double doors into a beautifully decorated connecting hallway, with thick-pile red carpeting, mahogany wood panelling on the walls, and the occasional artwork that bore the hallmarks of mass production. The whole place stank of fresh varnish and paint, and some of the stone busts of Roman emperors placed at regular intervals against the walls were still wrapped in transparent plastic.

A cold dread gripped me as I realized that I was deep in the belly of the beast that was Henderson, and that immediate escape was looking less and less likely. I followed Warden toward a set of heavy airlock doors that I presumed led to some kind of landing bay. "Is . . . Mr. Henderson around?" I probed.

"No," she said, with just barely perceptible relief. "He has left it to me to see you and Daniel off. A lot of things currently require his attention. He has made the spontaneous decision to expand into off-world operations."

"Take it you don't approve."

She stopped, startled by my statement, and turned. "What? What on earth makes you think that?"

"I dunno. You just seemed like you didn't approve. Admittedly I don't yet know what it looks like when you do approve of something, but I can take an educated guess."

She leaned in so close I had to lean back a little. Her face was still neutral, but very red all of a sudden. "I am completely in support of all of Mr. Henderson's decisions. If your intention is to drive a wedge between me and my employer, then you will not succeed. Are we clear?"

I glanced behind myself, in case there was some kind of agent provocateur standing there that she was addressing instead of me, then displayed my palms. "Crys-tal?" I said, baffled.

Scowling, Warden placed her hand against a security scanner. A high-pitched hiss burst out from the hinges of the airlock door, which grew quickly into a roar of wind as the thick steel slowly parted, revealing the docking platform.

The Ubatsu building was near enough the tallest building in Ritsuko City, which was a very competitive field. The nature of a bubble city ensures that there isn't much room for expanding outward, but expanding upward is always an option until you reach the legally enforced buffer zone between the city and the glass ceiling. Ubatsu reached as close to that buffer as it dared, and from the rooftop docking bay I felt I could throw a stone straight upward and watch it ping off the plexiglass shield.

Then I saw the ship parked in the center of the bay, and froze where I was, midway through the doorway. My jaw hung loosely like a little hammock in which my tongue tossed restlessly as I sought the words.

After Quantunneling started tearing the transport industry apart, most shipbuilders realized that there wouldn't be much money in selling practical designs anymore. Not the kind of ships star pilots favored: sleek and maneuverable with plenty of missile tubes and fast-enough engines to outrun enemy ships weighed down by too many missile tubes.

No. All of a sudden, anything that merely desperately needed to get somewhere could be there at half the cost and zero time, so they couldn't make money selling ships for transportation anymore. Not long afterward, the only new ships getting built were luxury yachts that rich brackets used for vacation cruises. And with opportunities for commerce growing exponentially, there were a lot more of those rich brackets popping up. Everyone except star pilots was making money hand over fist. Even street buskers looked down on each other if they couldn't hire a backing vocalist or two.

And new money being what it is, ship designers competed for a while to create the ship that reflected the least possible amount of taste in its owner. They made pleasure ships with gold-plated hulls, custom nacelle rims, observation lounges with bar and karaoke facilities . . . and every single one would immediately brighten up the day of any pirate who happened upon them midflight.

This became clear fairly swiftly, and decadence was toned back down a little in favor of a degree of practicality, so the newer ships tucked some plying fast engines in between all the jacuzzis. Daniel Henderson's brand-new ship was not one of those. Mr. Henderson had presumably done very little research, and had chosen the ship on the basis of the best being the most expensive. The ship before me was the very one that many pirates had affectionately nicknamed "The Dinner Bell."

"Oh, Christ," I said, still staring. "It's the Corona Platinum God of Whale Sharks."

Start with something shaped vaguely like a jar. A huge, thick, curvy jar with very few aerodynamic properties, the kind of thing they sell yeast extract in. Then make it the size of a house so that its curved, spidery landing legs are visibly straining under the weight. Then find some way to give the jar a tumorous disease that covers it with observation bubbles, each housing a bedroom or some decadent facility or another (it's a very strange disease). Finally, cover the whole thing in highly polished metal, colored a vibrant aquatic blue.

Warden was beside me. "Is it seriously called that?"

My gaze continued following the ship's bulky curves as I spoke, and my voice seemed to come from far away. "Corona went through all the metals, silver class, gold class, and platinum class. Then they went through titles, king class, emperor class, up to god class—then they started using the names of fish. This was the last one Corona made before they started reining it in."

"Yes, well, Mr. Henderson does have a tendency to indulge Daniel," said Warden.

I turned to her. "No, what I'm trying to say is, this is a really, really bad ship to be cruising in. It's a deathtrap."

One of her eyebrows sprang up like a gazelle hearing a tiger fart. "My understanding was that the manufacturer has a good reputation for preventing mechanical failures."

"It's functional, yeah, but look at it. It might as well have a big sign trailing out the back saying 'Pirates Please Kill Us and Take All Our Stuff.' And it would only move like a whale shark if the whale shark was on dry land. In Earth gravity."

"I see," said Warden, elongating the ee. She looked up at the ship again, and frowned. "I would remind you that you assured us that you were willing to fly, I think your exact words were, 'anything with at least one wing.'"

I looked sadly at the ship's stubby wings. They looked about as conducive to flight as a cocktail stick lodged in a swan's throat. "Nobody flies these things anymore, I'm telling you."

"Urgh! I told you, Dad!" said a familiar voice from surprisingly close behind. "I told you you should have gotten me the red one."

Daniel had come out onto the bay by the same door we had, wearing a silvery flight suit of the kind some star pilots still wore if they were too cheap to buy a shaving mirror.

Henderson wasn't far behind, wearing a different reindeer-patterned sweater from the one he'd had the day before, combined with slippers and a pair of white shorts so short that were it not for the belt, I would've mistaken them for boxers. The creature known as Carlos was bringing up the rear, still wearing its specially tailored tuxedo like an unusually formal set of goalposts.

"Good morning, Mr. McKeown," said Henderson, grinning like a shark. "You look . . ." He hesitated as he took in my appearance, which had been done no favors by a night in a cave with no changes of clothing. ". . . Present. You were saying something about this very expensive ship I picked out?"

"He was saying it's lame!" said Daniel, just as I opened my mouth. "He was saying that it's a load of multiplying subtraction." He glanced at me as he used the words, and seemed downhearted by my grimace of distaste.

Mr. Henderson was still smiling, but there was a sadness in his eyes. As he locked gaze with me, he absent-mindedly picked wool pills off his reindeer sweater with his cassowary-talon ring. "Do tell us your professional opinion on the ship, Jacques."

"It's so lame, isn't it, Jacques," said Daniel, nodding to himself. "Dad should've gotten me the red one, shouldn't he. God, he is so stupid, isn't he?"

This was probably a good time to start representing myself in this little negotiation. I made a loud throat-clearing sound that inadvertently came out sounding a bit squawk-like. "Obviously it's a very sound purchase—that shade of blue is the very latest in aerodynamic innovation, I've heard—but this model does tend to get attacked by pirates a lot."

Daniel's demeanor changed instantly. His eyes sparkled, although they could just have been reflecting the flight suit. "Oh my god. You think we might see pirates? That would be so awesome!"

"Well, I think that settles it," said Henderson, clapping his hands. I don't think he'd been paying attention since his last contribution to the discourse. "Have a nice time up in space, Danny, and I know you'll get lonely without your dear old dad, but know you've got the best star pilot in the universe to protect you." He kissed the top of Daniel's head.

"URGH I HATE you," replied Daniel, out of reflex.

"I love you too," said Henderson, smiling at me as Daniel made a particularly loud, embarrassed noise.

Warden, who until this point had drifted into the background in a way that seemed to come very naturally to her, subtly drifted back out again. "Mr. Henderson, perhaps we should not entirely dismiss Mr. McKeown's feelings? The important thing is Daniel's safety, after all."

"Oh, I agree, Penny. That's why you're going with them."

Warden blinked twice. "Sir?"

"You wouldn't expect me to leave Danny alone with a complete stranger, would you? He might end up getting sold as meat to some planet of primitive alien scumbags. I need someone I can trust up there. More importantly, someone Daniel trusts."

"Yeah, it's fine, can we go now?" said Daniel petulantly.

Warden looked at him, then at Henderson, then back to her pad, which provided no help. "Mr. Henderson . . . I have a great many duties as your personal assistant."

"All taken care of, Penny. Cindy's taking over. Aren't you?"

Carlos slid aside with a sort of stone-like grinding noise to reveal that a young woman had been behind him all along, in a demonstration of background blending as yet unrivaled. She looked essentially identical to Warden, except younger, and smaller by a factor of around 10 percent. She was also paler, and all her facial features seemed to be arranged with infinitesimal precision like a bone china tea set.

"Ms. Warden," she said, clutching her own tablet.

"Ms. Sternall," said Warden. An awful lot was being said in their curt greetings and locked gaze, to the point that I felt grateful that neither woman was holding a broken bottle. "Mr. Henderson, with respect, Ms. Sternall has not been my assistant long enough to fully grasp all the subtleties . . ."

"Oh, she'll figure it out. I gave her all your login details," interrupted Henderson, waving a hand. "Besides, you're getting promoted. Surprise!"

"To what role?" asked Warden, in the tone of one who had just been asked what form of execution they preferred.

"To head of Henderson Lunar and Extrasolar Enterprises! You couldn't expect me to be the one to oversee the operations. The thought of spending much more time in one of these off-world colonies makes me want to spit up blood. I left some paperwork in your cabin; check that over and you can get straight to it when you get back, yeah?"

"Can we GO now," suggested Danny, whose repeated attempts to walk briskly into the ship had all been aborted when nobody had made any motion to follow.

"Er, I just need to stop back at the Quantunnel booth, get my stuff out of storage," I said, pointing a thumb over my shoulder, uncomfortably aware of the tense stare-down still going on between Warden and Cindy.

"No need," said Mr. Henderson firmly. "The ship has its own onboard Quantunnel booth. It's got all the mod cons, you know. Now, are there any last misgivings you wish to raise?"

There was an impatient edge to his voice. Carlos, I noticed, could move pretty subtly when he wanted to: at some point he had moved to a point between me and the door by which I'd entered, responding to some shrewd instinct. When he saw me looking, he slowly folded his arms like a medieval fortress raising a pair of drawbridges.

I gave in. "No, boss," I muttered.

"Good! I'm sure Danny will have nothing but wonderful things to tell me." He patted me lightly on the shoulder, and I felt the little sting of an extended cassowary talon. I met his gaze, and it was a stark contrast to his tone of voice. After a moment, he gave Warden the same look, and she swallowed quietly.

Daniel pressed a shiny black remote that was still wrapped in a gift ribbon, and the airlock door hissed open with a smooth, almost seductive motion, folding down to form a set of shallow steps. Daniel walked reverently in, glancing back at Ms. Warden, who was walking slowly and stiffly as if her legs were moving with no apparent input from her conscious mind.

Henderson and Cindy watched from the edge of the docking bay, waving with a varied mixture of earnestness and sarcasm. Carlos just stared, and I had a distinct impression that some part of his mind, buried somewhere in all that muscle, was taking meticulous notes.

I followed Warden up the steps into the shining-clean airlock, and a not-unpleasant new ship smell reached my nostrils. I pressed the button to close the exterior door behind me, and appraised the two people I was now sharing an awkwardly small space with. Warden seemed frozen; her expression hadn't changed since her stare-off with Cindy, and she was gripping the datapad with white knuckles. Daniel was staring at me like a hungry man regards a sandwich artist.

My options were becoming fewer by the moment, I realized. I might have to kidnap them.

CHAPTER 9

I HAD TO admit, the buyer of the Platinum God of Whale Sharks certainly got their money's worth, assuming what they wanted to buy was a brief period of obscene luxury and comfort followed by a prolonged one in the company of pirates. Daniel had immediately bolted off to inspect the bridge, Warden had drifted off on some errand of her own, and I was looking for the Quantunnel booth.

On the way, I found myself mentally cataloging all the problems that would arise in an emergency situation. The walls were covered in decorated silver plating, and the floor with thick-pile red carpeting, all of which would have to be hastily torn off if I needed to access components in the infrastructure. None of the interior doors locked, and there was no dedicated security or regroup room. I stumbled upon one of the observation lounges in my search, and not a single item of furniture, not the beanbag chairs or the snooker table or the karaoke machine, was bolted down. So in the event of gravity failure or depressurization, everything would go flying. The snooker table alone would rack up an impressive body count.

In the back of a small reading room—packed with Jacques McKeown's entire body of work, naturally—I found the Quantunnel booth. For one heartening moment I thought I had found an obvious escape route, unsupervised, but the moment I booted up the interface and started searching for a destination, I was halted by a request for a passcode. Operation Kidnap was back on the table.

Fortunately, all booths had to have unrestricted access to U-Stor spaces, thanks to a law that was passed after one poor bracket was denied access to his medication, so I scanned my key ring tag and the shutters promptly opened. I toyed with the idea of sealing myself inside again, but swiftly dismissed the thought and instead recovered my gun. After a little digging, I found my shoulder holster and put it on under my jacket. This, I decided, was a concealed-carry situation.

Overpowering Daniel I didn't see being much of a problem, but Warden would be something of an X factor. I'd have to take that datapad away from her, for a start. I had a feeling that, at the first sign of ill intent, she'd use it to hack the universe and erase me from existence. I'd probably just have to wait until she was asleep, assuming she slept and didn't just recharge herself from a wall socket every night.

Once there was no one to interfere with where I took the ship, it would just be a matter of picking an amenable pirate family, going to their turf, and being a bit too obvious. On this ship, that would be the easy part. It really was a boarding waiting to happen.

A day ago I had thought that being a pirate wasn't even a last resort. How naive I had been way back before the multiple threats to my life (in which I included every individual second spent in the company of Mr. Henderson). It was a stark and hungry existence, even more so than charter piloting; at least then you could always live off abandoned meals in the Sushi Station, as long as you got there before the janitors.

But at this point it was a matter of survival, and no one could blame me, especially after the treatment I'd had at the hands of Warden. I pictured her explaining the situation to the police. "He took me hostage until he could run off with a pirate gang!" "And you did nothing to provoke him, madam?" "No! Apart from directly and indirectly threatening to kill him several times and deliberately ruining his life so that he was forced to run off with a pirate gang."

That gave me pause for thought. I stopped in the middle of a connecting hallway. Escaping the ship and joining pirates really was a fairly obvious move on my part. Warden must have considered it. What if she'd already hacked the universe to make all the pirates want me dead, too?

I heard a ladylike sigh of frustration that seemed very familiar and noticed that one of the doors in the hallway was ajar. Through the crack, I saw Warden sitting on the edge of a bed—a bed, naturally, not a recessed bunk, because large pieces of furniture are exactly what I love taking up floor space when I have to run to the bridge for an emergency course change—inspecting the contents of a briefcase, which I assumed Henderson had left here for her.

Right. This was an opportunity. I just had to start building the persona of a broken-down star pilot resigned to his predicament with absolutely no intention of moving in a piratey sort of career path. I rapped upon the door with two knuckles. "Anyone in?"

"What do you want?"

I took that as an invitation and pushed the door open wide, remaining in the door frame. In keeping with the rest of the ship, it was a very pleasant bedroom, straight out of a luxury hotel, with a wide, circular viewing window representing another crucial weak point in the hull. Warden was facing away from me, still reading the paperwork in her hands. I flicked the little switch in my head and coughed politely. "Hey. Can't tell you how relieved I am that Henderson didn't want to tag along in person."

She didn't look at me. "You came in here to tell me that you can't tell me something?"

Not a promising start. "If we keep our heads down, stay in the Solar System within the reach of security services, I don't see the trip being a problem. What I was saying about pirates earlier, that was, you know, worst-case-scenario talk. In case you were worried."

"I see."

"It's like how you have to turn your phone off before making a trebuchet jump. It's very, very unlikely to teleport us to an evil parallel universe, but anything we can do to reduce the chance . . ."

"Don't let me keep you from the preflight checks," she said pointedly, still not turning to look at me.

I felt I'd planted enough seeds of innocence for now. I turned to go. "All right, see you later. And congratulations on the promotion, by the way."

There was a rustling crash of paper in distress. I spun around. Warden was suddenly standing upright, facing me and clutching her datapad in her usual professional pose, but the paperwork she had been looking at was now strewn all over the floor. It had been flung with such force that some sheets were still drifting around the room like large, rectangular snowflakes.

"Mr. McKeown," said Warden, with a dangerous quaver in her monotone voice. The datapad was shaking.

"Ms. Warden?" I noticed that, with no actual conscious thought on my part, I had put up my hands in a surrender gesture.

"I appreciate that I have made life difficult for you." She framed each syllable carefully, as if navigating a verbal minefield. "But both of us are mutually trapped in this extremely dangerous situation, and your smug sarcasm is not helping."

I felt the switch in my head turn back the other way. My hands dropped. "I nearly got plying lynched because of you! And trapped in a cave! All you had to do was make a sexy video, which you put way more effort into than was necessary, by the way! I wasn't even being sarcastic! Why would you think I was . . ." My monologue switched tracks midjourney as I read the minuscule changes in her expression. "Is this promotion not a thing we like? Why wouldn't a promotion be good? It's got *pro* right there in the word."

Somewhat softened—in the sense that quartz is somewhat softer than diamond—Warden looked away. "Henderson has made me a divisional head."

"Yeah. Well done you."

"He made Brian Pritchard a divisional head, too."

I was still trying to read her face, but she had reined her emotions back in, and it was like trying to make a picture out of a particularly nondescript cloud. "And we don't like Brian Pritchard?"

"Brian Pritchard was my predecessor as Mr. Henderson's assistant. Just under a year ago, he began serving nineteen consecutive life sentences."

"So, no, then?"

Warden sat gently back down onto the mattress and stared at the papers splayed across the carpet. "The UR's current government have been making a concerted effort to combat corruption. Since they came into power, there have been several high-profile investigations into the Henderson organization's activities," she said. "Each time, all incriminating evidence has mysteriously led to only one of the company divisions. Each time, the head of that division has taken full responsibility. Each time, Mr. Henderson's lawyers have convinced the jury that Henderson himself knew nothing about it. It has been a continuous pattern. He now refers to the process as the 'naughty-ectomy.'"

"Ah," I said, understanding at last. "And I take it that Henderson is actually more closely involved than the official record states?"

She passed over one of the loose pieces of paper. "Look at this."

It was a rather poor-quality satellite picture of a bubble city. I didn't immediately recognize it on sight, but the tacky pseudo-Arabian Nights architecture gave it away: it was New Dubai, the colony on the desert moon Sigma

14-D. At the bottom was some writing in a red spidery hand. "*P: Investigate potential market for all the incredibly illegal things we sell. Mr. H.*" Then he had drawn a little smiley face.

"This is why Mr. Henderson has given me these instructions in a non-electronic format. All of these papers are going to be burned."

"Not necessarily. You could—"

"No, McKeown, they are. They are going to be burned because I am going to burn them. Mr. Henderson will instruct me to, and Mr. Henderson's instructions must be carried out."

I leaned on the door frame, arms folded. "Mr. Henderson also instructed you to employ the real Jacques McKeown for his son's birthday. But you actually haven't. You got one over him there."

She glared at me. "And along with the video shoot, that knowledge is why I did not sleep last night."

I raised a finger. "Hang on. So you've only been Henderson's assistant for less than a year?"

She looked a little ill. "Henderson has never had an assistant for more than a year. I only found that out after I was promoted. Before then, I mainly looked after Daniel's affairs. Henderson hand-picked me from the administrative team of his corporation, and—"

"Whoa," I interrupted, swapping my raised finger for a raised hand. "What do you mean, you looked after Daniel's affairs?"

She reddened and looked at the floor, shifting her weight. "Daniel had been falling behind at school, and Henderson . . . I was looking for a way to rise closer to the inner circle; I didn't know the full extent . . ."

"Oh, go forth and multiply," I breathed, wide eyed and grinning. "That is beautiful. You were the plying *nanny*."

She stiffened, rage flashing in her eyes. "I was not a nanny! I was a tutor and a personal assista—"

From the hidden speakers in the ceiling, there came the sound of a string quartet experiencing a momentary burst of loud enthusiasm, followed by Daniel's voice. "This is your captain speaking," he said, his mock-professional tone wavering with barely contained excitement and impatience. "Would star pilot Jacques McKeown please report to the bridge for space adventure time."

I sighed contentedly. "Well. Little Lord Dointleroy is calling. Let's talk about this later." As I unfolded my arms and turned to leave, the zip fastener on my open flight jacket brushed my holstered blaster pistol, rattling audibly.

Warden glanced up just in time to see me holding my jacket closed in about the most obvious way possible. Her eyebrows went up, first one, then the other. "Mr. McKeown, is that a gun?"

I thought quickly. It probably wasn't worth trying to deny it. So I went the opposite direction.

"Uh, yeah," I said beratingly, as if she'd merely asked me if I was wearing trousers. I held my jacket open, then snapped my fingers to signal realization. "Oh, I know what you're worried about. Don't fret, it's only a blaster pistol, see? Energy based. Won't leave stray projectiles knocking holes in the hull. Anyway, like I said, I'm needed on the bridge so I'll see you later bye."

Then I turned smartly around and walked away, crossing my fingers and hoping to God that she'd drop the matter. It had always been the best technique for getting out of awkward conversations with Mum.

CHAPTER 10

THE BRIDGE WAS grandiose, of course. It was a circular chamber within the largest front-facing observation bubble, with a magnificent captain's chair in the center, artistically realized entirely in curved lines and silvery mock leather. In front of it was a complicated-looking horseshoe-shaped console about fifty times larger than it needed to be. A cursory glance on my way across the room revealed that the console had little to do with controlling the actual ship and seemed mainly concerned with disco lighting effects and adjusting the backrest.

"Is this, like, the best ship you've ever piloted?" asked Daniel proudly, gazing at me from over his illuminated control panel.

I rotated in my chair and looked down at my own controls before answering. There was a two-joystick steering system, and every other function was controlled by a touchscreen in between. No pedals, no gauges, no separate controller for externals. I had to flip through three menu screens on the touchscreen to find the controls for the weapon countermeasures. There might as well have been a button that unrolled red carpets for boarding parties.

"Well, it suits my purposes," I said, guardedly. Daniel beamed. "Are we ready for takeoff?"

"Ooh! Not yet." He pressed one of the illuminated buttons in front of him and leaned a little too close to a nearby mike. "Prepare for takeoff!", he shouted, before sitting back and grinning at me expectantly.

I drummed my fingers on my station. "That was it, was it?"

"Did I do it all right?"

"Uh. Yeah. Textbook." I turned back to my touchscreen, checked the external cameras to make sure the bay was clear, and activated the engine.

The ship lurched forward as an apparently slightly poorly-angled takeoff jet belched into life, and I narrowly escaped gouging my eyes out on the two joysticks. Then the landing legs rapidly withdrew into their housing like startled trapdoor spiders and the ship lurched the other way. I wrestled with the sticks until the angle was somewhat corrected, and the ship bobbed clumsily on a cushion of thrust like a fat person trying to get comfortable on a beanbag chair.

"Wow," breathed Daniel appreciatively. "Listen to that engine purr. Like a cat."

If there was anything about this ship that was like a cat, it was its willingness to do as it was told. Not the engine, which was greedily consuming about three times as much fuel as a ship this weight would realistically need, projecting the energy from the thrusters the way an overfed pig projectile vomits swill back into the trough. It climbed up into the sky in the manner of an overweight cherub with undersized wings, correcting its course with the occasional well-timed fart. Daniel was enjoying the view of the city, sitting proudly upright like a benevolent overseer.

I set a wobbling course for the airlock at the very apex of Ritsuko's plexi-glass dome, which reminded me that we needed to call in for clearance. I eventually found the communications tab, after several touchscreen swipes and pop-up advertisements, and hailed the upside-down control tower.

"Golf Whiskey Sushi Zero Zero Niner One calling Apex Tower," I said in my professional voice. "Requesting exit to Big Black, over."

"Apex Tower to Golf Whiskey Sushi, exit request acknowledged," came the tower controller's voice. "Stand by, your vessel will be scanned."

I was chummy with a lot of ground control and tower boys, since we'd all been thrown on neighboring trac-heaps after Quantunneling came about, so I had a pretty good idea what was coming next. I took a deep breath and waited.

"Apex Tower to Golf Whiskey Sushi. Seriously? Over."

I let the deep breath out again. "Golf Whiskey Sushi to Apex Tower. Don't worry, it's not mine. Over."

"Exit granted. Opening internal airlock access. Have fun with the pirates. And with explaining the blaster damage to whatever plying fatheaded rich bracket you're flying that thing for. Over and out."

I risked a look back at Daniel while the ship was in the airlock and we were waiting to be cycled out through the inner and outer doors. He was still watching me with a huge excited smile on his face, like a dog on their first car trip before they've come to associate such things with the vet.

"That was so cool how you were talking just then," he said, jiggling up and down. "All that star pilot banter, it was like actually being in one of your books. Hey, do you think, after the trip, we could go to one of your star pilot bars and meet all your drinking buddies?"

I tried to picture how that would turn out. An underage client walking into somewhere like the Brandied Bracket and announcing that it's okay, he's being accompanied by his friend Jacques McKeown. My mind's eye was suddenly flooded with shoe leather. "No offense, Daniel, but I'm only being paid to fly."

"Oh. Sure. That's cool. You can just drop me off at Dad's new place when we're done. And then I can tell him all about the time I had."

That was the first time I began to wonder exactly how many layers of intellect I was up against. What game were Daniel and I playing here? Poker or Guess Who?

When the outer airlock was open I took the God of Whale Sharks upward, and I was almost lurched out of my chair again when we escaped the effects of Ritsuko's artificial gravity field. Once I'd killed the thrusters and jiggled the joysticks into line, the ride became comparatively responsive. The ship certainly benefited from being in zero gravity; now all it needed was six or seven weeks' work by a team of men with angle grinders.

Below us, Luna seemed a lot smaller, especially with the Earth hanging directly overhead like a yellow disco ball. The black infinity on all sides gave the usual dizzying vertigo for a second. I took my customary moment to meditate on it, then began plotting a course. That ran into an immediate roadblock.

"So, you haven't told me where you actually want to go," I said.

"Ooh! We should go to Earth first."

I turned and looked at him again. "I was under the impression you were after a more exotic adventure than the place where you live."

"Oh, we just need to make a quick stop. It's cool."

"I can't land on Earth. I haven't got the paperwork," I revealed. "I can't get the paperwork without six months of background checks, and they've got a lot of tricky legislation for people trying to land unauthorized. 'Tricky legislation' is the name they have for surface-to-air missiles."

"Nah, it's cool," said Daniel, *cool* being the default position of the entire universe, apparently. "We don't have to land. We just need to pick up one of my, er . . . friends. In Cloud Castle. You can just fly us close to Earth and I can use the Quantunnel booth."

Cloud Castle. I'd heard rumors about it. An exclusive gated community for the ultrarich residents of the United Republic, attached to a point halfway up one of the space elevators they used to get workers up to the satellite surveillance network. It made sense that the Hendersons and their friends lived there. The only reason someone with the money to leave Earth wouldn't do so would be if they never had to set foot on the ground.

"You can't Quantunnel to Earth from orbit," I pointed out. "Earth's Quantunnel network doesn't allow offworld transport. It's their law. We'd need to land first."

"Oh. Well, it'd probably be cool if we just landed quickly."

My fingers were drumming on the joystick. "I doubt the authorities would see it that way, Daniel."

"No no no, we have to. It's really important. Come on, it's really easy to just quickly land and pick something up and go. Dad's friends do it all the time."

"These friends of your dad," I said. "Do they tend to be . . . burly sorts? In suits? With guns? 'Cos I have a pretty good idea of why they don't get hassled."

"Do you want to meet them?"

I paused for a moment, digesting this, then rotated one hundred and eighty degrees in my chair and placed my hands tentatively on the joysticks. Then I made a snap decision and rotated one hundred and eighty degrees right back. "Was that a threat?"

"What?"

"I'm not asking in a doint-waving counterthreat kind of way, you understand, I genuinely couldn't tell if it was a threat or not."

"No, it wasn't a threat, seriously," said Daniel, but he kept smiling earnestly.

I wasn't prepared to call it. "It's fine if it was a threat. I respond well to threats. It clears the air. I just like to have a grip on the situation."

"Okay, it was a threat."

"Are you only saying that because I said it was fine?"

"Um. Maybe."

I stared into his wide, trusting, admiring eyes, his big, beaming smile. There was always the possibility that he was on the level and had been only saying innocent things that I, in my paranoid way, had taken for veiled threats. And even if he wasn't, would Mr. Henderson care that much for Daniel's complaints? How much did he dote on his son? Enough to buy him whatever he asked for, but spending money was something he seemed to do pretty casually. And he didn't care enough to do thirty seconds of research and realize the ship he was buying was total pirate bait. There was a distinct possibility that Daniel did not actually have any power here.

Power to have me violently murdered, that is.

I placed my hands on the joysticks and sighed. "Shall we just stop off on Earth, then?"

"Yay!"

CHAPTER II

THANKFULLY, AS PARANOID as the United Republic could be about non-Terrans, they were still slightly more paranoid about their own citizens. Almost the entirety of the satellite surveillance network around Earth pointed inward, and it didn't take long to find a gap in the coverage big enough to squeeze even the Platinum God of Whale Sharks through. After that I was able to mask our presence by hiding in the upper pollution layer.

One of the broader societal effects of Quantunneling, I'd noticed, is that people became much worse at giving directions. The best Daniel could offer was that Cloud Castle was "in the sky somewhere." Although Quantunneling probably wasn't entirely to blame.

Fortunately, a space elevator is a difficult thing to miss, and even with smog reducing visibility to roughly the distance between my face and the tip of my nose it didn't take long to find the thick silvery-blue cable snaking off into the clouds in both directions. Then it was just a matter of hugging close and following it downward.

The first sign that we were drawing close to our destination was when the yellow clouds began turning green, then to a rich, healthy blue, apparently due to artificial coloration. The next sign was when the clouds began to thin and we almost ran straight into an artificial sun, attached to the space elevator with a gigantic steel brace.

Past that, we found ourselves in a massive sphere of clear air, apparently maintained by a complicated array of powerful fans that were making a determined effort to use up what energy the planet had left as quickly as possible. In the center of this space was Cloud Castle, and it was clear that, for all the things Mr. Henderson had had to say about bubble colonies, he can't have been completely averse to the concept.

Cloud Castle was a network of tightly bunched spherical habitats clinging to the space elevator like a colossal glass raspberry on a branch. I peered into the domes as we flew past and saw a succession of neatly spaced white houses and perfectly-kept green lawns, interspersed with gleaming white surveillance poles, each with row upon row of cameras along its length. As we passed by human figures, lightly dressed in fashionable pastels, their tiny faces turned to look, suspicious. Shortly, the cameras began doing likewise.

"We're drawing too much attention," I said, uncomfortably. "Where's the plying docking bay?"

"Oh yeah, it's in the middle somewhere," said Daniel. He made a very strange gesture that involved bending his wrist right back and pointing to something below and to the left of him. "That way."

"Thanks," I said, smiling with both rows of teeth.

The ship circled the dome cluster like a mosquito who'd shown up at an orgy and was trying to decide which buttock to sample first. We must have been spotted by every resident in the place by the time I noticed a set of bay doors in the roof of a small, white dome marking the nexus of six large habitats.

The ship hovered close to the doors and my hand hovered over the communicator as I concocted a lie to tell the ground control people. If I could come up with something that would get us inside, I could figure it out from there. The never-fail method was to put on the falsetto voice and claim to be going into labor, but that tended to be overkill . . .

The bay doors began to open, sliding apart like the jaws of a Venus fly-trap. I hadn't even sent a hail signal yet. I glanced back, but it seemed like Daniel hadn't either. Not unless he was in the habit of keeping a communication device up his nose.

It didn't seem like a friendly welcome. It reminded me more of a sleeping bear lazily opening one eye as a much smaller animal attempted to sneak past. And now it was scrutinizing me and trying to decide if it was in the mood to get up and start mauling.

Still, it was an opportunity. I maneuvered the ship carefully inside the circular hangar and came in to land on one of the many unoccupied parking bays. There was only one other ship: another luxury yacht, slightly more understated than ours, with the gleaming sheen of a vessel that was very frequently cleaned but very rarely flown. The residents of Cloud Castle clearly had few reasons to travel anywhere else.

Nobody came out to greet us, but we hadn't been shot down by surface-to-air missiles, which was a plus. I'd probably have been immediately blown out of the air if I'd shown up in the *Neverdie*. The obvious pointless decadence of the Platinum God of Whale Sharks had earned us the benefit of the doubt.

I watched the bay doors ominously slide closed; then my touchscreen drew my attention with a pop-up window and a little beep. "The Quantunnel booth's connected to the local network," I reported. "So who is this person we're picking up, again?"

I heard the sound of aluminum foil being crinkled, and turned to see Daniel standing up out of his chair, straightening his jumpsuit, and brushing off imaginary dust. "It's just a friend," he said.

"Look, if you're bringing one of your dad's toughs aboard to menace me around, just say so."

He smiled, baffled. "What?" He was adjusting the clasp on his chest as a man in a tuxedo would adjust his bowtie.

"It'd honestly be a relief at this point. I know where I stand when I'm under a henchman's shoe."

"Uh," said Daniel, uncomprehending. "I'm just gonna go and get her. I'll be literally one second."

Then he ran off, leaving me with my advancing worries. *Her*, I repeated, in the confines of my own head. The plot thickened. I wasn't immediately relieved, though. No reason to assume Mr. Henderson wouldn't have female henchmen, just as willing and able to put their shoes on my face as the men.

I was startled from these thoughts by a burst of energetic violin music coming from my console. The touchscreen flashed with the words "Incoming Call: Cloud Castle Ground Control."

Glancing up, I looked through the view screen at the interior wall of the docking bay, in the upper half of which was a wide viewing window. Two sets of heads and shoulders were visible, silhouetted against severe fluorescent lighting. The shoulders were either wearing big epaulets or hunched up with anal retention.

My hand hovered over the Receive Call button. It was probably safe to assume that Terran ground control wouldn't be as easygoing as their

Lunarian counterparts. For one thing, I didn't know them personally and couldn't blackmail my way through with knowledge of late-night drinking indiscretions.

Fortunately, I wasn't trying to gain entry. I only needed to stall them until Daniel returned with whatever fresh hell he had prepared for me. That gave me the advantage. Stalling bureaucrats is easy; half the time they stall themselves without you even having to ask. But failing that, the best technique is to pretend to be extremely stupid.

I got into character by slackening my jaw and staring boggle-eyed at the touchscreen as I mashed the receive button with a knuckle.

"Your vessel has been scanned," came a pompous voice. "One or more of your crew members are lacking the necessary permissions for entering or landing upon United Republic territory."

I found myself wondering when it had gone out of fashion to refer to it as *planet Earth.* "Hello?" I replied, lowering the pitch of my voice an octave and talking like my tongue had grown three sizes larger.

"Entering United Republic territory without valid permissions is grounds for immediate detention and interrogation under the Prevention of Terror Act," continued the official.

"Whaaat?" I slurred, leaning into the touchscreen as if I didn't know that the mike was incorporated into the headrest of my chair.

"If you do not submit valid permission documents, immediate action will be taken."

I waited for roughly the amount of time it would take an average person to start wondering if I'd hung up, then repeated, "Whaaat?"

A pause. "State whether you are the captain or the pilot of this vessel."

"Do you want to speak to the captain?" I spoke as slowly and loudly as possible, enunciating as if I'd been taught to speak on a consonant-per-year basis. "He was here a moment ago."

"State whether you are the captain or the pilot of this vessel." The tone was completely unchanged.

"Why do you keep saying the same things? Are you stupid?" I was deliberately trying to provoke frustration, partly to aid with the stall and partly out of curiosity about whether there was anything remotely close to a human being behind that voice.

"Please identify yourself immediately," it said, which did nothing to resolve the debate. "Failure to comply will—"

"I don't think I can help you. You should talk to the captain," I said. "Could you hold for a minute while I find him? I think this is the hold button." Then I hung up.

I leaned back and placed my feet up on the console, crossing my ankles. Elegant little play, the idiot routine. It gets the target frustrated, but not confrontational frustrated—the kind of frustration aimed mainly at yourself and your lack of patience for the disadvantaged.

They'd probably call back, but it might not be for a while. First there'd be however long it took for them to realize that they were not on hold after all, but were waiting patiently on a disconnected line. They might call back immediately at that point, but chances were good they'd double-check the scans, make some effort to contact someone else, or initiate some other time-wasting bureaucracy that meant they wouldn't have to attempt to communicate with me again

The steel rods holding the docking bay access door closed suddenly slammed aside, with such unnecessary violence that the *clang* was audible from my cockpit. I started, failed to disentangle my ankles, and fell right off my chair.

By the time I'd gotten my legs sorted out and gotten back into a position to see outside, the bay's access door had just completed the final part of the rather technical multistage opening sequence. A small team of eight armed men, decked out with black body armor and concussion rifles designed for use in riot control, jogged into the docking bay with military choreography.

I watched, open mouthed, as they trooped underneath the ship and out of sight, presumably making for the external airlock door. What the hell kind of spaceport has a plying SWAT team ready for deployment in case there's a momentary issue with the paperwork? What the trac kind of terror threat were these measures designed to combat? Malmind cyberserkers masquerading as very stupid rich people?

From the belly of the ship I heard a short, polite knocking on the external airlock door. This formality over with, it was immediately followed by a harsh pounding of rifle butts. How long would the hull on this decadent pile of trac actually hold out? I was starting to feel like the bag of chocolate buttons inside a cheap Easter egg.

Subconsciously, my hand had already drawn my blaster from my shoulder holster. Blowing the invading soldiers away wasn't what I'd consider the rational course of action, but the sight of it could at least start a conversation.

I scurried out of the bridge and down the two sets of carpeted steps to the circular "foyer". The inner airlock door was open. I considered closing it, but that would only delay the inevitable and ensure further damage to the ship. A ship could still fly with a smashed-open external airlock door—you just had to make sure you only ever entered or left the ship within an atmosphere—but there'd be no escape with both doors forced open. Not unless everyone onboard was prepared to seal all their orifices shut.

The external airlock door was still holding, but the wheel lock quivered with greater and greater energy with every hit. I pointed my gun at it, planted my feet, and waited. Hopefully my greeting would expedite matters.

Boy, I thought as I waited. It would be so embarrassing for these guys if it turned out I did, in fact, have the necessary permission papers and could produce them the moment they stormed in. This was not a particularly helpful thought to have. After all, even if I did, they might not necessarily be in the name of Jacques McKeown . . .

And then it hit me. Warden was still onboard. She'd convinced the chip-ID system that I had the name of a traitorous novel-writing bracket everyone wanted to kill. Convincing the immigration database that I had a visa would probably be a hell of a lot easier.

The crew quarters were only one level up. I took the stairs three at a time and shoulder barged my way into Warden's quarters. She was still sitting on the bed, going over Mr. Henderson's paperwork, and was startled to her feet by my sudden entrance. "Mr. McKeown? What on earth are you doing? What is that banging noise? Answer both questions."

I took a deep breath. "I'm bursting into your quarters waving a gun. Second answer, there are some United Republic immigration staff wanting to see paperwork that I don't have."

"I see." She sat down again and crossed her legs. "I expect the relationship between the two matters is that you think I can assist in some way."

"Nail on the head. Can you?"

She returned her gaze to her work nonchalantly. "Were I inclined to, yes."

I squeezed the grip of my gun. This helped me cope. "Why wouldn't you be inclined to?! Do you know what those drones are going to do when they get in here?"

"I know what they're going to do to *me*, Mr. McKeown. Absolutely nothing, because I am a citizen of the United Republic and a resident of this community. What they will do to *you* is capture and interrogate you until you confess to your involvement in anti-Terran terrorism."

The banging noise was getting more sonorous. I got the impression that the team outside had made a decent-enough dent on one part of the door and had all started concentrating on that. "I'm not the slightest bit involved in antiterror Terranism! I don't give a trac about what Earth does!"

"I doubt that fact matters as much to the gentlemen outside as meeting the monthly quota for antiterror operations," said Warden. "As long as your signing hand is still functioning by the end of the week, they may even be able to earn a funding increase."

I tried playing one of the big cards in my hand. "You know Mr. Henderson isn't going to be terribly pleased about his son's special treat being ruined by his hero getting arrested and tortured."

She placed a hand on her chin thoughtfully. "Actually, Mr. Henderson has long borne a grudge against the immigration department. I may be able to shift the blame entirely to them. It can hardly be considered my fault that you failed to apply for the right permissions."

"*May*," I repeated, triumphantly stabbing a finger at her as if I were pinning the word to a corkboard. "You said *may*. You can't be certain he won't take it out on you."

"And you can't be certain he will. Welcome to your new life on the ocean of uncertainty that is the Henderson Corporation." She met my gaze, one side of her upper lip stabbing upward in distaste. "I've had to put up with it for a lot longer than you have."

My chest deflated, and my arms fell loosely to my sides. My gun brushed my leg like a faithful dog reassuring its downhearted master. "Back to plan A, then," I muttered, turning to go. I stopped in my tracks when a particularly loud clang signaled that the first opening had been created.

"Of course, I would become more inclined to assist if something was offered in return," said Warden, with maddening calm.

I reluctantly turned back around as if mounted on a slow lazy Susan. "What do you want?"

"Your pistol," she said, nodding toward my dangling hand. "I have been feeling more and more often in the last few days that I need a means of defense."

"Do you even know how to use a blaster?"

"I don't intend to fire it, Mr. McKeown. I would just feel more comfortable with it in my possession."

I looked down at my gun. I fancied that it was looking up at me with big, brown puppy-dog eyes. Below me, I heard the whine of bending metal. I reached for one last attempt at reason. "This gun may be the only defense we'll have if pirates get onboard."

"That was precisely my thinking. And the specific pirates I am concerned about are the very recently recruited ones who may or may not already be on board the ship."

I gave in. While I wasn't sure what game I was playing with Daniel, I knew exactly which one I was currently playing with Warden: some hybrid of chess and Russian roulette, and I didn't have the rule book. I toyed briefly with the idea of starting a game of Clue with her in the starring role, then sulkily threw my gun onto the bed.

The airlock's exterior door rattled aside with some difficulty, having significantly changed shape since the last time it had opened, and the lead soldier found himself standing in the entryway with his rifle still poised stupidly in midsmash. Ms. Warden's datapad was directly in front of his face, displaying an official-looking certificate with a large and ominous seal.

"I am Penelope Warden, divisional head of the Henderson Corporation and registered notary, here are my credentials," she said, pausing for the briefest possible amount of time for each comma. "All interactions with my client Mr. Jacques McKeown must now go through me. I am his representative for all matters related to his application for asylum."

The soldiers leaned in, in finely honed military unison, to read the small print. With their all-black helmets and shiny black body armor sculpted into the shape of ideal human musculature, they looked like a blackberry bush swaying in the breeze. They were all wearing black balaclavas under their helmets that only exposed the eyes, but those eyes were conveying enough confusion to make up for the rest of the face.

"Asylum?" asked the one in front.

I was standing behind Warden, trying not to look like a schoolboy getting his angry mother to confront the headmaster. I waved cockily, and some of the gazes turned to me.

One of the soldiers—it was hardly worth differentiating them—decided that the best approach to Warden was to pretend she wasn't there. I wished

I'd thought of that when we'd first met. "Do you or do you not have the necessary permissions to enter the United Republic?" he asked gruffly, with a menacing glare.

Warden immediately sidestepped to intercept it. "My client does not currently possess the necessary permissions. However, United Republic law states that an entrant without permissions may remain in transit regions for a period of twenty-four hours in order to lodge an application for asylum."

The soldiers started grumbling antsily, having psyched themselves up for a bout of skull cracking that was slipping ever further from their grasp. One of the shrewder pairs of eyes said, "But that's only if he's actually eligible for asylum."

Warden was ready for that one. She smartly swiped the certificate on the pad aside to reveal a highlighted section of legal document. "Indeed. United Republic law states that an individual becomes eligible for asylum if there is strong evidence to the effect that their physical well-being is under threat by a ruling authority."

"And is it?"

"It is. Mr. McKeown is in extreme danger of being physically brutalized by a team of eight government soldiers for not possessing permission papers."

The shrewd one figured it out first. "You mean us?"

"The law of the United Republic states only that the threat be created by a ruling authority," said Warden, folding her datapad under her arm and standing fully straight to signal her victory. "It does not state that the ruling authority cannot be its own. And we have all the evidence we need that the threat exists, because I am currently addressing it."

The men had been defeated by the very bureaucracy they zealously enforced, and they knew it. They shifted guiltily, looking sadly at their weapons, as if they'd just realized that they'd shown up in tuxedos to a beach party.

But then the shrewd bracket started with a realization and threw up an upward-pointing index finger. "Ha! Wait a minute! There's a fault in your logic!"

Warden's half smile of triumph froze. "Is there."

"You say he's eligible for asylum because we were going to physically assault him. But if we *don't* physically assault him, then he's not eligible at all, is he!"

A moment's absolute stillness, then Warden sighed in irritation through her teeth. "I should have realized. You're right. You are entirely authorized to brutalize Mr. McKeown as long as you do not brutalize Mr. McKeown."

She let that sink in for a moment, the two parties staring at each other across the ship's threshold. The shrewd bracket's shoulders slowly sagged.

"Well, he still has to leave," said the team leader.

"Absolutely," said Warden. She turned to me. "Daniel's picking up Jemima, I take it?"

"Yeah. Possibly. Who's Jemima?"

"Mr. McKeown will be out of your hair within a couple of hours. In the meantime, don't hesitate to leave." She probably intended to remain standing defiant as the door closed in the soldiers' faces, but it got stuck halfway. We stared at each other through the gap for a while before the soldiers quietly walked away, muttering.

The one bringing up the rear looked briefly over his shoulder. "We like your books, by the way."

CHAPTER 12

IT WAS ABOUT an hour before Daniel returned. I used the time to beat the dents out of the exterior airlock door as best I could, which made me quite nostalgic for the days when enemy pilots could actually afford ammunition. The selection of tools available on the ship was of course pathetic, so I was using a meat tenderizer I'd found in the breakfast nook.

So Warden had figured out that I was planning to cross the Black. Her having my gun was going to make it difficult to maintain control of the ship if I started flying it to suspicious places, but she obviously didn't know me well enough yet if she thought that would make me give in. She herself had made it impossible for me to return to Ritsuko City. I'd just have to take a more delicate approach, or, failing that, threaten to beat her to death with my own severed leg.

I tried the opening and closing mechanism a few times. It worked relatively smoothly. It wasn't going to be completely airtight, but we still had the internal door, and I probably wouldn't need to do any EVA work. Even if I did, the gap wasn't enormous; it wouldn't suck *all* the air out of the internal atmosphere if I worked fast.

I tested the opening mechanism one more time and saw Daniel at the entrance to the docking bay, accompanied by (presumably) Jemima. Who, to my relief, was not the ironically named ex-wrestler bodyguard my imagination had been furnishing, but a girl his age, with bright pink hair and a baggy hoodie matched paradoxically with tight black leggings.

"I thought you were coming back in the Quantunnel," I said.

Daniel's face was very red, and sweat glistened on his brow. He started a little at my question, having been gazing fixedly at the girl. "What? Oh, I wanted to show it to her from outside first. It's cool, isn't it, Jemima?"

She was looking over the ship's ample curves. "So this is yours?" she asked. Then she glanced nervously over her shoulder at the docking bay entrance.

He took a step closer and pretended to appraise the ship, arms folded. "Yeah, that's my ship," he said, trying to sound nonchalant but emphasizing the *my* weirdly. "I just got my own ship now, no big deal."

I leaned on the door frame and stared at them. His eyes kept flicking over to her, studying her reaction, but her own gaze was reserved only for switching between the ship and the door by which she'd entered. "Wouldn't it be, like, really obvious to pirates?"

"That's what I said," I interjected, unable to help myself.

"Is that what happened to the door?" she asked, nodding shallowly toward the dents.

"Oh my god," said Daniel, dropping the aloof act. "Did we miss it? Did pirates try to board while we were gone?"

I gave that question the awkward silence it deserved. "Not while parked in a docking bay, no."

He laughed a little bit too much. "Oh yeah, of course. Not while parked." He coughed, reassembled the aloof look, and pretended to have noticed me for the first time. "Oh, hey, Jacques. This is Jemima. Jemima, this is my pilot, Jacques McKeown. He's just a friend of mine, y'know. Maybe you've heard of him; he's written some books?"

Jemima had been watching behind her during most of the introduction but now gave me her full attention, quickly looking me up and down. "You're not Jacques McKeown."

She didn't say it with the tone of one triumphantly revealing subterfuge. It was a matter-of-fact statement, mixed with the slight bafflement of one wondering why no one else has seen what seemed obvious to them. Even so, I jumped and almost lost my balance. "What?"

Jemima shrugged. "Well, y'know, the real Jacques McKeown wouldn't come out and fly other people's ships, because he, like, writes books full time."

Daniel laughed a bit too much again. "No, really, it's actually the real, actual Jacques McKeown. My dad got hold of him for me."

"Well, your dad was probably, you know, lying to you. Like he did when he said he didn't break Mr. Peterson's legs for giving you a failing grade."

Daniel seemed about to say something, but then fell silent as a thoughtful look crossed his face. Apparently this extremely compelling point had not occurred to him.

It was time to flick the switch in my head. I laughed good-naturedly, making a pretty convincing job of it, if I do say so myself. "I know how it looks," I said, smiling in a crinkly eyed favorite-uncle kind of way. "But you'd be surprised how little money novels make these days. And a writer's life is never going to be enough for someone who's used to space adventuring, is it?"

She touched her chin, looking at me with reassuring uncertainty. "But . . ."

The entrance to the docking bay opened noisily, and Jemima almost jumped out of her skin. She let out a sigh of relief when she saw that it was only one of the soldiers, smartly relieving a single member of the armed group that had been watching us vigilantly for the entire hour.

"Hey, can we go inside now?" she said, with one last look behind her.

Daniel beamed at the suggestion. I moved out of the doorway to let them in, keeping an eye on Jemima. I offered a cheery wave to the armed guards, then "closed" the exterior door.

All throughout and following takeoff, Jemima stood over me to watch the scenery from the best spot. But once we were out of Cloud Castle's designated clearing and back in the real clouds, the scenery was swiftly reduced to flat, unbroken yellow like we were flying through custard.

"So, is it, like, a Santa Claus thing?" she asked. Most of her jitteriness seemed to have mysteriously evaporated since our departure.

"What?" I said.

"You know, like, you're not Jacques McKeown but you're one of Jacques McKeown's helpers?" She gave a little twitch at the corner of her mouth, the sort of thing nervous people do that will only turn into a full smile if someone else smiles first.

Daniel obligingly burst into another of his desperate, overlong laughs. Of course he was hovering around, too. He had to maintain a constant orbit of about three feet from Jemima. A little Goldilocks band of his very own, not far enough to separate from her but not close enough that she might pick up on his incredibly obvious crush.

"I am Jacques McKeown," I said, flatly. I'd been trying to get into the mindset of the real Jacques McKeown, and after a couple of dry heaves, I had concluded that he would be pretty testy by this point. Luckily, that would require very little acting.

"No, seriously, he is. Dad checked him out on the ID network and that was his name," said Daniel, confirming Ms. Warden's story.

"Well, that doesn't actually prove it," said Jemima. "Jacques McKeown probably doesn't write books under his real name, 'cos all the other pilots want to kill him and stuff. I heard about that on the fan site. It kind of sounds like a name someone made up because it sounds like a piloty kind of name."

"Which could easily be the case, if the owner of the name's father was a pilot and wanted their son to also be a pilot," I pointed out. This was true of my own dad. He'd been a full-time courier for Speedstar Transport before star piloting officially became a thing, and it's always easier to con people with the truth.

"I guess," said Jemima. Then, "Oh wow." Her eyes flew to the view outside.

The pollution clouds parted like hideous yellow curtains over a nighttime window and the Platinum God of Whale Sharks burst back out into the blackness of space, nimbly slipping through the same gap in the surveillance net as before. The infinite spangled emptiness had never looked friendlier. For one thing, it gave me something to distract the passengers with.

"I've never seen stars like that before," breathed Jemima, rapt.

"So what do you think of my ship?" asked Daniel, brushing some imaginary dust off a section of ornamental railing. "You think it's so lame, right? My dad picked it out. I told him to get the red one but he can be so stupid . . ."

"It's really cool," said Jemima, deforming her face against the curved plexiglass above and to the right of me.

"Yeah, it is, isn't it?" said Daniel, changing his tune with the ease and smoothness of a freight train trying to switch tracks while halfway past the junction. "It cost, like, half a million or something."

Jemima finally peeled her cheek off the window, leaving a patch of pubescent grease and hair dye. "What? Oh . . . yeah, the ship. It's really . . . nice. What are you going to, you know, call it?"

"Call it? Oh. Uh. What would you think if I called it the *Jemima*?" I felt a surge of regret for having given Warden my blaster, because I had a sudden longing to put the end in my mouth.

"Oh," said Jemima awkwardly. "That's . . . cool . . ."

"Hey," I said brightly, leaping to the rescue as star pilots tend to do. "Where do you crazy kids want to go, anyway?"

"Oh, yeah," said Jemima, relievedly looking away from Daniel's eager face. "I was going to say, I can't stay out too long. I didn't actually tell my mum that I was going out."

"It's cool. I probably wasn't going to stay out very long either," said Daniel hastily. "Where do you want to go?"

Jemima glanced back at space through the plexiglass, like a diner trying to pick from a menu. "I'm fine with wherever you want to go."

"I'm literally fine with wherever—"

"Erm, excuse me," I interjected, before the discussion continued its round trip to nowhere fast. "Did I hear you say you only need me for a few hours?"

"Oh, well, if you want to hang out for longer . . ." said Daniel.

"No no no," I interrupted, nipping that one in the bud immediately. "It's fine. I was just under the impression that I was being contracted for a few days here."

"Not all in one go," he said, nonplused. "It's a school night. I was just going to take a, you know, test-drivey thing and then you can drop us off and Dad can call you in at the weekend some time."

"Yeah, that should work out. My mum's usually away at weekends," said Jemima quietly.

A little shoot of hope sprouted forth from the black bean of my internal mood. Drop them off? As in, they're not even going to supervise me taking the ship back to the Ubatsu building? I could have crossed the Black and been safely surrounded by fellow pirates before the night was over. And bringing them the Platinum God of Whale Sharks might even buy me a spot in a top bunk right off the bat.

There was still the matter of Warden, but maybe she'd want to be dropped off somewhere, too. If she didn't, I could always "drop her off" in one way or another. Trac, I thought. That was a dark thought out of nowhere.

"Well, how about just a tour of the Solar System, then?" I said aloud, lent energy. "A flyover of Saturn's rings is something you have to do once in your life. Hell, you're still young. Let's do it twice for kicks."

"That sounds awesome," said Jemima, not looking away from the view.

"Awesome, yeah," parroted Daniel. Then he felt confident enough to move an inch closer and initiate a bout of hover handing.

I set a course for Saturn, gunned what passed for the main thruster, and gripped the joysticks with a silent sigh of relief. There was something very pleasing about not having to kidnap the two children. Even disregarding the complications it would have created, I'd be plied if I wasn't starting to like the little brackets.

Daniel was still a little doint, obviously, but the knowledge that he had partially been doing all of this to impress a girl sort of recontextualized him a bit. There was a certain pathetic lovability about it, like a dog holding its bowl in its mouth.

And Jemima's reaction to seeing space had made me feel a little warm inside. My first gaze into the abyss had been similar, and it was something I saw so rarely these days, now that people thought they could get the experience just as well from immersion simulators. Or by going out onto their roof garden in the middle of a quiet night and looking up.

We flew past Luna, glancing briefly at the lights of Ritsuko City, under the colossal plexiglass shell that the moon wore like a sparkling monocle. Jemima remained by my side, hypnotized by the stars. So of course Daniel stuck around, fidgeting with his fingers. In contrast, I don't think he'd looked out of the window at all since Jemima had come aboard. His attention alternated between being focused entirely on her and combing his fingers through his highlighted forelock.

Experience transporting tourists had taught me that the scenery tends to get samey very fast, and right on cue, Jemima resumed the discussion, after Luna was behind us and the view was awash with blackness again. "So are you really, truly Jacques McKeown?" she asked, turning and half perching on my console.

"He totally is," answered Daniel on my behalf.

"I bet he can't prove it," she said. She seemed more excited, bobbing on her heels and clasping her hands. "Ask him something about the books. Something, you know, only Jacques McKeown would know."

"I will! Okay. Um. In what book . . ."

An alarm sounded. My touchscreen started flashing red, and the console in front of the captain's chair gibbered urgently. A few crucial seconds were lost as I navigated the swipe menus looking for the damage report, then I clicked my tongue. "One of the rods in the engine compartment isn't cooling."

"Is it supposed to?" asked Jemima, eyes wide.

I stood up. "Well, considering that they're cooling rods, yes. Don't worry, this is pretty common. Nine times out of ten, it's just misaligned. I'll be gone about half an hour to fix it. Daniel. Jemima." I put a hand on one shoulder for each of them. "I need you to step up for me. I won't be long, but if any more red lights come on, I need you to stay calm, be strong, and let me know as soon as possible. Can you do that?"

Daniel's chest swelled. "Yes, sir!" Jemima nodded.

"Good. Stay here."

I jogged out of the bridge, then slowed immediately to a walk when I was confident that I was out of sight. There was no reason to start worrying until at least five of the cooling rods were down. On top of that, I knew perfectly well why the rod had deactivated: because I had told it to.

Every time I started work with a new ship, I made a point of learning the quickest way to make an alarm go off that doesn't actually damage the ship. It was always handy to be able to manufacture myself a coffee break on short notice. And on this occasion I had to swiftly reacquaint myself with Jacques McKeown trivia before the grilling continued.

I headed for the reading room. I wouldn't be able to read all of the plying things, but I had a familiarity with the events in the books, mainly because most of the bitter conversations I'd had in the Brandied Bracket drifted to the topic of which McKeown books ripped off whose stories. I'd just have to hope that giving the titles and the blurbs a quick once-over would give me enough to bulltrac with.

I met Warden in the corridor outside the reading room, and she followed me in like a cat hanging around expecting to be fed. "What was that alert sound?" she demanded.

I made a beeline for the bookshelf. "Minor engine fault," I said casually, not looking back at her. "Two-second fix. Don't worry about it."

"So nothing's going wrong?"

I ran my finger along the garish spines. There were only about thirty books in McKeown's entire canon, but the shelves had been supplied with every book in every edition, format, box set, and special-edition re-release, with the searing attention to detail of a true psychotic fan.

"Nah," I said.

There was a surge of energy, and I felt a stifling heat on one side of my body, as if someone had opened the door of a preheated oven. Instinctively I dived away from it, landing on my back in time to see a sphere of amplified blaster energy splatter across the Quantunnel booth in the corner.

The last few tendrils of orange-white energy slithered inside the booth's control panel. It gave a little electronic belch, and then hot slag began to drool from around the screws and the gaps between keys.

I looked at Warden. She was holding my blaster outstretched, her mouth tight and determined. I could see that the gun was on the now potentially ironically named Solve All Immediate Problems setting. Both she and I flinched as she fired again, the shot melting one of the upper corners of the Quantunnel booth's shuttered doorway and ensuring its permanent uselessness.

"How about now?" she asked coolly.

CHAPTER 13

I WAS STILL lying on my back by the bookshelf, propped up on my elbows. On instinct I made an attempt to quickly move into a standing position, which was immediately aborted when I found myself staring down the barrel of my own gun. Not for the first time, but on this occasion, someone else was holding it.

"What are you doing?" I asked, displaying my palms and trying not to sound too interrogative.

"I'm making a career change," she said. "I'm going to kidnap Daniel and Jemima, and you are going to help me."

Her voice was the same as always, condescending and professional, but the end of the gun was shaking, and I could see lines of sweat escaping from her hairline. I hoped she hadn't gone insane. I could always handle sane people. Sane people are predictable. It's practically the definition of the word.

I was about to ask why she was doing this, but that seemed like a fatuous question. "Is this about being made a divisional head?"

"I am not going to end up like Brian Pritchard. I will not allow myself to be filed away until Henderson needs another scapegoat. Stand up."

I did so, keeping my hands where she could see them. She was smart enough to stay a good two arm lengths away, keeping the gun trained on me. "Okay, so what exactly is your plan, from this point?" I asked.

She moved to the door and gestured with the gun, instructing me to head through it. "You will fly this ship to an area outside planetary surveillance and make contact with a pirate organization cognizant enough to deal with that can be trusted to take us in and shelter us from the authorities and from Henderson."

I walked the hallways as slowly as I felt I could get away with, but she didn't take the bait. She didn't try to hasten me by jabbing me with the barrel. She kept the gun out of my grabbing range and matched my speed. Together we shuffled along the expensive carpet like a pair of slugs negotiating the floor of a salt factory.

"You know, you'll laugh when you hear this," I said hopefully. "But I was actually planning to do something along the same lines."

"Yes, McKeown, I am fully aware of that. So all you have to do now is continue according to that plan with the slight modification that we are now partners in the crime."

I stopped and turned on my heel, and she promptly froze, hand tightening on the gun. "So you don't have to keep pointing the gun at me!" I said, exasperated. "We're on the same page, right?"

"That will remain to be seen," replied Warden, gun unmoved. "Proceed to the bridge."

I got halfway through turning around again, then stopped. "We don't need the kids. We can just drop them off when they're finished sightseeing and make for the Black. Then it's barely even a crime."

"Don't be dense, McKeown. Henderson would have us blasted out of the sky for disloyalty alone. While we have his son, we have leverage. We can release them as soon as we are out of Henderson's reach."

"All right, so maybe we're not on the same page. What do you mean, release them? So we'll cut them loose as soon as we're in the middle of the Black and give them twenty euroyen for the rickshaw home, will we?"

"You're good at improvising. I'll let you come up with something."

By this point we were outside the door to the bridge, and from the other side I could hear scrips and scraps of the most stilted and awkward conversation in the history of courtship. I turned around, keeping my back to the door, and was pinned into place by the gun, still aimed squarely at my chest.

"Once we go through this door, there's no turning back," I advised. "There'll be no more chances to change your mind. You know perfectly well we could do this without bringing the kids into it. But when we go in there and tell Daniel that he's being kidnapped, Henderson will be after us both for the rest of our lives."

Hints of emotion rippled across her face. A twitch of an eyebrow here, a wobble of the corner of the mouth there. She took a deep breath, and all was stone again. "Henderson is not all powerful. Until recently, I thought that he was. I'd never seen any scheme of his not go entirely according to his desires."

She paused lengthily. She was either meditating on the thought or waiting for my prompt. "And then what?"

Her eyes narrowed. "And then, I saw him swallow that a two-bit out-of-work star pilot could actually be Jacques McKeown."

"All right," I sighed. "Fine. You didn't have to make personal comments. And you can be the one to tell them, then, since you're insisting."

"Fine." She jiggled the gun barrel. "Open the door."

I turned around and did so. Daniel was sitting in his captain's chair, and Jemima was standing nearby, leaning on his console with arms folded. As we entered, they both boggled at us like deer in headlights.

"Whoa, is that a gun?" asked Daniel, pertinently.

"What's going on?" asked Jemima. Her hands gestured uncertainly behind her. "I've got . . . I'm supposed to be back home . . ."

I looked back at Warden, gathering my hands behind me, looking at her with polite expectation. Bits of her face were quivering again, as if every individual muscle was taking part in a heated debate over whether this was still a good idea. "Well?" I said. "Isn't there something you'd like to tell our passengers?"

Maybe I shouldn't have needled her. Her scowl hardened with determination. "Daniel, Jemima," she said. "I am kidnapping you. Remain calm and make no attempt to resist, and you will be returned unharmed to your families in due time."

The kids maintained their boggle-eyed looks as if she hadn't said anything at all. Then Daniel smacked both his hands over his eyes with what sounded like quite injurious force, and he emitted the same "URRGHH" sound he'd made at the dinner. Which, with all the ways he could have responded, was frankly not the one I would have put money on.

"What?" Jemima asked him.

"My dad is SO embarrassing," he wailed. "He's making Ms. Warden pretend to kidnap us because he wants to make it exciting. URRGH. He's ALWAYS INTERFERING."

"Your dad is really weird," said Jemima.

I leaned toward an unmoving Warden and whispered as close to her ear as the gun would allow, "Seems like I was wrong back there when I said that that was your last chance to back out."

Her face flashed thunder at me. Teasing her probably wasn't doing me any favors, but I was tired and letting Pragmatism have a rest while Spite had a go on the steering wheel. "I assure you," she declared to the kids, "this is not an act. Take your phones out, turn them off, and give them to me." To me, she said, "Get into the pilot's seat. Set a course."

I shrugged, and made my way around the perimeter of the bridge to the pilot console as Jemima in the center watched, worried, rotating like a lighthouse.

"Do you have any specific guidelines for what direction to take?" I said, swiping onto the navigation map.

"Just get us out of system surveillance," ordered Warden, placing a hand on my chair's backrest while trying to keep the gun trained on both of the kids at once. "Then make for the pirate base you think best suited for our needs."

I rubbed my chin as I inspected the poorly detailed representation of what was colloquially referred to as "the Black": the portion of known space that fell outside the policed zones surrounding the Solar System and every other major human settlement. A significantly large majority of the galaxy that only I and my peers were willing to attempt to cross without Quantunneling. "And our needs are to find a pirate clan that won't immediately strip us for parts the moment we show up in a glittering bonanza yacht," I said, partly to myself.

"Yes, Mr. McKeown, that adequately describes our needs."

Den and Mark would probably be the best bet, I thought. Our relationship was based on mutual dislike, but they technically owed me one. "Right then," I muttered, plotting a course for the asteroid belt near Cantrabargid. Warden leaned over my shoulder, watching my inputs carefully.

"Um, hi," said Jemima, directly behind us.

Warden spun and pointed my gun at her. Jemima cringed apologetically, holding out a smartphone in a pink case that matched her hair.

"Sorry," said Jemima. "Here's my phone. But, er, hey, if this is something Mr. Henderson arranged, could we do it, you know, some other time, only I didn't tell my mum . . ."

Warden sighed like a housewife whose nervous dog was terrified of the vacuum cleaner and took the phone. "I'm afraid I do not care about how your mother feels about it, Jemima. Mr. Henderson did not organize this and I am actually kidnapping you."

"She says she's actually kidnapping us," called Jemima back to Daniel.

"Well, she isn't," said Daniel stubbornly. "It's my stupid dad."

Warden stood politely still as Jemima held her chin, frowned, and scruti-nized Warden and the gun. "Are you sure? I mean, this is exactly the sort of thing that tends to happen with, you know, people who work for your dad."

"No, it's totally my dad."

"But can you be sure?"

"Yeah, 'cos he's telling me so."

There was an audible *snap* sound as Warden and I both whipped our necks around to look at Daniel. He was holding a slim, expensive phone to his ear and listening with eyes rolled heavenward.

Warden's face, already pale from a lifetime of staying in doing adminis-tration, turned the color of an unpainted papier mâché project. Then she moved with the suddenness of a jumping spider, launching herself at Daniel's phone. She misjudged the height of the metallic railing around the captain's chair and face planted into the deep-pile carpet.

Her head rose, after an embarrassed second of stillness, to meet the gaze of a startled Daniel, who was almost leaning far enough back in his chair to turn himself two-dimensional. He held out his phone toward Warden. "He wants to talk to you."

And then, she was on her feet again. It was that fast. There was no messy struggling to get the limbs into place; she simply zipped upright. There was maybe the briefest glimpse of a transitionary phase, during which she ap-peared to be in the fetal position about one foot off the floor, and then she was standing, smoothing down the creases in her business attire.

All eyes were on her as she took the phone and, her hand shaking almost imperceptibly, held it to her ear. "Yes," she said, after listening for a few tense moments. "Yes," she added, gaining confidence. "Ye-es," she clarified.

Her conversation with Henderson continued in this rather monotonous fashion until she suddenly glanced at me. "Yes," she reiterated, thoughtfully. She offered the phone. "He wants to talk to you."

Her complexion was far beyond merely pale. She looked like all her blood had been replaced with correctional fluid. I took the phone from a hand resembling a bunch of cold chicken bones in a surgical glove.

I took the phone and felt a little spark of hope. Warden was weakened, dividing her attention between too many factors. Perhaps this was the op-portunity to throw her back into the clutches of the bear while I made a run for it. I brought the phone to my ear.

"I already told him we're working together on this," said Warden, apparently reading the look on my face.

"Hello, Jacques," came Mr. Henderson's voice, dangerously level. "How is Daniel's trip going?"

I'd been preparing some statement along the lines of "oh god she's gone insane send help," but Warden's comment closely followed by Henderson's greeting had derailed my words on their way to my mouth. "Whurt?" was all I could manage.

"Jacques, could you do me a favor?" said the familiar voice on the phone, entirely devoid of Henderson's usual good cheer.

"Mr. Henderson," I said, trying to get things back on track.

"Could you look behind you? Could you do that for me?"

I was peering over my shoulder before it could even occur to me to disobey, and I found myself staring at a blank section of bulkhead by the door, allegedly gold colored but more like the color of urine. "Why?"

"Now look down."

I did so, straining uncomfortably. I saw only the backs of my shoes, or at least the small percentage of them that extruded from the ridiculously thick carpet. "Yes?"

"What you're doing there, Jacques, is watching your back. And I just wanted to give you a head start, because you're going to be doing a lot of that from now on. By which I mean watching your back. Jacques."

"Oh," I said, grimly. "Mr. Henderson, whatever Warden said . . ."

"Oh, don't get me wrong. It's heartwarming, it really is. You and her running off together, love triumphant across the class divide." There was a wobble in his spiteful tone of voice that was probably more to do with murderous rage than being touched by the romance. "I've got a lump in my throat. Have you got a lump in your throat, Jacques?"

I couldn't decide what aspect of this conversation was the most horrifying. "What?"

"'Cos if you do, I've got a whole room full of knives expressly designed for removing that sort of thing. Now, I know you're a man who's had a lot of empty threats, so I won't waste your time. First thing I'm going to do now is call your publisher and see exactly how much trouble I can make for you, yeah?"

I hastened to get a word in edgeways. "But! But . . . what about . . . Daniel?"

"Oh, I thought that went without saying. I'm going to have all my best talent hound you to the edge of the universe, and then, as long as not a hair on Danny's head has been harmed, I will make your deaths as quick as I can be bothered to make them. Oh, but I hate planning too far ahead. Maybe I'll just wing it, yeah? See you soo-oon." He hung up, with furious speed.

I grimaced, despondent, at the dead screen of the phone. I shared a stony-faced, tight-lipped glance with Warden.

"So embarrassing," said Daniel.

CHAPTER 14

"WELL. THANKS A plying bunch," I muttered, hands on the joysticks, bitterly jerking them like a cuckolded farmhand at the cow's udders.

"For what?" asked Warden, perching on the console beside me, for want of another chair. She'd only just returned from throwing Jemima and Daniel's smartphones out of the airlock, and the airlock still wasn't properly sealed, so her hair had become a lot more tangled.

"Getting me caught up in your psycho-div kidnap plan."

"We already agreed that we both had an interest in fleeing to the Black."

"I didn't agree to saying as much to Henderson's plying face," I pointed out. "And I want it on record that I was completely against bringing the kids into this." I half turned in my chair and meaningfully caught Jemima's gaze.

"Is this some kind of good-kidnapper, bad-kidnapper thing?" she asked, twiddling her fingers.

"If it makes you feel any better, McKeown," said Warden, pushing every word out of her mouth like a bitter cherry stone, "I am the one who has flung themselves into the unknown. You are the one who has experience with the Black. I am not the one who has friends among pirates."

"Friends?" I repeated. "I give them things they want and they don't blow me up. They're not on my plying Christmas-card list."

"Maybe you should, you know, park somewhere and think your plan through properly?" called Jemima. Two factions had naturally formed within the bridge around the only two available chairs. Daniel was still in the captain's seat, with Jemima perched on one of his armrests. He had crammed himself aside in case he accidentally were so ungallant as to touch her posterior with his elbow.

"Ugh," said Daniel, bored. "Please don't go along with my dad's stupid plan to take over my holiday like he always does."

"I don't know, dude, I think it might be for real," said Jemima conspiratorially. "You saw how she went for your phone. She went, you know, mental."

"Dad just didn't want the surprise being spoiled. She's probably taking us to some lame pizza restaurant so he can sing 'Happy Birthday' and be really embarrassing."

Warden watched them, testily. She was holding my blaster loosely by her side. My chair was on casters. At any moment I could have made a swift kick, followed by a swift grab, and then she'd have to stop pretending to be the one in charge.

And then I could wave my doints around like a big, strong man before going back to doing exactly what we were already doing. Because any victory I could have over Warden at this point would be a hollow one with Henderson on our tail. Like it or not—and that was a pretty huge and emphatic "or not" as "or nots" go—I was going to have to see this kidnapping thing through. But that didn't mean I couldn't grumble as I flew the ship and tried not to think about being savaged by reindeer sweaters.

After a couple of hours of awkward nonconversation, we reached the trebuchet gate that served the Solar System. This was the first step in getting some serious distance between us and our many problems on Earth and Luna.

Trebuchet gates were the answer to long-distance space travel before quantum tunneling came along. They were massive corkscrew-like devices that harnessed the kinetic energy from the movements of nearby star systems to slingshot individual ships massive distances within a sort of static warp bubble missile. Most of the galaxy was littered with the things. In fact, the standard definition of "known space" was "everything within a certain distance of a trebuchet gate." They had the advantage over quantum tunneling in that you didn't need to have another device at the destination point for them to work—you just had to be prepared for whatever unknown horrors you might end up stranded in the middle of.

Quantunneling could claim every other advantage, of course. Like lower energy usage. A lot of space environmentalists had complained that the trebuchet gate system had accelerated the life cycles of several stars by many millions of years and had robbed their systems of the chance of ever sup-porting life. And then there was the issue that trebuchet jumping was an inexact science at best, and that there were still one or two cases per year of ships being hurled directly into solid objects and being reduced to two-dimensional stains on the surface.

Still, I'd always felt that the danger and gross overuse of energy was part of the romance and adventure that gave star piloting its allure. A small chance of death was the spice of life. Nevertheless, I opted not to mention any of this to my passengers.

The trebuchet gate was visible through the viewing dome. I started mov-ing us along the illuminated spaceway leading up to it, which had originally been intended to manage the queue, and which was now, of course, deserted. I was about to key in to the gate's automated systems when I felt my phone vibrating in my pocket.

It must have been able to refresh its battery now we were near a modern electrical system with wireless charge support. I glanced at Warden. She was keeping her eye on the kids as they took in the sight of the trebuchet gate's coiling form. I subtly nudged my phone halfway out of the pocket to see the screen. "Unknown Number," it said.

I made a snap decision. "Bathroom break," I said, getting up.

Warden glanced at the view screen. "Can it not wait until we're out of the system?"

I glanced over my shoulder when I was already halfway to the door. "Nah, it's smartest to be as biologically evacuated as possible before starting a trebuchet jump," I said. Again, it was easiest to con people with the truth.

Once I was in the corridor with my back to the closed door, I took the call, holding the phone like it could turn red hot and burn my ear at any moment. "Hello?"

"Is this Mr. Jacques McKeown, the author?" The voice was female, busi-nesslike, and sounded slightly worried with just the mildest injection of spite.

I looked back at the door for an instant, as if I could somehow see Warden through it. "Yes, that's me," I said unhappily. "Who is this?"

"Emily," said the alleged Emily, as if I should have known that. "Emily from Blasé Books. Your publisher. I've sent you emails?"

"Ohhh," I said, nodding slowly as my eyes darted around. "Yeeeeah. Emily."

"Is this a bad time?" asked Emily. I'm fairly certain there was sarcasm in there.

"No, no, not at all," I said. "What's this about?"

"Is that all you have to say, Mr. McKeown? We've been trying to open a dialogue with you for years. You never reply to emails, you refuse to give us your phone number . . . but you're happy to give it out to some very strange man you're doing some kind of contract work for?"

I assembled a few puzzle pieces in my head. "Henderson called you?"

"I think that was what he called himself, yes. He was really very angry about something. I didn't catch the full details. The moment I got a word in edgeways I asked for the number he had for you."

I rubbed my eye with my free hand. "Did he tell you to . . . do something to me? Something I wouldn't like?"

She didn't seem to be listening. "It really is very maddening that we have only now been able to talk one to one. It's really very unprofessional. And might I suggest, Mr. McKeown, that perhaps you wouldn't need to take contract work if you would finally allow us to pay you for—"

"Emily, please, listen. This man, Henderson, what did he tell you to . . ." I finally parsed the sentence I'd interrupted. "Uh. Pay me for what?"

"No, Jacques, Henderson doesn't want to pay you anything. Please pay attention; it's really very rude. We are the ones who are trying to pay you."

"Pay me for what?" I repeated patiently.

"For books! Remember? Those books we publish? That you write? Honestly, what else would we want to pay you for? Look, I have your number and your chip ID now. Can I just transfer the money to the associated account?"

"Yes," I said. The word escaped before it had even had a chance to cross my mind. I was, after all, still a star pilot. "But hold on. Are you saying that Mc. . . that I haven't been paid for a book?"

There were some slightly adorable shocked noises before the reply came. "For goodness' sake, Mr. McKeown, what on earth kind of income do you have that you haven't noticed? We haven't paid you for *any* books. Not until now. Every time we email we ask for your bank details, but all you ever send to us is manuscripts. We even tried searching the bank databases for your name and address, but that came up empty. Really very unprofessional. Have you considered hiring an agent if you're so busy?"

"Sorry," I said, dreamily. My head was starting to spin. I leaned on a bulkhead for comfort.

"It's all right, Mr. McKeown. It's just that the tax people were starting to ask questions about all this money we allegedly paid you still sitting in our account. Oh, and since you're answering the phone now, I wonder if you'd like to hear a couple of appearance offers. Some of them could be really very effective . . ."

My arm suddenly lacked the strength to hold my phone up. It fell to my side, causing the call to automatically end. I'd just stolen from the real Jacques McKeown. I'd plied him up on behalf of all pilotkind.

My arm strength suddenly returned and the phone came back up again so I could check the balance on my account. Then I had to bring my other hand up to swipe across because the number wouldn't fit on the screen. It was the kind of amount that makes you immediately terrified of the inevitable karmic backlash.

Right on cue, the door beside me flew open, and Warden was there. Her eyes flicked from the phone in my hand to my face, and she bared her teeth. "Who were you talking to?" she demanded. Then something approaching concern crossed her face. "McKeown, you've gone white. Who was that on the phone? Henderson? You should've gotten rid of it."

I couldn't help myself. Right then and right there, I had to share it with someone. It was too big for one mind to toss around alone. And Warden might have been right up there on my least favorite people in the universe list, but she was the only one who knew who I really was. "Not Henderson. Publisher Jacques McKeown has never gotten around to collecting his money. Henderson told them I was him, so they've just sent me everything they owed him."

Warden's brow immediately made like a car crash. She was born of the corporate environment, of course, so this clearly made even less sense to her than it did to me. "You have stolen McKeown's royalties?"

"Yeah," I said. A slightly insane grin pulled my lips apart now that I had sounded it all out, and I laughed. "Yeah! That plying story-stealing bracket, profiting off us all while we're eating out of the bins. Looks like we got the last laugh!"

She rolled her eyes around, thinking. "Except, if what you're saying is true, he has not profited at all. He has not accepted any money for exploiting you people."

A few unpleasant thoughts dropped into my mind with echoey, ominous plops. My elation was still there, somewhere, but now it felt like someone listening to very loud music at the back of a funeral service. "Yeah . . ."

"But now *you* have."

Her statement hung in the air for a moment, then some kind of missile struck the ship, and we were both flung into the bulkhead. I laboriously disentangled myself from Warden and made it most of the way back to my console, just in time for another missile to fling me off my feet and cause my face to smash into the back of my chair.

"We're under attack!" relayed Jemima. She was almost fully crouched and clinging to the center railing with both hands.

Daniel was still sitting in the captain's chair, propping his chin on his hand indifferently. "Now he's just trying way too hard."

I threw myself into the pilot seat and checked the damage report. The ship informed me with large flashing red letters that it had "sustained damage." This plying ship had the computer interface of a poorly researched movie. But none of the major functions seemed to be damaged and there were no hull breaches. I suspected it was a warning shot, even though such things are traditionally supposed to miss.

I brought the ship around to face the blips on the radar and saw a cluster of buff-colored ships arranged in a threatening attack pattern. I saw two of them break from the group and move across into a flanking position, covering both sides of the route to the trebuchet gate.

"It's not pirates, is it?" thought Jemima aloud. "We're still in the policed areas, aren't we?"

"No, it's not pirates—it's my dad," insisted Daniel.

"He may have a point," muttered Warden, suddenly beside me again. "Henderson will be sending mercenaries. But . . ."

"But they shouldn't have found us this quickly," I finished, distracted by my display. I had brought up a zoomed view of what seemed to be the leading ship. It looked familiar, but I couldn't quite place it. It had the faintly organic design I associated with the just barely spacefaring extrasolar races, who were still more comfortable with designing plows and combine harvesters than spaceships. But there were also custom augmentations more consistent with human aesthetics—a sleeker nose cone, an out-of-place set of silver fins.

The pilot hailed us with a video call, and an image immediately came up of a hulking figure completely silhouetted against firelight. Nevertheless, I recognized him immediately. An open fire in an enclosed atmosphere will lead to death or the need for a supremely expensive air filtration system. Either of which requires a psychotic level of devotion to your image.

"Angelo," I said, by way of greeting.

"Address me not by that name, steward of falsehood," boomed the man I had last seen getting his armor polished at Frobisher's laundry. "Bad enough that for years thou would sully the same air as I, professing hatred for deeds thou thyself had committed. Bad enough that, without thee addressing me with such familiarity."

"Friend of yours," said Warden quietly, very slightly a question, but mostly identifying aloud with no small amount of relief.

I was almost relieved, too. My list of potential threats had been fluctuating so wildly lately I'd almost forgotten that all my former colleagues still wanted me dead. There was something comforting about knowing that at least one state of affairs remained stable. "Listen, A—er. What would you rather I call you, then?"

He shifted in his seat, and for a moment, a flicker of firelight revealed that he was leaning on the hilt of his sword. "Address me as Nemesis, as I name thee Traitor," he growled. "Address me as the avenging hammer of justice, brought down upon thee as though all pilotkind doth hold the hilt."

Behind me, I heard Jemima audibly untense. "Oh, thank God. This whole thing actually had me going for a while. I really literally thought we were being kidnapped for real."

"I told you. It's so fake, isn't it," said Daniel.

The emotionless blackness of Angelo's silhouetted face glared at me. "Um," I said. "Listen. Mr. Nemesis . . ."

"Your companions would mock me?" he hissed. All those years of hunting jungle monsters to lay their carcasses before his uninterested alien queen had made his hearing pretty sharp. "Inform them that I would not spare thy household to reduce thee to stardust, Traitor."

I shushed the children, then made a gesture with my hands as if holding up an invisible volleyball. "Okay. Hear me out," I said to the unmoving black outline on the screen. "I actually have a really large amount of money . . ."

Angelo's ship, still visible in the zoomed-in view, launched a missile. A white triangle expanded rapidly, filling the view as the torpedo sped toward us.

I slammed on the joysticks, and the Platinum God of Whale Sharks—or the *Jemima*, depending—immediately began to speculate upon the possibility of taking evasive action. The ship's components finally reached enough of a consensus and she began lumbering into a barrel roll, at which point an explosion in her underbelly accelerated it a bit.

"Face thy death with dignity, Jacques McKeown," said Angelo. "Do not waste thy final moments with bargains. Use them to decide which of thy many names shall adorn thy tombstone."

I checked the readout. According to the one warning window that wasn't a pop-up advertisement, we had a hull breach. It was in food storage, which was easy enough to section off from the rest of the internal environment, but most of the ship's inventory of potato chips and ice cream was now lost to the pitiless void of space.

Warden took the opportunity to address the communicator. "Enemy vessel. There are innocents onboard this ship."

"She's right, there are," I said, nodding rapidly.

"Thou would hide behind children," sneered Angelo. "Your dishonor knows new depths with every passing second."

"Trying way too ha-ard," commented Daniel in a singsong voice.

"It's not very realistic with the whole medieval-talk thing, is it?" added Jemima, not quietly enough. "It's really, you know, twentieth century."

"Listen," I hissed, leaning close to Warden. "Push the innocents thing. These guys are big on honor."

She nodded and turned back to the communicator. "Enemy ship," she said. "Would you be willing to spare the rest of us if McKeown surrendered to you alone?"

I immediately shoved her away and started making static sounds with my mouth. "Pssssh! You're breaking up! Stay on the line! Krsssssssh pkssssssssssh." Then I ended the call and opened and closed my fists at Warden a few times before finding the words. "What is wrong with your brain?"

"I was merely assessing all available options," she said coldly.

I gestured to the ships. "Those brackets are all-or-nothing lads," I said. "It's like seeking forgiveness and asking permission. They might have let you go if you hadn't been so unclassy as to ask them."

"Nevertheless, we seem to have given them pause for thought."

Together, we looked at the ships, hanging silently and unmoving in space. And then, after a couple of seconds' contemplation time, every single one of them started emitting volleys of blaster fire.

This time, I was somewhat more prepared, and the engines had warmed up a little, so I was able to use the sheer distance between me and them to anticipate where the shots were going and carefully arrange for the ship to be elsewhere. But the distance was closing fast.

The Platinum God of Whale Sharks actually had a fairly competitive top speed. It was just getting there that was the problem; the thing accelerated like manure making its way out of a cow's arse. I pulled both joysticks back with one arm and used the other to set everything I could find on the touchscreen interface to maximum. I could only hope that Angelo and his friends wouldn't be able to get into close range before our speed topped out.

I scanned the nearby area. Nothing but space. With a few asteroids to weave around, a bit of texture, I'd be in my element, evasionwise. Even without my usual suite of pre-programmed movement sequences, give me a few tons of rock and I could wipe any pursuer off like trac on a tea tray. On a level playing field—and open space is about as level as it gets—then it comes down to who showed up in the best ship. In this case, that debate would end with one word. The word was *kaboom*.

The trebuchet gate was the way out. All I had to do was make a beeline for it, setting its firing angle as I approached, then get ourselves launched the moment we were in range. The beauty of the system was that it was impossible to tell precisely where we'd be flung to. But before I could do that I had to get into a position where there wasn't a throng of hairy murderers between us and the gate.

We reached top speed, which was helpfully indicated by the entire ship vibrating violently and ringing with the musical squeaks and pings of screws coming undone. Angelo's little lynch mob of a fleet kept in hot pursuit, just far enough away to be the size of murderous crows on the viewing screen. I was dodging their missiles with well-timed rolls, but it was only a matter of time before that wouldn't cut it anymore. Turning at this speed, in this ship, was like pushing a boulder up a hill.

But that gave me an idea. I scrutinized Angelo's ships through the rear view. They were stocky attack ships, well armored, built for making head-on attacks and soaking up damage. Well suited to Angelo and other overcompensating warrior types of the opinion that dodging is for girls.

All of which meant that they, too, were at a disadvantage at speed. They could deliver a nasty frontal charge to get them in the thick of it as fast as possible, but they lost confidence if the charge went on too long. They couldn't maneuver well.

"Hold on to something," I warned, flexing my hands like a concert pianist in preparation. I felt Warden grip the back of my chair urgently.

"You know, this is actually getting exciting," said Jemima, obediently clutching a length of railing. Daniel grunted and swung his chair back and forth, bored.

I waited for the brief pause between volleys of missiles as the pursuers let their tubes cool down, then made my move. I put both joysticks up, and the ship began to pitch forward, describing a downward arc.

Just as I knew they would, I saw our pursuers begin to plot a similar path, curving downward to get us back into their sights. But at that moment, I dropped our speed to zero. The ship was no better at decelerating, but its turning jets became more and more effective as we slowed, rolling us into a tight little spiral as Angelo's ships sailed away above us, no doubt wondering where the hell we'd gone.

Then, when our ship was pointing upward, squat nose cone aimed at the dissipating vapor trail Angelo's fleet had left behind, I put the speed back up to maximum.

That was where it all went wrong. Instead of the expected burst of acceleration, there was a smoky cough from somewhere behind us, something important-sounding made a rather distressing noise, then the engines fell silent.

The touchscreen flashed red and bleeped to itself for a few seconds as I drummed my fingers on the joysticks, frozen in a dynamic piloting pose worthy of a dramatic escape.

Warden broke the silence with a polite cough. "What was the plan, McKeown?"

"No one ever looks up," I muttered.

"Excuse me?"

"If we could have gotten out of their sight and ended up above them, they wouldn't have figured out where we'd gone until it was too late. 'Cos no one ever thinks to look up. We would've been halfway to the gate by the time they realized."

"I see. So what went wrong?"

"The engine failed."

"And why did it fail?"

I read the words flashing red before me. "Engine Overheat Error," it read. "Probable cause: coolant rod deactivated by user."

"It just did," I said through my teeth.

Angelo and his hunting party rose back into view like an elevator full of grizzly bears arriving at my floor. I palmed the touchscreen rapidly, but it seemed to have frozen on a red screen stating that, for our comfort and convenience, all engine functions had been disabled for cooling. I took issue with the "comfort" part.

"Make thy peace, Jacques McKeown," said Angelo, appearing momentarily onscreen again.

"I'm not Jacques McKeown!" I revealed loudly, when their missile tubes began to glow. "They're making me pretend to be Jacques McKeown for that doint back there!"

"Yeah, I knew that," said Jemima. Daniel looked over his shoulder, wondering what doint I was talking about.

"Pathetic," intoned Angelo.

"Well, he's obviously not the real Jacques McKeown," said Jemima. "Jacques McKeown's, like, really rich from all the books and doesn't need to come out into the open like this." I nodded rapidly as the phone on which I'd seen my new bank balance started feeling very warm in my pocket.

Angelo's guns still hadn't fired, so perhaps we'd at least given him a moment of consideration. The big, sweaty fish was biting at the hook; it was time to start reeling. "You have to admit, there's room for doubt, isn't there?" I said, keeping my face placid and tone civil, being the better man. "Whatever you think is most likely, there's at least a chance that you're about to kill four innocent people. Half of them children. And then who'll be the one with no honor, Angelo?"

Angelo lowered his head even further and burbled out an angry, animalistic noise from the back of his throat. But it was a defeated sound. Either he'd been talked around, or the moment to atomize us all out of spontaneous berserker passion had been lost. We'd drawn it out too long.

Then, a new ship screamed by overhead, mere yards from the tops of our vessels. Everyone on the bridge reflexively ducked, and I saw Angelo almost knock all his teeth out on his own sword. The newcomer then decelerated, executed a tight, flashy turn, and joined our little discussion circle, like a flashy young stud in a leather jacket arriving at the singles bar.

It was the filth. The Interplanetary Security Service, the "policed" part of the phrase "policed section of space." Their ships were unmistakable—metallic blue and almost perfectly cone shaped, the most powerful engines available at the back, tapering down to a point at the front, where a selection of blasters and torpedo cannons awaited the unwary troublemaker. They'd suffered massive cutbacks as a result of—what else?—quantum tunneling, and ever since then had had a rather psychotic eagerness to poke their noses in at the first sign of conflict.

But there was something odd about this one. Instead of immediately hailing every ship in the vicinity with an ear-cracking siren and a reading of the rights, it was just hanging there in space, silent and unmoving after its flashy entrance. I briefly met Angelo's gaze as we both wondered where this was leading.

And then a projector mounted above the ISS ship's cockpit window burst into life, displaying a gigantic holographic screen across space directly in front of its nose. An immediately recognizable face appeared, grinning, its orange skin neatly juxtaposing the ship's blue coloration.

"Henderson," I realized.

"A good morning to you all," he said. His voice was coming through the ship's comm system slightly out of sync to the movement of his lips on the holographic screen. "Don't mind me if you were in the middle of something. I'm just going to sit here murdering every single person that tries to harm Danny."

"How the hell did he find us?!" I hissed, partly to Warden and mostly to myself. "Trac. He must have figured out we hadn't left the system yet, and of course we were stupid enough to just head straight to the most obvious trebuchet gate."

"Possibly," said Warden quietly. "Or possibly it's because I texted him and told him where we were."

I banged my forehead against the touchscreen, as a consequence of all the strength flooding from my upper body. "Why did you do that?" I asked, lips deformed against the glass.

"Think, McKeown. Henderson's main interest is keeping Daniel safe. If your former colleagues truly intended to destroy our ship indiscriminately, then our desires temporarily aligned."

"Oh. Of course. Sound thinking. Maybe next we could dissuade muggers by handcuffing ourselves to a Bengal tiger." I threw myself back in my seat and waved my hands manically. "Hey! I've got an idea! How about we all stop ringing up the plying supervillain!"

"What stake hast thou in this dispute?" demanded Angelo.

Henderson smiled without humor. "I'm just a father who's concerned that his son isn't having the best holiday he could possibly have with his new best friend, Jacques McKeown."

"DAAAD," screamed Daniel, covering the top of his head with both hands. Jemima, who'd been standing in front of him watching the display, flinched at the outburst.

"Is he truly the traitor Jacques McKeown?" asked Angelo, jabbing into the communication screen with an index finger like a German sausage.

I tried to think of precisely the right thing to say that would appease every party, but my thought process took slightly too long. "Oh, I should hope so, the amount he cost me," exclaimed Henderson, filling the pause. "*Traitor* certainly seems to fit the bill."

"Then thou shalt bear witness to his destruction," replied Angelo, his voice descending gradually into a vicious hiss.

"Sorry if I'm being stubborn, but actually, no, I don't think I will. I don't think you're going to blow up that ship. I think you're going to do that thing where you go inside the ship and take everyone alive, and then bring them to me. You're going to do that because I'm telling you to."

A few of the ships in Angelo's party were rotating slowly toward the ISS ship, anticipating a change in the dynamics of the situation. "And for what reason should we obey thy commands?" asked Angelo, an offended edge to his tone of voice.

"Boarding! That's the word I was looking for. Sorry, I've a lot on my mind. What was that? Oh, well, let's say, thirty thousand of those stupid moon dollars you have?"

I could still feel Warden's hand on my chair's headrest, gripping hard enough to pull the upholstery tight. There was nothing we could do but watch the exchange like a pair of frightened kids hiding behind the sofa while their parents argue.

"Begone from this place, Terran worm," growled Angelo, to my simultaneous relief and increased tension. "There is no honor in thy grubby offerings."

The permanent half smile froze on Henderson's face. Clearly he was used to the discussion ending after money came into it. I got the feeling we were about to see what happens when an unstoppable force meets an immovable object. "All right. I like this, it's cute. Fifty thousand. Come on, boys, that'd buy a lot of cheap wine and back-alley hand jobs."

Angelo and the cadre of John Carter types from which he'd presumably constructed his lynch mob were a prideful bunch. Tribal living on hostile planets drums that into you. And while they were star pilots, they weren't hurting for euroyen as much as the rest of us. This was partly because they preferred to catch their own food, and partly because they often had side gigs taking suicidally dangerous bounty-hunting jobs. And while Henderson's offer wasn't dissimilar to such a contract, they did it more for the honor and the chance to relive the glory days. Not for money, and certainly not money being dismissively tossed at them as if from a strip club patron.

Soon, all their weapons were trained on the ISS ship. I very much doubted Henderson was actually inside it, but after honor and pride Angelo's lot were pretty big on symbolism, too.

"Perhaps thou should slither away now," said Angelo. "And butt thy nose elsewhere, lest we slice it from thy face for thy tone."

Henderson's smile had now entirely disappeared. He shifted in his seat, planting his chin upon his hand to regard the enemy he had just created for himself, and his bottom row of teeth ground back and forth. "Well," he growled. "This is what happens when you try to meet someone halfway."

The screen disappeared. All was still. I glanced nervously at Warden, and she returned an identical expression. "What happens now?" I asked.

"He's probably going to run away or start shooting," suggested Jemima. "I mean, that sounded like the sort of thing you say just before you do one of those two things."

As it turned out, she was wrong: neither of those things happened. Instead, I noticed movement on the outside of the ISS ship and commanded the interface to zoom in.

It took me a moment to recognize Carlos. It was the first time I'd seen him without his tuxedo: he was on this occasion entirely unclothed except for some kind of shiny black shorts for modesty's sake. He crawled his away along the ship's hull toward the nose cone, moving across by bending and straightening his massive arms like some kind of giant red caterpillar with a fist on each end.

He paused briefly when he reached the outside of the cockpit window, then jumped. He launched himself with such power that the ISS ship was sent spinning in the opposite direction. His body sped horizontally across space, leaving what looked like a red comet tail composed of what I think might have been hairs.

His target seemed to be a ship right in the middle of Angelo's armada, which, like the others, hadn't moved, because they were all waiting to see where this was leading. Carlos almost missed it, but he extended a hand as he went past and managed to grab one of the torpedo tubes. He spun around it a few times, then, momentum sufficiently built up, brought one of his fists down upon the top of the ship.

It went straight through the hull and up to the "wrist." Then the entirety of Carlos's mass clambered inside the hole. He had a cat's ability to inexplicably fit through small gaps.

On the communication window, I saw Angelo, all poise and posturing forgotten, slapping at something offscreen, presumably his own communication device. "Brothers!" he cried. "Answer my call! What ails thee?"

All we could hear from our end was a combination of static and indistinct crashing and groaning noises that were equally likely to have come from comms interference, from metal being torn apart, or from people being torn apart.

What we could be sure of was the look on Angelo's face, bathed in the glow of the video screen as he watched live feed that we couldn't see, and it was ghastly. His tanned complexion was turning the color of a normal person's skin.

The sound suddenly became an earsplitting roar of wind, and at that same moment, I saw Carlos emerge from the hull of the stricken ship like a jet of pus spurting from a burst pimple. He kicked away toward another target and the ship, now empty of life, began to gently spin as it drifted away.

This time, the ship Carlos was streaking toward had the presence of mind to start firing, as did most of its colleagues. The area of space immediately surrounding Carlos became a confusing mess of blaster fire, torpedoes, and crisscrossing vapor trails. Carlos either took every hit and suffered no damage or employed some arcane movements of his insane body to ensure that at no point was any part of him in any of the uncountable firing lines.

Halfway to his apparent destination, his path of movement suddenly turned a sharp ninety degrees. But it didn't seem to have anything to do with having been hit by a blast, as the new path was just as straight and determined as the first.

"Tell me," I said to my equally transfixed crewmates, "that that plying thing did not just kick flip off a torpedo."

The originator of the torpedo—and Carlos's new target—registered all of this too late. The pilot made an attempt to get out of the way, but their engine wasn't warmed up. With spooky accuracy Carlos shot straight up their torpedo tube without even touching the sides. Angelo immediately called the stricken ship, whose pilot managed to get almost a whole word out before that audio feed also descended into loud crashes and violence.

I caught Angelo's gaze after he switched the feed off. He scowled, his upper lip curling around his nose like the bread of a steak sandwich. "You may have this fight alone, coward," he growled, before cutting communication.

His ship peeled away from the gathering and sped off in the general direction of Ritsuko. His surviving allies quickly followed his lead. Soon our ship was alone with the ISS vessel and the two drifting ships whose pilots were now too dead to escape.

Carlos emerged from the top of the second ship he had taken care of, and he clung to the hull, mournfully watching his potential targets disappear, like a child watching their mother get back in the car without them on their first day of school. Then what passed for his face slowly turned to look in our direction.

Warden jerked into life. She threw an order in my general direction—"Call Henderson"—and ran for the captain's chair. I hailed the ISS ship, and in the same time, Carlos leapt onto that ship's hull, preparing to steppingstone over to us.

The communication screen sprang to life with a new feed, and Henderson's face appeared. I hadn't been able to make out the scene behind Henderson when he'd been on the holographic screen, but seeing it on the communicator, it surprised me. He was sitting on the captain's chair of a bridge considerably more efficiently laid out than mine, and I saw uniformed ISS agents behind him, some nakedly resentful, some hovering nervously around, making sure he was satisfied with their performance.

Which meant he actually was onboard that ship in person. That made sense, if his bodyguard was here, too. It was a risky thing for a professional in a dangerous lifestyle, and that further meant that he was taking Daniel's abduction a lot more seriously than his manner of speech suggested. I felt myself shiver with intimidation.

"Henderson," said Warden. Henderson did not smile.

I looked behind me. Warden was standing behind the captain's chair, holding Daniel tightly by the shoulder with one hand and holding my blaster to his temple with the other. Daniel, for his part, was directing his usual resentment toward the face of his father. Jemima had been vaguely hovering around the room and was settled safely away from Warden just next to my position.

"So, what's the plan, Penny?" asked Henderson, his chummy tone of voice inconsistent with his rock-solid face. "'Cos I can see you've clearly got this all worked out."

"Call Carlos back," said Warden. Carlos, somehow informed on the events by means I couldn't even guess at, was still perched on the top of the ISS ship's hull, watching us intently like a pointer dog. "Daniel will be returned to you when we are outside your sphere of influence. But if you make any moves against us while we make for the trebuchet gate, he dies."

"Ugh, will you please stop it?" moaned Daniel. "We all know it's an act and you're just embarrassing yourselves."

There was an awkward pause, then Henderson's face broke out into a wide, warm smile. "Ah, you're right. This was all completely set up and you're not actually in any danger at all."

"Why do you always have to mess with everything I do?! I HATE you!"

"Oh, forgive an old man for wanting your trip to be exciting. But do your dad a favor, Danny—just go along with it. We've put so much effort and money into all the actors and set pieces; it'd just break everyone's hearts to know you saw through it so quickly."

"URGH," went Daniel, rolling his eyes. "Fine."

"Oh my god," murmured Jemima, audible only to me. I looked at her quizzically. "It's not an act. It's all real, isn't it."

I glanced briefly over at Warden before answering. "Yeah."

"Is she going to kill us?"

I had something snarky prepared, but then I caught the look on Jemima's face, and some long-forgotten instinct made me think better of it. "Not if I can help it," I whispered sincerely. "I'll stop it before it comes to that. Promise."

"Well then, let me just get back into character," said Henderson jovially. He disappeared downward off the screen, apparently rolling forward off his chair, to the confusion of the ISS officers behind him. Then he rose back into view with a face like a gathering storm. His eyes flashed white hatred from the shadows formed by his lowered brow.

"Take us to the gate, McKeown," said Warden, still holding the gun to Daniel's head and not breaking eye contact with Henderson's image.

I didn't need telling twice. I slid us into forward thrust, and the ship accelerated apologetically past Henderson's ship and toward the massive corkscrew that still hung patiently in the background. I was acutely aware of Carlos's eager gaze boring into us as we swept past, ready to spring at the slightest instruction.

"Penny?" said Henderson conversationally. "You're going to die."

Warden pretended she hadn't heard. But I almost heard the *click* of all her joints locking solid.

"I know, philosophically, we all are, eventually," added Henderson. "I'm just saying that you probably have more reason to philosophize about that than others. We're going to find you. We'll know how far the gate sends you and we'll find you."

"McKeown," said Warden. "Do you know how to make a fire-and-forget jump?"

In the back of my mind, my survival instincts immediately leapt to their feet and started swearing and banging a drum. "Yeah," I said warily. "I've never done one, but it was covered at flight school."

"Please explain what it is, for the benefit of anyone who might be listening?"

Suddenly I felt like I was back in my childhood home, relaying messages between parents. "You try to cancel out of a trebuchet jump just as the gate begins to fire. It makes the gate's firmware crash, and you get launched right as the gate starts decalibrating. There's always an element of randomness to a gate jump, but this gives it a much wider range. And it's impossible to track."

"So you know what to do now, don't you."

I sighed. "I was kinda hoping I didn't. 'Cos it sounds like you want to hurl us into a completely randomly chosen point of the Black."

She tensed up more, if that was even possible. Her hand tightened audibly around the gun. "Are you unwilling to do it?"

I turned in my chair and took the controls. "No, no, I'll do it. Just thought maybe you might like to save a bit of time and shoot us all in the heads instead."

No one replied. The trebuchet gate grew larger and larger in our view. On the video feed, Henderson watched, face still, like the crowd watching the condemned prisoner walking up to the scaffold.

Then he suddenly shot forward in his seat, eyes blazing. "How the hell do you think you're going to walk away from this, Warden? Walk away from me?! You think you can hide out there, in space, of all places?" He slapped himself on both cheeks in mock concern. "Oh, whatever shall I do? Surely I can't just find some scumbag who'll take money to hunt you down? Who in the Black could possibly fit that bill? Oh, that's right!" He slapped his forehead. "Absolutely anyone!"

I killed the feed. We were inside the corkscrew now, and a giant metallic spiral filled my view. The gate's automated systems interfaced with the ship's computer, and the instruction panel appeared in the middle of my screen. After setting the destination as vaguely as possible for a spot in the middle of the Black, a countdown from thirty began.

They had indeed covered fire-and-forget jumps long ago in my pilot training, mainly to tell us not to do them. But the trouble with teaching people not to do a thing is that you have to tell them about the thing first. So I knew that it could be fairly easily achieved by repeatedly jamming the gate's Cancel button when half a second of countdown remained. I watched the numbers tick down, my knuckle hovering over the touchscreen.

"Um," said Jemima quietly, close to my ear. "Could you be honest? How likely is it that this will kill us all?"

I kept my gaze fixed on the countdown. "Well," I murmured, speaking as slowly as I dared. "I wouldn't put it above one percent. And. Below three percent."

"You wouldn't put it between one and three percent?" summarized Jemima.

"No," I replied, drawing the syllable out a good few seconds.

"Would you put it at more than three percent?"

A set of metal rings appeared around the ship and began to spin in opposite directions, knitting the warp bubble around us. My hair stood on end as every airborne particle in the ship's atmosphere held perfectly still.

"Tell you later!" I shouted over the growing roar of the activating trebuchet cannon, before smashing the Cancel button.

For one confusing moment, the ship seemed to be several million light years in length and facing in twenty different directions. Then reality reasserted itself, and we crossed the Black.

CHAPTER 15

I WENT THROUGH the usual disorienting sensation that accompanies a trebuchet jump, and once I'd firmly established where my body ended and the
rest of the universe began, I took stock.

I'd had worse trebuchet jumps. I was still sitting in the chair, miraculously,
although it had rolled a good six feet away from where it had been previ-
ously, and there was a large, painful bruise on my forehead that seemed to
correspond in size to a patch of grease on a nearby bulkhead.

Jemima and Warden were both picking themselves up from various sec-
tions of floor. Daniel's chair had been heavy enough to stay where it was, so
he was still in it, although it hadn't fully stopped spinning. His face looked
a little green.

"Urgh," he said, it being his catch phrase. "We could have gotten, like, hurt
from that. That was against, like, health and safety or something."

"Where are we?" barked Warden.

I moved my chair back to the console by the traditional method of repeatedly digging my heels into the carpet and hip thrusting madly. "Well,
I can tell you it's not a worst-case scenario, because we're still alive," I said,
leafing through the navigation menus.

"Answer the question," said Warden testily, looming over me again.

I looked at the tiny icon that represented our current location. Then I
looked at the other icon indicating the asteroid belt near Cantrabargid,
where I'd last seen Den and Mark. Then I looked at the yawning black gulf
of barely charted space between the two and emitted a little sigh.

"We're here," I said, pointing helpfully. "We want to be there."

"How long will that take?"

"Assuming we aren't attacked on the way?" I said.

"Well, that would just make things quicker, wouldn't it?" asked Jemima, appearing at my other shoulder. "That's what you, like, wanted to do, right? Join up with pirates? And once you do that, we can go home, right?"

"Uh. Yeah," I said, nodding slowly.

What I did not mention was that while a lot of pirates in the Black were reasonable ex-pilot types just trying to get by, it was still a very large and completely unregulated region, and some parts of it were more unregulated than others. Solar System authorities had sent a couple of census workers around the Black to get at least some idea of who was out there and what they were doing, and several of them had never been heard from again. I'd heard that one of the census shuttles had been found drifting, with a load of severed limbs tied to the rear nacelles like grim wedding party ornaments.

"But if that doesn't happen, I'd say it's a four-hour travel time," I said.

"BOOOOR-IIIING," interjected Daniel informatively. "I don't wanna go wherever Dad's got set up. It'll be boring."

"Dude, it's not set up, it's real," said Jemima, desperately staring at the gun in Warden's hand.

"It is set up. My dad said it was. Ms. Warden isn't even any good at pretending. She used the exact same voice when she was making me clean my room."

"Set the course," said Warden to me through her teeth.

"Right you are, Mary Poppins," I replied, under my breath.

"Four hours, then," said Warden, addressing the room. "We should take the opportunity to get some sleep."

"I'll just nap in the pilot's chair," I said, pulling the peak of my cap low.

Warden eyed me suspiciously. "Why?"

"Because if we do get ambushed by something, then I don't want to have to run up however many plying flights of steps dodging beanbags and popcorn machines to get back to the controls," I spat.

"Very well," she said, after mulling it over at length. "Daniel. Jemima. Come on. I'm going to lock you in one of the cabins."

"Erm," I interjected as I noticed Daniel immediately perk up. "Maybe . . . put them in separate cabins," I suggested. "So they don't conspire with each other."

"Thank you," mouthed Jemima.

Warden mulled this one over, too. "Perfectly sound reason twice in one minute?" she said suspiciously. "Don't strain yourself, McKeown." She must have been in a good mood, or at least drifting over to the manic side of bipolar.

"I'm not going to bed!" protested Daniel as Warden waggled the gun toward the door. "I'm not tired! This is stupid."

"Daniel, do as you are told," said Warden, holding the gun uncomfortably. I didn't think she'd actually shoot him with it, but I wondered if she'd go as far as a pistol-whip.

"Yeah, come on, Dan, please," said Jemima fearfully, touching his arm in a way that made Daniel's eyes bulge out like a pair of sweaty cue balls. "I want to see, you know, what your Dad set up. Maybe it'll be . . . fun?"

"Okay," said Daniel meekly, reddening.

Warden was shepherding the pair of them out of the room with little sweeps of the gun but stopped at the door. "McKeown, give me your phone. We need to get rid of it before it's traced."

"I know! Stop fussing, all right?" I snapped. "Just concentrate on locking the kids up. I can get rid of my own phone. I'm not stupid."

She opened her mouth to attempt some devastatingly witty response to that, but then aborted and went for a tired sigh instead. "Fine. Don't forget."

Soon I was alone on the bridge, with no company except the background chorus of stock electronic bleeps and hums that were piped through the PA system apparently for atmospheric purposes alone.

I leaned back, interlaced my hands behind my head, and watched the passing stars until they started to lull me into a doze, and my thoughts returned to Jacques McKeown. The traitor to pilotkind believed by a growing list of people to be me, including his plying employers now.

But the greatest of all sellouts hadn't reaped any of the traditional reward of selling out—I had. And I didn't want to think about whether or not this meant I had also stolen the title of traitor along with everything else. I'd just have to let that hang over me until the opportunity arose to donate it to charity or sprinkle it all away from the top of a tall building.

I just couldn't get my head around why he'd never taken it. Was he just dense? He was smart enough to write the plying things and steal other people's life stories. Didn't add up. Had he been screwed by his agent or the publisher? No, the publisher had been trying to find him. And they said he didn't have an agent.

Maybe, and this was getting really speculative, he just felt bad. He was just some star pilot doing some amateur writing on the side to make ends meet, and the success snowballed on him. It seemed likelier, but then again, according to the publishers he'd never collected *any* money. Not even from his earliest books, before he was popular as both author and hate figure.

No star pilot would turn away cash. That was just a fact. We'd all gone long past the point that pride had to be sacrificed for survival. So . . .

. . . So there was always the possibility that the real Jacques McKeown wasn't a pilot.

I had almost put myself to sleep with the nice, calming background noise of constant dread when my phone burst into life, sending me into a brief seizure that almost toppled the chair.

I worried my phone free of my pocket. No caller ID, again. The words *don't forget*, in Warden's strict tones, echoed in my ears for a moment. But what the hell, I thought. She wasn't the boss of me, and there's always room to dig yourself a little deeper. I answered.

"Take it you got there alive, Jacques?"

Still bleary from partial sleep, I needed a moment to recognize that voice that I'd heard before, but never from this phone. When I did, it sparked off a new round of seizures that sent me straight off the chair and onto the floor. "Henderson?" I said, propping myself up on an elbow.

"Jacques, Jacques. We're both men of the world. Well, you're not—you live on the moon—but we understand each other, don't we? It hit me while I was saying to Penny that thing about how any scumbag in the Black would sell her out. I thought to myself, wait a minute, I know just the guy."

"What?"

"Geez, does living in low gravity make your brain float away? I mean you, Jacques! You're the right guy in just the right place to ease a concerned father's mind."

"Didn't you have a vendetta against me not too long ago?"

Henderson was doing that thing where he appeared completely deaf to any voice other than his own. "Now, I did a little bit of thinking after our earlier conversation, and I want to float some guesswork past you. Tell me, this whole idea to kidnap my son, was that really something you and Penny agreed on, equal partnership style?"

Henderson was sharp. Dangerously so, like a knife hanging off a kitchen worktop in a household with young children. I looked all around before answering, to make sure Warden wasn't still hovering behind me like one of the brides of Dracula. "No. I swear."

There was a pause. "Okay, so either you're telling the truth, or you're lying and you've decided you want out. That's cool. Either suits me. What was it that killed the romance? Is she frigid? I'm pretty sure she's frigid."

I winced. "I—"

"I'm just messing with you, Jacques. That was the other thing that didn't add up. You and her, running away together? You just didn't seem like her type. I always pictured her settling down with some kind of filing cabinet with a dildo strapped to the top. But anyway, now we all know where we are, I have a proposal."

"Go on," I said.

"Wow, you are just turning on her like a revolving door, aren't you. It's a simple deal—turn on the Quantunnel booth in your ship, set it to the one in my spaceport on Ritsuko, let me and my boys come in and take everyone home. You do that, I wipe the slate clean and forget all about you. Seriously. Next time I see a poster for your books I'll say, 'Who's that? Why have I never heard of such a popular and obviously extremely sensible writer?'"

I finally got a word in edgeways. "Warden blew up the Quantunnel booth," I said quickly, uncomfortably aware that I was, as I spoke, proving that she had been extremely smart to do so. "With a gun."

"How on earth did she get hold of a gun?"

"I have no idea," I said immediately.

"Actually perhaps I should have said 'how *off* earth'?" He made a little muttering laugh at his own joke. "Hm. This complicates things. All right, new deal. I'm sorting out some scum on my end. I'll let you know where they're going to be, you just tell Penny whatever lie you need, let the scum onboard, they take everyone away, you try not to look too much like a target, and then you can go wherever you want. Sound good?"

I only half heard his words, because all my instincts were fighting each other inside my conscious mind. The scrappy survival instincts were all completely in favor of the proposal, but they were being fought on all fronts by the much older instincts of a star pilot. All of which were saying that, leaving aside Henderson being as trustworthy as a thirdhand EVA suit, betraying a woman to the archvillain that she was attempting to escape from was simply Not What Star Pilots Did. In response, a convincing case was made that this was a pretty sexist thought to have in a modern universe, and besides, Warden was a woman only on a completely technical level.

Henderson broke my silence. He made the effort to sound reasonable. "Look. I'm offering a clean break out of this, Jacques. I know it's what you want. And as long as Penny and Danny end up back with me, I could give two fetid shits for where you go after that."

I bit my lip. "What about Jemima?" I probed.

"Jemima? Danny brought Jemima along?" He made a chuckle I didn't like the sound of. "He's coming of age fast, that boy. Now I know why her mother's been on the news so much today. Actually, that might work out really well. Hold the scum!" His last three words had been muffled, apparently directed at someone else in the room with him. "I'll let her know. She's got some clout with the UR government. Well. I say clout. She runs it."

My eyes widened like balloons attached to air tanks as I translated this in my head. "Jemima's mother is the president of the United Republic," I said, tonelessly.

"Yeah. She's an uppity little bitch. Haven't quite been able to get her under the thumb, yet. But she'll be all over this. She'll send the Navy SPEALs. Yeah, you know what? Forget everything I just said. I don't need to make a deal with you. You can make all the deals you like when the navy burst in and shoot you in the knees and pin you to the floor. Catch you later, then."

After he hung up, I stared at my deactivated phone for close to a full minute. Then an actual reasoned thought penetrated the din of chattering voices in my head, and I embarked upon a short walk down to the airlock to finally get rid of the phone.

On the way, I tried to focus my mind. I wasn't going to even try storing away the new knowledge that Jemima was the president's daughter. I was very firmly ordering that to the back of the queue of things my brain needed to process. The only concrete fact that mattered was that we were now on the run from the entire plying UR Navy as well as Henderson. If either of those parties tracked down the ship and boarded it, I gave myself even odds that I wouldn't immediately be shot in the face for being too visible.

That was when a plan started unfolding. Henderson wanted Warden dead but didn't seem to care as much about me. Suddenly we weren't as "in this together" as I'd assumed. So if I wasn't onboard to be captured when the cavalry arrived, Henderson probably wouldn't give me another thought.

I reached the airlock, and opened the inner door just an inch to toss my phone through, receiving a vicious blast of ice-cold suction before I could slam it shut. Then I opened the external door remotely, and my only means of communication disappeared into space, along with all my prepaid minutes.

That was the solution. I was already in the Black; I was where I wanted to be. I just had to get off this plying ship. Leave it to drift in the middle of nowhere and let Henderson and the UR Navy scoop it up like dog dirt. Sure, it was a betrayal, but getting two minors back to their parents practically made it heroic.

If the Platinum God of Whale Sharks had had escape pods, I would have been in one already, waving goodbye to this whole tangled mess. But that was just another safety measure the manufacturers apparently felt would have spoiled the party. I'd have to flag down a pirate vessel. I was honestly surprised they weren't already circling us like hyenas, but one would show up sooner or later. Where things would get complicated would be persuading the crew to attach an umbilical but do basically the exact opposite of a boarding. They'd probably want to do the more conventional kind of boarding and clear the place out, if not hijack the entire ship, which would definitely get in the way of my plan to quietly slip away into the night.

Once I was back in the pilot's seat, I devoted all my thought to the matter, there being little else to do besides watch the stars fly past, and eventually remembered that I was, as of recently, a multimillionaire. Money was the ultimate persuader. What I wasn't sure about was what kind of value Solar System currency would have out here in the Black, where transactions were mainly done through either bartering or theft. Still, I'd heard of arms dealers who went into the Black soliciting custom from pirates, so euroyen must have at least some value. And regardless, a million of any kind of currency turns heads.

I performed a wide sensor sweep. Not a single blip. My concern for the absence of life around here was growing. But then, the Black was a big place. And we were currently deep in a large section of it I'd never set foot in. I usually flew tourists to Cantrabargid because it was near the rim of an outlying policed zone and conveniently close to a trebuchet gate. I hadn't been this deep in the Black for a very long time.

I started casting an even wider sensor sweep. I picked up a handful of populated planets within a few hours' flying range, but most of them were still around the hitting-each-other-with-swords stage of civilization, last I'd heard. Humanity was still the most advanced spacefaring race, representing most of the traffic on what few spaceways had been established. *Spaceways* being probably an overgenerous term for "someone drew a line from one policed zone to another and did a quick one-time check for black holes."

Finally, I found a blip. Right on the edge of the *Jemima*'s communication range. A small vessel, but I was sure they could fit me in somewhere.

I leaned close to the mike, to ensure no one else onboard would hear me, and sent out a standard directed signal on a hailing frequency. "Hello? This is civilian vessel . . . *Jemima* calling unidentified craft," I said enticingly. I dispensed with the sign-offs and official-sounding voice; the Black tended to be less formal.

Something vaguely communicationesque burst from the speaker, any possible sense lost in thick static. I winced, lowered the volume slider with my index finger, and messed with the frequency adjusters with my other digits.

A video feed swam into focus in the middle of my view. The signal was all over the place. The interpreter seemed to be cycling through every color and shape it could think of on the basis that at least some of them would be correct. But there was a collection of flesh-toned patches in the middle that roughly correlated to a human face.

"Hay-lo?" came the staticky voice. It was high pitched and evocative of the mentally simple.

"Hello?"

"Hay-lo," it repeated, with more confidence.

"Hi, I need you to listen really carefully," I said. "I've been kidnapped by this crazy Terran div and she's making me fly this ship, but she's gone to bed now and for various complicated reasons it's vitally important that I get off this ship without her knowing. So here's the deal—if you come here quietly and let me onboard your ship, and fly me away without anyone noticing, I will give you money. I've got a lot of money kicking around. It'll buy you a lot of goods from merchants who do dealings in policed zones. All I ask is a lift to the closest thing there is to a spaceport around here. What do you say?"

There was a thoughtful pause, punctuated with a clicking and humming which was either the static or someone stalling for time.

"Hay-lo," they said, finally.

I wasn't sure how to take that. It wasn't a hostile reaction, it wasn't telling me to go and stick it, but it didn't seem to be getting the ball rolling, either. "Hello? Who am I talking to?"

"Hay-lo?"

"Who. Are. You. Who. You."

"Me-uh? Ohhhh. Me-uh pie-let."

"Okay. You pilot. Now we're getting somewhere. I don't suppose there's anyone else on there I could talk to instead of you?"

"Cap-ton."

"There's a captain?"

"Cap-ton, yay-us."

"Can I speak to the captain?"

"Cap-ton pie-let. Me-uh pie-let. Me-uh cap-ton."

I rubbed my eyes. There was something very odd about the way they were talking, besides the obvious. Not exactly like a foreigner with only a passing familiarity with the language, more like a non-human whose vocal cords had never been designed to speak the necessary syllables. But the feed had gotten slightly clearer, and it was definitely a human face in there.

"Okay, let's start from the bottom and work up," I muttered to myself, then spoke as clearly and loudly as I dared. "Money. Mon-ey. Do you know mon-ey?"

"Mun-ay, yay-us!" said my correspondent, nodding. That seemed to get through. "Mun-ay foo-ud."

"Yes! Money buy food. Lots of food. I have money. Come get me. You have money. Yes?"

"Coo-um yu-oo?"

I was reminded of conversations I'd had around closing time outside the Brandied Bracket. "Yes. Come me. Get money. Buy food."

"Yu-oo foo-ud, yay-us."

The feed cut off, ending the discourse. But I could still see the other ship on the long-range scanner, and after a moment, it began to move slowly toward my location at the center of the screen.

I slowed the ship in preparation for the rendez-vous, gradually enough that hopefully no one onboard would notice the change in engine noise. Thankfully the ship's designer had made a lot of effort to suppress the engine sound, along with every other feature that might have been conducive to flying the plying thing.

Every time I'd ventured into the Black, I'd met pirates. The reasonable kind, like Den and Mark. Because of this I had assumed that the Black was densely populated with them. That had certainly been the case back in the

Golden Age. But the pirates I'd interacted with since had very rarely been in the mood to update me on the politics of the region.

I did know that pirates had been feeling the pinch as much as anyone, with fewer lootable ships passing through space, and word was that more and more of them were ditching the life in favor of going native on extrasolar worlds. So if there had been changes, they probably weren't in the pirates' favor.

All of which led me to wonder at this point who or what I had just enlisted and whether or not this was as great an idea as it had seemed. I considered holding out for a better class of rescuer, but I find it rarely helps to dwell.

The other ship entered visual range with surprising speed, but then, it seemed like a pretty sleek model. As far as I could tell—it was so coated with grime and layers of frozen dust that I almost mistook it for an asteroid. The main giveaway was that an asteroid is quite a cohesive object, and wouldn't have so many bits looking like they were ready to fall off. Nor would there be a single black smear rubbed out on the windshield, presumably for looking through.

I was staring at it for so long that I completely forgot to hail it. The Incoming Call icon was flashing on my touchscreen. I poked it with one finger, not looking away.

Then my view was filled with a fresh video feed, and I saw the person I had been speaking to, now unobscured by blurring or static. My first thought was that it had been quite some time since I'd last eaten. This was relevant, because if I'd had any food inside me it would probably have immediately ejected itself from whichever orifice was nearest.

I was right—there had been a human face. What I hadn't picked up on was that it didn't actually belong to the onscreen person wearing it. It was tied on with what looked like a length of stripped copper wiring.

"Coo-um yu-oo," said the pilot. It was a leathery green mass that seemed to be having trouble deciding on a shape. One large yellow eye was staring earnestly at me through the mouth hole of the disembodied face.

"Uh," I began. The part of me that wasn't shrieking endlessly directly into my mind's ear was idly wondering if the owner of the face had also contributed those dried-out limbs and lumps of unidentifiable flesh hanging from every extruding component in the background. "You're. The captain?"

"Cap-ton. Mun-ay. Foo-ud."

"Yes, those were the basics, weren't they. Look, sorry to have brought you all the way over here, but I think I might have slightly misunderstood the situation vis-à-vis, erm, human body parts . . . not that there's anything wrong with . . ."

"Coo-um. Yu-oo. Mun-ay." At more or less this point I realized that the distortion of the creature's voice, which I had at first attributed to a bad signal, was in fact the result of trying to speak through a near-constant flow of viscous dribble.

I pantomimed glancing off camera. "Oh! Look at that. Turns out I didn't need help after all. Thanks for coming anyway, though. I actually have a fairly urgent appointment somewhere that isn't here, so . . ."

"Yu-oo. Foo-ud."

I ended the call abruptly. Then I sat perfectly still for a moment, clutching the two joysticks, waiting to see how quickly this was going to escalate. The other ship hung in space in front of me, unmoving, watching like an owl.

Nothing happened for some time. Then I very, very gently pushed the joysticks and began turning away, warming up the engines to begin accelerating.

The other ship opened fire. I wasn't sure with what—it looked like a jagged ball of garbage being projected from a bent torpedo tube. But it struck the Platinum God of Whale Sharks right in the underbelly, followed by a sprinkling of components that had broken off the attacking ship with it, and the damage was real enough.

There was another breach. I remotely sealed off a depressurized section of corridor that led to one of the communal toilets and made a mental note to put a sign up. But the blast had given the ship a head start on the acceleration process, and the recoil from shooting the missile had sent the other ship into a gentle spin, so I took the opportunity to gun it.

Keeping my gaze fixed on the controls, I heard the swish of the bridge door opening, then the rhythmic thumping of women's shoes on thick carpet, and Warden materialized at her usual position behind my shoulder. "What hit us?"

"No idea!" I blurted out. "Complete ambush from something I never saw coming or spoke to." I winced at myself, but Warden was fixated on inspecting the ship in the rear view.

"Pirates?" she asked.

"No. Don't think so. Never seen anything like it before this moment. Did I mention that?"

She sighed angrily. "I was laboring under the impression that you had a working knowledge of the Black, McKeown."

"Not every single inch of it! Whose idea was the plying fire-and-forget jump? What do we do now?"

"Just outfly them!"

By now the Platinum God of Whale Sharks was going flat out. The other ship had matched speed with no difficulty and was keeping leisurely attack distance. It was clearly a very top-of-the-range star piloting ship, much more so than Angelo's, and easily outclassed us even in a state of disrepair. Experimentally I attempted an evasive move, but our pursuer mimicked it with the nonchalance of a man whistling and holding his hands behind his back. "Great plan!" I barked. "You got some actual flyable ship hidden in your underpants?"

"McKeown—"

Another garbage missile burst from underneath the enemy ship, along with another handful of dislodged fragments. It moved only slightly faster than the two ships, but even so I wasn't going to be able to shake it off with my ship's rotation speed.

"McKeown, you are the star pilot here," reminded Warden urgently.

"Right," I muttered. I couldn't think of a way to finger the touchscreen with both hands clutching the joysticks, so I leaned forward and rubbed my nose back and forth across the glass. "Launching weapon countermeasures."

There was a muffled *clonk* and several hundred strips of aluminum foil were projected from the rear of the God of Whale Sharks, which I recognized as the absolute bare minimum weapon countermeasure system mandated by safety regulations. The garbage missile brushed straight through them like a movie star passing through the crowd outside a premiere, before the explosion hit like a barrage of flashbulbs.

Instantly the ship dipped forward and the steering went wonky. I assumed something had happened to the port nacelle. I was immediately proven right when I saw a large piece of it drifting past my view. Our top speed and maneuverability had been cut in half.

"Okay, that didn't work," I said grimly. I wondered how long it would take my hungry friend to reload that makeshift cannon of his.

"Think of something, McKeown!" instructed Warden.

"Oh, good advice, thanks for keeping your end up." I gave up trying to keep the ship under control and let it enjoy its twirling death spiral to nowhere as I worked the communicator to broadcast on the universal distress frequency. "Mayday! Requesting assistance!"

"Well, *I* could have done that," said Warden, folding her arms.

"Any ship in broadcast range! We are under attack by an unknown vessel! Please respond!"

I listened fretfully to the uninterrupted bed of light static, and then an icon appeared. A signal was coming in from very close proximity. I opened a channel. "Hello?!"

"Foo-ud. Foo-ud. Foo-ud."

"I wasn't talking to you!" I blocked the communication and boosted the signal. The broadcast would reach a wider range at the expense of sound quality, so I'd have to speak as clearly as possible. "We're on a very expensive ship! We have tons of money we just don't know what to do with! Come and kill this thing—there are fabulous prizes to be won!"

Still nothing. This was within expectations. Flying across the Black was like riding on public transport late at night—the smarter move is to keep your head down and ignore any sign of trouble. But whatever it was on that ship must have been almost ready for another shot and I was out of ideas.

Then, Warden pushed my head away from the chair-mounted mike. "This is Jacques McKeown's ship," she said urgently. "This is an urgent request for assistance from a ship being piloted by Jacques McKeown."

"What are you—" I began, but I was silenced when she shoved her fist into my mouth. The return communication was still static across the board, but it was a very slightly intrigued static.

"Run long-range ID scans on our vessel and you will detect that one of the chip IDs onboard is attached to the name Jacques McKeown."

The communicator held its breath. Then the response requests started popping up like drops of rain on a pavement.

"What did you say you wanted?" said the first one.

The ship shook again, and the screen went dead. Another piece of something damaged—probably related to the computer system—spun merrily past the front viewing window. The ship rotated until it was entirely upside down, and the engines couldn't do much more than phut, like a tortoise desperately wriggling its limbs to right itself.

And there, directly above us, was the ship piloted by that face-stealing monstrosity, arranging itself like a vast and terrible foot preparing to stomp down upon the struggling tortoise. I was twisting the joysticks around like the handles of an out-of-control spacehopper while Warden was bent forward almost double, practically lying across my lap as she scoured the touchscreens for a useful function.

The creature's ship dipped slightly. Its cannon was swinging loosely off its housing and it was split and curved backward a little at the end, but when I saw something within its depths start glowing redly, I knew that it would hold together for its final, fatal shot.

There was a blast, and another cloud of loose bits broke off from the vessel. And when I was still alive a few seconds later, I tentatively lowered my hands from my eyes and saw that the explosion had come from the enemy ship's opposite side. The missile intended for us exploded inside the cannon, and a succession of follow-up blasts Swiss cheesed the enemy ship in seconds.

"What happened?" wondered Warden aloud. She yelped slightly when the enemy pilot's face mask, slightly burned at the edges, plopped against our viewscreen.

Something off to the starboard side fired one more shot into the wreckage, removing what little integrity it had left and reducing it to a cloud of rust flakes. A new ship moved into view: a converted ship-to-surface cargo transporter, a little worn, but not showing the kind of neglect I had now learned to associate with face-wearing green monsters.

With the computer down I didn't have any means to contact our rescuer, but it looked like they were aware of our difficulties and were preparing to connect an umbilical. A scuffed white tube concertinaed out from the ship's underbelly in an ever so slightly suggestive way.

I turned to Warden. "I need my gun back."

She jumped and immediately pointed it at me again. "Why?"

"I have to go down to the airlock and greet whoever just saved our lives. There is a significant chance we have moved from the frying pan to the fire to the waste disposal unit, and I would appreciate having some control over the situation."

"Valid point." She straightened up and pointed my gun upward, supporting it with her other hand. "We'll both go and greet them."

"Oh, for plying out loud," I moaned, as she marched me down through the ship with the usual stubborn foot shuffling on my part. "We're in the Black now, aren't we? This is where I wanted to be. What do you think I might do if I get my gun back—hijack the ship and take it to exactly where it already is? Not to mention the engine's totaled."

"Me having this gun, McKeown, seems to be the only reason you have to assist with any agenda other than your own. I will continue holding it until you are a little more used to the idea."

"You don't know me, Warden. I'm not just some merc with a price and no morals. I'm a star pilot. From back when that actually meant something."

"A star pilot who, five sentences ago, confirmed their intention to become a pirate."

I scoffed. "You actually counted the sentences, didn't you."

"There have been plenty of moments when you were out of my sight," she continued. "Anyone could have contacted you in that time."

I scoffed again, louder. I made sure to maintain a look of weary contempt on my face.

After briefly checking on the kids—Jemima nervous but keeping it together, Daniel expressing his boredom with one elongated, inappropriately loud word—we made our way down to the airlock. The umbilical had already been attached, and with the external door forced open, there seemed to be somebody in the airlock already. They were patiently knocking on the interior door.

"Surely you don't expect me to be the one in front, when you're the one with the gun," I said, when she stood well back, taking aim at the inner door.

"I will be aiming over your shoulder," she said. "Just don't make any unexpected moves. Open it."

There was another patient knock upon the airlock door. I sighed and reached for the touch plate by its side.

And in the nanosecond before touching the Open panel, I remembered the old boarding trick. The one that comes in handy if you suspect the crew of the ship you're boarding are prepared and may be armed and waiting on the other side of the door. The one where you only partially pressurize the umbilical, then throw loose objects at the airlock door to simulate knocking.

As the interior door opened, I caught a momentary glimpse of a small pile of tennis balls floating in midair before there was a sound like a clap of thunder and I, Warden, and several cubic meters of the God of Whale Shark's internal atmosphere were blasted forward through our airlock and onto the soft floor of the umbilical, which rolled us around like a bouncy castle.

I got up on all fours, which was difficult since the floor yielded hugely every time I put my weight on it, and glimpsed my blaster overtaking me on the left with a merry bounce. I glanced back at Warden. She was rolling around just behind me like a clump of sensible laundry circling a tumble dryer.

Opportunity knocked. I made movements not dissimilar to a breaststroke to navigate the distance between me and my spinning blaster pistol. When I was close enough, I shoved my hand down into the soft floor, creating a slope that the gun could slide down into grasping range.

This plan was scuppered when a foot, clad in an EVA suit, came down into the narrowing gap between the gun and my hand. Instinctively I grabbed the suited ankle and heard the sound of a different blaster pistol leaving its holster, directly above my head.

My gaze traveled up the EVA suit and arrived at the face of a young woman, with grease smeared on her face and her hair tied back. Her blaster was aimed smartly at the center of my forehead.

"Hiya!" she said, brightly. "Did you know that everybody wants to kill you?"

CHAPTER 16

SHORTLY AFTERWARD, I found myself in the mess hall of the newcomers' ship, tied to a metal chair with loops of spare electrical cable. Warden and Jemima were tied to similar chairs on either side of me. Daniel was also there, but our captors had opted to put tape over his mouth after a short amount of time in his company.

The ship interior was quite junky, as they go, the walls covered in loose engineering panels and each corner piled with spare bits and pieces casually kicked aside. The floor was little more than a rattly gantry, providing an only slightly better walking surface than the layers of pipes and cables underneath.

I was right at home. This was a far cry from the Platinum God of Whale Sharks; this felt like a ship that people actually lived in. Very much like my own, although I had an obligation to keep it somewhat tidier for the tourists. And the *Neverdie* wasn't plastered with Polaroid photographs, all virtually identical: a smiling young couple, their heads pressed together and one or both of them holding the camera.

The woman I had met in the umbilical was sitting on a fifth chair, turned around so that she could lean forward onto the backrest. She had stripped off the EVA suit to reveal a set of well-worn mechanic's overalls and was vaguely aiming her gun in our general direction.

"We just got married a few weeks ago, actually," said the woman, who had introduced herself as Pippa. No one had said anything about her marriage, or anything at all, but things had been silent for a while and she looked like she would scratch claw marks into her chair if she didn't mention it. "Had the ceremony at Salvation Station, where we met. That's it there." She indicated one of the many completely identical photographs. "Aren't many wedding dresses in the Black, obviously, but Peter said I should just show up and whatever I was wearing would be a wedding dress. He's so smart. He's the pilot, you know."

"I think I gathered that," I said. "Where did you say you got married?"

"Salvation Station. All the girls made a big layer cake for the reception by pressing a load of emergency rations together . . ."

"What's Salvation Station?" I interrupted.

"It's where we live," she said testily, like I should have known that. "It's where a lot of people live. Are you really Jacques McKeown?"

"Actually I'm not," I said.

"Yes, he is," said Warden, apparently on instinct.

"He isn't really," offered Jemima.

"Ymmph hmmph mph," added Daniel.

At that point, the male half of the newlyweds returned from across the umbilical and appeared at the airlock door. Peter was a tall, thin man whose head protruded from the EVA suit like a tortoise's from its shell, and he had short, stubbly hair and spectacles. He was holding a large cardboard box with both hands.

"Well, the ship's mostly intact, but it'll need to be towed back to the station for repairs," he announced, dropping the heavy box to the side of the door. "Found a whole bunch of Jacques McKeown books, too. Rare editions and the like. I thought maybe we could sell them to that guy who's building that hate cathedral."

Pippa practically leapt across the room and draped her arms over his shoulders. "That is such a clever idea. You are such a clever man. Mwah."

"It's because I have you to inspire me," said Peter, with the self-assured grin of a man who knows he's the master of his domain.

"Oh you are so sweet, I just want to dine on your flesh, mwah mwah mwah."

I coughed politely, and Peter seemed to acknowledge our presence for the first time since he'd entered the room. "So, what's the story? Is he really McKeown?"

Pippa offered us an embarrassed smile, without disentangling from her husband. "Seems to be some confusion around that, actually."

"You know what we should do? We should take him to Salvation. Rob's got one of those hand-chip-scanner machines. We can look at his ID and that'll settle it."

"Brilliant idea, mwah. How do you keep doing it? Mwah."

"Oh, stop. It was your brilliant idea to answer the distress call, mwah."

I heard an abrasive sound next to my ear and noticed that Warden was grinding her teeth. She was also sitting in a cringe with her knees and elbows drawn in tightly, as if trying to extrude as little of her body as possible into the ship's dingy atmosphere.

Peter laboriously detached himself from his wife. "What I don't get is what Jacques McKeown would be doing in the middle of the Black getting shot at by a Zoob."

I was about to say "Yes, let's all discuss how little sense that makes," but the last word of his sentence changed the words forming in my throat. "Zoob?"

"Yeah, you know, the little green—"

"I know what a Zoob is. Are you saying that thing that attacked us was a Zoob?"

Thinking back, it made sense on certain levels. The Zoobs were a race of just barely sentient small blob-like green creatures with one large, adorable eyeball and a mouth just about equipped to speak in simple, broken English. They were native to some oceanic world where another, equally barely sentient species had begun preying on them aggressively, and after their plight was revealed by a popular documentary, a lot of them were "rescued" from the planet.

There had been a period—some time before Quantunneling came about—when it had been fashionable for star pilots to adopt Zoobs as a sort of onboard pet, as they were very clearly aliens, but were also friendly, adorable, and just intelligent enough to put saucepans on their heads and run around asking who turned out the lights.

I'd never kept one on the *Neverdie*. A couple of my colleagues had them, and I'd seen them while visiting for poker nights, that kind of thing. From those encounters, I'd realized I wasn't a Zoob person. They were cute, yes, but so are talking teddy bears, and talking teddy bears can be turned off. Some pilots found it endlessly amusing to teach their Zoob how to play 52 Pickup, but I hadn't seen the appeal.

I relayed all of this to Warden and Jemima. "Most of the pilots I know put their Zoobs up for adoption after Quantunneling," I concluded. "They were too expensive to feed and the spaceport didn't allow them."

"Mm, yes," said Pippa, sitting on her chair again. Peter had disappeared into the cockpit to fly us to whatever this Salvation Station place was. "A lot of the guys who've crossed the Black brought Zoobs with them. That's what caused the whole problem here."

"What problem?" asked Jemima.

"Wasn't any easier to feed Zoobs out here in the Black after Quantunneling hit. Impossible to make them understand why they weren't being fed on time, either. Turns out Zoobs are only willing to do the cute-mascot thing as long as their needs are being met."

"Oh, trac," I breathed.

"Didn't understand why everyone had to go hungry when there was nice fresh meat all around the place. Not sophisticated minds, you see. Well. Sophisticated enough to wait until the crew are sleeping or looking the other way before they start biting throats out. Then they take over the ship and fly it until it falls apart. It still happens now and then, even now we know all this. People get attached to their Zoobs, convince themselves that theirs must be the exception."

I tried not to think about the handful of Zoob-owning friends of mine who'd crossed the Black, and who I never seemed to hear much from these days.

"Anyway," said Pippa brightly, slapping her thighs as she stood up. "Not going to dwell on nasty things like that. I'm on honeymoon! I'm gonna check on my Pookie Bear."

She left us, presumably so that she and her husband could continue being completely insufferable with each other, and we were unsupervised in the mess hall.

"If we can get out of these ropes," I muttered, leaning into our little semicircle, "then I think we can make a move."

Warden immediately untensed and glared at me witheringly. "And what kind of move would that be, McKeown? A move out into the vacuum of space? Or a move to hijack a ship from two armed pirates, without weapons?"

With superhuman willpower I kept my tone polite. "You are welcome to make your own suggestions for escape plans if mine are so full of flaws." "The main flaw in your escape plan is that we don't need to escape. These people are taking us where we wanted to go all along, to what seems to be the center of the pirate presence in the Black. Frankly, now that I know that there are women there, I am considerably reassured."

I blinked. "Of course there are women there. Why wouldn't there be women there? You think women can't be pirates?"

Warden took on that very specific tense posture unique to upper-middle-class white people being called out on saying something politically incorrect. "Of course not."

"Anyway, my point was, yes, we were planning to meet with pirates, but not pirates who, thanks to you, now think that I'm Jacques Mc-plying-Keown."

Warden straightened her back, sniffing. "That seems to be solely your problem."

"But . . . isn't that enough?" asked Jemima.

Warden and I both looked at her as if we'd been having a row in the kitchen and the dishwasher had suddenly demonstrated the ability to speak.

"Sorry," added Jemima hurriedly. "I know I'm just, you know, the hostage. But it seems to me like he's brought you all this way, and if he's going to be in danger, don't you think you, you know, owe him something?"

Warden didn't reply straightaway. Her mouth had taken on a very curious shape. It was like taking a freeze frame of the moment when a contemptuous sneer is halfway to turning into a look of slack-jawed surprise.

"Sorry, I shouldn't have interrupted," said Jemima, dropping her gaze.

I coughed. "Aren't you going to answer the young lady's question, Ms. Warden? I think it's a pretty good one."

She scowled impotently, and I think at that moment I was more cheerful than I'd been in years. But Jemima, having suddenly drawn attention to herself, brought a lingering question to the forefront of my mind.

I turned to her, straining against my bonds. "Hey, is it true that your mum's the president of the UR.?"

Jemima and Warden both started at the question. Jemima colored and looked at the floor, while Warden seemed to freeze again, eyes glazing over. She sucked on her suddenly dry lips. "I see."

I swung my head back and forth a few times, to take in both ends of the spectrum of embarrassed looks. "Wait, you didn't know? The galaxy's most organized psychotic?"

"Many things required my attention!" she protested. "I was hired to single-mindedly look after the interests of the Henderson family and corporation! All I knew was that Daniel . . . How did you know Jemima's the president's daughter?"

"Henderson—" I was going to add *told me*, but my better instincts kicked my mouth shut an instant too late. Her sudden question had caught me off guard.

Warden's eyes narrowed. "When did Henderson tell you? Did you call Henderson and offer him a deal?"

"No!" I said truthfully. "I didn't call him. I seem to be the only one who doesn't think calling Henderson will solve all my problems—"

"So he called you, then."

"Of course he didn't."

It was hopeless. She must have seen enough of my barefaced-lying face to be able to identify it on sight. "This is why I am not indulging your escape plans, McKeown. This, Jemima, is why I don't owe him anything. He will sell us out the first chance he gets."

I wasn't letting that lie. "Not us. You. I will happily sell you out the first chance I get because you are going to get us all killed. And I think that's as obvious to Jemima as it is to me."

"Do you know what I think, McKeown?" said Warden archly. "I think you're trying to score points with her now that you know she has influence."

I almost choked on my own snort of rage. "Oh! You know, until this moment I didn't think 'projection' was actually a thing. You only started throwing words like us around since I told you who her mum was. The only one trying to score points here is—"

Jemima hopped in her chair, slamming all four legs on the grating floor with a violent clang. "Could you please stop talking about me like I'm the— like I'm the prize money?!" she yelled.

Warden and I were both frozen in midrecoil, staring at Jemima in shock. Her face was red and her mouth was quivering.

"Now, maybe you can't trust Mr. Captain Not Jacques McKeown but he's the only person here you, you know, know anything about and you shouldn't just assume you'll be able to, to make friends with the pirates," continued Jemima. Her voice was quavering, and her eyes glistened. "And you, maybe you can't trust Ms. Warden either but you probably can't trust Dan's dad either and Dan's dad isn't here and she is. So I think you should both just maybe remember that we've all been tied to the same chairs and that tying people to chairs never leads to good things. Okay?"

I looked down at the cables binding me to my chair, as if I had briefly forgotten their existence. "All right," I muttered. "Let's just stop bickering and figure something out."

At that moment, the cockpit intercom burst into life, firstly with static, then with male and female giggling, before the male voice managed to pull itself together. "Hey, uh, sorry to interrupt," he said. "Stop it, Pippa, you're terrible. Salvation's in visual range. Have a look."

The set of vertical shutters opposite our little semicircle of chairs turned sideways, permitting a view of the space outside. Salvation Station was presumably the large space station whose open airlock the ship was curving gently toward.

The last pirate hangout I'd been to was Old Freeport, way back before Quantunneling pulled the rug out from under the star piloting game. It had been little more than a collection of old decommissioned or shot-down vessels welded together with permanent umbilicals. The docking bay had basically just been a large cargo container with one side sawn off. It had a certain surviving-against-the-odds charm, but it was the kind of place where the ramshackle bar wouldn't sell you a beer if you didn't have a gun visible on your hip. And even then it was considered poor etiquette to drink all of it, rather than throw it in the face of the person next to you and start a fight.

I'd been expecting Salvation Station to be something along the same rickety lines, but to my surprise, it was an actual space station. With a donut-shaped residential promenade built around a power facility and administrative center in the core, the kind of design modeled after a giant chariot wheel with prominent hub spikes.

To my further surprise, it appeared to be relatively new and extremely professionally constructed. The hull shimmered with metal plates that hadn't yet built up the layer of dust and grime that gave hulls actual character.

But it was built to last. The plating was thick and reinforced, steeply curved to efficiently disperse explosive damage. There were mounted turrets all around the top and bottom of the ring, covering every possible angle of approach. The nearest ones turned and watched us suspiciously, waiting for a false move. In the distance I could just about see a perimeter defense consisting of towed-in asteroids with more mounted turrets, which Peter and Pippa must have already moved us through.

All in all, as much as one would expect from an outpost designed to be placed smack in the middle of pirate territory. Except there were pirate ships everywhere, and whoever was operating those turrets seemed completely tolerant of them. The smaller ships were much more in keeping with what I expected of pirates, being mostly well used and heavily decorated rust buckets repurposed out of old ship-to-surfacers. They hung around the station the way a group of toughs might congregate around the outside of a swanky nightclub.

"Pretty swanky," I commented, summarizing all of the above.

"Did they build that?" asked Jemima.

"Of course not," said Warden. "Pirates don't build space stations."

"Oh, what, so they stole it?" I sniped. "How do you picture that working? Cut the bicycle lock and pull it here on a tow cable?"

"Well, I don't know! As I have said before, McKeown, you are ostensibly the expert on pirates here."

"Yeah, I know. And speaking as such, that thing was definitely built here. If it was patched together from hijacked ships it would look like a rusty mirror ball, and if they'd dragged it here it'd have brought half the region's interstellar dust with it. They must have been secretly shipping in materials for years."

"But I thought pirates were all really poor and stuff," said Jemima. "'Cos teleporting means no one has to fly through the Black anymore except pilots and they're poor as well."

"You've certainly picked up on the salient points," I said, eyes not leaving Salvation Station as it grew bigger and bigger in our view. "I don't know what to tell you. This is all new to me."

The station went out of view as the ship turned in order to dock, and the next thing we saw was the interior of the bay. It was not dissimilar to the one we had briefly occupied back at Cloud Castle, in terms of layout and cleanliness, but that had been the cleanliness of an old construction that was very rarely used. This was a new construction absolutely teeming with life.

Almost every docking space was occupied by a pirate ship, and almost all of them were unloading. Pirates of every shape, size, and species, helping each other carry crates, sacks, and sheets of building material into the space station proper.

The ship landed rather inelegantly—as if Peter and Pippa were distracted by something—but once the floor had stopped vibrating and our chairs had stopped moving around the room like a slow barn dance, the ship was at rest on the floor of the docking bay. After a second, the background hum of the engine ceased, the kind of white noise that's only noticeable after it stops.

"Right," I said, leaning forward. "Here's the plan. Before they come back—"

The cockpit door swished open and our captors returned, Pippa holding her blaster and Peter holding mine. They were each covering us with one hand while warming their other hand in each other's back pocket.

"Okay, never mind," I muttered, leaning back again.

▲▲▲

The four of us were escorted from the ship and across the docking bay by the happy couple, who it seems also understood the importance of staying out of grabbing range. From what I could gather, this appeared to be a fairly standard take-them-to-our-leader scenario, but the process was slowed down considerably by Peter and Pippa greeting every single person we passed, on infuriatingly cheerful first-name terms.

Warden walked just ahead of me. She was looking all around, scrutinizing the details and no doubt finding ways to work them together into some scheme to completely ply me over.

I glanced back at the kids. Jemima walked head bowed, seemingly embarrassed with a dash of good old-fashioned fear, but Daniel, still gagged, seemed to have nothing but fascination for our surroundings.

We moved straight from the docking bay to an enormous area with ceilings as high as a cathedral, and it took me a moment to shake off my preconceptions of pirate stations and realize that it was intended to look very much like a spaceport concourse.

There were troughs with plastic plants. Benches. Clear signage indicating directions to the toilets and exits. The walls were lined with several levels of shops, although most of them were still under development. Darkened shop windows half obscured various arrangements of stepladders and protective plastic coverings. Most of them had a prominent sign out front, bearing the words Your Business Here in garish red lettering.

So that was one way it differed from Ritsuko spaceport, and the other was that it wasn't lined with endless rows of out-of-work charter pilots trying to solicit work. The pilots were there, but they were happy. They swarmed about the place with purpose, chatting, laughing, working together to build this place as one, big, single-minded family. It was the kind of camaraderie I hadn't seen since the pre-Quantunneling days. Somewhere beneath the endless buzzing fear that I was about to be crucified, I felt the stirrings of intrigue.

It seemed like we were being led toward a small cluster of people in one of the larger nexuses of the concourse, in the middle of a wide clearing that the pirate workers were steering clear of. I soon saw why: some filming was taking place. A young woman in a technician's overalls similar to Pippa's was carefully holding out a phone horizontally, framing a shot of the older man in front of her.

He looked familiar, but then, there was a sort of universal quality to his appearance. He wasn't in overalls or flight gear, like pretty much everyone else, but a fatherly red-and-black checked shirt with the sleeves rolled up. A middle-aged paunch bloomed out from blue jeans, cinched unreasonably with a belt.

Either his full beard had turned prematurely white, or he had mastered that ruddy, twinkly eyed look that allows older men to inexhaustibly project a younger bearing. Up close, I realized that the area around him had not been vacated because of the filming. It was because he projected the kind of presence that filled a room.

"Rolling," said the camera holder.

The man being filmed, who had been standing with tightly pressed lips and neutral posture, was suddenly wearing a huge, winning smile and arranging himself to look like he was about to chummily bear hug the air in front of him. "Investors, business owners, visitors, boys and girls," he said, in a voice like honey dripping off a Cuban cigar, performing various sweeping gestures to generally indicate the scenery. "Welcome to Salvation Station. An island of peace, safety, and entertainment, right here in the middle of the Black. Enjoy the mysteries of unknown space the traditional way, with real star pilots, and assured of total—"

"Plying hairy trac-holes!" someone shouted, ruining the take. Then I caught a lot of reproachful looks, and realized that it had been me. I must have reflexively blurted it out after I realized who the man was. I'd been holding the image of his face in my mind's eye and de-aging it until the beard was dark again and the laughter lines faded.

Having already ruined the take, I figured I might as well voice my conclusion. "You're . . . Robert Blaze."

His expression shifted from mild annoyance to faintly embarrassed pride. Warden glanced at me questioningly, one eyebrow raised.

Robert Blaze was the person who the average nonpilot thought Jacques McKeown was. The archetype. Not some media-constructed, lantern-jawed action hero, but an ordinary, regular guy who just happened to be the greatest star pilot who ever lived. The original. The first star pilot to resign from the big transport corporations and go it alone as a freelance bounty hunter, charter pilot, and mercenary. Savior of a hundred worlds, veteran of a thousand planetary wars. But the word on the space lane was that he'd mysteriously disappeared shortly after Quantunneling put us all out of work.

My first instinct was to shake his hand, but as my arm shot out, I noticed just in time that the hand I was proposing to shake was missing, replaced by a hook. I was able to change the gesture midway into a respectful tilting of my cap, and out of nowhere, I remembered that Robert Blaze had been one of the first pilots to adopt a pet Zoob.

"And your reputation precedes you as well, Mr. McKeown," said Blaze. The way he said the last two words was like a glimpse of a concealed blaster inside someone's jacket. I remembered with a jolt that McKeown's books had stolen more stories from the life of Robert Blaze than any other pilot, by a very wide margin. "Assuming you are Jacques McKeown, that is; I've been hearing conflicting reports."

This wasn't the ideal way to meet your hero, and my stammering failure to reply gave Warden her opportunity. "He is Jacques McKeown," she said, stepping forward. "You can do whatever you like with him. In return, I request sanctuary. My name is Penelope Warden. I am highly skilled in the areas of IT and business management, and can be a great asset."

"Oh, that was the plan, was it?" I hissed bitterly. "Nice. Great start for your new life of not being a backstabbing henchman to a crime lord."

Blaze waited until I was finished, then addressed Warden. "On the run, then, Ms. Warden? You'd be surprised how often we get this. Half the funding for this place came from fugitives. First time we've ever been paid in hostages, I should add." He noticed that Daniel still had tape over his mouth and smartly pulled it off with a single sweep of the hand. "Is he Jacques McKeown?"

"Yeah," said Daniel, as if it were a stupid question. "My dad says he is and my dad's really really important and he paid for all this so if you don't—"

The tape went smartly back onto his mouth. "All right then," said Blaze. "And are the kids with you, or are they pack-in bonuses?"

"Uh . . ." began Jemima.

"I'd like them given safe passage," said Warden. "As part of the reward for McKeown."

"Well, I'm sure that can be arranged," said Blaze, speaking as if he were merely taking everyone's lunch order. He turned to Jemima. "Assuming he is McKeown. Is he McKeown?"

Jemima still hadn't closed her mouth from back when she'd said "uh." I saw her glance at me, then Warden, then back to Blaze. She chewed her lip, calculating, but her eyes were apologetic. "I . . . um. Yes."

"Jemima!" I cried. Plying perfect—as if I didn't have enough to deal with, suddenly the Terrans were ganging up.

"Three against one," said Blaze, smiling at me.

"I'm not plying Jacques McKeown!" I yelled.

Blaze's smile shifted into a more sympathetic one. "All right then. If you're not Jacques McKeown, who are you?"

I launched into a summary of events, jabbing an angry finger at each of my companions in turn. "*She* works for *his* dad who's this megarich super-villain and she thought she'd hired Jacques McKeown for *his* birthday but she plied up and hired me to pretend to be Jacques McKeown, then the moment we were in space she decided she didn't want to work for his dad anymore so she made me help her kidnap them and fly us out here." I took a deep breath, getting pretty heated, and jabbed a finger at Jemima. "And *she's* a friend of *his* who's waiting for the chance to have some kind of role in this narrative."

"Hey!" protested Jemima.

Blaze had been standing with his little smile, holding his hook behind his back, displaying the patience of a saint as my words washed over him, along with the occasional droplet of saliva. He turned to address Pippa and the camera technician, who seemed to be what passed for the jury. "Is it me, or does that story ring just a little bit truer than Jacques McKeown suddenly coming out into the open and taking private gigs?"

"Yes!" I said, nodding very quickly.

"Yeah," said Pippa. "You'd think he'd have enough money, wouldn't you."

"Ye-es," I said, nodding slightly slower this time.

"Scan his ID chip," said Warden, scrambling for a foothold. "You'll see."

"Ah, that was the original plan, wasn't it," said Blaze. He nodded to Peter, who had mysteriously disappeared early in the conversation, and had now returned with a handheld chip scanner attached to a tablet device. Craftily he was able to scan the back of my hand while I was still holding them both out in an explanatory gesture.

"Jacques McKeown," read Peter from the tablet.

The atmosphere around this little discourse was feeling more and more claustrophobic. The background noise of construction work was beginning to sound like a flock of crows circling me in anticipation. "Okay, look . . ." I began.

"Well, that clinches it," said Blaze, looking at the proffered tablet screen with amusement. "You cannot possibly be Jacques McKeown."

"No, but listen," I added, before fully parsing his sentence. "What?"

Blaze turned his back on us and walked a few idle steps away, taking in the sight of what was fairly safe to assume was his creation. "Jacques McKeown isn't the novelist's real name. I happen to know that for a fact. If we'd scanned your ID chip and seen any name other than Jacques McKeown, that wouldn't have told us anything. But from this result we can deduce one thing: that Jacques McKeown is the one person you cannot possibly be."

He turned, and gave a little twinkly eyed laugh at the looks on our faces. "I'm sorry. Forgive an old retired star pilot who has to amuse himself where he can. The truth is, I knew you weren't Jacques McKeown from the moment you walked in. I just wanted to see who would lie to me."

Warden's face remained emotionless, but sweat appeared on her forehead with an almost audible *phut*. "Captain Blaze . . ." she said. I wondered if she was going to switch tacks immediately or continue trying to persuade him to have me killed.

"Oh, I'm not going to make an issue of it," said Blaze, laughingly waving his hook in a way that could probably have seriously injured someone standing nearby. "You don't have to buy your way in. Out here we take every pair of hands we can get. I'll get someone to take the kids home; we're not monsters. And of course there's always a space here for another pilot."

Having been led into what had felt like a lion's den, I stood blinking as the lion served the tea and started talking me through his record collection. "Really?"

He squinted at me, touching the point of his hook lightly to the side of his mouth. "I try to keep track. Forgive me, I forget the name, but . . . you were Cantrabargid, yes? The Malmind War."

"Yes!" I said, thrilled, but that didn't seem like enough. "Did you . . . like that one?"

"Textbook planet saving, I'd say. What've you been up to since then?"

"I, er, was living in Ritsuko City," I admitted. "Charter piloting. Day trips."

He winced. "Well, that's actually good. You're exactly the kind of person I need to reach. The kind who needs to know about this little enterprise we've got going on here." He turned and took a few steps away again, gazing up at the cathedral-sized partially constructed concourse.

I took the hint and started walking with him, and we commenced a slow tour of the station, Warden and the kids following awkwardly behind. "So what is this enterprise?" I said. "If I may ask." I mentally added the words *please may I ask oh trac I just want this conversation to go on for the rest of my plying life.*

"What does it look like?"

"It looks like a spaceport."

"Yes, a spaceport. But what about it would you say makes it different from the spaceport back in Ritsuko City, or New Dubai, or anywhere else in the policed zones?"

I cast a look around, frowning. "There aren't any Sushi Stations?"

Charitably, he considered this, head tilted to one side. "Not yet, no. But I meant more about the people." He was leading my gaze toward a small group of three pilots, amiably chatting and leaning on a tool chest set up outside an unfinished cafeteria.

"There are pilots," I hazarded. "And they actually look like they belong here. And don't seem to be contemplating suicide."

He punched me playfully in the arm, thankfully with the non-hook hand. "*Ex-actly!* That's exactly what we're creating here. A place where pilots belong. What are you achieving back there, in the Solar System? What are any of the star pilots achieving?"

"Not a whole lot," I admitted.

"No. Everyone made the same mistake when Quantunneling started. They tried to hold on to how it used to be. Hung around the colonies on Luna and Mars because they were the hub of our glory days. But we have to face the fact that back there just isn't where star pilots are needed anymore."

He was right, of course. Star pilots had been essential for space colonization, back in the day; the big transport corporations weren't well suited for navigating the perilous Black. Star pilots were small, fast operators who knew the territory best, so eventually we were couriering everything and everyone that needed to get to the outlying colonies. But then there was Quantunneling, and after that, seeing star pilots sitting on every available surface in the Ritsuko City Spaceport concourse was like seeing a magnificent new building still surrounded by rusty scaffolding.

"The answer was staring us in the face the whole time," continued Blaze. "The Black. This vast region of space, untamed, unmapped. This is where star pilots are supposed to be now."

"But . . . we've always done things in the Black," I said. "Everyone's saved at least one planet out here, right?"

"Yes, and nothing changes. No offense meant. We sort out a squabble, kick the Malmind off another world, but then what? Squabbles remain. The Malmind find another planet to pick on. I'm not talking about being directionless mercenaries with vigilante leanings. Or treating the Black like most people see it, like some dark patch that we just have to work around. I'm talking about making something out of it. Shaping it into our own image. A place built by star pilots, for star pilots. No disrespect, no begging for clients, and no Quantunneling."

"Isn't that a Quantunnel over there?" said Jemima, pointing.

My attention had mostly been directed at Blaze, with everything else disappearing into a barely registered pink fog from about a six-foot radius around him, but now Jemima had stepped into that radius and I followed her finger.

At the far end of the concourse—there technically wasn't one, since it was ring shaped, but there was a large, circular area that seemed to be a focal point, like the diamond on an engagement ring—was what was undeniably an incomplete, spaceport-sized Quantunnel gate. Two workers in a cradle suspended next to the unfinished horizontal beam were laying new tiles in between laborious measurements.

"Well, all right, so there's one Quantunnel," said Blaze jokingly. "Putting it together's a nightmare. Did you know, it has to be exactly the same size as the gateways in all the other spaceports, accurate to at least one-third of a millimeter? Otherwise it just doesn't work."

He caught the look on my face, which must have been similar to the look a child wears when they come downstairs unexpectedly on Christmas Eve and find their parents eating the cookies meant for Santa. He gave me an awkward attempt at a reassuring smile.

"Look," he said. "I know what you're thinking. But we have to be serious. We want to be officially recognized as a government of the region, and we need trade, tourism, and immigration. We can't do that if we don't have some kind of connection to the policed regions."

"Right . . ." I said, unconvinced.

"I promise you it'll be the only one. This isn't the only place to visit around these parts; there're other stations. Colonies. Racing centers. Quite a few native planets. All accessible only by the traditional means." He patted me on the shoulder and winced slightly when he caught the whiff coming off my long-unlaundered set of clothes. "Join me for dinner tonight. I'll give you the full picture. Until then, make use of the facilities. Have a wash, find a change of clothes, make yourselves at home. I'll see if we can get some fresh tape for the boy's mouth."

CHAPTER 17

A SUDDENLY MUCH friendlier Peter led me to what was apparently going to be the hotel section of the station, showing absolute indifference to any topic of conversation other than his marriage. Outside the door of one of the mostly finished staterooms he saluted chummily and gave me my gun back. I was momentarily startled by the way it came so abruptly back into my possession but swiftly transferred it to my shoulder holster before the universe noticed.

The room was just a hotel room, and despite the lack of windows, seemed comfortable enough. There was a double bed and a writing desk that could have come from any hotel resort in the galaxy, if they hadn't been bolted down. The room smelled strongly of fresh paint and there was no hot water, but it was still better than sleeping in the *Neverdie*. At least the bed was a bed, not a blanket thrown over a stack of unclaimed suitcases. And I was woken from my brief nap by the sound of construction, rather than a knife fight over the last parking bay.

Peter knocked on the door an hour before dinner, and handed me a number of shrink-wrapped objects. "Rob said to give you these," he said. "Had to guess at your size."

The first package was a pair of distressed jeans. The second was a T-shirt bearing the words "I Found Elation on Salvation Sation."

"Take it you'll be keeping your flight jacket?" he asked.

Pilots understood pilots. Wearing anything other than your own flight jacket, with its unique pattern of wear and tear and custom sewn-on patches, was like losing your keys and breaking into the wrong house. "Of course."

"Dinner's in the main refectory, just next to the Quantunnel chamber. And that lady friend of yours was out in the hall, looking like a French poodle got lost at the dog track. Said to tell you to hurry up. See you at dinner."

I considered this information, then went back inside, leisurely changed my clothes, and took an additional ten minutes or so to carefully comb my hair to just the right level of endearingly scruffy. Then I came out and met Warden.

Either she hadn't been offered a change of clothes or she'd opted out for some characteristically paranoid reason, as she was still in her office attire. She offered me a scowl as I appeared, which I found absolutely delicious.

"Cheer up," I said, in a maddeningly good mood. "Mission accomplished, right?"

"Maybe," she said. "But this isn't exactly what I was expecting of a pirate community."

"Oh, well, I'm so sorry," I said dryly as we made our way through the surprisingly wide hallways of Salvation Station. "Let's leave immediately and roam around the Black some more until we find a pirate clan that's slightly more to your taste. What is your problem? We're in the Black, they've taken us in, we got what we wanted."

"I did not say it wouldn't suffice, McKeown. I simply have a concern that these people may not be pirates at all. They seem bent on founding a governed colony recognized by human authorities."

"Is this seriously happening? You, Warden, are about as far from a pirate as you are from being pleasant company, and you're complaining that these pirates aren't piratey enough? I'd have thought you'd be all for it. Bringing law and order to the wild lands and all that."

Enough contempt radiated from her single raised eyebrow to match a thousand mothers-in-law. "McKeown. The whole reason we came here was to *escape* the law. From the very human authorities Blaze and his ilk intend to welcome with open arms."

I genuinely hadn't thought of that, but I wasn't about to drop the good mood. "That's serious long-term-problem territory. Anyway, he said we aren't the only fugitives here. Maybe they're working out some kind of amnesty thing."

"I'm assuming as much, but that is one of many questions I have for Blaze. I've already taken note of several areas that may need better management."

I blew out through my lips. "You are so plying Terran. It seems to have gotten along perfectly well so far without your divine insight."

"Why are you so enthusiastic? You saw it. Blaze is bringing quantum tunneling to the one place in the universe where they haven't yet made pilots obsolete. I think he intends to turn you and your colleagues into some kind of living museum."

"Look, Robert Blaze knows what he's doing. Robert Blaze never puts a foot wrong." That had been part of the theme song from his short-lived Saturday morning cartoon series.

She nodded. "So it is hero worship, then."

"Maybe it is!" I barked. "So what? Oh, you've probably never had a hero. Probably far too human a concept for the amazing android PA to understand."

"You mean gynoid, McKeown. Androids are male."

By now we were in the concourse, and I'd noticed that the many passing technicians and star pilots were giving us funny looks every time she addressed me by that name. I stopped in front of her and leaned forward confrontationally. "Will you stop calling me McKeown? Hardly need to keep the subterfuge going now, do we."

We continued in silence for a short while, me fizzling with renewed energy and Warden biting her lip in consideration. Soon, the door to the refectory was in sight, directly opposite the unfinished Quantunnel gate as promised. It was a suitably grand archway, and a professionally made plaque overhead read Welcome Center in indented letters. Over that, though, someone had tacked a piece of notepaper bearing the words Temporary Refectory.

"Did you pick up on anything interesting in Robert Blaze's conversation?" asked Warden, peering at me coyly with a hand on her chin.

"You mean besides his grand, radical scheme to change the face of the Black and bring a new lease on life to the disaffected pilots of the universe?" I said patiently. "No, not especially."

"I meant specifically in relation to Jacques McKeown."

I rolled my eyes back and forth, replaying the conversation in my head, or what I could remember through the haze of completely heterosexual man crush. "What are you getting at?"

"I thought he seemed very quick to accept that you aren't actually Jacques McKeown," she said, with a look in her eye reminiscent of a biblical serpent. "Rather strangely quick."

"Yes, well? That should be blatantly obvious to anyone with an ounce of sense. For one thing, I don't have horns growing out of my skull."

"The phrase I picked up on was 'I happen to know that for a fact,' in reference to Jacques McKeown being a pen name. But how would he know that for a fact? Or that you weren't Jacques McKeown from the moment you entered the room? Unless . . ."

"Unless he knows who Jacques McKeown is," I finished, my walk slowing and my voice turning monotone as I completed the thought.

Warden coughed. "Or."

It looked for a minute like we were going to make the entirety of the remainder of the conversation solely through meaningful looks and eyebrow waggles, before I resolutely stepped in front of her and did the confrontational-lean thing again. "Not possible."

"It would explain why McKeown has never taken his payment," she said, not making eye contact. "It would make more sense if he were somewhere remote, away from banking networks, where currency is less useful."

"That doesn't mean . . ." I waggled an index finger in the narrowing gap between our faces. "Robert Blaze cannot be Jacques McKeown. Jacques McKeown has ripped off Robert Blaze more than any other—"

I stopped as I listened to my own words. "Almost as if his stories were closer to hand than others," said Warden, voicing my sudden thought.

The meaningful-look-eyebrow-waggle conversation resumed for a few seconds before Warden tactfully stepped around me and continued toward the refectory. She was the one with renewed energy now, and she walked with a smug flounce in her hips.

I entered the Welcome Center just behind her. This seemed to be one of the areas of Salvation Station that was closest to completion. It took up most of the concourse level of the station's central core and, like a cathedral, had a tall ceiling with a skylight. A bright imitation-sun lamp had been placed above it, casting down heavenly beams of light.

It illuminated a vaguely circular room ringed with reception desks and tasteful classical pillars. The floor was marble, or a damn fine imitation of it, and there was a large logo in the center that I could only presume was the intended symbol of this startup nation. It showed a ship, a sleek, traditional star piloting model not dissimilar to the one associated with Blaze, flying around a patch of space with stars, leaving a vapor trail that looped around it like a lasso.

Around it, several rattly metal folding tables had been set up, each one flanked by benches that seemed to be intended eventually for communal seating areas, almost completely occupied with pilots and technicians. Since the tables were arranged in a circle there was no place of prominence, but Blaze seemed to be carrying one around with him, and he stood out like a messiah at a last supper.

He stood and gave us an enthusiastic greeting as we entered, gesturing to two vacant seats at either side of him. Jemima and Daniel sat past the empty seat on his left. Jemima was sitting with her elbows drawn in as closely as possible to avoid nudging the hairy technician on her left. Daniel seemed to be occupied with eating an entire bowl of rehydrated mashed potatoes.

"Come in, friends; take your seats," Robert Blaze announced grandly. "The dining is presently rather simple fare. Once we have proper connections to the rest of human civilization, we can start bringing some talent in to run the restaurants, but until then, I hope this will suffice."

Most of the food had the plasticky sheen of preservatives powerful enough to sustain it through lengthy storage, the sort of thing normally intended for school cafeterias. But it more than sufficed. I'd forgotten how long it had been since I'd eaten properly. I loaded up a plastic plate with fries, baked beans, rectangular mini pizzas, and dinosaur-shaped chicken nuggets.

"Try the wine," suggested Blaze, filling my plastic tumbler from a large jug. "Again, we haven't properly stocked the bars and clubs yet, but some of our boys and girls have an interest in homebrew."

I obediently tried it. It slammed down into my stomach like a stone slab, throwing up dust and fog that flooded my head. "Mmm," I summarized. "I could get behind it. Don't usually see wine with a head on it, do you."

Blaze smiled happily as I filled my tumbler to the rim. "Now, I want both of you to have a full understanding of what we're trying to build here," he said. "I've shown you around, and I like to think it speaks for itself. I'll answer whatever questions you have."

Even through the haze of drink that I was endeavoring to thicken, I could sense that immediately throwing McKeown-related accusations around probably wouldn't be a good idea. If anything, that would be something more for the coffee-and-cigars phase of the meal. So I decided to start soft and steer the questioning gradually in the right direction.

Then Warden got there first. "Mr. Blaze, how long have you and the others been working on this station?"

"Please. Call me Rob. We set the first foundations just under a year ago. My crew and I had been roaming the Black for some time, ever since

Quantunneling came about. We saw the writing on the wall pretty quickly and thought we could live out our days adventuring, foraging for what food we could find on planets with organic life."

"And you were wrong?" deduced Warden aloud.

His features clouded over somewhat. "We managed for a while. But *organic* is one thing, and *edible* is quite another. When food began growing scarce, certain members of my crew became . . . difficult."

I was in mid gulp and slammed my tumbler back down as I remembered a conclusion I'd reached earlier. "Your Zoob!" I said, only slightly slurred. "Did the Zoob bite your hand off?"

Blaze looked at me tolerantly but warningly. "Yes. I was the only member of my crew to get away alive. There were four others, besides Zoobster. All of them were close friends. As I believed Zoobster to be."

I endeavored to crawl back inside my cup. "Sorreeee."

"It's quite all right." He snapped back into cheerful, charismatic mode. I wondered if he had a switch inside his head, too. "I realized something had to be done. At first, it wasn't much more than a conjoining of effort with others who had crossed the Black, an organized attempt to take down Zoob-infested ships and push back the competing pirate groups. Our numbers kept growing with disillusioned pilots, and we began to feel that perhaps we had a greater calling."

"But you are a pirate organization," said Warden.

"I won't deny it," said Blaze cheerfully. "We need to eat. Trade for building materials. We'd do honest work out here if any was available. The gratitude of a saved planet doesn't go a long way to pay the fuel bills."

"I hear that!" I interjected, probably too loudly.

"But we also have a code," said Blaze, looking serious. "One we already had. The unwritten conduct of a star pilot: to help the innocent and fight for what's right. We don't kill, and we don't steal what's truly needed. Sadly, there are plenty of pirates out here who do not see things the same way."

"Surely you must have realized that connecting with the rest of human society will mean having to face justice for the breaking of spacefaring laws?" asked Warden.

"Of course we're aware of that. Very intelligent question." He offered Warden the kind of winning smile that would melt the thighs of a hundred space princesses, but it bounced off her like a paper dart against a stone statue. "Like I said, a lot of our money comes from fugitives seeking shelter.

Frankly, we need to explore every available opportunity for funding. One of our top priorities, when we negotiate trading and transport connections, is to secure an intergalactically recognized amnesty for all crimes committed by our settlement team."

"Do you believe you will get it?"

"I believe we're creating something here that human society wants," said Blaze. "I believe they will want it more than justice for a few minor misdemeanors."

"I see," said Warden. "The pirates who do not share your code—do they ever attempt to attack?"

"You saw the defense system on your way in, didn't you?"

"But how do you tell the difference between them and the members of your own community?"

Blaze shrugged. "So far, we get by just from everyone knowing each other. We have a man on every turret eyeballing the ships as they come in. I realize we will need something more efficient . . ."

"Yes, you do," interrupted Warden. "I have a contact at Argus Armaments. They've developed an automation system for turrets I could get for you at cost. You can make your turrets automatically fire upon any ship that does not transmit a unique code, which you give to all your friendlies."

Blaze was stroking his beard, intrigued. "That certainly does sound more efficient. We should have a serious talk about that in future."

"How are you for onboard armaments? Computer systems?"

Blaze gave Warden a sidelong look. "Penelope, wasn't it?" He filled the glass in front of her with wine, which she politely ignored. "I'm slightly afraid to ask who you used to work for, but I'm starting to think that their loss was my gain."

Meanwhile, I'd been drinking increasingly and was starting to feel resentful, as if my date was chatting a little too flirtatiously with the waitress. "You've got no idea," I said into Blaze's ear, one hand on his shoulder to keep myself steady. "He'sh why she did thish whole kidnapping thing."

"Yeah, uh, I totally won't press charges about that if you don't want," said Jemima. Daniel said something indistinct through a mouthful of dinosaur chicken nuggets.

"I imagine you would be more worried about the theft you have committed," said Warden, spearing me with a meaningful look.

I frowned. "What theft? You mean the ship? We didn't blow it up."

"I was actually referring to your recent windfall."

"Ah!" I slapped the tabletop hard enough to make all the plates rattle. I realized I'd been handed the perfect opportunity to move toward an answer on the Jacques McKeown mystery. I leaned toward him, watching for changes in his face. "I short of acshidentally nicked Jacques McKeown'sh money. Like, all of it."

Blaze seemed nonplused, but this was probably more to do with the way I was leaning into his personal space, carefully scrutinizing him with narrowed eyes. He politely leaned away. "How did you do that . . . accidentally?"

"Funny shtory," I said. Keeping my head up was starting to take some effort, so I briefly rested it on his shoulder. "Hish pub-lush-er mishtook me for the real Jacques McKeown and shent me all hish money he wash shupposhed to get for all hish traccy booksh he wrote."

"All his money?" asked Blaze, half smiling with his mouth and half frowning with his eyes.

"Dunno why he'sh never claimed it." I shook my head back and forth, grinding my chin into his shoulder. "He doeshn't return their callsh or shomething. I'm not about to shtart looking for the real one, I tell ya that. I mean." I stepped the scrutinizing look up a bit. "HE COULD BE ANYWHERE."

"Well, quite," said Blaze mollifyingly. "You know, that's actually really interesting."

"Yes, well, returning to salient points . . ." said Warden.

Blaze ignored her outright. "If that was all the money he's ever been owed for every single book, it must be a pretty huge sum."

"Yep," I said, draining my tumbler and holding it out meaningfully as Blaze reached for the jug. "Don't even know what to do with it all. Maybe keep enough to keep myshelf going and give shome to a charity for pilotsh or shomething."

"Well, they do say charity begins at home, you know," said Blaze, looking up at the light coming down from the skylight.

I twigged what he was getting at after a few false starts and slammed my tumbler back down, creating a momentary little homebrew-wine fountain that seriously contaminated my fries. "Oh hey! Yeah. Thish ish totally a charity for pilotsh, ishn't it. Well. Maybe your uncle Shanta Jacques McKeown Claush will put a little preshent in your shtocking if you be a very very very very good boy."

"More wine?"

"Ooh! Good shtart."

CHAPTER 18

AND THEN I woke up.

Which is to severely understate the massive amount of effort that went into it. My metabolism had been fighting a battle on the Russian front that was my liver since the moment I'd passed out, and it was frankly astonishing that I was even alive. My return to consciousness felt like an enormous sunken ship finally breaking surface after an all-night salvage operation.

And then the chain snapped and the wreck crashed heavily back into the waves as the first pain in my head exploded. I don't know what they were making that homebrew wine out of, but the last time I'd had a headache this bad was after getting trapped in a fuel compartment for an hour without a breathing mask. My throat made a noise like the rumbling death throes of a trapped cow.

"Oh, you're awake," said Warden.

I lifted my head, which was a fairly weighty salvage operation in itself, and saw Warden sitting primly next to a fire.

That helped flood some emergency activity into my limbs. I sat bolt upright. "FIRE!"

"Yes, that is a fire."

"Put it out! You can't have fires on space stations!"

"Good advice, but if you take a moment, you will notice that we are not currently on a space station."

My sudden movement had summoned a swarm of spots before my eyes, but once they faded, I saw that she was right. I was lying on coarse sand, and the fire was in a ring of red stones in the center of a jungle clearing. The trees were a deep burgundy, and had grown into tentacle-like curves entirely uncharacteristic of trees of terrestrial origin. Through the gaps between the black leaves overhead I saw a fire-orange sky, lit by two small rising suns.

The next thing I noticed—for there was quite a long queue of things to get through—was Jemima, sitting on the third point of a triangle formed by me, her, and Warden around the fire. Both the women were giving me faintly accusatory looks.

Next on the queue was a painful throbbing in my hand, which was readily explained by the bloody bandage wrapped around it. The question of where I was was suddenly elbowed out of my head by the persistent ache. "What happened to my hand?"

"Robert Blaze cut your ID chip out while you were unconscious," said Warden.

"What?" I cradled my hand as if it were Robert Blaze's feelings, wounded by the accusation. "He wouldn't do that!"

"He kinda did," said Jemima. "Sorry."

"But . . ." I poked at the reddest part of the bandage, and felt pain, but not the reassuring bump of a subdermal chip. "He's . . . a good guy."

"He was apologizing a lot," said Jemima.

"Yes, it took quite a lot of rationalization on his part," said Warden. "It was quite instructive to watch him going through the thought processes."

"Why didn't you stop him?!" I yelled.

"Jemima tried," said Warden.

Jemima glanced at her. "We both did, didn't we? That's why he put us down here. He said we needed to cool off. And he said to tell you when you woke up that he did say that he has to take every opportunity for funding he can get." She rolled her eyes upward as she remembered his words. "And that you'd probably have been totally persuaded to let him have all the money if you'd given him time, so he was just, you know, cutting that whole part out."

I inspected my hand mournfully. "He's got my chip. He's got access to my bank account. Trac."

"Well, he wouldn't, would he?" said Jemima, frowning. "ID chips record your DNA and physical details and check they're still correct before they can be scanned. Don't they?"

"Not off-world, Jemima," said Warden, like a middle-school teacher correcting an oral presentation. "Once a Lunarian chip is extracted, a dedicated hacker could copy its information and paste it into a different one, and it would work perfectly well. Off-world chip IDs only record basic identification and do not make biometric security checks."

"Why not?"

"Maybe because our government isn't run by paranoid fascists?" I suggested. Then I remembered what company I was in. "No offense."

"For what? Oh. Right. Mum's thing." She talked about the government of the UR like it was a Tupperware party that she was afraid to walk through, in case several middle-aged women pinched her cheek and asked if she had a boyfriend yet.

"Hang on a sec," I said, looking around the clearing. "Where's Daniel?"

"Still with Blaze," said Warden, staring at the fire and allowing the slightest quantum of shame to drift into her voice. "Henderson had been broadcasting an offer of reward. I think Blaze worked out Daniel's identity fairly quickly."

"That's it," I said, snapping the fingers on my wounded hand and immediately regretting it. "That's what Blaze is doing. He's protecting us. He's hiding us on this planet until Henderson's men have come and taken Daniel back."

"Well, if that was his plan, he could've just told us," said Jemima. "Without waving guns around and forcing us onto a shuttle."

"Or stealing your ID chip," pointed out Warden.

"He had to have a good reason," I insisted. "He's the original star pilot. He's a hero a million times over. He—" I realized something as I was looking at Jemima, and my sentence screeched to a halt.

"He . . . cut out your ID chip?" finished Warden in very nearly a sing-song voice. "He . . . exiled us to an alien planet?"

"He doesn't know about Jemima," I said, the words marching from my mouth in an ominous monotone. "Henderson said he was going to tell Jemima's mum that we'd taken her hostage."

"If it were known that the daughter of the United Republic president had been kidnapped and taken to the Black by off-worlders," thought Warden aloud, "then the president would undoubtedly call for a large-scale naval operation."

"No she wouldn't," said Jemima, with bitter conviction.

"I rather think she would," said Warden.

Jemima hugged her knees and fiddled with the flaps on her sneakers. "Well, you don't know her."

"How about we just assume she will?" I suggested. "Because if she does, a fleet of UR face stompers are going to show up at Salvation Station looking for you, and when you're not there they're going to tear it apart!" I was on my feet and pacing now. "Did Rob say when he was going to pick us back up?"

Warden made a contemptuous sound. "I, personally, am not holding out hope for that. And I don't see what you think you possibly owe him at this point."

I stood over her, and she remained seated, politely looking up at me as if I were merely taking her order. "It's about not grouping everyone into either assets or obstacles, all right? I don't care what Blaze did or why he did it; Salvation Station is bigger than just him and I don't want to see it getting stomped."

"It's rare to see you so passionate," muttered Warden, almost without moving her lips.

"Right!" I backed off, quivering with adrenaline. "Now. There's got to be something on this planet that can get Jemima back in the Black."

Jemima, who had spent the entire discourse since her last contribution staring at the fire with her knees drawn up to her chest, suddenly unfolded like a trapdoor spider striking. "Now *you're* doing it!" she yelled.

"What?"

"Talking about me like I'm . . . an asset!" She dropped into a silent huff for a second before changing her mind and jumping out of it again. "I mean, this always happens to me. I wanna do things, you know? I wanna see things and hang out with people. But Mum only ever takes me out of the house so I can, you know, stand next to her while people take pictures."

My hand was aching and I had decided I wasn't having any more of this Terran trac. "Jemima, forgive me if the lives of the people on Salvation Station are more important to me than your desire for a proper holiday."

She backed down, cowed. "I know, I just . . . You could ask how I feel about all this. I'm not just some thing that has to be moved around and rescued, you know?"

And then the undergrowth behind her burst outward and she was grabbed by a furious cyborg warrior.

It had been human, or at least humanoid, but most of its flesh was covered (or replaced) by a mixture of metal and plastic. Except for a pair of red-tinted cybernetic goggles, its head was unaugmented, and its gray lips were pulled back into a grimace of hatred as it clutched Jemima around the waist.

She yelled and struggled, her elbows bouncing off the cyborg's head and neck with no apparent effect. The intention seemed to have been to pick her up and drag her away, but it had underestimated either her weight or her unwillingness to keep still.

I was already on my feet and had drawn and pointed my blaster before I'd fully digested the discovery that I was still carrying it. "Jemima!" I called. "Head down!"

She got the idea, and with the cyborg's arms still fastened around her chest, she curled into the fetal position. The sudden concentration of weight bent the cyborg at the waist, and at the same moment, I fired the gun.

The ball of energy struck the cyborg on the top of its bald scalp and tunneled through to its pelvis, leaving a ruined furrow of white-hot metal and melted skin. It dropped instantly, and Warden helped Jemima struggle out from under the dead weight.

"What the hell is it?!" cried Jemima, clutching at Warden fruitlessly for comfort.

I kicked the body onto its back, and the two darkened red circles in its implanted eyes gazed blankly up at me. On closer inspection, it seemed like the head and a sizable chunk of the upper chest were all that remained of the original life form, and everything else was artificial. The limbs were titanium skeleton held together with pistons that looked powerful enough to crush diamond. The power unit was located in the belly area, with a coolant feed pipe leading from just underneath to between the legs. And then I was certain of what I had only suspected up to then. There were very few organizations of cyborgs designed with such a puerile sense of humor.

"This trac just got calculus," I breathed, poking at the ruined body.

"What do you mean?" demanded Warden, who had been standing around stunned and useless for the whole encounter, but was now standing over the corpse with me trying to seem important.

"It's a Malmind cyberserker," I said.

"The Malmind? The augmentation collective?"

"Yeah. They take over planets. It's kind of all they do, actually. This is one of their infantry units."

"Why would an infantry unit for a hive mind be out here by itself?"

I glanced fearfully around at the surrounding jungle. I didn't see anything, but the background hum of animal noise could have been masking the movements of any number of stalking cyber-Frankensteins eager to evangelize their collective in a way that did not involve pamphlets. "It wouldn't."

I kept my gun ready. "We should move. And put the fire out. It could draw attention."

"Hey. Erm." Jemima, more excited than traumatized, was crouching by the body. "It, you know, it died kinda easy, didn't it?"

"It's a powerful gun," I said, still holding it as I stamped at the burning sticks. Although I did notice that it wasn't on the highest setting, and I'd seen cyberserkers shrug off worse in the past. I nudged one of the body's fleshy parts with my toe, and found it rather soft and yielding. Maybe this one had been assimilated more ineptly than usual?

"Yes, and with limited charge, as I recall," said Warden huffily. "Perhaps you should put it away for now. In fact, perhaps I should . . ."

"Yeah, no, never again," I said, shoving the blaster deep into my armpit region. She was right, though—there couldn't have been more than a couple of full-strength shots in the cell, which amounted to about nine or ten of the piddly little stun blasts. "Come on."

"It was . . . weird, though," said Jemima, frowning, once we were crushing our way through overgrown vegetation with no particular preference for direction, as long as it moved us away from all traces of murder cyborg. "I mean, it wasn't pulling or trying to hurt me. It was just sort of holding on."

"Perhaps it was malfunctioning," suggested Warden, wearing a fixed grimace as she negotiated thick foliage and low-hanging branches in desperately inappropriate clothing.

"It's possible," I said, taking point and keeping a close watch on the up-coming jungle, which thus far had been lifeless in a simultaneously reassuring and worrying way. "That might be a good sign, actually. Maybe it got separated from the rest of its unit? If it got far enough away, it would get some serious lag."

"How do you know so much about them?" asked Jemima.

"Fought against them in planetary wars, back in the day," I said, trying to sound casual. "Kicked them off Cantrabargid. That's the routine—they try to take over a primitive planet; the nearest star pilot helps the locals fight them off. No big . . ."

We suddenly reached the edge of the jungle and emerged into the bottom of a wide orange valley that snaked away into the distance. A narrow stream of water ran through the center of a wide riverbed. This must have been the dry season of a flood calendar not dissimilar to the one on . . .

"Oh, trac," I said, taking in the view. "We're on Cantrabargid, aren't we."

"Yeah, I think Blaze said something about leaving us somewhere appropriate," said Jemima. "Wow. It's actually really, you know, beautiful here, isn't it."

I didn't join her on that particular reverie, but locked eyes with Warden, who was wearing another of her neutral expressions. This was the one I'd come to associate with smug derision. "Go on then, say it," I said.

"Excuse me?"

"You were going to say something like 'Oh, clearly you did an extremely thorough job of kicking the Malmind off Cantrabargid.' And it wouldn't have been the least bit constructive."

"I can't imagine why you would assume I wanted to say such a thing," said Warden, with a subtly different neutral expression. "I think that indicates your feelings more than mine."

"It must have been alone," I insisted. "Yeah. Now I know we're on Cantrabargid, it's all making sense. It was a straggler from back in the war. Been wandering alone without instructions since the retreat—what's that noise?"

I'd become aware of a rumble rising from the background wind, which was now separating into a thousand thuds of feet upon rough ground. I saw dust rising in the distance, where the valley snaked around and curved out of sight.

A vast, broiling mass of life poured into view like a flash flood. A giant quilted bedspread of a thousand shades of nutty brown bore down the valley toward us, following the stream.

We sheltered behind a convenient boulder as the stampede passed. It was a mass of furry creatures, bipedal and equipped with the usual accoutrements of a primitive race: tatty loincloths and spears, some of them riding large, bull-like domestic animals that had hair hanging over their eyes. They were all about three feet tall and bore a slight resemblance to upright sloths. They sped past us without even a glance, in a state of crazy-eyed, panicked mass exodus.

The rumbling continued. I peered around our convenient boulder and saw what they were running from.

No doubt about it now. It was the Malmind, out in force. A whole plying invasion unit, the kind that only has to position itself next to a village, march from one side to the other—and then there isn't a village anymore. There was a rectangular cohort of cyberserkers like the one we'd just encountered, augmented humanoids, and in front of that was an advance unit of converted sloth creatures with controllers bolted to their grimacing faces.

They were marching after the fleeing natives in the kind of perfect step unique to cybernetic hive minds, with no regard for terrain or obstacle. This boulder we were hiding behind wouldn't even slow them down.

"What do we do?!" asked Jemima.

"Perhaps you should kick them off the planet again," said Warden.

"How about you go out there and see if your standup set gets any laughs?!" I snarled.

She didn't have a chance to deliver a no-doubt-unhelpful retort before we were interrupted by an urgent mooing sound and a spray of gravel. Some kind of vehicle had pulled up next to us—a sort of four-wheeled chariot pulled by a pair of the buffalo-like creatures I'd seen a couple of the sloths riding.

The driver was, of all things, a human woman. A young one, early twenties or even late teens, but it was hard to tell through all the war paint on her face. She was Caucasian, but tanned to a shade about halfway between latte and espresso, with blond hair tied into rough dreadlocks. She was wearing garments not dissimilar to the ones that the sloths had on, by which I mean she was wearing two of them, one around the chest and one around the hips. Neither of which were covering as much as they did on the sloths.

"Get in," she commanded.

We did so, the Malmind horde barely fifty yards away and closing, and the chariot jerkily took off. I'd gotten on last, old habits dying hard, and now found myself directly behind some kind of ballista mounted to the back of the chariot.

"Use it," instructed the driver, not looking away from the reins.

I considered the Malmind horde. A hundred lurching tech zombies loaded with enough augments to stop a bullet and absorb moderate blaster fire. Then I looked at what I was expected to slow them down with. The ballista's bolts were blunt, wooden, and each about a foot long and two inches wide. I might as well be throwing my shoes at them.

"This isn't going to do trac," I said.

"Above," said the girl at the reins irritably. She evidently wasn't the most erudite conversationalist.

But I could see what she was drawing my attention to. Above, on top of one of the valley walls, a number of sturdy-looking red boulders had been arranged precariously on the edge. The one in front was held in place with a wedge attached to a mechanism with a prominent red and white target painted on it.

I immediately swung the ballista around and let a bolt fly. It sailed under the target and shattered against the rock wall.

"You need to aim higher," shouted Warden over the noise of the chariot, clinging to both sides for stability.

"Yes, all right! I've played Joogie Launch too!"

I went through the awkward—but surprisingly intuitive—process of loading another bolt, and pulled the trigger again. The second shot clipped the side of the target, and after a bit of umming and ahhing among the components, the mechanism decided that this would suffice. A counterweight dropped and the wedge was pulled out, sending a parade of boulders trundling directly into the path of the Malmind horde.

They were slowing down. They must have seen what I was trying to do after the first miss and realized—with the eerie, instantaneous calculation of a machine mind—that they weren't going to be able to get ahead of the rockfall in time. By the time the rocks swept across, blocking our view of the army, they had stopped completely.

"Yes!" cried Jemima, sitting beside me and pumping a fist. "We beat them!"

The carriage gave a sudden lurch of speed to narrowly avoid an errant boulder, and I had to grab her shoulder to stop her from falling out.

"Not beaten," said the driver gruffly, whipping the reins again. "Just escaped alive."

I turned in my seat to look at the strange girl again. Despite her youth, she controlled the chariot with practiced skill. And while the two suns of Cantrabargid had tanned her almost to a Henderson level of dull orange, her flesh didn't look overly leathery or muscular. My curious gaze scanned up and down her body, then a little further down. Then I noticed Warden watching me, and I hastily took it all the way down to the wooden floor. "This is a . . . very well-made chariot you have here," I offered.

"Yeah," said the driver over her shoulder, slightly baffled.

The mass exodus of sloth things for which we were apparently serving as rear guard made its way through the valley, passing the jungle we had woken up in on the right, until the walls of the valley began to sink into the ground and the terrain shifted into flat, rocky plains.

The Malmind didn't seem to be following, so the column of fleeing sloths became more of a miserable march, with the chariot slowing down enough to go a little easier on the rough terrain. It meant we could finally have something resembling a proper conversation, which we were well overdue for.

"All right," I said, mentally stacking up my list of questions. "What is this all about? That was the Malmind, wasn't it?"

"The metal men drove us out," said the girl. "Took our village. Some were caught. They were made like them."

"Yep, sounds like the Malmind, all right," I said.

Warden took over for the next obvious question. "And who are you?"

"Alice," said the native girl. "I live with the Ruggels. I was left on this planet when I was twelve."

The Ruggels presumably being the sloth-like creatures all around us. "When you were twelve?" I asked. "So that would've been, what, nine, ten years ago?"

"Why do you ask?" inquired Warden, one eye narrowed.

"So what happened to the Zuvirons?"

By this stage, the chariot had slowed down to a walking pace, so Alice was able to look away from the road for long enough to give me a protracted sidelong stare. "The what?"

"You could hardly have missed them," I said, slightly aghast. "Dominant species? Eight feet tall? Four arms? Always going on about honor and swords?"

"Never seen anything like that," said Alice. "Only ever Ruggels."

Jemima, who had been kneeling upright on the side of the chariot, taking in the sight of the seemingly infinite orange plain stretching to the horizon, chipped in. "Maybe this isn't actually the planet you thought it was?"

That would have been an appealing thought and one I would very much like to believed, as it would have meant my time spent fighting the Malmind alongside the Zuvirons hadn't been a complete waste, but it just didn't sit right as the two familiar suns beamed down. "It looks exactly like it, though."

"Perhaps the Malmind have a type of planet that they prefer?" suggested Warden.

I slackened my jaw at her in contempt. "Warden. They're an intergalactic machine intelligence that turns all sentient life into more of themselves. They are not fussy. They do not hold out for a planet with nicer beaches." I looked up into the sky again. "I dunno, though. Maybe it is just a massive coincidence. Nothing new under the suns, is there."

"I can't believe there was ever a war fought here," said Jemima in a breathy voice, drinking it all in. "It's so peaceful."

"Yeah, that's how you can tell that there was a war fought here, Jemima," I said.

The procession slowed. The Ruggels at the head of the march must have established a campsite, and by the time we arrived, most of them had staked a claim on a few square feet of space, throwing down as bedding whatever items they had been able to grab in their escape. Six or seven were working to gather brush for a fire, while another handful were gathering large stones to form a circle for it to go in. There was little conversation beyond the occasional squeak. They seemed to have a remarkably good instinctive grasp of their assigned tasks and sleeping areas. I suspected that scent marking might have been involved, and resolved to be cautious about sitting down.

As we dismounted from the chariot, Alice had a relieved reunion with what I presumed to be her adoptive family. Four of the Ruggels, three full sized with gray streaks in their fur, one little more than a pup, hurled themselves at her and snuffled around her limbs fondly.

We could hardly escape notice at that point, and the Ruggels approached us with sniffing, brown-eyed curiosity, keeping a wary distance of a couple of feet. Jemima outstretched a hand to pet one of the smaller ones, but it shied away and hid behind what may have been its parent.

"How were you abandoned here?" I asked Alice, when she had shaken off the affectionate greeting. The Ruggels remained close enough that they could pass for a large, furry skirt.

"My parents were studying the Ruggels," she said, idly stroking a proffered head. "They left me with them when they went off into the jungle. Didn't come back."

"Is that so," said Warden. I looked at her questioningly, and she raised an eyebrow in reply.

"You can stay here tonight," said Alice, pointing to a vacant area on the outskirts of the camp where, by some prearranged signal, some bedrolls had been set up. "Tomorrow, we take our village back."

It hadn't sounded like a rousing clarion call to action, but the fire roared into life with remarkably good timing, and an adorable squeak of defiance sounded throughout the campsite.

CHAPTER 19

IT SURPRISED ME that, having spent the afternoon fleeing for their lives, the Ruggels were intent on having a bonfire party the same night. But from what Alice was saying, it seemed like a cultural thing.

"Most important time to celebrate," she said, as food was served and a ring of Ruggels joined hands around the fire. "Bad days are there to remind us of the good ones."

The food consisted mainly of haunches of meat, presumably from the domestic cow things I'd seen, with some wild fruit and root vegetables, but I found it surprisingly palatable. We ate reclined around a large ground-sheet, with the food laid out in unhygienic piles in the middle. Warden excused herself fairly swiftly after consuming the bare minimum required for continued survival, while Jemima went to sit by the fire, swaying gently as she watched the younger Ruggels dance. I found myself alone with Alice, which presented an opportunity to ask something that had been nagging me.

"You said your parents brought you down here, then disappeared on some kind of expedition," I said, putting down my current haunch.

"Yeff," she replied, her mouth full.

"How did you get down here? On a ship?"

She nodded.

"Is the ship still around?" That was the first of my two big questions.

"Hasn't been used since then," said Alice, suddenly wary, having perhaps anticipated what the second of my two big questions was going to be.

And here it came. "Can we borrow it?"

She smiled deviously, in the way a child would when they are about to run to the teacher with a cry of *telling!* "You mean, can you take it."

I gave an embarrassed and hopefully friendly sounding laugh. "If you don't know how to fly it, then it's not much use to you, is it. I could fly it. I'm a pilot. And I have a rather pressing need to get back to where I was before."

"If you don't know where it is, then it's not much use to you, either, is it," she said, imitating my voice.

"It's back in the Ruggel village," I deduced. "Where the Malmind are."

She cocked her head coyly. "Help us chase them out. Then you can get what you want."

I couldn't deny that I was thrumming with excitement at the thought. Helping primitive people fight off the Malmind was something so perfectly attuned to my narrow skill set that only the word *serendipitous* sufficed. But through that giddy excitement, I sensed a note of resentment in Alice's last few words, and some bitterness in the way she was tearing meat from the bone in front of her with her teeth.

"I could fly you off here as well, you know," I offered.

Baffled, she made a show of looking at the many reveling Ruggels within our field of view. "And go where?"

I shrugged. "Fair enough."

But she didn't seem to want to let it drop. She had put her food down now and was staring at me, reclining on her side with her arm as a pillow. "So where are you going back to?"

I was about to say "Ritsuko City," in the prideful way we citizens of the first and biggest off-Earth colony tend to use, but then I remembered the whole marked-for-death-by-entire-peer-group thing. "There's a space station full of people like me," I said, looking up into the night sky as if I'd be able to see it. "If we don't get back there, a lot of trouble might be coming their way."

"Are they your friends?"

I looked sadly at the fraying bandage on my hand. The dark red stain in the middle was like a single eye, staring back like the reproachful gaze of a kicked puppy. "I have to assume so."

"Why?"

I was too sleepy and full of greasy food to wrestle with philosophy. I rose to my feet, brushing the dust and sand from my jeans. "Can I get back to you on that one? We can talk about taking the village back first thing in the morning."

She shrugged and returned to the food pile as I gingerly stepped around the numerous sleeping bodies of the older and better-fed Ruggels who weren't joining in the festivities, making my way to our assigned sleeping area. Warden was there, sitting on a stone with crossed legs, making notes on her tablet.

"Hey," I said, staking a claim on a bedroll by sitting on it. "I think I know how to get us off this planet."

An eyebrow raised, and Warden's skittering finger halted abruptly on the surface of her touchscreen. "Oh?"

Now holding new cards that she didn't know about, I felt my mood improve further. "Unless you're more interested in your tablet, of course."

"McKeown . . ." she began, warningly.

"Alice has a ship. She can't fly it, and it's in the Ruggel village under Malmind control, but we can have it if we help them retake it." I blinked once. "And you can stop calling me McKeown now, you know."

"I don't know what your real name is."

"You must know, because you changed it on the ID network."

"I think you know perfectly well why that wouldn't clarify the matter." She sighed through her teeth. "Do you trust them?"

"I trust them more than the Malmind, and we have to trust someone. Could you just drop the plying aloof thing? I am trying to get us all off this planet. You could at least get onboard. I'm not asking for gratitude, because I appreciate that that would be like asking a Slignn for tap-dancing lessons."

"Forgive me if gratitude is not the first thing on my mind," said Warden, meeting my gaze sternly, "when, after finally finding a place that can shelter me from Henderson and where I can make a real difference, I am immediately exiled to an alien planet because someone couldn't keep their intoxicated mouth shut."

I unfolded two fingers, firstly as an obscene gesture, and secondly to count them off. "Okay. One. You were the one who brought up McKeown's money at dinner. And two. I just told you I have a way to fix this. What is your problem?"

She broke off her gaze. I could almost have said that Warden looked guilty. It was a very, very brief glimpse, and was swiftly replaced with a more familiar neutral look with the usual mix of contempt and grudging tolerance, but I was sure I'd seen it. "McKeown, something is not right about this whole situation."

I nodded, exaggerating a stupid grin. "Yeah! There is something pretty not right about the Malmind occupying the Ruggel village. That's why I'm proposing we do something about it."

"I mean, the entire situation. The Malmind, the Ruggels, Alice, the whole planet. There's something wrong."

I frowned. "Well?"

Her mouth did a few laps around the lower half of her face as she picked through the best words to use. "It's too . . ." Her hands came up, jiggled around, then went down again. "Cute."

I treated her to a long pause, maintaining eye contact throughout, then echoed, "Cute."

"Too . . . obvious," she tried. "Too clear cut, perhaps. I get a sense that one or all parties are trying too hard."

I sighed and leaned back. "That's your reasoning, is it? Sorry, Ruggels, we can't avenge your lost and wounded and help you retake your ancestral home, nor accept your gift of a ship that will let us get off this planet, for I'm afraid the psycho-div over here thinks you're too cute and trying too hard."

"I did not say I was not in favor of such a deal," she said, tightening her mouth and spitting each word. "I am trying to make you understand that there may be more to this situation than first meets the eye. A number of things have not been adding up."

"Like what?"

She indicated straight downwards "This camp has been put together from what little could be seized at a moment's notice from the Ruggel village, yes?"

"Yeah?"

"So why, among the items grabbed in those first moments of panic and flight, were there three human-sized bedrolls?"

I looked down and inspected the rough cloth beneath me. It was definitely too big for a Ruggel. And looking around, I saw that all the sleeping Ruggels were using properly proportioned bedrolls. "Maybe they're not actually bedrolls," I said. "Maybe they had some other purpose. Like, carrying stuff on one of those domesticated animals they have. It's just a big, thick sack, right? And anyway, Alice said her parents were here, too, at some point. Three humans, three bedrolls."

"It doesn't explain why they brought all three, if only one human currently resides here," said Warden. "There's more. What about those mechanisms you used to cause the rockfall when the Malmind were chasing us?"

"What about them? They're a fairly standard defensive measure for primitive cultures. The Ruggels must have been expecting an attack at some point."

"But I can't think of any reason why the Ruggels would also paint obvious targets onto them," said Warden. "I mean, *they* knew where they were and that they had to be shot. Painting targets on them just draws attention to them. The Malmind could easily have spotted them, perhaps even used them against the Ruggels."

"What exactly do you think that indicates, Warden? That the Ruggels were in on their own invasion? They were probably just being thick. They can't be the brightest stars in the cosmos. If they were, they'd have invented the internal-combustion engine by now."

The party seemed to be dying down, along with the fire. Most of the Ruggels had drifted off to their sleeping area. Warden and I watched the silhouette of Alice against the dying embers, dutifully helping the more civic-minded creatures tidy up the remains of the banquet.

"There's something strange about that girl, too," said Warden.

"Ugh." I mimed being knocked backward by an invisible wave of stupid and lay back on my bedroll, hands behind my head. "Will you just leave me out of your plying paranoid trac?"

She leaned over me, not taking the hint. "What kind of parents leave their child with the primitive species they are trying to study? For that matter, what kind of parents bring their child to an uncivilized planet in the first place?"

I rolled over and closed my eyes determinedly. "And who would leave their child under the supervision of an impostor and a psycho-div? Some people just haven't got a Parents of the Year Award on their priority list. Is what I would be saying if I hadn't gone to sleep. Snore snore."

"But didn't they tell anyone where they were going?" pressed Warden. "Hasn't anyone noticed that they're missing?"

I gave up and rolled back over, propping myself up on an elbow. "You know what I think this is all about? I think you're afraid of niceness."

That shut her up. "I . . . what?"

"Oh, I understand. Working with Henderson, you probably get used to niceness being the prelude to . . . cassowary disembowelment. So when you see a perfectly straightforward situation, the nice, blameless, simple people being ousted by the evil Malmind—and that's pretty damn provably and unambiguously evil, take it from me—your first instinct is suspicion. You tell yourself there's got be some hidden cassowary talon coming out of nowhere."

"Do not think you understand me, McKeown."

I grinned at her discomfort. "But it's not just that, is it. You're afraid of people being nice and uncomplicated because that means you'd have to be nice to them. And you couldn't abide that, could you. You'd think it would show weakness. You're afraid someone might get too close and see where the armor ends and the weakness begins."

"Spare me your boneheaded pop psychology," snapped Warden, tightening her folded arms even further.

I settled back down to sleep, my point well made. "You only say that 'cos you know I'm right."

She left a thoughtful pause long enough to let me think she was going to let me have the last word for once and I could finally get some shut-eye. "So what about you?"

"Hm?"

"If it's pop psychology we're doing, have you considered that your problem is that you find it impossible to move on from your past glory days?"

"All right, you've got me there. I do think the Golden Age of star piloting was more agreeable than whatever the hell color of age you'd call this one."

"But that's why you've been so eager to trust, lately. Why you refuse to accept that Robert Blaze betrayed you. Why you will so readily accept the situation on this planet. The chance of going back to your old fantasy life is being dangled over your nose, and you roll over like a dog."

I sat up again. It'd been a while since I'd done this many sit-ups in one session. "Well, at least there has been one thing in my life I took pleasure from! At least I'm not dead inside! And if rejecting your paranoid moon-landing-conspiracy evidence makes me a stupid doggie on a leash, then call me Mr. Woofy. Frankly."

"I never said I had hard evidence," said Warden, remaining infuriatingly composed as always. "Only a few nagging doubts."

"Emphasis on the *nagging*. Well, I'll tell you what. You come with me and Alice to recon the Ruggel village tomorrow morning, and if we see a massive soundstage with buildings painted onto canvas sheets, then I'll admit you were right all along."

"Fine!"

"Er, why don't you two, you know, get a room," said Jemima, approaching our sleeping area.

Warden and I gave her matching grimaces at the notion, and she smiled, embarrassed, before taking a seat on the last remaining bedroll. She seemed flushed and out of breath, but she hummed happily as she made to remove her big, fashionable shoes.

"And where were you?" I asked.

"Oh, I just . . . joined in with the dancing for a bit," admitted Jemima, still taking deep breaths to bring her heart rate down. "Phew. They're just so cute, aren't they."

"Yes, Warden was just saying how cute they are," I said, arms folded sulkily, realising that the specter of a decent night's sleep was drifting further away with every passing second.

Jemima beamed. "You know something? I really like it here." Her face turned serious. "We're going to help them, aren't we? Against the cyber things? You've fought them before."

"Yes," said Warden disapprovingly. "That seems to be the sole point on which we are all agreed."

Jemima gave a little snort, downgrading it to a nervous smile before it could break out into a full laugh. "Wait, both of you agree? How did that happen?"

"Alice has a ship," I reported. "It's back in the Ruggel village. We help them retake it, we get a way off this planet."

Jemima's upbeat mood visibly went down the drain. Her hair's vibrant pink tint seemed to spontaneously darken a few shades. "Oh. But . . . we don't have to leave straightaway, do we? They might need more help. You know. Settling back in."

"I rather think we do," I said, becoming annoyed. "Because your mum's thugs are going to be showing up at Salvation Station pretty soon, and if you're not there, there's gonna be a lot of face stomping that could otherwise have been avoi—"

"My mum isn't sending thugs!" cried Jemima, flailing her hands for a moment before composing herself. "She probably hasn't even noticed I'm gone! Stop thinking you understand what my mum is like! And anyway, the people at Salvation Station cut your chip out! Stole all your money! You don't owe them anything!"

"Jemima . . ." I began, but that sentence went nowhere.

"And you," she said, turning her pointed finger to Warden. "Where else do you have to be? Your plan was to join the pirates, wasn't it? And then the pirates turned you out and left you on this planet. You don't belong there. And you can't go back to Earth, either."

Spent, she slumped back down, thrusting her face into the space between her knees. Over the mass of quivering pink hair, Warden caught my gaze meaningfully.

"It's just . . ." continued Jemima, uprighting herself with second wind acquired. "Everywhere up in space it's just been people trying to kill you and use you and neither of you have anywhere to live and nobody else cares! Why is it such a stupid idea to just, you know, stay here a bit longer? Here there's just . . ."

". . . killer cyborgs," I said.

"Jemima," said Warden, with what amounted to warmth for her. "Just because you want to rebel against your mother . . ."

"I'm not trying to rebel against my mother!" said Jemima, swatting Warden ineffectually on her padded shoulder. "I'm just saying you're totally overreacting!"

"Jemima, your mother probably already believes that you have been kidnapped," said Warden, brushing her swatted shoulder with quick, severe strokes. "Just because she can be distant does not mean she has no concern for you at all."

"Yeah," I said, feeling like someone with actual emotions should probably get involved in the conversation. "I mean, when I was a kid I thought my mum didn't love me 'cos she'd never buy me a cream-filled crepe from the bakery when we were walking past. She always pretended she couldn't hear me yelling. I thought she didn't care. But then I got older and I realized she just didn't want me to turn out fat and hideous, like her."

"And besides," said Warden, bulldozing me right back out of the conversation. "You are more than just your mother's daughter. You are part of the public perception of a nation's president. And with that, you are a symbol of the nation. Any perceived affront upon you is an affront upon that nation, and I am certain they will respond accordingly."

"I didn't ask to be the symbol of a nation," spat Jemima, returning her chin to the cradle on her knees as she submitted to our combined assault.

"Yeah, I imagine those pilots on Salvation won't remember asking for a jackboot facial, either," I said, rolling over to turn my back on them. "I don't think that's on any of their plying day planners. Now I really am going to sleep."

And I really was.

CHAPTER 20

IF THE PLANET we were on wasn't Cantrabargid, it was an uncanny doppelgänger. It had the suns, the terrain, and the thirty-hour rotation cycle, which meant I could get a generous ten hours of sleep and have a bit of a lie-in before the sun rose.

But then I was well fed and energized, and was willing to be generous with the benefit of the doubt. Conditions for the evolution of life were strict enough that suitable planets tended to be a little bit samey.

And it may even have been Cantrabargid after all. It was a pretty big planet, and I'd not seen huge amounts of it the first time. Maybe this was another set of rocky orange plains on the opposite side of the planet from where the Zuvirons lived. Contrary to bad fiction—like Jacques McKeown's—very few habitable planets have exactly the same terrain from pole to pole, but there's no reason there can't be two deserts.

Mind you, they both had to be pretty damn big deserts. The Malmind War had seen skirmishes eighteen miles wide. And after a punishingly long hike along the top of the valley wall in the cold morning sun, I stood atop a rock spire that served as a vantage point, and the desert was still stretching from horizon to horizon.

"Stay low, McKeown, you'll be seen," said Warden, crouching beside my perch.

"The Malmind don't look up," I said, attempting to memorize the layout of the Ruggel village, nestled in the huge, bowl-shaped crater that seemed to mark the beginning of the valley. "Design flaw. That's why it was always star pilots having to deal with them—they're very easy to bomb."

"He's right," said Alice, who was kneeling unafraid at the very edge of the valley wall. "When they don't fight, they just stand around like farm animals grazing."

The bowl must have once been a lake, which had long since shrunk down into the little watering hole around which the village was built, just as the valley must once have been a mighty river that was now the little stream. The houses were squat, uniform dwellings constructed from rough slabs the same color as all the surrounding rock.

Crouching low enough to squeeze inside Ruggel-shaped doors was apparently too complex an operation for an individual Malmind cyborg to process by itself, so most of them were following preset patrol routes along the roads and alleyways dividing the houses. The few patches of pale white flesh that were uncovered by cybernetic implants had been universally burned a vibrant pink by the sun.

"They don't appear to be doing anything," said Warden, showing off those keen observational skills.

"They're just occupying," I said, climbing down from my perch for the sake of a more face-to-face discussion. "They don't care about holding a village. They care about adding to their numbers. They're waiting for the Ruggels to come back and try to retake their homes."

"Which we will," said Alice defiantly.

"Not much chance of a surprise attack, then," said Warden unhappily.

I blew air out of my cheeks and looked down at the village again. From there, the Malmind could see along the valley for miles. An approach from that direction was far too obvious. But the walls of the crater were too steep. An invading force would need climbing equipment, and the descent would be slow. It would be almost as obvious as a frontal assault.

"How did the Malmind take the village in the first place?" I asked Alice. "This is about as defensible as it gets."

"I don't know," she replied. "It all happened so fast. They came out of nowhere."

"How conveniently unspecific," said Warden, giving me one of her looks. Alice scowled, confused.

My gaze drifted to a patch of dusty silver-white that was poking up from between a couple of houses. Some old sheets had been thrown over it to help it blend in with the rest of the village, aesthetically speaking, but a nacelle is a difficult thing to disguise. It had to be Alice's parents' ship, unused for however many years, but intact enough to be beaten into a flying state, I was certain.

"This would be so much easier if I had a ship," I thought aloud, then turned to Alice. "If I could get in there alone, get to the ship, maybe— "

"Nope," she said, with irritating speed. "Village first, then ship. Earn trust."

I sighed. At some point, when the Ruggels had been teaching her essential survival skills, there must have been a few basic lessons on contract negotiation.

"You may have raised a relevant point," said Warden, charitably. "It could be possible for one or two individuals to sneak into the village unnoticed, by climbing down from the cliffs."

"And then what?" I asked. "Break out the kung fu?"

Warden surveyed the village, tapping her chin with one finger, then used the same finger to point. "What's that?"

She was indicating a cylinder of tarnished silver that had been erected in the center of the village, on the bank of the watering hole. It was about ten feet tall and held upright by a number of twisted metal limbs. About halfway up the cylinder, there were four extruding rubber tubes, currently dangling unused.

As we watched, one of the Malmind cyborgs, in response to some kind of signal, lurched up to the cylinder and placed one of the tubes into its mouth. The tube immediately stiffened as some hideous substance was passed through it into the cyborg. Like many things about the Malmind, there was something indecent about the whole process that seemed completely unnecessary.

"That's weird," I said.

"What is?"

"It's the hub cylinder. Dispenses nutrient fluid that keeps the units running. Also the top part is a signal booster, receiving messages from the Malmind central core and passing them on to the local forces. It's the focal point of every Malmind expedition. But it's weird."

"What is?" repeated Warden patiently.

"They're usually kept somewhere out of the way, 'cos they're such an obvious weak point." I rubbed my chin. "Maybe it needs to be near a water source?"

"So we destroy it, and they are helpless!" said Alice, punching her palm in triumph.

I shook my head. "If they don't get orders from the core, they'll just continue following the last order received. And they can go for days without nutrients. They'd still have more than enough capacity to make us into Christmas decorations if we went in noisy."

"But what if they were receiving different orders?" asked Warden.

I looked at her questioningly, and she jiggled her tablet in response. Ply knows how she had been able to hold on to that thing all this time. It was probably because it was the closest thing she had to a soul.

"You said it was a signal booster," continued Warden, double-checking what I presumed to be the suite of hacking tools she had installed. "If I can get close, I may be able to override that signal. If I can figure out what kind of machine code they use, I may even be able to reprogram them. If not, I can at the very least shut them down with code they don't understand."

"How close is close?" I asked.

From some mysterious pocket in her outfit she produced a double-ended USB cable. It was about two feet long. "This close."

I cocked an eyebrow at the village below us. "Are you honestly volunteering for the solo mission? 'Cos I am fully onboard with that plan and plying thrilled at the prospect."

She took that on the chin. "No, McKeown. Two of us should still be able to maintain the element of stealth. As the resident veteran of Malmind combat, I propose that you come with me in an advisory role."

"Yeah, yeah, I figured as much. I'm just a little concerned that 'help retake the Ruggel village' has suddenly turned into 'single-handedly retake the Ruggel village.'"

"We'll be ready with more rockfalls if you need to make an escape," said Alice. "But don't think about trying to take the ship." She patted her loincloth, which jangled musically. "I always keep the keys with me."

"Didn't even cross my mind," I said, and I meant it.

"I'll go back to the camp and get the climbing gear," said Alice, making to leave.

"Now?" said Warden. "Shouldn't we wait until darkness?"

I shook my head. "Nope. Malmind have enhanced vision. We'd be the only ones with a disadvantage in darkness, so we should do it now. Unless you're having second thoughts in the cold light of day."

"None at all," said Warden. She watched Alice scamper off back along the trail, and I could immediately tell that she was waiting for her to be completely out of earshot. "So."

"Yes?" I said, with an exaggerated encouraging tone.

"Among what few bare essentials could be grabbed in a single panicky moment as they were ousted from their homes by a belligerent force, there was also apparently some climbing gear."

I gestured to the village with an open palm. "They live surrounded by cliffs! And sloths climb a lot! It's probably an important part of their lives!"

"What about the ship?"

"That will be an important part of our lives, or at least the continuation of them. What are you getting at?"

"It seems odd that she would always be carrying the keys to a ship that she claims to have not used in close to a decade."

I peered out toward the ship in question, still sitting visibly between Ruggel dwellings. Now that I was focusing on it, I noticed that some potted plants had been arranged around it artfully. "It hasn't been flown, no. But there's no reason she won't have been going inside it. Maybe that's where she sleeps. Maybe that's where she keeps the bedrolls and the climbing equipment."

"Well, as long as you are satisfied, then forget I said anything," said Warden.

"Way ahead of you." I halfheartedly scanned the village yet again. "I mean, what do you think this is going to turn out to be? A VR simulation they put us in while we were asleep?"

"Of course not. Jemima and I were both awake for the whole trip from the station to the planet."

I raised my eyebrows. "So . . . maybe it's just me who's in a VR simulation."

Warden shrugged. "You aren't, but there's no possible way I can prove that to you."

"Hm. On second thought, a VR simulation would have more emotions than you." I glanced back along the trail. The location of the Ruggel camp was indicated by a column of campfire smoke in the distance, like a single pencil mark across the orange sky. "Do you think Jemima will be safe in the camp?"

"Safer than in the surrounding desert," said Warden, also staring at the smoke. "To the extent, I am hoping, that she will be dissuaded from trying to escape when we have to drag her back to her responsibilities."

"And yet, here you are, having run away from all of yours."

"I only did so after careful consideration led to the conclusion that fleeing was the most logical course of action for me at that time," she said, sounding more than a little rehearsed. "She is merely being immature."

I nodded. "Funny. You ever think, between the three of us, we've sort of created a little impromptu family unit?"

I had never heard a syllable infused with as much utter loathing and disgust as the next one to come out of her mouth. "No. I do not."

I blinked. "Me neither."

After Alice returned with some ropes and climbing hooks, and immediately left again to wrangle up some more boulders for the valley escape route, Warden and I made our way around the lip of the crater, seeking the best spot to rappel down to.

We found it in a small courtyard, right next to where Alice's ship was parked, backing onto the sheer cliff wall and decorated with a small well in the center. It seemed to be the point of least Malmind concentration and was well sheltered by buildings and the ship. And directly above it there was a sturdy elongated boulder a few feet from the edge of the cliff, around which I began looping the rope.

"You ever rappelled before?" I asked Warden, as she was standing nearby pretending to look useful.

"Have you?" she asked, instantly getting on the defensive.

"Once or twice." I tied the rope into the standard star pilot's hitch, optimized for pulling cargo around in zero gravity. "Always from ships, though." I pulled the last loop tight with a flourish and gave her a smile.

It wasn't returned. "You're really enjoying being the most qualified person for this situation, aren't you."

"Only now that I can see it's bothering you," I said, passing the rope through my belt loops and feeding the rope down the cliff. I could see a sentry in a position to spot us once we were low enough, but it wouldn't be a problem if we timed our descent to match the moments when it turned its back. "Okay. Hold the free end of the rope behind your back, like this. Keep your legs spread apart on the way down. Although I have a feeling you'll have difficulty with that part."

She followed my directions resentfully, and the two of us carefully backed off the ledge. The hard part is always the requisite moment of terror when you learn whether or not the rope is going to take your weight, but after that, it was simple enough, even with only ten minutes of training.

About a third of the way down, I cast a look over my shoulder at the village below. "Okay, stop a second," I called.

Warden did so awkwardly, her sensible shoes scratching upon the rock. But I had to admit, she was doing pretty well for someone in office attire. "What is it?"

I cocked my head. "Lookout on the roof of the two story building." I presumed it was some Ruggel equivalent of a town hall. "We go much lower, he'll spot us. We wait till his patrol turns around."

"Fair enough," said Warden.

The ropes went slack.

We were in freefall for a bloodcurdling couple of feet before we stopped sharply. The pair of us bounced freely on the ropes like a pair of rubber spiders before securing our feet on the rock wall again.

"What the hell happened?" I hissed, sweat dripping into my eyes.

Warden was looking up. "I suspect the tall rock you chose as our anchor just toppled onto its side," she said, in a small voice.

"You sure?"

"Fairly."

I followed her gaze. The morning sun was moving overhead, and the cliff we had descended so far was a sheet of black, silhouetted against the brightening sky. And at some point since the last time I'd looked at it, the mass of black appeared to have grown a nose. Our two ropes dangled down from it like lengthy snot trails.

"Uh—" was as far as I got before I noticed that the nose was growing longer, and that I was still moving slowly downward as it did so.

"Our weight is pulling the rock off the cliff," said Warden flatly.

"Plying porous rocks!" I said, kicking off the wall for a big jump down. "New plan! Get down now quick smart like!"

The two of us started bouncing our way down the wall with all consideration of stealth forgotten. My feet slammed into the cliff again and again, jarring my ankles and sending little bursts of dust and sand sprinkling down upon the courtyard below. The friction from the rope burned the skin from my palms.

When I was about three-quarters of the way down, I risked a look up. The rock looked like it was more than half over the edge, and I could see it being pulled left and right in time with the hops of Warden and me.

Ply it, I thought. This is the kind of thing we keep ourselves in good health for.

I let go of the rope and spread my arms wide. The rope whizzed through my belt loops, sending me into a spin and whipping painfully against my stomach, but I forced myself not to panic. I went limp, closed my eyes, and recited something familiar and comforting in my head. I opted for the standard preflight checklist from the old Speedstar employee manual.

I'd only gotten as far as *ensure that all tray tables and footrests are stowed* when I hit the ground. My spread-eagled body thudded onto the sand like a flipped pancake landing back in the pan, with an involuntary grunt from my lungs taking the place of the appetizing sizzle.

Flat on my back, I watched Warden daintily make her way down the rest of the wall with considerably less concern, now that the anchor was relieved of my weight. I passed the time by flexing each of my muscles one by one, testing for broken bones.

By the time I'd gotten as far as the feet, she was standing over me. "Are you all right?"

"One more sec." I rolled my ankles and went down the toes, curling each one in turn. "Seems like it."

Against expectations, she offered a hand to help me up. "Gratifying to know that chivalry still exists."

I rubbed at my bruises, which took a bit of work, because it felt like my entire body had been bruised simultaneously. "It would only count as chivalry," I said in a strained voice, "if you were a woman."

I turned, then made immediate eye contact with a six-foot-five, armor-plated cyborg warrior.

It was directly between us and the narrow passage that was the only way out of the courtyard. It froze when I noticed it, perhaps to send an update on the situation back to the central core and wait for new orders, before outstretching its arms and lurching forward. Its one uncovered eye was wide with frozen hatred.

I felt rock behind me. With no input on the part of my conscious mind, I had apparently backed up against the cliff. Out of the corner of my eye, I saw Warden dangling from her rope again.

"McKeown," she said. "Pull."

I got the idea, grabbed the trailing rope I had recently fallen from, and swung off it as the raw skin on my palms screamed in protest. As the two of us pulled and dangled like bell ringers, and the cyborg drew ever closer, I became certain that the rock was going to turn out to be completely secure, just to make this as wantonly cruel as possible.

Then the sudden slackening of the rope sent me into the dust again, with Warden joining me for the second round. A moment later, a viciously heavy thud launched us both about six inches off the ground. There was now a very large rock in the courtyard instead of a murderous cyberserker.

"Oh, calculus. It saw us. Now the whole collective knows we're here."

"It knows that we are at this position," said Warden, dusting herself down primly. "Therefore, we endeavor to be in another position."

"There's only one way to go!" I said, indicating the narrow alleyway, whose far end my imagination was already furnishing with hordes of approaching cyborgs.

"We can climb onto the ship." Warden made for Alice's shuttle, pushing aside part of the protective sheet to reveal the maintenance rungs going up the side.

"Good call," I admitted, making to follow. The top of the ship was only about four feet lower than the roof of the nearest house, and a rooftop traversal was probably the smart approach. When we were both carefully crouched on the smoothly curved roof of the ship, I could see that the cyborg sentry was no longer on the town hall roof. It may even have been the same one that was now twitching under a huge porous rock.

I made to clamber onto the next roof, but Warden stopped me with an outstretched hand. "Hold."

"What?"

"Examine the ship as best you can from here and see if it remains entirely consistent with Alice's story."

I screwed my eyes shut, then opened them as wide as I could, a massively exaggerated blink. "What is wrong with you? Have I built up enough chivalry points that I can give you a little smack?"

"Doesn't it seem rather small for a three-person family embarking on a scientific expedition?"

I eyeballed the ship. Not that I wanted to give her the satisfaction, but it did seem a little on the poky side. As far as I could tell, it wasn't much more than a runabout, the kind of thing mainly used for transferring people and cargo from orbiting ships to planet surfaces. It had, however, been modified for interstellar travel.

"I think they must have been working from a larger science ship," I speculated.

"That immediately forgot about them after they went missing?"

"Well? It's a big universe, these things happen." I made to climb onto the next roof and leave the issue behind. "Hell, my graduating class at flight school had two missing persons by the end of the field training course. There was a policy against sending anyone to look for them, you see. Apparently they once lost a whole class that way when a black hole wandered onto the course."

I opted to stay low, and lay on my stomach at the edge of the building's roof, scouting the village center below. The maintenance cylinder wasn't far, but then, there was nothing in the village that was particularly far from anything else. A hop down to ground level, then about twenty yards of open ground to the edge of the watering hole where the cylinder had been set up.

Easy enough if there hadn't been so many murder cyborgs around, re-maining stubbornly in their patrols. I'd been hoping that we'd drawn enough attention by being spotted in the courtyard that the way would be clear, but I should have realized the Malmind were too smart for that. Actually, to look at it, none of the cyborgs were distracted at all.

"Hm," I said. "Why aren't any of them investigating the courtyard?"

"Perhaps they put it down to a freak rockfall," suggested Warden, crouch-ing awkwardly next to me out of refusal to go fully prone. "Or they know we're here but don't see us as a threat."

"I can tell you right now that they don't see us as a threat, but they should see us as nice, fresh materials for them to get their claws all over. I don't get it." I made an attempt to shrug from a prone position. "But I'm not about to ask them to explain themselves."

"So what now?"

I held up a finger and watched the patrolling cyborgs carefully for about a full minute, before lowering the finger ceremoniously. "I'm pretty sure there's a window in the patrols. Not a long one—we'll have to sprint to the cylinder, but we just have to get between it and the lake. There should be a blind spot there."

"I might prefer that we stake our lives on more than just *should*, McKeown."

"All right then, there *is* a blind spot," I said, trying to sound confident. "None of them are watching the lake. I doubt they're expecting the Ruggels to come retake their village in plying submarines."

"On your mark, then."

I waited for the opportune moment, then swung my legs off the roof and dropped the short distance to the ground. The stone floor was more loose than I'd anticipated, and I threw up a noisy skitter of gravel as I landed, but I couldn't let myself dwell. I kept the silver pillar in the center of my vision and ran, not looking around or checking to see if Warden was following.

When I arrived at the cylinder unmolested, two things immediately became clear—firstly that Warden was indeed following closely behind, and that the blind spot between the cylinder and the lake was not going to be big enough to fit two people. I stood with my back pressed tightly against the metal, and Warden appeared in front of me, flustered from the run. I think we both realized at that point that the only way both of us would be totally hidden from sight would be if she crushed her body against mine and we started sloppily making out.

We met each other's gaze, and the silence drew on, dangerously close to the point where a cyborg might turn around and spot her, if it hadn't already passed.

"Kneel," she instructed.

This was unexpected. "No," I replied, sweating.

"I need to stand on your shoulders."

"Ohhh. That makes more sense." I dropped into a squat, and Warden swiftly stepped on, first the right foot, then the left. She was not a heavy woman, but she was still wearing tight and pointy dress shoes (presumably to match her personality), so as I laboriously pushed myself upright again, my shoulder muscles gained new appreciation for the plight of cocktail olives.

"Something is approaching," advised Warden from her new vantage point.

"Nghap," I said in acknowledgement, gritting my teeth.

Her voice lowered. "A cyborg is heading straight toward the cylinder."

I couldn't move around the cylinder to see it, and even if I could, my peripheral vision was blocked on both sides by a combination of Warden's shins and the growing number of spots before my eyes. Instead, I just closed my eyes and attempted to will myself thinner.

From the opposite side of the pillar, I heard heavy footfalls approaching with the terrifying perfect rhythm of a cyberserker, scattering gravel with every creaking thump. They stopped mere feet away from our position.

I held my breath and went back to the Speedstar preflight checklist. *Ensure docking bay is clear. Activate hazard lights. Verify presence of copilot. Verify consciousness of copilot. Verify sobriety of copilot—*

From inside the workings of the column I heard the gurgling of liquids moving around, followed by a series of greedy gulps from the cyborg. A few drops of viscous nutrient fluid landed in the dirt. Then I heard an armored foot turning on its heel, and the cyborg stomped away.

Above me, Warden released a held breath. "I wasn't noticed."

"You plying were by me," I spat, attempting to push her feet up with my hands to alleviate the weight and almost succeeding in giving myself stigmata. "Can you access the signal booster up there?"

"Ah, yes. It seems like this whole top part lifts up."

"Well plying do be burgy dur," I said. Then I concentrated, blocked out the pain, and tried again. "Well plying see if you can do your hacking thing before you plying nail me to the ground!"

I heard a click, and a squeak of hinges, and felt numerous spikes and lifts of pain as she shifted her weight around, working. By then, I'd discovered that some alleviation could be found by digging my feet into the sandy bank of the watering hole and pushing against the cylinder as hard as I could, and soon I'd dug an impressive pair of furrows.

By that time, a minute had passed. "You having trouble finding the port?" I inquired.

"No, not exactly," she replied, her voice muffled and echoing. "McKeown, what is this signal booster supposed to look like?"

I thought back to my war days. I'd seen them a few times, but only ever scorched and mangled and lying in the wreckage of a bombed-out Malmind stronghold. "I think it'll be a sort of boxy thing with a bunch of spiked aerials coming off, connected to a power source by wire."

"Right," said Warden. A long pause followed. "Is there any other appearance they can take?"

"Well, what are you looking at?"

"Nothing."

"What?"

"I can see the top of something that I believe to be the nutrient tank."

There were two reverberating taps that I assumed were her knuckle against the tank. "But nothing else. The entire top part of this cylinder is hollow."

I let the cogwheels in my mind turn for a few seconds, then I dug my feet in harder and pushed upward with all my remaining strength. Warden gave a little yell and fell head-first into the cylinder's interior, kicking her legs madly. Relieved of the burden, I spun and looked around the tube.

"Trac," I said, then I said it a few more times with increased volume. "It's a plying traccing decoy!"

The Malmind had come out in force. The entire street (for want of a better word) was now packed with cyborgs, in both humanoid and Ruggel flavors, a dense forest of sunburned flesh, lusterless fur and black synthetics. And every single one was staring directly at me.

I popped back into the blind spot more for my own comfort than anything else, thought quickly, then jumped. My fingers fastened around the lip of the open compartment beside Warden's struggling form. My body was about as past its prime as a packet of sandwich ham two weeks after opening, but I could at least manage one pull-up, if I used one of the feeding pipes as a foothold.

The space above the nutrient tank was, indeed, hollow—or at least had been before I'd shoved Warden's upper body into it—and was just about large enough for me to fit my legs in. So that left me and Warden's legs perched visibly on top of a minuscule siege tower, surrounded by the horde.

No member of said horde had moved. Neither were they looking at us. I knew that they tended not to look up, but one of them must have seen where we were.

"McKeown!" cried Warden, still trying to correct herself. I dropped and gently but firmly filled her mouth with my knee. I met her furious gaze as she sank her teeth into my jeans, then put a finger to my lips.

The Malmind horde was starting to move. They were shuffling slowly around each other in a mystifyingly complicated pattern, like a choreographed dance production at a home for the elderly. When all of them had shuffled into place, they had taken the form of a rectangular block, transforming from a mob into a regiment.

Then they began to move directly toward us, the two different body sizes marching with two different beats. The smaller feet of the converted Ruggels were a quick, skittering cymbal tap to underline the slower snare drum of the humanoids.

Unconsciously, I had already drawn my blaster from inside my jacket. I still had enough charge to score lethal hits on maybe four or five cyborgs, assuming perfect shots to the heads or crotch reactors. Less if I wanted to hold back two shots to avoid being taken alive. I looked back down into Warden's unhappy eyes, and consoled myself that at least my penultimate act in life would be an immensely satisfying one.

The Malmind stopped. The rank of cyborgs was inches from the cylinder. I could look down and see the bald spot in between the cranial implants of the topmost soldier. I took careful aim at it, waiting for the first attempt to topple our perch.

Then the horde divided itself neatly into two, and both halves turned smartly and marched off in opposite directions, away from us and along the banks of the watering hole. Within moments, we were alone, but I waited until I'd watched the entire army meet each other on the far side of the water and stomp toward the valley, out of the village. Only then did I untense myself and withdraw my knee from Warden's mouth.

"That was uncalled for," she said, spitting up loose threads of distressed denim.

"They've all gone," I relayed.

She gave a mighty burst of effort and withdrew herself from the cylinder the way a cat does from a kitchen sink after you turn the tap on, landing on the ground in an alert crouch, scanning the surroundings. Meanwhile, I lowered myself gently and dropped onto the ground beside her.

"Trac," I said, to fill the silence. "I knew they didn't make their signal boosters that obvious. Should've realized."

"Yes, you should," said Warden, dusting off her knees. "So where is the signal booster?"

I exposed my bottom row of teeth and released a frustrated sigh through them. "I don't know. It could be anywhere. I'm a little more confused about why they didn't attack us. They must have realized we were there. They must have."

Warden looked up at our little unused siege tower. "Apply logic, McKeown. If this tower was truly intended as a decoy, then the purpose of a decoy is to engage the enemy elsewhere while your forces pursue their true agenda unchallenged."

"Which means . . ."

Although we lacked the benefit of being part of the same emotionless hive mind, Warden and I could demonstrate remarkable synchronicity at times. In this case, with no planned choreography whatsoever, both of us turned our gazes to the valley path the Malmind forces had taken, then grabbed each other around the shoulders and yelled in each other's faces.

"THE CAMP!"

CHAPTER 21

SOMEHOW, THE JOURNEY along the valley felt like it had been a lot shorter when we were leisurely walking it in the early morning cool. Running at full sprint under the increasingly baking sun made it an arduous cross-country run for which my body was even less suitable than it had been for pull-ups. I tried not to think about the rockfall traps we saw untriggered along the way.

The Malmind were not as hampered by human limitations as us and must have gone into their fastest speed-lurch mode the moment they left the village, because we failed to catch up with them. And by the time we arrived at the camp, they'd already been and gone.

All the possessions and sleeping equipment remained, but there was not a single sign of life, and everything was scattered and torn, as if a multitude of heavy feet had stomped pitilessly through it. The ashes of last night's fire were scattered across the ground like a comet tail.

Warden and I picked through the wreckage, but we didn't find a single body, alive or dead. With the Malmind, this was about the worst possible sign.

"Jemima has been taken," said Warden gravely.

"Alice, too," I added, punching my palm.

"Yes, willingly or unwillingly." She met my gaze.

I waved an arm in irritation, letting my hand flap loosely like a surrender flag. "Let's not think about that straightaway. We need to know what direction they headed. Look for tracks."

That was easier said than done. If we'd been surrounded by a nice sandy desert, whipped over the centuries into smooth, undisturbed dunes, then the trail would have been so obvious they might as well have paved it.

But these were the rocky plains. I could just about hazard a guess that they were heading northwest, toward the cliffs that the valley opened out into, and that was only from the direction indicated by the campfire ashes. "They cannot have gone far, McKeown," pointed out Warden.

"I know!" I put my hands on my hips and searched the horizon, but there was nothing so helpful as a rising dust cloud or neon sign. "Things would be so plying different if I had a ship, right now. We could spot them easily from the air."

"What about Alice's ship? Could you get it working without the keys?"

"Nah, can't do that."

"Why not?"

I was about to reply "because I just can't," but that didn't seem like a satisfactory answer, even to me. The truth was, I probably could get it going without keys, especially if it was an older model from before the recent updates in security measures. Pretty much anything more than six years old I could get inside with nothing more than stiff wire and half a tennis ball. But that wasn't the point.

"I just . . . feel weird about taking it."

Warden dropped the torn bedroll she was checking under. "Are you serious?"

"It's a pilot thing. I . . . it'd be like wearing someone else's flight jacket. It's just. Eurgh. Not something you do."

"McKeown." She trotted smartly up to me and jabbed a finger into my sternum. "You may have regressed into that stupid cowboy code-of-honor fantasy life you used to lead, but I, personally, do not wish to attempt to explain that to the president when she finds out what happened to her daughter. So we are going to take that ship. Understand?"

I sheepishly backtracked out of finger-jabbing range. "All right, all right. I know. Was just kinda hoping I could get through my entire life without breaking every single one of my principles."

"Good." She began striding for the valley.

"So," I said, jogging a little to keep up. "Having walked all the way to the village and back, the plan at this point is to walk all the way there again?"

"Barring alternatives," she replied through her teeth, without slowing.

"Right. What an absolute plying model of efficiency this whole operation has been."

▲▲▲

It was rubbing up against noon by the time the village was back in visual range. We were making our way back through the valley this time, rather than along the side, for the sake of being close to the stream. This was doing very little good for my feet, which seemed to have gone up two or three shoe sizes since I'd woken up that morning.

"'Stupid cowboy fantasy life?'" I asked, when it occurred to me to do so.

"Let it go, McKeown," murmured Warden distantly. She was probably doing even worse, with those sensible shoes in this terrain, but she was courageously holding it all behind the façade of emotionlessness. Beads of sweat gave it away.

"What would you plying know," I said, more to myself than to her "At least we had a dream. At least we were trying to be part of something bigger than ourselves."

"And what was that? Your ego?"

"It was about helping the weak! It was about justice! It was about showing people less advantaged than us that they didn't have to cave in to being brutalized."

She grabbed me around the throat and slammed me against the valley wall. She wasn't strong, but the attack had caught me off guard and I lost my balance. I thought she might have been trying to make a point, but she kept me pinned there, one hand on my chest, as she peered around a nearby outcrop, a finger to her lips.

"They're in the village," she reported.

"Who are?"

"Who do you think? The Malmind."

I edged my way behind her, inserted my head into the space just above hers, and peered around the wall. Sure enough, I could see the little black dots of Malmind cyborgs patrolling the village, just as they had been doing before. Even at this distance, they could be easily identified by the way they walked like stunned ostriches queuing up at the lunch trough.

"It's not possible," I whispered.

"And yet, there they are."

I let myself fall backward away from the outcrop and leaned on the cliff wall, thinking. "There's no way they could've gotten back to the village this quickly without us noticing."

"Do they have much stealth capability?"

I gave her a withering look. "Warden, look at them. They move like dinosaurs with their feet trapped in buckets."

"Then the only explanation is that they must have another means of getting into the village. Other than the valley path or descending from the cliffs, either of which, as you say, we would have noticed."

Even as she said the words, I could feel a couple of loose threads in the depths of my mind, straining to reach each other. "Wait a second," I said, pacing in as wide a circle as I could manage without walking out into the open. "Alice said the Malmind came out of nowhere when they first took the village."

"If we can trust her version of events."

"Stop it. So if we assume they didn't attack from the front, or from above, then that leaves . . ."

My finger waggled in front of me, chopping the air up into thin slices. "Yes?" prompted Warden.

"Well."

"Well what?"

"Well. In the little courtyard we rappelled down into. There was a well."

"Well?"

"Yes. A well."

"I meant, well, as in, where are you going with this?"

I stopped the waggling of my finger and pointed it skyward as I met her gaze. "Why would there be a well? The village is plying built around a dirty great watering hole. They don't have any need for a well. As well." I dropped my finger to symbolize the dropping of this extremely good point.

"So perhaps it wasn't a well," said Warden, her speech slowing as she came around to my line of thinking.

I think it was me who started running first.

▲▲▲

The pains in my feet temporarily forgotten, I headed away from the village and then took a left turn out of the valley, following the cliffs to the area that the scattered campfire ashes had been vaguely pointing toward.

I almost walked straight past it when I found it, as it was naturally hidden behind a sort of S bend of extruding rock, but the draft gave it away. There was an entrance to some kind of cavern network that seemed to slope downward under the valley.

"I knew it," I said as Warden trotted up to see. "This is where they took the others."

"There must be caverns running under the village," said Warden, panting a little. "And the well must have been an access point."

"Right. Maybe the Ruggels use them as a tomb or something. I'll bet the real Malmind signal booster is down here somewhere."

"And presumably also the prisoners. Surely they won't have been converted so quickly. We can rescue them."

"Right!" I held up an open hand. "High-five."

"Stop it. Let's go."

Although hard to spot, the cave entrance was surprisingly wide, enough to walk two abreast. The tunnel widened even further once we were in.

I had some experience with Cantrabargid's caves, and had always found them rather disappointing, as natural features go. I'd rarely seen one that was more than just a pathetic little crack in the side of a mountain, scarcely of use for much more than a weapons cache.

But this cave was about as accommodating as they get. It was a flat tunnel that maintained a semicircular roof along its entire length. Which gave credence to the idea that it was manmade, or at least Ruggel made, but at the same time, the walls were rough and the tunnel snaked weirdly. Perhaps it was a natural tunnel that had merely been widened.

A short way into the tunnels, what little light came in from the entrance had faded to nothing, but we could see a glow from the corner just ahead, which we swiftly found to be coming from a series of flaming torches marking a path that someone must have very recently taken.

"The Malmind can see in the dark, I think you said?" asked Warden, inspecting a flame warily.

"Yeah, so I guess if they were the ones that lit these, then we know they were moving prisoners through here."

We continued, following the illuminated path. I was losing faith in the idea that the Ruggels had dug this out. It was far too big, and the torches were old, used, and placed too high for a sloth to reach. I supposed the tunnels must have predated them, and that was confirmed when we found an ancient stone casket in a recess in the wall.

"Well, you were half right," said Warden, inspecting it with hand on hip. "Someone used these tunnels as a tomb. Rather large for a Ruggel, of course."

She wasn't exaggerating. The casket would have been rather large for a family of four. Weathered lettering was carved into the side, each character about eight inches high.

"Wait a second," I said, crouching nearby. I ran my fingers along the carving, finding the lines that were obscured by time and meager torchlight. "I recognize this language."

"What does it say?"

"Um. When I say I recognize it, I mean I know what it is, I can't translate it. It's Zuviron." Cantrabargid's warrior race had a famously inefficient written language. I couriered a couple of messages for them during the war; they had each weighed two tons and had to be carried with the winch. "So I was right. This is Cantrabargid and this is Zuviron land. So what the hell happened to them?"

"McKeown," said Warden, hushed and urgent. She had gone on ahead a few yards. "I hear something. Just ahead."

We crept to the far end of the current length of tunnel, where it opened up onto the second level of a vast, cylindrical chamber, which presumably had to be this large to accommodate the many Zuviron tributes to the dead carved into the walls.

I can't imagine that the Zuviron dead would have been mollified by them now, not after their tomb had been abused into its current state. The lowest level of the chamber, below our perch, was absolutely swarming with Malmind cyborgs. Some were patrolling, some were standing perfectly still, and others were queuing politely at one of the six nutrient-dispensing cylinders scattered throughout the crowd.

In the very center of the floor was a sight that I only recognized from rumors. It was a tulip-shaped tower of mysterious electrical components, trailing black cables like the numerous tentacles of an eldritch abomination. At its base was a range of screens and keyboards that had much of the church organ about them, ringed by a humming server farm laid out like a druidic stone circle.

"Well," I said, after swallowing hard. "Now we know why they didn't need a signal booster in the village."

"Why?" asked Warden, not looking away from the spectacle.

"Because this is the Malmind central core. From which every Malmind unit in the entire galaxy is controlled and monitored. I heard it tends to move around a bit. I guess it's currently on Cantrabargid."

Warden put a hand on her hip again. "Well, let me congratulate you a second time on what a thorough job you did saving this planet from them."

"It was years ago!" I barked, before reflexively ducking, checking, and double-checking that the Malmind hadn't heard me. I continued in an urgent whisper. "What was I supposed to do? Become their king? They used to bite each other's noses off as a greeting!"

"Doesn't seem to have helped them."

I felt a pang of guilt at that and became uncomfortably aware of the desecrated Zuviron tombs all around us. But that made me wonder why I hadn't seen any Zuviron cyborgs. It was hard to assume that the Malmind couldn't see the usefulness in a few battalions of brick trac-houses. Maybe they were too useful and were all off-world conquering planets as we spoke. Or maybe the Zuvirons hadn't let themselves be taken alive. That seemed very "them."

But as my gaze, driven by my thoughts, ran along the walls of Zuviron memorials, I saw something. A little way along the elevated path that ran around the room's perimeter, I could see that several sarcophagi had been hauled out of their recesses, and the spaces were now blocked off by fizzling force fields.

I caught Warden's eye and cocked a head toward it, then the two of us made our way along the path, staying close to the perimeter wall. When I reached the first improvised cell, I could almost feel the buzz from the force field generator as a physical thing sandpapering across my nerves. There must have been enough charge in it to atomize a pregnant Zuviron tribe mother.

But as I peered through it, I saw a huge number of closely packed, fearful Ruggel eyes staring back from the darkness. Then there was a sudden eruption of furry bodies, and Jemima appeared, looking a little sunburned but otherwise unharmed.

"Oh my god!" cried Jemima, almost running straight into the force field to greet us. "They said no one would ever find us here!"

"Where is Alice?" asked Warden suspiciously, inspecting the other cells and finding only Ruggels.

"She escaped," said Jemima. "None of us have been converted because they've been busy trying to get her back."

"Escaped? How?" Warden was inspecting the force field generators and saw as I had that they completely covered the mouths of each recess with no gaps.

"I dunno," said Jemima. "She wasn't in this cell."

"Wait a second," I displayed a finger. "Who said no one would ever find you here? Because I know Malmind cyborgs, and they're not chatty."

"He did." Jemima pointed toward the lower floor of the chamber as best she could without sticking a hand through the force field.

I knew who she meant even before I looked. There was a human figure at the bottom of the control tower, so small between the huge, glowing screens and components that I hadn't noticed him earlier. He was sitting in a rather ordinary wheeled office chair, his hands rattling dexterously on the many keyboards. To my own self-disgust, I felt momentarily starstruck.

It was him. Malcolm Sturb. The former boy genius turned teen software mogul turned adult galactic scourge. By now, he was in his late twenties or early thirties, and was of average height and average build, save for a paunch consistent with a white-collar worker unaccustomed to exercise but very much accustomed to having a Danish pastry with their morning coffee. He was wearing an ordinary polo shirt, slacks, and a massive, ornate metal crown constructed from geometric shapes.

The man who had created the Malmind—ostensibly after growing bored with VR war games—was right in front of me. The brain. The master controller.

And I had a gun.

I pulled it from inside my jacket to coincide with my thoughts, and my excitement rose. Jemima's bulging eyes shone out from the darkness like a pair of headlights. "Are you sure about this? Is there any charge left in that?"

"There's more than enough," I said distantly. "And yes, I'm sure. I know what would be the best use for it."

"Really?" Jemima bit her lip. "Are you sure you want to use it up? I mean, you might need it later."

"I'm talking about killing Malcolm Sturb!" I hissed. "Ending the Malmind! The galactic scourge gone once and for all! I can finish the fight that

I and every other star pilot have only ever chipped away at for decades. What better use are you imagining for half a charge of blaster cell?"

By the end of my question I was already turning the blaster up to Solve All Immediate Problems and taking aim for the slumped figure silhouetted against the multiple screens. But Warden clamped a hand around my straightened elbow. "McKeown, if you fire that gun, every single hostile entity in this chamber will immediately know our position."

"Warden," I said, adopting her tone of voice. "It won't matter because all the hostile entities in the room can't do trac unless the central control hub is functioning, and the central control hub in question will be spread across the floor like jam on toast."

Her eyes flicked around as the cogwheels turned, then she released my arm. "Very well. Proceed."

I was about to, but I noticed a commotion in the cyborg mob. Sturb suddenly spun around in his office chair as his minions parted neatly. Alice was being brought forward by a pair of the humanoid cyborgs, each holding an arm. She was making up for that by getting as much motion as she could out of her legs, but they weren't touching the ground.

"Ah yes, the native girl," said Malcolm Sturb. I hadn't heard that he had a voice like one of those early twentieth century horror movie villains. "You are proving an annoyance again and again. Converting you first has now become a necessity."

"You can't make me keep still for it," said Alice through defiantly clenched teeth.

"I only need one minion to hold each limb," said Sturb matter-of-factly. "Unless you are hiding several thousand vestigial ones, I do not see this as an issue."

As if to illustrate his point, two cyborgified Ruggels ran up with perfect synchronicity and latched onto her shins. Even from a distance I could see the fear rising in Alice's eyes as Sturb took a step forward, toying with his fingers menacingly.

"We will . . . be avenged," quavered Alice.

Sturb folded his arms. "Girl, you are the only thing that even comes close to intelligent or physically threatening among that entire teddy bear collection you call a tribe. Honestly, who or what do you expect to be avenging you?"

And that sounded like as good a cue as any. I stood at the edge of the platform, spread my legs to optimal heroic-pose width, took a moment to make sure I was dynamically silhouetted against the glow from the force field behind me, and yelled, "STURRRB!"

Every face in the room turned in my direction. I must have made for quite an impressive sight, elevated above the Malmind horde with gun drawn and legs akimbo. It was the sort of situation that called for a one-liner.

"SUCK IT!" I roared, and pulled the trigger.

It had been a while since I'd had a chance to fire my blaster at full power, and I'd forgotten how much of a kick it had. A roaring ball of swirling energy burst from the barrel and smashed into a mob of Malmind cyborgs like a bowling ball into pins. I saw Sturb flinch with the impact, but it had missed him by several feet.

Once the moment passed, I realized that the reason I had missed so hugely was less about the recoil and more about Jemima, suddenly standing next to me and pushing on my wrist with all her strength.

"Jemima?!" I said.

"It's a real gun!" she called, apparently not addressing me.

"Real gun?" said Sturb, suddenly very pale and dropping his villainous accent. "You let him get this far carrying a real gun?" He directed this question at Alice, who had been freed by the cyborgs but was making no effort to escape or fight.

"You're the one who's supposed to take their weapons away. You're the villain," said Alice.

"Excuse me!" said Sturb petulantly. "It says quite clearly in the guide, if the participants are not disarmed in the first encounter, any available person should take the opportunity to do so when possible."

"I didn't know he had a gun!" Alice protested. She, too, had dropped the slightly alien lilt from her voice.

My legs were starting to get stiff from my heroic pose, and I still hadn't gotten my head around the situation, until Warden piped up. "McKeown. Look."

She was kneeling by the edge of our perch, and I saw what she was indicating. The cyborgs I had fired upon were reduced to scattered, fizzling pieces on the ground, surrounded by their completely unperturbed brethren. I saw a lot of scorched servos still whirring by themselves, and a lot of mechanical body parts with scraps of waxy fake skin hanging off them. What I wasn't seeing was much in the way of organic tissue.

"I don't believe these to be cyborgs at all," said Warden. "I think they are entirely robotic."

I thought back to the first one I had killed when we'd arrived on the planet. Its insides had been far too red hot and melted to properly inspect, but now that I thought back to it, the rubbery, dead look on its face could probably be explained by it being both made of rubber and not alive.

I hopped down into my newly created smoking patch of destruction, crunching motors and gears beneath my shoes. "Could someone please explain to me what is going on? Are you telling me that none of this has been real?"

The person I had assumed was Malcolm Sturb blustered indignantly. "Of course it's real! This is a genuine planet-saving experience straight from the Golden Age of star piloting. I mean, you can forget about VR. This is realer than real."

I let him finish, counted to three, then made my point. "I meant, not real in the sense that no one's actually being turned into cyborgs or in any danger at all."

He adjusted his crown. "Well. No. Not until you showed up swinging a real gun around, anyway."

I turned to Alice. "And presumably you weren't raised by sloths, either."

She picked awkwardly at her fur bikini and reddened. "No. But I am classically trained."

My scowling gaze then moved to a row of cyborg Ruggels, who were still standing nearby with frozen shocked expressions and their little arms held out. After a few seconds of concentrated glare, one of them caved, relaxed their arms, and morosely unclipped their fake cranial implant. That spurred the rest of them to do the same.

"Well, I feel like a plying chump now, don't I," I spat. "Ruggels. You even made the name cute. What are they really called?"

"We are Spercubulans," said the nearest ex-Ruggel, making me flinch. It spoke with a rather alarming voice that sounded like a death metal singer had given up his career to spend the rest of his life chain-smoking in a public bathroom.

"Deep space nomadic mercenaries," explained Alice, staring at the floor. "They do any work for pay. It's part of their honor system."

"Yeah," growled another Spercubulan, producing a switchblade from some kind of pouch like a marsupial's. "So you better not ruin this gig for us, or we'll cut yer."

"So what happened to the Zuvirons?" I asked, turning back to Sturb.

"Ugh. Suppose there's no reason to hide anything at this point, is there." He turned back to his cluster of keyboards and entered a lengthy password into one of the many competing screens.

There was a whining of hydraulics, and then a large Zuviron wall painting (depicting warfare, predictably) began to rumble, before sliding upward into a hidden recess and revealing a doorway marked with black-and-yellow stripes.

And beyond that was an elongated corridor, partly lit by wall-mounted torches and partly by numerous screens and hardware bedecked with glowing LEDs. I saw row after row of workstations like scaled-down versions of the one Sturb used, and at every single one, there sat a Zuviron. Each stared fixedly at a screen, with all four arms occupied with a controller of some kind. At least one of them that I could see was wearing a helmet with two cans of energy drink attached.

"Four arms, very good for working the controls," said the Sturb actor, as if that was the only thing that needed explaining. "Each of them can control two robots at once."

I recognized a couple of Zuviron warriors I'd fought alongside in the war. None of them looked physically unhealthier, I had to admit, but none of them were on their feet or engaged in a life-or-death grapple for their future, which, for them, was pretty unhealthy in a sense.

"Zovok," I said, addressing someone I had last seen tying the spinal columns of two cyberserkers into a knot, somehow without killing either. "What are you all doing here?"

He didn't even look at me. "We do what we have alwaysh done," he said through his tusks. "We fight for honor. We fight for glory."

I grabbed his naked thigh urgently. It was like slapping a beached whale, and he didn't even react. "But it's not real!"

"Honor demandsh that we fight and prove who ish the mightiesht," muttered Zovok reasonably. "Honor shaysh nothing about having to actually be in danger ash well. Thish way we have honor and don't loshe good breeding shtock."

I flung a hand back at the actors and depowered robots behind me, who had gathered to watch the whole scene passively from the doorway. "They're desecrating the tombs of your dead!"

"What need have the dead for honor?" asked Zovok. "Shuch shentiment ish usheless when Zovok ish jusht four hundred pointsh from the achievement."

I gave up and stomped back to the Malmind chamber, not stopping until I was close enough to address Jemima, who was still crouched guiltily on the upper path. "And you knew about this?"

"Well, I figured it out after they brought me here," she admitted. "When I noticed there wasn't really a force field. It was just fluorescent tubes and a buzzing noise. They came clean, and I said I'd play along."

"Why?" asked Warden, standing near her on the ledge and just as nonplused as I.

Jemima shrugged. "It was fun."

I clutched my temples for a moment. "We are trying to get you back to Robert Blaze before the UR stomps all over his station!"

Jemima scowled. "I keep telling you . . ."

"Robert Blaze?" said Alice, her attitude changing instantly from embarrassed guilt to urgent concern. "Is he in danger?"

"Do you know him?" asked Warden.

"He's the one who set all this up!" said Alice. "Gave us all these jobs."

Warden looked to me. "Is that right."

"Blaze did this?" I reiterated. I felt a growing sickness in my stomach, and I returned Warden's gaze. "We need to get off this planet right now. Me and Robert Blaze are going to have to have words."

The Malcolm Sturb impersonator touched his index fingertips together nervously. "You're not going to get him to shut all this down, are you?"

I gave him a withering look. "Do you know, I rather thought I might."

He looked hurt. "But . . . why?"

I splayed out my arms. "This is obscene! You've turned star piloting into a plying theme park! It's like prostitution on a planetary scale! I actually thought I was making a difference. I actually thought you were Malcolm Sturb!"

"I am Malcolm Sturb," said Malcolm Sturb.

"No, I meant the real Malcolm Sturb."

"I am the real Malcolm Sturb."

I scrutinized his face. I had never met the real Malcolm Sturb in person, but I'd seen plenty of photographs, usually just above or just below words like "The Enemy" and large sums being offered for reward. And the likeness between those and the man in front of me was, on reflection, uncanny. A great deal of complicated feelings started wrestling for space like baby birds in a nest, cheeping obnoxiously.

"Oh, trac, you are, aren't you," I said.

"Yeah, I just said."

"What the hell are you doing here?"

He seemed offended. "Trying to earn a living! Do you know how much it costs to keep a galaxy-spanning hive mind going? I had to uncyborg most of them just to get by. There isn't as much traffic around here as there used to be. You know what I blame? Quantum tunneling."

CHAPTER 22

WHEN I WAS a kid, my dad cheated on my mum. Just the once. As he said at the time, it could hardly have been avoided: he was French. The solution they hit upon to patch the whole mess up was a family holiday in Luny Land, which basically did the trick and ended up being one of the happier times in my childhood.

But I have a very clear memory of the journey there on the tube train. One of the most excruciating trips I've ever taken, right up there with that short lived nuclear waste dumping contract. Sitting in absolute silence for hours, with both my parents opposite each other, maintaining fixed, tight-lipped eye contact. I didn't dare to so much as ask for my coloring crayons in case the argument started again.

I bring this up because I was distinctly reminded of it by the atmosphere in Alice's borrowed shuttle as I flew Warden and Jemima back in the direction of Salvation Station. Except that Jemima had taken my role, while Warden and I were both sitting with arms folded, staring straight ahead, in perfect imitation of my mum.

Several hours in, I decided I was going to have to start talking about it, because otherwise I was going to grind all my teeth down to slivers. I unfolded my arms and took the joysticks, not to correct the steering, but because I suspected I would need something to grip. "Well?"

"Well what?" said Warden, in the passenger seat beside me.

"Haven't you got anything to say?" I said, it being the only thing I could think of to say. "Something along the lines of 'I told you so?'"

"Since you bring it up, then yes, I did say that something seemed wrong," she said, archly taking an interest in her armrest as she did so. "I admit I didn't think we had stumbled into an amusement arcade."

"I don't get why you had such a, you know, problem with it," said Jemima, in the tiny living space behind us. To my annoyance, she had insisted on leaving the Malmind lair through the gift shop and was now wearing a bright pink T-shirt bearing the words "I Was a Cantrabargid Captive!!"

I half turned in my seat and rested an elbow on the headrest to give her the full force of my glare. "Are you serious? Did you even see what was going on down there?"

Jemima gave one of those nervous quasi-smiles that weren't sure if they were going to break out or not. "I saw a lot of things, yeah. I saw a lot of people who seemed to be, you know, perfectly happy with it all."

I turned around and got my eyes back on the metaphorical road. "Well. I'm not happy. What you saw was exploitation. It's offensive to me and the entire calling of star piloting."

"Oh, what, so you want to try to shut down something that helps people just because it offends you?" said Jemima hotly. "Like what my mum does with all those newspaper companies?"

I kept my eyes on the view screen, but held up a single waggling finger. "It is not. The same thing."

"Why?" she insisted, in that infuriating teenage way.

I let the finger continue waggling for a few moments as I sought the words. "Warden. Tell her."

"Tell her what?" said Warden sniffily. "I agree with her that the arrangement seems to work perfectly well for all concerned. I'd rather discuss what plan we have for getting her back to her mother before the navy arrives."

"She's not going to send the navy, I keep telling you," insisted Jemima, after a tut and a sigh.

"You don't know that," said Warden dismissively.

Jemima stood up straight so quickly that her head sank an inch into the ceiling padding with a *thunk*. "Why does everyone think they know my mum better than I do?!" she raged, before stomping off toward the toilet door at the stern. "She's only been president for two years! I've had her for, like, sixteen!"

She slammed the toilet door shut behind her. I heard a clank as she sat huffily down on the toilet lid.

We flew in silence for another ten minutes, me glowering at the small cluster of stars we were making absolutely no significant progress toward, and Warden pretending to be taking an academic interest in the specks of cosmic dust that drifted past.

"Someone should talk to her," I said, hinting spitefully.

"People only ever say *someone* when they mean *you*," said Warden.

"All right, you should talk to her!" I snapped. "You know how to talk to kids. You were Daniel's tutor."

"Personal assistant," she said tightly, firing the syllables as if from a staple gun. "I can instruct children, yes, but I think this requires a different level of communication."

"I can't go back there. I'm the pilot."

"I didn't mean you. If the aim is to talk her out of her arrested develop-ment, I'd rather the blind not attempt to lead the blind."

"Listen here, you div—"

The debate ended suddenly when the control console blared an alert in my face to the effect that a ship nearby had locked its weapons onto our shuttle.

The view through the windshield was just the usual endless black with twinkly bits, so I flicked on the augmented-reality flight aid. The view became filled with bright green lines, wrapping themselves around the contours of a fleet of ugly black attack ships arranged in a grid that filled the view screen. More and more of the ships were locking weapons onto our shuttle, but no one was firing yet. The sleeping dragon had merely opened an eye and seen what appeared to be a fly buzzing around a turd.

"What the trac?" I said, reflexively.

"I think it might be the United Republic navy," said Warden. "It appears that Robert Blaze and his colleagues are in something of a strawberry jam situation."

"Never understood that phrase," I muttered, before addressing the toilet door. "Hey! Jemima! Wanna come see how much your mum doesn't care?"

She didn't reply. I heard the faint sound of tinny music. She must have had her ear-buds in.

"Whatever," I said, switching to the communication controls. "This should save a bit of time." I directed a broadcast to the nearest convenient ship. "This is . . . uh . . . a passenger shuttle we borrowed. We have the president's daugh-ter onboard our ship. Not a prisoner. That part is crucial. Not a prisoner.

Ready to return her when you are. Over." I put a hand on the mike and turned to Warden. "Anything you want to add?"

I was answered by a burst of static, and then the voice of a woman, speaking with extreme measured politeness with more than a hint of eroticism. "Attention. Thank you for coming within missile range of this United Republic naval battleship. We are currently maintaining a perimeter around this region of space. Please reverse and seek alternative routes, as any attempt to encroach further will be treated as hostility. If you would like to learn more about the United Republic Navy, including current maneuvers and job opportunities, please contact . . ."

"Just one thing," said Warden. "The UR Navy mostly consists of unmanned ships."

I flicked the communicator off with a frustrated grunt. "Right. So that was plying pointless, wasn't it. And we'll never be able to break through a naval perimeter in this . . . thing."

"There may be a gap in their coverage," suggested Warden.

"And there might not be. And once we've gone all the way around looking for it, it'll be too late. The rescue fleet will have torn Salvation Station apart looking for something to rescue." I tapped my forehead rapidly as I thought aloud, and it soon began to hurt. "There's got to be someone we can call, let them know we've got the person they're looking for. Surely you've got contacts in the government?"

"Yes, but I threw my phone out of the airlock when I resolved to kidnap Mr. Henderson's son."

"Oh yeah," I said. "And I did that too, didn't I."

"Not before . . ."

"Not before he called me and told me about Jemima, no, but I did after that. Give me some credit." I blew out my cheeks. "Okay then. Forget calling someone. We've got to find a way past the perimeter without being noticed."

"It occurs to me that a Quantunnel would be enormously useful at this point, if Blaze's people have completed their gate," said Warden.

I felt the usual surge of anger I felt whenever someone suggested using a Quantunnel, but managed to redirect it to a different part of my brain, and the energy boost sent a sequence of wheels turning. "Hang on. We can't Quantunnel. But what's the next best thing to Quantunnels?"

"Don't milk it, McKeown. Do you have a plan?"

"Trebuchet gates," I said, slightly miffed. "There's a trebuchet gate very close to Cantrabargid; that's why I always used it for my charter tours. We can reach that and get launched with time to spare."

"That would propel us too far, surely."

"There's another crafty little hack you can do with them, kind of like the opposite of what we did last time," I said, running the numbers through my head as we spoke. "You activate the launch before it's fully charged, and you can get thrown a shorter distance with slightly more accuracy. I think I can get us within the perimeter, maybe even right up close to Salvation."

"Is it safe?" asked Warden.

"No," I said, having anticipated the question. "Although I'll be plied if I can think of anything else to do. Except maybe fly all the way back to the Solar System and drop Jemima off to her mother directly."

"NO," said Warden, loudly.

"No, I'm not a fan of that one either. Trebuchet it is."

My wounded hand started throbbing again as we neared the Cantrabargid trebuchet gate, and I started to wonder if going back to the Solar System was actually as impossible as it had seemed. Without the chip I wasn't legally Jacques McKeown at present, and those star pilots who wanted me dead had probably all lost interest in the matter around the time their weekly fuel bill showed up.

"McKeown," said Warden suddenly.

I snapped out of my reverie. "Hm?"

"Concentrate, McKeown, we are nearly there."

Sure enough, the rather old and poorly-maintained trebuchet gate was filling the viewscreen, a giant, metallic pacifier hanging in space. "All right, let's see if I can actually pull this off," I said, mostly to myself, as I got to work interfacing with the gate and making the navigational calculations.

So, I thought. Why not go home to Ritsuko City? The fact was, I supposed, that I wanted to be here, and I wanted to save Robert Blaze. I liked the idea of a place for pilots in the universe. What I'd seen on Cantrabargid was making me go off his specific vision pretty plying fast, but I still wanted to save him. That, and now maybe kick him in the doints a few times, as well.

"What exactly is the risk here?" asked Warden. Her voice seemed to be particularly abrasive on this occasion.

"It should be easy as long as I can stay *focused*." I peered at the numbers before me, and my thoughts drifted almost immediately away again. I was in pain, tired, and coming down from angry adrenaline. My brain had thrown itself onto a mattress in a sulk, curled up, and was refusing to respond.

I screwed my eyes up tight and opened them again, a technique that has never, ever worked in the entire history of man. The wall of figures I was proposing to ram our shuttle through swam momentarily back into focus, but Warden's constant staring threw me off again. I saw her glance behind her—Jemima was still in the rear toilet listening to what sounded like theme songs from Japanese cartoons—and release an irritated sigh.

"McKeown, I think we should have sex."

I did the eye-screw thing a second time, then a third, then clenched my fists. "I am trying to concentrate on this jump so we don't end up crushed up against Salvation Station's hull," I said measuredly. "That statement did the opposite of helping."

"Don't be willfully dense," chided Warden. "It is obvious that built-up frustration is affecting your judgment, and if it will ensure our survival, I am willing to make a sacrifice."

I sat back in my chair and stared at her. She had the same stiff posture and cold tone of voice as always, not exactly throwing herself into the task of seduction. "Make a sacrifice? Oh, aren't you just plying full of the milk of human kindness."

She curled her mouth disgustedly. "You are physically attracted to me. It was increasingly obvious when we were being forced to work together on that planet. I'm only suggesting that we optimize our current resources."

"And you honestly think that getting within a plying light year of your current resources would ease my tension? I'd be afraid of something getting bitten off."

She straightened her back, offended. "Your embarrassment is wasting time. I am willing to brave this unpleasantness; I am only asking to be met halfway."

I gave her a sidelong look through narrowed eyes, and she shifted uncomfortably. "Ohhh," I said. "I know what this is all about." She didn't respond, although she maintained glaring eye contact. I continued. "This isn't about throwing yourself on the sacrificial altar of my libido. You're not that magnanimous. You're the one with the frustration built up and you're the one that secretly wants to ply me rotten."

She colored. "McKeown . . ."

"Scratch that—you just want to ply *something* rotten. But you can't let yourself think that, oh no. That would be showing far too much emotion for the plying psycho-div. So you've got to convince yourself that you really don't want to and that you've got no choice so that you're free to have all the dirty hate sex you want without fear of ruining your image."

She was squirming in her seat, limbs locked, and I fancied she was about to start sweating poison like a tree frog. "What . . . on Earth . . . makes you think . . . that I would want to . . ."

She was having problems getting her mouth around the words, so I took over again. "You brought it up, you plying nutcase. Are you like this because of Henderson? You have to build up a big wall because if it ever cracks he might see your weaknesses? And now everything you've suppressed is rushing to the surface and overflowing the dam and you just thought, hey, here's this rugged star pilot over here who might be able to stick a finger in the hole to stop the leak—actually, that was a bad choice of words . . ."

"*McKeown*," she intoned. The straining dam had given a little squirt. "How could I possibly be attracted to you?" She pronounced the last three words the way one would pronounce *louse-ridden*.

I folded my arms, springing the trap. "I never said you were. I just said you were after dirty, consequence-free sex with whatever was convenient. How strange that your mind should go there—"

"*Enough*. I am not the *slightest* bit attracted to you. I don't even know who you *are*!"

I raised my eyebrows, surprised. She let out a long breath, then almost immediately drew it all back in.

"That's why I keep calling you McKeown!" she continued. "Because when I went to change your name on the chip ID network, I discovered that there were *three* names already on it! And not even the authorities seemed to know which one you were born with!"

She slumped in her seat and turned away. I thought the outburst was over, but then she suddenly sprang back into life like a mantrap. "When I came to that spaceport, looking for a pilot, I was convinced that I would not survive to the dawn. It was my last, tiniest scrap of hope. I was going to present a random bum to Mr. Henderson and introduce him as Jacques McKeown. I was certain that Henderson would see through it in an instant and we'd both be meat for the cassowaries."

"Charming." But I wasn't sure if I was more offended by her willful endangerment of my life or use of the words *random bum*.

"But then we got through the dinner, and I realized that I'd stumbled upon the perfect candidate entirely by accident. Someone who can wear any disguise he wants because there's nothing underneath. You just adapt. You become whatever you need to be."

"Thank . . . you?"

"It was not a compliment!" She was practically screeching now, and her hands were bobbing madly as she sought the words. "You are a cockroach, McKeown! You get dropped into a situation and you scrape together whatever you need to survive a little bit longer! You've got no idea how to plan. How to build anything or make something of your life. Your only conviction is the desire to live a stupid space-hero fantasy! I don't understand how someone can be so adaptable and at the same time so intent on clinging to the past!"

She deflated a little, bracing herself on the armrests, and I thought the storm might have passed but then recognized her posture as that of someone midheave during a protracted vomiting session.

Sure enough, the hands came up again. "And if I have occasionally found you interesting solely on some academic level, then it was only because I have never been able—"

Something seemed to get through to her conscious mind and she immediately clammed up, wrapping her arms around herself and shrinking in her seat. It was like a misbehaving umbrella finally closing and snapping into place. Her eyes focused determinedly on the viewscreen in front of her. Only her beet-red complexion remained as evidence of her rant.

I chewed on my lip as the silence dragged on. Then I gave a little cough. "Feel better?"

"Yes," came a tiny little voice from somewhere inside the tightly folded package of her body.

"How was it for you, darling?"

"Just launch the plying ship, McKeown."

CHAPTER 23

THERE WAS A sickening surge of turbulence, a disorienting dance of light and color across the view screen, and the shuttle emerged lurchily from the short-range trebuchet jump.

Salvation Station was very close. In fact, it was filling most of the view.

I slammed on the braking thrusters, knowing full well it wasn't going to stop us in time, and yanked on the stick. The shuttle spun into a full turn, and we found ourselves hurtling backward along Salvation Station's armored hull.

The actual distance between the shuttle and the station was hard to determine when the view screen showed nothing but blurred metal plating. I thought it would be safe to bank away, whereupon one of the shuttle's fins smashed into what I supposed was one of the station's defensive turrets, and we went into a violent spin.

The shuttle's artificial gravity drive kept us from being thrown around, but the spinning view brought me perilously close to redecorating the interior a lovely shade of puke. I was leaning so hard on the pitch controls that I heard a *crack* and one of the screws in the control bank popped out and pinged away.

Finally, the thrusters caused the spin to slow, and I went through the dance of overcompensating and counter-overcompensating. Eventually, the shuttle leveled out smoothly, and I let my muscles untense in relief.

Moments later, they all tensed back up again when I realized we were heading straight for Salvation Station's main docking bay, upside down. We'd slowed significantly, but not enough to stop us from passing through the force field and falling into Salvation's internal gravity.

The shuttle's roof hit the floor of the docking bay, and that was all we saw through the view screen as we skidded gradually to a halt, throwing up sparks as we went. I could feel the fins smashing through numerous loose objects, which my imagination decided must be the legs and torsos of numerous innocent bystanders.

Then we stopped, and the shuttle rocked back on its curved roof, letting us see the docking bay properly. It was the same one that we'd arrived in the last time, but it was now completely deserted but for a handful of ships. We'd been plowing through crates that seemed to have been prepared for loading.

There was a beep as the shuttle liaised with Salvation's internal atmosphere, and the gravity was switched to match the rest of the station. The ceiling immediately became a floor, upon which Warden and I landed in a pile.

"How very smoothly done, McKeown," said Warden from somewhere underneath my left leg.

"No, I guess you were right," I said, still groggy from the trebuchet jump. "We probably should have plied each other senseless first."

I struggled out of the knot of limbs and managed to get upright, then made for the airlock door. The toilet slid open and Jemima crawled out, looking rather green about the gills.

She looked up at me blearily as I struggled with the airlock door handle. "Upside down," she mumbled.

"I knew that," I replied, turning it the other way.

Once out in the docking bay, I could confirm that it was almost completely deserted. One or two technicians and pilots were coming and going via the main access to the concourse, hastily dropping supplies near the parked ships, but that was all. They must have noticed our entrance, but they appeared to be far too occupied to care. They glanced only briefly at the crates we had destroyed during our landing.

The next thing I noticed was the Platinum God of Whale Sharks, which was squatting on a parking space in the corner like a huge, fat dog sitting somewhat alert. A freshly brushed dog with a brand-new collar, because repairs had been made to the damaged hull and nacelle. The breaches were patched to a semiprofessional standard, and the entire ship had been recently spray-painted a vibrant red.

I was walking slowly up to it, brow furrowed and jaw slack, when I heard a familiar voice call one of my names. "Mr. McKeown! You're back!"

Daniel was there, clutching a small box of what looked like souvenirs, which he immediately set down so he could scamper over. "Did you win?"

"What?"

"Mr. Blaze said you had to go off for a while to fight evil and right wrongs." His eyes were shining. I noticed he'd discarded his silver jumpsuit in favor of a brand-new flight jacket adorned with Salvation Station logos, which was at least slightly less pretentious. "Is all the evil finished then?"

"Working on it," I said, distantly. "Where is Mr. Blaze?"

"Jemima!" shrieked Daniel, noticing his crush appear from the inverted shuttle in the background. Without even a glance back at me, he trotted straight over to her, screeching to a halt the moment he was in the three-foot hover radius. "You missed everything! Mr. Blaze fixed our ship and he's been teaching me how to fly it! It's actually really easy!"

"DANIEL," I shouted, loud enough to echo around the docking bay. He gave a little jump and returned his gaze to me. "I said, where is Mr. Blaze?"

"Oh, he's just outside," said Daniel, gesturing to the doors that led to the station's main concourse. "He's really worried about something; he keeps trying to get people to leave."

I passed into the concourse and saw Blaze immediately. He stood addressing a small group of his crew as others hurried past in both directions, carrying crates. He gave a steady stream of orders in his reassuring voice, without barking or forgetting to say please, although his shoulders were hunched and his eyelids were heavy with exhaustion.

He noticed my appearance almost immediately. His eyebrows went up and the lower corners of his mouth pulled away from his teeth, in a smile that anticipated an awkward conversation. He extended a half-open hand. "Mister—"

I punched him. Grabbing his proffered hand and pulling him forward added considerable stopping power to my flying fist, which sent him right onto his back, bleeding from a split lip. But I kept holding his hand, and once he was on the floor, I transitioned his weakening grip to my wrist and showed him the bandage he had given me.

"What was all this about?!" I said, pointing, not having improved my ability to come up with spontaneous, dramatic one-liners.

"You . . . have every right . . . to be angry," he said, with some difficulty. A couple of technicians who had been moving upon my flanks stopped short as Blaze waved with his free hand. "Look. I may have given the impression that . . . our project was better funded than it is. That's why I took your chip. We had debts we needed to pay straightaway, and . . . I thought you would see the logic if I gave you time to cool off."

"Yeah, I guessed that much," I snarled. "How about you see if you can cool off my fist before it hits your face?" I raised it for another punch, but a burly pilot appeared from the throng and seized my arm by the elbow.

Blaze was getting up, with the assistance of two members of his entourage. "I take it you weren't impressed by what we're doing on Cantrabargid," he said grimly.

"Impressed?!" I echoed. "It's an insult! You're turning the Golden Age of star piloting into a plying theme park!"

He straightened his back, and his eyes set to a-twinkling again, but this time it was a sad twinkle, like the glistening of light off held-back tears. "The Golden Age is over. That's what I need you and everyone else to understand. We can't deny that and we can't change it. What we can do is commemorate it."

"Oh, right," I said, nodding. "With bikini girls and cuddly toys?"

"No, it's not an accurate re-creation of that specific war. But it's the same basic story as every other planet that star pilots have saved. We're just compressing all of those histories into one. The spirit, the true meaning, of what you did for Cantrabargid, and what all the other pilots did for all those other planets—that's what's going to live on. That's all that matters."

"But it's not *true!*" I insisted.

He folded his arms. "Look, you can't just tell people not to be bored. You have to meet them halfway. We've spiced it up for broader appeal so that the message can reach as many people as possible."

"But . . ." I faltered. "Malcolm Sturb should be in jail, at least."

"He's changed. A lot of things have changed." Blaze's chest puffed up with melancholy passion. "Quantunneling changed everything. Either you change with it, or you spend your whole life scuttling around the wreckage of everything else that couldn't change. Like some kind of . . ."

"Cockroach," said Warden from somewhere behind me. I very deliberately avoided looking at her. "Can we move on? Is the station being evacuated?"

Blaze deflated, crestfallen. "Yes. A Terran fleet is approaching from multiple directions."

"We noticed," said Warden, deadpan.

"But there's a gap in the perimeter, and we're getting as many of our people through it as we can before they arrive." He seemed to notice the growing crowd of onlookers and waved them away. They immediately returned to their escape preparations.

"A gap in the perimeter, you say," said Warden, giving me an accusing look.

"You know full well it would have taken too long to check," I said, from the corner of my mouth.

"At first, I thought they were the fleet that had come to get Daniel back," said Blaze. "I'd already called his father and told him where he was."

"For a reward," I interjected.

He sighed. He didn't look guilty, just sad. "But they haven't responded to any of my offers to return him. I fear this may be our debts being called in sooner than I expected."

"The United Republic don't even interfere with Ritsuko City, and that's right on the Earth's doorstep," said Warden. "They have even less interest in the finances of deep space pseudo-colonies."

"Yeah, they're here for Jemima, not you," I clarified.

Blaze's brow furrowed. "The girl? Why?"

"She's the president's daughter." His eyes bulged, and I felt moved to interrupt as he opened his mouth to say something incredulous. "Yes, she really is the president's daughter. And not that you deserve it, but we've brought her back here so that you can hand her over before this place gets turned upside down, and in return, you can—"

I was raising my voice over an engine roar that I had, up to this point, been attributing to one of the remaining ships in the docking bay heading off to join the evacuation fleet. But then I remembered that there was only one ship in the bay whose engine sounded like the drawn-out, dying fart of a beached whale.

I darted back a step and stood, stunned, in the entrance to the docking bay as the Platinum God of Whale Sharks lurched out of the station. The engine noise ceased abruptly as the ship passed through the force field into the vacuum of space, then bobbed sickeningly and sped out of sight. Jemima and Daniel were nowhere to be seen.

My hands clenched pointlessly at the air. My first instinct had been to run forward and yell something along the lines of "come back," but that already felt stupid. Instead, I let my arms drop and my entire upper body slumped forward.

Warden appeared in my peripheral vision, so I jabbed a finger in her direction. "You know," I growled, "for an oppressive regime, you lot are really plying bad at keeping the children disciplined."

"Yeah, we saw the Whale Shark," said Peter, his voice emanating from Blaze's speakerphone. "It broke off from the evac fleet and was heading toward Black Central Point."

Blaze gripped his phone tightly, his knuckles whitening. "That's not a safe zone," he said. "We haven't cleared the pirate clans out yet. There might even be Zoobs." The point of his hook rattled nervously against his phone's touchscreen.

"You'd almost think something had given the impression that the Black was a fun place where there isn't any real danger," I said, leaning against a nearby pillar with arms folded.

"There's something else," said Peter. He was all business, so presumably Pippa wasn't in the room with him. "We did a check on the incoming fleet. It's a couple of hours away still. But it's not just Republic Navy."

Blaze met my look. "What is it?"

"It's mostly Republic, maybe eighty percent, but they've made up the numbers with, er, mercenary talent."

"You mean star pilots," I said.

"Yeah," he admitted sheepishly. "Looks like they've hired every contractor in Ritsuko City."

"Yes, that all sounds to be in order," said Warden, fiddling with her datapad. "Even a partial perimeter would severely tax the Republic Navy. Since civil disobedience is the bigger problem, a lot of the government wonders why they even need an interstellar navy at all."

Blaze's legs gave out under him, and he sat on the floor, staring at his phone. His face was as gray as ash. His mouth opened and closed silently like a kicked dog mournfully licking up spilled peanut butter. "The very people I'm doing all this for," he mumbled. He looked up, a little bit of that Robert Blaze fire sparking and dying in his eyes. "I can't let it all be for nothing. I can't let them rip apart the one thing that could have helped them. That's not star piloting. Is it?"

I'd been angry at him, but that anger was being drowned out by my feelings at seeing my biggest hero plop down on the floor, defeated. It was like seeing my dad cry, only without being able to blame it on the cheap whiskey. I coughed uncomfortably. "Could we conceivably just call the navy and tell them Jemima isn't on the station now?"

"I see you're not familiar with United Republic antiterror procedure," said Warden down her nose. "If we tell them that, it will only make them wonder why we're so keen for them to not come here."

Blaze shook his head, eyes wide. "We can't let them search the station top to bottom. It's practically wallpapered in stolen goods."

"And if they can't find Jemima, they will certainly be looking for reasons to justify their incursion," said Warden thoughtfully, tapping her foot.

I sighed. "We're going after Jemima."

"We are," said Warden. With her usual infuriating lack of expression, I wasn't completely sure if she'd put a question mark on the end or not.

"We'll bring her back," I continued. "And then the navy can take her and go away happy. And then we can have a very fruitful conversation about the future of your whole project out here."

He stared up at me in wonder, his eyes not quite doing the twinkle thing, but certainly on twinkle standby. "You would do that for me? Why?"

"Gratitude," I said.

"For what?"

I held out my uninjured hand. "For very kindly returning my ID chip."

The twinkle standby ended, and his face darkened a little. But he dug into his jeans pocket and produced a brown envelope, stained with a little blood. I checked its contents. A tiny piece of plastic the size of a rice grain. I'd never seen an ID chip outside the skin before, but it seemed legit.

"Right," I said, closing my fist around the envelope. "I'm gonna need a couple of lads to flip our shuttle over."

I started heading back to the docking bay, gesturing to a couple of the burlier, less argumentative-looking members of the throng, but Blaze quickly rose to his feet. "You know that you're not actually entitled to Jacques McKeown's money?"

That made me stop, and I gave him a thoughtful look over my shoulder, the kind a chess master makes when his opponent wanders straight into an unbelievably obvious trap. "Yeah. Remind me how you know that?"

All expression immediately left his face in a very deliberate kind of way, so that he and Warden, standing next to each other, were like a pair of Buddha statues. But I'd already seen that momentary flash of guilt.

I pointed at his face. "Conversation. Later."

CHAPTER 24

MY CONFIDENCE DRAINED somewhat after the shuttle had been uprighted and Warden and I had set off, bound vaguely for the Black's central point. The shuttle had taken more damage than I'd thought, probably from when the nacelle had hit the turret gun on our way in. It was trundling up to top speed like a rickshaw driver ten years past optimal retirement age.

Of course, the Platinum God of Whale Sharks moved like a rickshaw driver twenty years past prime that had managed to run himself over with his own vehicle, so whether or not we would catch up with the *Jemima* (along with the other Jemima) wasn't so much an issueh as whether or not we could do so in time.

Blaze had lent us one of his more efficient scanning units, which was now taking up most of what little wiggle room there was in the cockpit, and I was spamming the blip constantly as we flew. The navy fleet lit up the screen like a perfectly laid-out semicircular flowerbed, with the star pilot fleet forming the uppermost section of the arc like an unwanted dog turd. The gap between them and Salvation was closing a lot faster than the one between us and the fat little blob that represented the *Jemima*.

"We aren't going to make it," I said darkly. "By the time we get there and back, Salvation'll be turned upside down."

"Perhaps there is a way to delay the navy," said Warden, who had been sitting thoughtfully in silence for some time, tapping her chin with a finger. "Can you contact them?"

I raised an eyebrow at her. "This shuttle's designed for ship-to-surface transport; it's only got short-range comms. We'd need to get in close to a manned ship. Assuming there are any manned ships."

"There'd have to be, for command and boarding. Almost certainly in the center." She pointed to the midpoint of the fleet on the scanner screen.

"So what do we tell them?"

"Just leave that to me, McKeown."

I eyed her with open suspicion. "Are you really that invested in saving Salvation? Trac, that sounded weird."

"It remains my best hope for a place to exist out here that can make some use of my skill set." She eyed the scanner screen. "Hopefully this venture will prove that. But a little more incentive wouldn't hurt."

She met my gaze. I felt my mouth tighten up. "What else do you want?"

"Do you remember the deal we made the last time you needed me to delay a United Republic military unit? I would like to make the same deal."

"You . . . want to hold onto my blaster again?"

"How many shots are left in it?"

I took it out of my shoulder holster and checked. I really should have taken the opportunity to find a new cell while I was on Salvation, but everything had been rather flustered. "Depending on the setting, it could stun maybe two or three people. Or blow one person's leg off. What do you want it for this time?"

"I wouldn't expect you to understand, Mr. McKeown. As we've established, you're not the kind of person who plans ahead."

She raised an eyebrow slightly, which was her equivalent of a cocky, trac-eating grin. I didn't like it.

"You are obstructing a United Republic peacekeeping force in the execution of urgent official duties," said a voice from the short-range communicator. It sounded bored, but not automated. "This statement is to be considered for all official purposes your one mandated warning."

Like a rubber mouse dangling before the face of a deceptively immobile cat, our shuttle hung in front of the large battleship that lay in the exact center of the naval fleet. It was only by hailing every ship within broadcast range that we had been able to identify the manned ships. For obvious tactical purposes, they were identical to the automated ones: sleek black lines and barely concealed weapon tubes, unpretentiously broadcasting on every visual level that something was about to get ground into space dust under the unfeeling jackboot of power.

Unintimidated, Warden leaned in close to the communicator, resting her folded arms upon the console. "My name is Penelope Warden, and I currently represent the ruling authority of the Salvation Station deep space colony," she droned. "I am formally requesting an explanation for your incursion upon sovereign territory."

There was a slightly stunned pause, then a fluttering of paperwork, before the poor bracket manning the ship's communication console replied. "Our orders are to search this sector and the pirate station and rescue the president's daughter."

"Then please submit your warrant so that the local authorities can assess the situation and come to an extradition agreement, as laid out in the Extrasolar Nation and Colony Diplomatic Protocols. In accordance with the same document, the station is considered a sovereign nation, meeting the requirements for population, government, and local law enforcement."

"Could you hold, please?" Then a click.

"Is that a real document?" I asked, while we waited.

"It was very hastily drawn up a long time ago, more for political point scoring than anything else," said Warden, not looking away from some dense, technical-looking documents on her datapad, of which she was busily refreshing her memory. "It's full of loopholes but has never been assessed or amended because the Republic has little interest in external affairs. I see no reason why—"

The comms unit suddenly ceased playing electronic smooth jazz with an ugly crackle. "Ms. Warden, is that you?" said a female voice.

Warden went white. "Ms. Sternall," she said, fighting to keep expression out of her voice.

It took me a moment to remember. It was the woman I'd seen with Henderson on the landing pad when we'd first taken off in the God of Whale Sharks. The one who had basically been a younger, slightly prettier clone of Warden, and who had taken over her duties after her "promotion."

"What a wonderful surprise to hear from you," said Sternall, with the kind of warmth that fails to make even an icecube sweat.

"Likewise," replied Warden, her lips quivering like she was about to throw up.

"So good to hear you're managing to stay active," continued Sternall. "But you don't seem to be fully familiar with the law. No extradition or warrant is required of a United Republic naval search-and-extraction excursion if it is taking place in United Republic territory."

Warden caught my eye, perhaps in a failed attempt to reassure. "But this is not United Republic territory."

"Oh, I'm sorry, if you'd read Extrasolar Nation and Colony Diplomatic Protocols properly, you would have known that, considering the impracticality of establishing embassies on every little extrasolar colony that has its own government, any territory occupied by an official United Republic ambassador to within a radius of fifty meters is considered a de facto embassy, and under United Republic responsibility, in order to ensure the safety of our representative."

"So?"

"So, in accordance with the Timmler Act, all close relations of United Republic presidents are automatically granted ambassadorial status while abroad," concluded Sternall with unshaking confidence. "This was made law after the incident with President Timmler's son and the urine fountain."

"Surely they can't actually do that," I whispered to Warden, practically mouthing the words. She appeared to have frozen. Were it not for the visible beads of sweat, I might as well have been talking to a mannequin for an extremely boring clothes shop.

"So, you have already had your warning," added Sternall when no reply came. "Please move out of the way so that we can take care of this internal matter."

"Jemima is not currently on Salvation Station," said Warden, closing her eyes tightly.

"Then you will have no objection to us searching it, very, very thoroughly. Because I'm sure you wouldn't be trying to hide something there."

The scanner reported that one of the ships in the fleet had powered up its weapons. And once it had broken that particular taboo, the rest of them quickly followed suit, sending their icons flashing like rows of Christmas lights. Warden was still silent and unmoving.

I sighed and took up the joysticks. "Well, so much for that."

Warden's hand snapped around my wrist apparently without moving through any of the intervening space. She squeezed so hard that all my fingers detached from the joystick at once. "*Wait*," she barked, delivering the word like an iron rivet being hammered home.

"Warden . . ." said Sternall tiredly.

Warden's fingers began flying across her datapad, her many short, sharp movements sending little sprinkles of sweat across the enclosed cabin. "According to your manifest, you are carrying a company of marines, armed and equipped for boardings, infiltrations, and suppression?"

"As I said, the search of the station will be very, very thorough," said Sternall, still smug but sensing danger. "The team will need to be equipped to suppress anything that obstructs their official duties. That applies to locked doors, security systems, walls, and human throats. All in accordance with naval regulations, as I'm *sure* you know." She delivered the emphasis on *sure* like a dagger under the ribs.

"And is each man equipped with regulation uniform and equipment?"

"I personally made certain of that, as is my duty. All fully cleaned and checked for optimal performance. Uniforms, helmets, body armor, boots—"

"Black leather boots?" interjected Warden.

"Of course."

Warden's datapad slammed onto her thigh like a winning touchdown. "Salvation Station has polished flooring, not carpeting."

Sternall made a little choking noise that might have been classified as a laugh by the broadest definition imaginable. "What has that got to do with anything?"

"Black leather boots will almost certainly cover the flooring in scuff marks. If firearms are employed, scorch marks will be left on walls and surfaces."

"So?"

"If you would go back to the Extrasolar Nation and Colony Diplomatic Protocols and refer to the section related to the maintenance of embassies and ambassadorial vehicles, it clearly states that all equipment and materials intended for redecorating official United Republic embassies must be fully rated for health and safety before use. And the safety record of marine-regulation footwear is very suspect. I can show you advertisements from the manufacturers themselves attesting to that." Her datapad was displaying a poster for leather boots, showing them crushing the face of a long-haired young liberal with great strength and efficiency. She was sitting with a relaxed posture again and was already bone dry.

Sternall was deathly silent, so Warden took the opportunity to put a few more kicks in. "Your operation cannot be permitted until your uniforms and weaponry are fully rated for use as decorating supplies.

As I'm sure you would have been aware, had you read the protocols properly."

I heard a sound that took me a second or two to recognze as a stack of papers being angrily thrown down. "Why the hell are you doing this, Warden?!" yelled Sternall.

Warden smiled and recrossed her legs. For her, she might as well have been thrusting both fists into the air as she ran a victory lap, hooting like a baboon. "I simply cannot in good conscience permit any operation to proceed without rigorous adherence to United Republic law. Although you may find that the operation is no longer necessary."

"How so?"

"Because by my estimate the checks will take at least six hours, and by then, Jemima will have been returned to you. And you will be able to take her home unchallenged. For some reason, I am extremely confident of that."

There was the sound of well-maintained fingernails tapping on scattered paperwork. "Fine. Six hours." Then the line went dead.

One by one, the little warning lights on the scanner scope, the ones indicating ships with activated weaponry, disappeared. Every ship in the fleet braked to a halt and deactivated engines. The dragon went back to sleep a bit at a time, lulled by the sweet music of bureaucracy.

Warden sank back in her seat and released a long, satisfied sigh like a deflating beach ball. A response that I was sure no amount of consequence-free, dirty hate sex could have provoked.

I gave her a knowing look as I set our course for the *Jemima*, and felt her irritation rise as she met my gaze. "Well," I said. "Look at Miss Adaptable over here."

She turned away. "There are, of course, many different species of cockroach." Her eye fell upon the radar screen, and she sat up. "The star pilot fleet is still moving."

I'd already noticed that. "They must be on Henderson's payroll, rather than the navy's. Don't worry about it. This is where I come in."

"I can tell what you're planning to do," she said. "And I don't think it will work. They've been paid, and money is all that matters to a mercenary."

I waved a hand. "A star pilot might look like a mercenary, talk like a mercenary, act like a mercenary," I said, "but they can't stop being a star pilot under all that. You'll see."

CHAPTER 25

AFTER COMPLETING MY transmission to the star pilot fleet, the damaged shuttle trundled its way toward the blob that marked the *Jemima*, and hopefully both of the kids. All the way, I kept my eye on the clustered pixels on the scanner screen that represented the fleets. The navy remained stock still, and I had a mental image of the onboard infiltration team mournfully unloading their blasters and taping cushions to the soles of their boots. The star pilot fleet was moving, but in many different directions, confused.

Warden suddenly leaned forward like a mousetrap springing and tapped the dot representing the *Jemima*. "It isn't moving."

She was right. We were catching up to it a lot faster than before. It seemed to have stopped dead a handful of light minutes from the Black's arbitrarily chosen central point. I would have immediately pushed the engines up a notch if they weren't already flat out.

"This is either a very good or a very bad development," I said, gripping the joysticks in the vain hope that they might rev like a motorbike's handlebar. "Or a bit of one and a bit of the other."

"No food, no plans, no knowledge of the area," said Warden. "Perhaps they have simply realized the futility of this gesture."

I tried to fit the idea of logic and rationality into my image of young people their age. It wasn't a comfortable fit. "Or maybe Daniel pushed the engine too hard. He can't have had many lessons."

Daniel had said that Blaze had been teaching him how to fly. We'd only been stranded on Cantrabargid for roughly a day and a bit, depending on how long the homebrew wine had kept me knocked out. And they would have had to repair the ship before anything else. I tried to calculate how much Blaze could have taught Daniel in that amount of time. If we went by how they taught it in flight school, he would still have been filling in multiple-choice tests on when it's appropriate to overtake on a busy space lane.

Probably safe to assume that he wasn't being taught by the book, then. It would certainly have been possible to learn how to start the ship and get it moving in a specific direction. Maybe even how to land it, as well. After that, it's mostly engine maintenance, spaceway code, and building up enough practice to get the muscle memory locked in.

But he was flying the God of Whale Sharks, and a big, complicated lady like that requires an experienced hand to guide it around the dance floor. He'd probably just overheated it. I tried to remember if I'd replaced that coolant rod I'd deactivated way back before we left the Solar System. I didn't have any specific memories of doing so. Yes, that had to be it. Daniel must have been trying to show off and the two of them were now sitting alone in the admonishing glow of red warning lights feeling like a pair of plying stupid doints.

Soon we were close enough to zoom the scanning view in a bit. The moment I did so, I noticed that the blob representing the *Jemima* was, in fact, two blobs, so close together that they had appeared to be one on the wider view.

"Oh, trac," I murmured.

"What?" said Warden.

I held up a finger to suspend the discussion for a moment, because we were about to enter visual range. I noticed a red dot in the distance ahead, so with the aid of the augmented-reality view screen, I drew a shimmering green rectangle around it with my finger, then stretched it out to ten times its size. The ships were blurry but unmistakeable.

"Oh, traccy traccy ply ply bracket doints and divs."

"What is it, McKeown?"

There was the *Jemima*, impossible to miss with its size and new paint job. One of the nacelles was hanging off, still attached to the ship only by a lump of twisted metal, partly charred black and partly glowing orange with heat. I was no crime scene investigator, but it seemed to me like the work of fairly standard weapon systems.

Presumably the weapon systems of the ship that was now attached to the Jemima by a filthy yellow-brown umbilical. It was slightly bigger, but not cargo-transporter-big, this was more toward the warship side of things. It was disk shaped, and whatever color its previous paint job had been, it was concealed under a brown crust of space filth.

"It's a Zoob ship," I identified aloud.

"The mascot creatures that turned violent?" asked Warden.

I did an ID scan of the *Jemima*. ID scans work by pinging another ship, and then the onboard computer does a quick internal search for the ID chips of onboard crew and lists whatever comes back. It was much more efficient than all that messing around with crew manifests we used to do, and made uncovering stowaways a lot easier.

Entirely within expectations, the scan came back to indicate that both kids were still on the *Jemima*. Of course, the ID-scan system couldn't tell the difference between a chip in the hand of an alive person and one that was lying in a pile of shredded flesh—or indeed in the adorable tummy of a satisfied Zoob.

We were in short-enough range for communication now, so I opened a channel. "Jemima? Daniel? It's me." It occurred to me that neither of them knew what my real name was. "The person you might as well think of as Jacques McKeown. If you're there, pick up."

The call was taken immediately, and we heard a voice almost identical to the one I had heard some time ago. "Hay-lo. Foo-ud."

I smartly snapped the communicator off and took up the joysticks again. "Okay, so either they're already dead, or there's a chance we have an opportunity to burst in at the nick of time," I said. "Airlock's blocked by the umbilical. But I'm pretty sure there'll be maintenance hatches along the hull we can use. Somewhere."

"Well, take your time," said Warden. "I'm sure the nick of time will be happy to wait."

I took us toward the *Jemima* as fast as I dared and did what's known as a bootleg turn, so that the starboard side of the shuttle was running parallel to the *Jemima*'s hull. I found what I was looking for on one of the *Jemima*'s flab rolls, not far from the bridge. It was a square panel, locked shut with a circular switch. The *Jemima* was lacking in a lot of standard safety features, but you basically can't have a ship without maintenance hatches. Only a very dense shipbuilder would construct a hull, then try to move all the infrastructure in through one airlock.

I positioned the shuttle so that our airlock door was over the hatch, then gently drifted toward it until the two hulls were pressed together. There was rubber padding all the way around our external airlock door, so technically the shuttle had an umbilical, albeit one about six inches long.

I killed the engine, squeezed awkwardly out of the pilot seat and around the scanning unit, and placed my hand on the handle of the exit door. Only then did it occur to me that I hadn't checked the rubber seal's integrity, and it could very easily have been damaged in the crash landing earlier.

"Fair warning," I said. "We may die horribly the moment I turn this handle."

"I beg your pardon?"

I turned the handle.

There was a terrifying blast as the internal atmosphere rushed to fill the small vacuum between the shuttle and the Jemima, but it ceased almost immediately. The seal was holding. I heard a little dainty pop from the hatch as the fail-safe deactivated, the one that prevents the hatch from opening in hard vacuum.

"That was hardly *fair warning*," complained Warden, now beside me.

"So far so good," I said reassuringly. I turned the circular switch and pulled. It didn't budge an inch, and my shoulder registered a complaint. "Aaaand there it is. Now it's bad again."

Without a word, Warden's hand joined mine on the switch, and we pulled together. No joy.

"Hang on. One more thing to try," I said, casting a look around the shuttle's interior.

"And then what?" asked Warden, tapping her foot. "We give up? Try to think of how we explain this to Blaze, Henderson, and the entire United Republic?"

"And then we try a different hatch, smart lady. Shut up." I found what I was looking for behind one of the panels in the tiny "communal area" behind the cockpit—the tool cabinet. Containing, among other things, a sturdy crowbar that looked like it had never been used.

I dug the end of the bar into the little gap between the switch handle and the door and pushed with both hands. Metal groaned under protest, and I could feel it starting to buckle. I paused, switched my grip, took a deep breath, then put all my strength into a full body shove.

The hatch flew open. And every single pound of pressure I had been expending upon the crowbar was delivered squarely to the middle of my face.

I fell onto my back, so the pain from landing on the solid floor could combine with the pain in my smashed nose to make me the filling of a lovely pain sandwich. I made to clutch my face, forgot I was still holding the crowbar, and almost brained myself.

Warden's face appeared in my vision once I could blink the tears away. "Do you need a moment?"

I sat up. I needed to anyway—blood was starting to run down my throat. I stuck the crowbar into the open hatch to steady myself. "No. No. All good. Ready for action. Rescue time." I crawled headfirst through the hatch before she could argue, keeping my sleeve under my nose to soak up the blood flow. As the saying goes, a star pilot's flight jacket has no stains, only stories.

The hatch led into the interim space between the outer hull and the internal walls, and it was through here that the manufacturers seemed to have threaded all the necessary cables and piping I might have needed to access during a technical issue.

Space was at a premium. We had to worm our way through gaps that remained punishingly narrow as it transitioned multiple times from vertical to horizontal and everything in between. The only light was afforded by slim cracks and vents in the internal walls, with the occasional diode and readout bathing me in ominous red. From somewhere around my feet, I heard the exertion sounds of Warden attempting to follow while maintaining her dignity.

After moving what amounted to about eight feet along the hull, I found a panel outlined in light, the same size as the one by which we had entered. I splayed my fingers across the square and pressed gently. Thankfully, it was as loose as a ceiling tile, as it was probably intended to be easily removed for the sake of basic maintenance. I pushed it open an inch.

The room beyond was one of the connecting corridors, I think one on the upper level that led to the bridge. It was hard to tell, because I could only glimpse a bit of it around the sweating mass of green flesh, and the underevolved mouth crammed with vicious spiky teeth, which were taking up most of the view.

I quickly pulled the panel closed again just as something that sounded like a wet, overinflated beach ball hurled itself against the other side and bounced off, gnashing random syllables.

"What's going on up there?" asked Warden, from somewhere behind me.

"Sorting it out," I replied.

The crowbar was still with me, so I held it in both hands and readied it near the panel. Blood continued to trickle from my nose as I took my sleeve away, and I was forced to make do with loudly sniffing it back up, which seemed to make the Zoob on the other side more and more excited as it slithered around in anticipation. I waited until the gibbering was coming from the furthest side of the room, then opened the panel an inch again.

The gibbering stopped. I counted to one, then shoved the panel with the crowbar as hard as I could, throwing it off and sending it skidding across the floor.

A split second later, the Zoob, hurtling toward me in midpounce, landed teeth first on the end of the crowbar. It had fangs all around the circumference of its mouth, like a lamprey eel. Every two-inch-long tooth was now fastened around the crowbar's shaft like an iris door.

I shoved it violently into the corner between wall and floor just below me, then pushed hard, so that my body slid into the room as the Zoob remained helpless. All the while it gnashed and gibbered at the end of the bar like a psychotic lollipop, staring up at me with its furious, bloodshot yellow eye.

So I pinned the creature in place with one foot and yanked the crowbar free, bringing a little festive shower of broken teeth with it. Almost immediately it began fighting to get its mouth around my foot, but only got as far as sucking on a loose shoelace before I brought the crowbar down, two handed, squarely into its giant eye.

It was like jumping on a beanbag and discovering a hitherto-unknown tear. White feathery matter, like scores of dandelion seeds, burst forth from the Zoob's wounded eye as it emitted a sound like the air being slowly let out of a balloon.

I just kept bringing the crowbar down again and again until the noise had fully stopped and the fangs around my shoe had relaxed. Warden's face appeared at the vent just in time for the last blow and the last little blast of white flakes.

"Maybe try not to breathe them in," I said, panting, as she daintily waved the drifting particles away from her face. "I have a feeling they might be spores."

She nodded and pulled herself into the room, staring at the remains of the Zoob with professional fascination. It now looked like one of those fake vomits you see at joke shops, but coated firstly with a sticky eyeball goo and secondly with a generous dusting of white fluff. "This is the life form that routinely wipes out entire star piloting crews, is it?"

I shook the filth off the end of my crowbar like it was a closed umbrella after I'd just come in from the rain. "Yeah," I said. "Looks like they're not hugely dangerous in a face-off. But from what everyone's been saying, they mainly rely on taking people by surprise—"

My eyes bulged as I parsed my own words, and I spun on my heel, swinging the crowbar through the space behind me. It collided awkwardly with the second Zoob that had just pounced at my exposed back and sent it bouncing along the corridor like a basketball, thudding hollowly with each landing.

It was smaller than the one I'd already killed and seemed to be wearing a disembodied nose on a strap around its face (not a nose that resembled Daniel's or Jemima's, I noticed thankfully). It corrected itself before it could bounce all the way into the far wall, then started hopping toward me, chomping in excitement. I planted my feet and readied the crowbar for a baseball swing.

Halfway to me, it stopped suddenly, shuffling awkwardly to a halt. It blinked stupidly at me for a moment, then tipped forward and landed face down with a slap. A hideous pink tongue, long and narrow, snaked out from underneath and fluttered greedily about the surrounding floor.

I wasn't about to question its sudden interest in the carpeting. I took a long standing leap off one foot and landed heavily on the back of its "neck" with the other. I took the crowbar in both hands and brought it down again and again, like a blind golf caddy with anger issues trying to put the flag back in the hole. Another cloud of white specks ruined the *Jemima's* expensive carpet.

"McKeown," said Warden, dusting herself off. "I think we should split up from here."

I leaned against one of the walls, wheezing, and held my chest in the hope that it would calm my heartbeat. "You don't . . . watch a great many horror films, do you."

"We will cover ground quicker that way. Every second may count if Jemima and Daniel are still alive." She gestured up the corridor with her head. "I will head toward the bridge. You go the other way and check the lower levels."

I banged the crowbar against the wall to dislodge a particularly sticky chunk of broken Zoob tooth, then frowned at her. "We heard a Zoob over the comms. The bridge is the most likely place they're going to be."

She produced my gun from inside her coat. "Good thing I asked to hold on to the gun, then, isn't it."

I considered this. "Can't argue with that." But I had a feeling she had some hidden thought processes going on, because she was actually proposing to put herself in danger, and I didn't recall having seen any blue moons or flying pigs on the way here.

She double-checked the charge meter on the gun, and seemed about to turn around and head through the next connecting door before she met my gaze. "Does your nose hurt?"

I touched it gingerly and winced. "It didn't until you brought it up, no."

She nodded and shut the door behind her. I made for the narrow stairwell to the next level down, and only then did it occur to me that I'd yet again been handed the raw deal. We hadn't been far from the bridge when Warden had suggested splitting up. So now I was having to search a larger section of the ship.

I made to do so anyway, it being hardly worth heading back and calling her out on it. But it didn't feel like her usual brand of pettiness, somehow. There had to be a bigger plan. Not for the first time, I wondered if when she looked at me, she didn't see a man, but some kind of giant chess piece with a target painted on its back.

The first room I checked on this level was the largest entertainment lounge, which I privately thought of as "the ballroom." The omnipresent deep-pile carpet was interrupted by a black-and-white dance floor in the center, served by an alarmingly elaborate lighting system. The room's perimeter was dotted with beanbag chairs, except for an area around the wall directly opposite the door, where the snooker table was set up, along with a row of bar fridges stocked with a variety of fizzy pops.

The wall coverings were a mess of vibrant colors from all my least favorite parts of the visible spectrum, and the entire ceiling was a domed, bulbous observation window, as if the decor was being harshly judged through the microscope of God. But besides every loose object having shifted slightly during our trebuchet jump into the Black, there were no signs of violence, nor indeed of the room having ever been used at all.

I turned to leave and try the next room when I sensed a noise. I say *sensed* because it came to me through the floor and the soles of my shoes rather than my ears. I hesitated, then "heard" it again. A dull, metallic thud.

I dropped to my knees and placed my ear against the cool tile surface of the dance floor, just in time to hear it again. It sounded like something heavy and blunt hitting something hollow and metal.

Then there was another sound just after it, a much softer one. It was so brief and strange that it took me a moment to identify, but I eventually concluded that it was either a small dog expressing disdain at his dinner dish, or the brief whimper escaping from the mouth of a terrified teenager trying not to make any sound.

I shoved myself back onto my feet—leaving another little sampling of nose blood on the tiles—and ran for the next set of stairs down, which led to a hallway connecting a couple of sleeping quarters. As I rounded the turn in the stairs, a symphony of crazy gnashing and murmuring reached my ears, and I was faced with what I can only describe as a wall of Zoobs.

The battleship that had attacked the *Jemima* must have been some Zoob attempt at organization, because there had to be at least fifteen of the little brackets, and as I watched, another one joined them from the open doorway that led to the airlock. Every single one was wearing some kind of body part that didn't belong to them. Mostly human, but I saw one with an orange furry trunk that must have come from a Magnerian bipedal mammoth.

Judging by the look of their bloodshot eyes and dull green pallor, most of them were rather badly malnourished. That was also given away by the fact that they were all stacked up outside one of the cabin doors, taking it in turns to hurl themselves violently at the small section of door that wasn't concealed by writhing green flesh.

The internal doors were only a light alloy. It had already bent enough that there was a clear gap, widening further with each impact. It didn't take a genius to guess why they were all so interested in this particular door. Through the gap, I saw a momentary flash of hot pink hair, desperately pushing some kind of barricade back into place.

The Zoobs were so excited at the prospect of getting inside the cabin that none of them paid me the slightest attention. That gave me some advantage, but bravely leaping into the fray like Errol Flynn, brandishing my crowbar like a sword, immediately felt like an incredibly bad idea. Individual Zoobs apparently weren't hard to deal with when they didn't have the element of surprise, but there were enough of them here to bite off all my limbs before I could wind up for the second blow.

I hopped from foot to foot, trying to think, as the Zoobs hammered the gap larger with each passing moment. That made the pain in my broken nose flare up again, which was even less conducive to thinking. I blocked one nostril and blew something red and lumpy out of the other, letting it splat upon the floor.

The Zoob that had backed off a little to make a run at the door suddenly froze and spun around to face me. A couple of other outlying ones did the same. Then three bouncing balls of green toothy death launched themselves in my direction.

I leapt back into the stairwell, in need of a choke point, and readied my crowbar for a swing. But they weren't even looking at me. Instead, they collectively fell upon the little blob of blood and snot near where I had been standing. They crawled all over each other like puppies fighting over the last free nipple, desperately slurping at it with their long, waggling tongues.

And that made quite a few things fall into place. Blood. That was all they wanted, nutritionwise. Maybe it was the only part they could digest. That would certainly explain why they didn't eat all those dried-up body parts, but mainly used them for accessorizing.

Apparently they were happy to forcefully take it from prey, but if any of it was lying around freshly liberated from a body, then that took priority. I'd been leaving a steady supply of drips from my broken nose since the moment I'd come aboard. There must have been a few on the carpet upstairs that had made the second Zoob hesitate.

The moment I realized this, I also realized, without a shadow of uncertainty, that Warden had figured this out around the time she had suggested splitting up. Because with my broken nose, I was a walking rally point for every Zoob I ran across. I made a frustrated burbling noise that sent more blood flying.

On cue, a growing separatist faction of the besieging Zoobs leapt for it and started slurping away. Now I had a plan, although not a plan I relished, because it hinged on the ever-unpleasant element of self-sacrifice.

I scooped up a decent amount of bloody mucus with my thumb and forefinger and flung it vaguely in the direction of the Zoob mass. Thickened by snot, the blood flew across the room much more efficiently, so this solution was unfolding ideally, broadly speaking. I threw more out, and after narrowly avoiding having my bloodstained fingers bitten off by a leaping

Zoob, I felt I had the undivided attention of the mob. The cabin door was forgotten completely.

I started backing up the steps, flinging more donations to the floor as I went. "Kids?" I shouted, over the burbling and slurping. "I'm luring them away! Just . . . make your way to the bridge as soon as it's clear. Warden's there."

A pair of eyes appeared at the ragged gap around the misshapen door. "Okay!" called Jemima.

The Zoobs were packed so closely together on the way up the stairs that they looked like a giant, writhing caterpillar. I had to keep swinging my crowbar to keep them from getting too close, even while I was dangling drippy enticements from my other hand. By this method I managed to get them up to the entertainment level of the ship.

By then, pain and blood loss were clanging numerous church bells inside my head, but I was managing to hold together the threads of a plan. All I had to do was get the Zoobs into the ballroom, hold them until the kids could get past into the bridge, then lure them all onto the umbilical and seal the inner airlock door. How I proposed to do that without sealing myself outside the ship with them was a bridge I could cross when I came to it.

There were already blood splats up here that I had left on my first way through, so I followed them backward into the ballroom and didn't stop moving until I was in the middle of the dance floor, standing over the little offering of blood I'd left there earlier. Gratifyingly, the little wandering Zoob dinner party followed me in, their enthusiasm for what must have become a rather samey series of meals undiminished. When I was fairly certain they were all in, I stamped my foot on the dance floor three times. I could only hope that the kids would guess that I was signaling them to move.

The Zoobs looked like they had almost polished off the last of the blood I'd left, and one or two of them had given up on getting a share of what remained and were making wayward glances around. They were in need of fresh encouragement. I reached for my nose.

Nothing came out. The reliable blood dispenser had dried up. Ah, I thought. Here, of course, we discover the glaring flaw in the plan—that it hinged on the use of more blood than one man should reasonably be able to produce while remaining upright.

I blew as hard as I could, but what came out was mostly snot. I flung it anyway, and it landed on the face of one of the nearer Zoobs. It made no attempt to consume it, and gave me a slightly reproachful look.

One by one, the crowd was realizing that there weren't going to be any more free samples, and that it was time to take the initiative and go to the source. One of them made an opportunistic leap, but I'd seen it coming and deflected it with a crowbar swing. It rejoined the mob, unharmed.

I had to move. But the Zoobs were fairly decisively blocking the way to the only door. Maybe there were vents or maintenance panels I could make an escape through, but I needed time to look for them. I glanced away, realizing as I did so that the Zoobs were waiting for me to do that, and saw the snooker table.

I darted toward it, just as the space I had been occupying was pelted with fanged green missiles. I reached the table at a full sprint, planted my hands on the baize, and used my momentum to swing my legs over and vault cleanly across. I crouched when I hit the floor, and as I rose, I smoothly tipped the table onto its side, reflecting briefly on the irony that this would not have been possible had it been bolted down.

One of the Zoobs had been close enough to be caught underneath what was now the snooker table's underside and burst messily, spraying spores in my face that I hastily swatted away. The rest started hurling themselves at the makeshift barricade, bouncing off with a series of dull thuds, like angry fists upon a wooden door in the middle of the night.

Sitting in extremely temporary cover, I gave the surrounding room a proper once-over. Accordingly, I couldn't see a single panel or vent that might represent an exit. Just big, solid, nicely decorated walls. Packed with beanbags and fridges full of fizzy pop.

The Zoobs didn't seem capable of clearing the top of the snooker table barrier with their pouncing leaps. But I doubted it would take long for them to figure out that I was glaringly vulnerable to being flanked from both sides.

So I stood up, peering over the table, and made a few token crowbar swipes to keep the frenzied horde focused. I felt like a castaway at sea discouraging sharks away from the lifeboat, except that the entire ocean was sharks. I needed a plan. The idea to create some kind of improvised pressure cannon from fizzy pop and snooker balls flashed briefly into my mind, and I dismissed it just as quickly.

I hit one of them with a halfhearted crowbar swing, and it flew sideways. That was mistake one, because it bounced off an artfully angled section of wall and landed near one of the fridges behind the barricade. A moment's terror passed as its blank, cyclopean gaze briefly met mine, then instinct took over. I darted out of cover to swat it back toward its fellows before it could react. That was mistake two.

Because all the Zoobs that had been making a frontal assault on the snooker table started streaming sideways toward me. I hastily dashed back into cover, hissing Pilot Math as I went, but the mistake was already made. A wave of Zoobs moved into sight from around the table. They seemed to have difficulty pouncing accurately when they were all packed together and interfering with each other, but it would hardly matter if they could just steamroll me en masse.

I swung the crowbar wide and low, and it didn't decelerate even as it hit every Zoob in the front line. It was like pushing inflated balloons around; they must have been boneless and mostly hollow. None of them seemed hurt. They just rolled with it and came back for more. It seemed like they had to be trapped and crushed to cause any lasting pain.

Speaking of which, I discovered that the Zoobs had actually been smart enough to flank my cover on both sides when one of them pounced me from behind and started chewing on my shoulder.

The padding in my flight jacket took most of the damage, but I could feel a dozen little points prickling my skin. I couldn't give it the chance to get a few more chomps in. I reeled, made another decision on instinct, and did a desperate forward roll into the bank of refrigerators. I landed on the Zoob, crushing it between shoulder and metal, and felt its "jaws" loosen.

But my victory came with the snag of leaving me sprawled on the floor on my back, and the Zoobs closed in like the tide. The light was being blotted out by a cloud of quivering round shapes all around my vision. The gibbering was reaching fever pitch, and I couldn't tell if it was coming from them or me.

I kicked with both legs and swung my crowbar around and around, like a baby refusing to be changed, but their numbers were too great. Something green and bulbous wrapped itself tightly around my shin, and the icy-hot sting of pain made me gasp.

Pain and sweaty hands worked together to make the crowbar fly out of my grip as I swung it wildly, and I didn't even hear where it landed. Their excitement was a pounding wall of frenzied noise. I felt a hundred sharp points, arranged in a circle, digging into my scalp, and blood traced a hot line from my forehead to my mouth.

I spat. In that final moment, I thought of Warden, and felt sick at the unfairness of it. I'd sometimes pictured myself bravely sacrificing my life to save another, but my preference had always been that it be someone I actually liked.

CHAPTER 26

THE SOUND I heard at the moment of death was a lot like a catastrophic shattering of glass. Instantly, the gibbering stopped, and the hideous, squeezing pain disappeared from my head and leg. I felt cold all over, along with a sensation like I was being lifted up from the floor.

It wasn't exactly how I'd imagined death. I'd always thought it was more of an ascending-tunnel-of-light, golden-angels thing. I at the very least assumed that it would be peaceful. This was the very opposite—I was freezing cold, something was roaring in my ears, and what felt like gale-force wind was blowing all around me. It was almost exactly like being caught in a depressurization event.

I opened my eyes to find them watering. I was alive, still in the ballroom, and caught in a depressurization event. There was a jagged hole in the plexiglass roof, only about three feet wide, but greedily sucking every drop of air, as fast as the life support system could replace it. This was the same kind of plexiglass that protected Ritsuko City from asteroids. Only a few inches thick here, but whatever had managed to punch through it deserved some kind of prize.

Zoobs and beanbag chairs were flying around the room like the balls in a bingo machine. I'd had the presence of mind to grab my snooker table, but soon I was upside down, feet stretched toward the raging hole. And in that position, I could see what it was that had saved my life.

It was Carlos, Henderson's bodyguard with the completely ridiculous physiology. He was still standing directly underneath the hole in the ceiling and had managed to stay in place by digging all his fingers into the dance floor, right up to the knuckle.

Still upside down and clinging to a snooker table, only two legs of which were retaining any kind of attachment to the floor, I caught Carlos's gaze. As neither of us was able to move or be heard over the wind, we communicated by look alone. He was almost impossible to read, but from what little I could glean, I was half tempted to let go there and then, and take my chances with the vacuum of space.

But before I could make my mind up, the growing cluster of beanbags and various other loose objects hovering around the hole in the dome crushed together tightly enough to form a rigid, temporary plug. The gravitons in the internal atmosphere reasserted themselves, and everything clattered to the floor. The snooker table tottered and landed back upright on its legs, with me tumbling around the side and ending up underneath.

The table's underside punished me for not keeping my head down with a ringing clonk to the skull, dizzying me for a few moments. By the time I had cleared the spots from my eyes, I finally peered out at the dance floor to see that Carlos wasn't there.

Something hit the floor heavily to my immediate left, and the snooker table was brushed aside as if it were a shopping bag being blown by the breeze. I looked up and saw something massive and fist shaped silhouetted against the light for a split second before I rolled, and Carlos punched the floor where I had lain, instantly turning thick-pile shag carpet into a sheet of wafer-thin cloth.

I'd had a feeling he hadn't shown up for a friendly checkup and a fist bump. I scrabbled away on my back with my feet and elbows, pain grinding away at my Zoob-stricken knee, unable to look away from his black, beady little eyes. With few options left to me, I tried to talk. "Carlos! D-don't kill me!"

Had it been a decent kind of enemy, I might have been able to provoke him into gloating or toying with me, which would buy me enough time to exploit the inevitable moment of weakness, but Carlos didn't even seem to register my words. If anything, he looked bored. This was his usual day at the office.

His fist swung around again, and again I rolled to the side, but he'd learned from my tactics. He let his own momentum spin him around and his other hand came out of nowhere, grabbing me around the injured leg gently but firmly.

For one insane moment I genuinely thought I'd gotten the wrong impression and he'd just been offering to put pressure on my wound. Then he swung me around like an Olympic hammer thrower.

The room whooshed past in a disorienting blur, then the entire side of my body slammed against the floor. The carpet was thick enough that it should have been like falling onto a crash mat, but it was also sprinkled with chunks of broken plexiglass. They weren't jagged like shards of glass-glass, but that was small comfort. Pain flooded my senses like ink in a tank of clear water.

I had just enough sense about me to drag myself toward the door, my injured leg now numb and useless, as Carlos lumbered toward me for the kill. My vision was clouding at the edges, giving me an almost literal form of tunnel vision in which Carlos was playing the role of an oncoming train.

I tried to think. My most dominant inward voice was screaming continuously that everything hurt and that I didn't want to die. A secondary level of thought was mainly listing all the swear words in my repertoire. But a third, much quieter level, struggling to be heard through the din in my mind, was able to direct my attention to Carlos's hands. In a slow-motion moment of desperate enhanced perception, I saw that his knuckles were raw and bleeding.

Between this and the hundreds of aches along the side of my body, I was gaining a renewed, fearful respect for plexiglass. It hadn't stopped the monstrous bodyguard, but it had made a crack. And any crack can be widened with the right tools.

One of the Zoobs, still stunned and woozy from being bounced around the room, was trying to steady itself about a yard away. Focus regained, I rolled myself over to it just as Carlos drew close, and I managed to knock it toward him with a sweep of my arm.

Carlos attempted to casually backhand it away, but once the Zoob was close enough to him to sense the fresh blood on his knuckles, it acquired a second wind with amazing speed. It clamped its teeth down on one of his massive fingers at the moment of impact.

Carlos must have had an astonishingly high pain threshold, because he didn't seem to notice until his hand came back from the swipe with the intended target still attached. He looked at it quizzically as it noshed away at his flesh, more confused than anything else. Then he tried to shake it off.

That was about the biggest mistake he could have made, because it sprinkled the floor around him with numerous fresh spots of blood. And for the many dazed Zoobs that were still scattered about the room, he might as well have been farting smelling salts.

I didn't wait for them to put the pieces together in whatever passed for their minds. I had already crawled to the next Zoob and swatted it toward the bigger target, making sure to use my less bloodstained hand. This one latched onto Carlos's mustache, which it chewed on experimentally in a bizarre moment of interspecies romance.

I'd gathered enough wits to shakily get to my feet, and kicked another Zoob into the growing fray with my good leg, bracing myself on a karaoke machine to take the weight off my bad one. By this point, my efforts were hardly necessary. Carlos was capable of getting a Zoob off his person with a single finger flick, but in the time it took for him to do so, two more leapt onto his bulk and started digging in.

He swept his fist along parallel to the ground, knocking back a wave of pouncing Zoobs with the force of a freight train, and of course they simply bounced off the walls and came back for more, unharmed. More attacked him from behind, and soon there were Zoobs all the way along both arms, clinging like barnacles. Trails of blood, sheer black against his red skin, left his body looking fully tiger striped. The more blood they drew, the more relentless the Zoobs became.

I'd already made it to the door, clinging all my aching and bleeding bits, but I paused at the threshold. Carlos was swinging his arms left and right madly, doing serious damage to the nearby decor but none to his attackers, and his motions became weak and quivery as the Zoobs sucked noisily on his exposed veins.

For some reason, all I could think of was the game of rock–paper–scissors. In a straight fight, Carlos destroys humans. Humans destroy Zoobs. And Zoobs . . .

Carlos collapsed to the floor, outstretching a massive hand toward me. I caught his blank gaze one last time before his eyes disappeared behind wobbling green blobs, and felt a sting of sympathy. Not for the pain and injury he was suffering, but because I'd finally seen an emotion I recognized. The one you feel when you have been denied your chance to succeed at the only thing you've ever been good at.

Then my aches and pains flared up again, and my pity disappeared. I blew a short raspberry and shut the ballroom door behind me as I hobbled for the stairs.

▲▲▲

I carefully climbed the stairs and found Jemima and Daniel loitering in the passage near the vent by which I'd entered. As I limped toward them, the door at the opposite end slid open and Warden entered. She gave a little double-take when she saw my wounds, and almost seemed about to display sympathy before catching herself.

"Are you guys all right?" I panted.

Jemima's wide-eyed gaze tracked a drop of blood as it fell from my scalp to the floor. "Uh. Yeah. *We* are."

"Daniel?" I asked.

The son of Henderson seemed physically unharmed, unless someone had impaled him on some kind of spike that went up his arse and all the way through to the top of his head, which was what his stance implied. His skin was chalk white, his eyes were the size of golf balls, and his mouth quivered, half shaping words in reply that never quite made it out of his throat.

"Daniel?" repeated Warden, placing her hands on his shoulders and snapping her fingers in front of his eyes. "It's Ms. Warden. You're safe now, understand? What happened?"

"They just grabbed onto the ship and came aboard," said Jemima. "Dan had kind of a close call, and then he went like that."

Warden glanced at her for the merest fraction of a second, then took Daniel's unresisting wrist and pressed his palm onto Jemima's chest, without warning.

"This may be serious," said Warden, as Daniel showed no reaction whatsoever. "This may mean additional trouble with Henderson."

Jemima folded her arms tightly and made an offended noise. "Oh, because Mr. Henderson's the only one that matters. You could be, you know, worried about Dan 'cos he's a human being."

Both my hands were occupied with clutching injured parts, so I gestured to the open vent with my head, sprinkling a bit more blood around for everyone to enjoy. "Argument won! Daniel Henderson is a human being. Now can we please get the hell off this ship? Don't ask me how, but Carlos showed up."

"Carlos?" said Warden as Jemima crawled into the vent, leading Daniel by the hand. "And you fought him off?"

I got halfway through adopting a smug, heroic stance before pain shot through my broken leg and made me cringe. "Sort of. The Zoobs did most of the work."

"Carlos," she repeated, stroking her imaginary beard. "I hadn't thought Henderson would be rash enough to take such a step."

I decoded something in her tone of voice and sagged in resignation. "You did it again, didn't you. You called him and told him where we were."

Warden gestured behind her, toward the bridge. "Of course."

I was far too pained and exhausted to do more than sigh at that point. "I really wish you would stop doing that."

"I would not expect you to understand, McKeown. As we have established, you do not plan ahead." Daniel's feet disappeared into the duct, and with a single shared look we wordlessly raised the subject of who was going next. "Are you going to require assistance?"

"Don't worry about me. Crawling I've about got down at this point. You go next. Chivalry's not dead, remember?"

She nodded, turned, and half crouched, then suddenly paused, and looked back at me. "Aren't you forgetting something?"

Another wordless exchange took place, and I fished the little envelope out of my back pocket. I felt the little lump of plastic with my fingers for a single sorrowful moment, then flicked it down the stairs to the lower hallway. This done, I followed Warden into the vent.

As I hauled my way through that tight space a second time, I heard a series of metallic thuds from deep within the ship. Then there was the hideous groan of rending metal. I swallowed. "Tell me Carlos can't still be alive. That'd just be unfair, wouldn't it?"

"I saw Carlos do many things during my employment," said Warden's arse as it wriggled through the space just ahead of me. "I would put nothing past him."

I heard another bang as Warden slid into the shuttle, this one more like a balloon bursting on a very large scale, possibly caused by that hull breach in the ballroom opening up again. The fail-safes were probably doing their best to isolate it, but all the same, I pulled myself into the shuttle as fast as I could and shut the airlock door.

The space inside the shuttle was at even more of a premium with the addition of two new passengers, despite them being underage. I propped an uncomplaining Daniel up against the cabin's rear wall and squeezed myself into the pilot's seat like toothpaste trying to get back into the tube. I couldn't fold my injured leg back in without the pain flaring up, so I just left it dangling over the armrest, where it would continually kick Warden in the arm, with any luck.

There was another sound of metal being tormented from somewhere deep within the *Jemima*, so without further banter, I detached the shuttle with a rather comical popping noise, cranked the speed all the way up, and yanked the steering column hard to the left.

So I almost ran us straight into the star pilot fleet.

They were hanging clustered in space like a gaggle of Roman emperors, waiting to give the thumbs-down as soon as the winning gladiator looked up. I recognized more than a couple. Jim Gunn's ship was there, as were the *Hopeless Endeavour* and the generous curves of Gareth the Overcompensator's freighter, always recognizable by its hot-pink spray job.

They were big names. Which meant they were also the most frequent targets of plagiarism by Jacques McKeown. And judging by the initial scan, every single one of them had their weapons powered up.

There was one particular ship that was even easier to recognize than the others. I hailed it, making sure to broadcast the call to every other ship in range. Angelo's musclebound silhouette appeared on the communication screen, lit from behind by fluorescent light this time, rather than an open fire. I had a feeling that this was a very serious gesture for him.

"Hast thou delivered what thou promised, knave?" he demanded.

"How nice to see you too, Angelo. Why yes, I am fractionally still alive." He didn't even respond. I sighed. "ID scan that ship. The Whale Shark, not the Zoob one harpooning it."

I could almost detect an increase in radiation in the area between the *Jemima* and the star pilot fleet as every single ship ran the necessary scan. I subtly edged out of the way.

"Jacques McKeown," read Angelo from the screen in front of him. "So, thou would abandon the man whose name thou stole aboard a vessel stricken with beasts? To do that even to a betrayer lacks honor."

That wasn't exactly the reaction I'd hoped for. "I—"

"Hold," said Angelo, suddenly leaning forward urgently so that his shovel-like face was illuminated by his monitor. "The creature known as Carlos. The one that slaughtered my comrades. It, too, is aboard?"

"Oh, ye—"

Angelo opened fire with every weapon at his disposal. Two rotary machine guns and two missile tubes sent streams of burning death into the *Jemima*'s exposed underbelly, reopening all the old battle damage.

Once he had broken the tension, every other ship joined in. The space between them and the *Jemima* became a solid cylinder of firepower that poured into the two connected ships like a stream of boiling water onto an ant's nest. If I hadn't moved the shuttle out of the way, we would have been reduced to a puff of shrapnel, spreading across creation for eternity.

The onslaught of missiles didn't even let up when the chain reactions started. Pounded into submission, the volatile materials in the engines and power reactors did what they did best, sparking off explosion after explosion that gutted the Jemima and the Zoob battleship, reducing them to clouds of white-hot metal and ruined internal fixtures. Half a glittering mirror ball sailed past our windshield. It was all rather cathartic.

Only then did the star pilot ships stop firing. Angelo sent one last shot into the silence, like he was putting a signature on it, or shaking off the last drop at the urinal. "Our dealings are complete," he said, grudgingly, and ended the call.

One by one, the ships drifted away, without a word. They were the crowd at the public hanging, dispersing after the adrenaline comes down, uneasy with the guilt of having been part of the moment.

"Jacques McKeown is dead," said Warden. "At least, as far as your colleagues are concerned. You must be relieved."

"Yeah, things'll be peachy until whoever he is brings another book out and all these guys ring me up wanting to know what the ply we were all doing out here today."

"You're . . . going to take me back, now, aren't you," said Jemima, sitting on the floor behind us with her back to the back of my chair.

"Yes, back to mum, or alternatively, we could have not come and left you with the monsters that were trying to eat you," I said, jiggling my injured leg. "You gonna complain?"

"I'm sorry, all right? We just wanted to see more," said Jemima weakly. "I never even left Earth until this trip. Just wanted to get an idea of what else was out there."

"And you did," I said, nodding. I felt I was well within my rights to get good and angry at her, but I was too exhausted to be anything but infuriatingly reasonable. "And then it tried to eat you. Because that's what it's like, this exciting star piloting life you read about. If you want the adventure and romance, you have to also accept that something might come along and start chewing on your head."

"Or invent something that makes it all pointless," added Warden.

I shot her a look that ricocheted straight off her stony gaze, then returned to Jemima. "In the meantime, we have to get you back to the naval fleet. You know, the one you said your mum wouldn't send?"

"She won't," said Jemima immediately.

"Tadaa," I announced, grandly nodding my head toward the scanner screen, and the swarm of pixels around Salvation Station that were all colored an official militaristic green.

I wish I'd had my camera out to capture her face. Her lips parted in wonder as she took in the sheer size of the fleet, but then she caught my gaze and leaned back. "Well, she only sent that because I'm part of her stupid image."

I groaned and slowly leaned forward until my forehead rested on the screen in front of me. "Of course you're part of her image. Doesn't mean you can't be important to her as a daughter, as well. It's possible to be more than one thing."

"Yes, take that from Mr. McKeown," said Warden, distractedly. She was half turned in her seat to eyeball Daniel's condition.

I didn't let her throw me. "I don't know your mum, but I'm pretty certain that she cares about your safety. That's what the United Republic's all about, isn't it? Keeping everyone safe?"

"*Secure* might be a better word," said Warden.

"I wish I could live in space," said Jemima. She was sitting with her back to my seat again, and from the way her voice was muffled, she must have brought her knees up to her chest. "I hate living in the UR. You're getting watched all day and all night. Mum keeps having people black bagged for complaining about it."

"Would your mother ever black bag you?" asked Warden.

"No ..."

"Then maybe *you* should complain. On behalf of—" Warden suddenly grabbed my dangling leg, and the pain was like someone banging a tin bathtub next to my ear. "McKeown. The fleet."

I grimaced. "What fleet?"

"The star pilot fleet. The ships that came to blow up the *Jemima* for us. It was not the entire star pilot fleet."

Jemima (the real one) appeared between us, one hand on each backrest. "So where's the rest of it?"

Warden pointed to the scanner screen. "They seem to be currently clustered in and around Salvation Station."

I squeezed the joysticks and set speed to maximum. "Trac. Setting course for whatever they've left of each other."

CHAPTER 27

SALVATION STATION APPEARED to be intact, externally at least, but hung alone in the middle of the Black without a single ship around it. The entire area covered by the ship's defense systems was utterly lifeless. The navy fleet were presumably all still cushioning their truncheons, and the residents of the station had all been evacuated to a safe distance.

The unaccounted-for component of the star pilot fleet was also nowhere to be seen. There were no gutted ships or floating bits of wreckage that I or the shuttle's scanners could detect, so apparently Salvation's defenses hadn't been deployed. And yet, the close-range sensor was absolutely lit up with blips.

"There," said Warden, pointing to the docking bay entrance as we neared it.

"Mystery solved," I murmured, worried. The entire bay was packed with star pilot ships of every size and shape. I recognized a couple, but these were mostly the smaller names, the ones who had fewer stories to rip off and consequently less investment in the lynching of Jacques McKeown. Very little care had been taken to park inside the lines, and we were forced to land the shuttle in the far corner, where the rear thrusters caused considerable trauma to a No Smoking sign.

We left the ship in pairs, Warden lending me a shoulder to take the weight off my leg—a gesture that should be attributed more to the need for expedience than anything else, as she was quick to point out—while Jemima pulled a still-catatonic Daniel along like a dogwalker with a particularly dozy terrier.

My concerns grew when we passed through the docking bay entrance into the concourse, because something had done serious damage to the doors. They were buckled and dented, and a large number of boots had made a concerted effort to widen the door frame. The nice new floor of the concourse beyond was tarnished with the very same scuff marks that would have so distressed United Republic regulations.

But at least it gave us a trail to follow, and finally some sign of life became evident. There was a noisy bustle coming from up ahead. As we rounded the curve, we saw a small mob of star pilots in the wide plaza in front of the Quantunnel gate. They were clustered around something. And it was very easy to imagine it being Robert Blaze sprawled upon the floor, getting a boot to the teeth every time he tried to explain that he didn't know where Jemima was.

I hurried as best I could with a dodgy leg and Warden weighing me down, but as we drew nearer, things recontextualized. I could see Blaze, not on his knees or stricken by tormentors, but standing upright in the middle of the throng, wreathed with fatherly smiles. And as we drew even nearer, the clamor of voices could be separated out into a storm of individual questions.

"How many more pilots do you need?" one pilot was asking.

"Where are the refueling stations?" asked another.

"I might have some outstanding convictions in Ritsuko; is that going to be a problem?" a third, rather anxious-looking pilot asked.

Blaze answered whatever questions he could make out with suave confidence, reassuring concerns and directing gazes toward features. Maybe I was a little delirious at that point, but for a moment, he looked like some kind of messiah in the marketplace, surrounded by love-struck peasants fighting to touch his holy hems.

"I told you," I said, heard only by Warden. "Star pilots are star pilots. Even when they're acting like mercenaries."

"Mm," she replied, heard only by me. "I can't help but feel that you will remember this moment differently if it transpires that Robert Blaze is Jacques McKeown."

As I mulled that one over, Warden detached from me, leaving me to lean on a nearby planter that I found much better company. "Gentlemen!" she said, in a schoolmarm voice that pierced right through the clamor and caused the crowd between us and Blaze to part like the Red Sea. "We have some internal station matters to discuss. If you would all feel free to explore, we can consider your futures here later."

Most of the pilots obeyed, spreading out to wander the evacuated halls, staring enraptured in all directions. The relief that radiated from Blaze when he saw the kids almost had physical presence. "Ms. Warden," he breathed, shaking her hand earnestly. "Mister . . ." He confidently stretched the same hand toward me, but it wobbled a little when he noticed the state I was in. "Dear god. Are you all right? What happened?"

I gave him my most sarcastic smile. "Ran into some old friends of yours. Zoobs. We found them just as they were making a very convincing case to Jemima and Daniel that the Black isn't as safe as they'd been led to believe."

He hung his head. "All right. You've made your point. Maybe it was presumptuous of me to start preparing the Black for visitors before it was fully secured. But we had no choice. Money is always tight. I had to create the Cantrabargid experience because we needed a source of income as quickly as possible."

"But that's not going to be an issue anymore, is it," said Warden, quietly enough to be heard only by the three of us. "Because you transferred all of Jacques McKeown's money from that ID chip before you returned it to us."

Two jaws hit the floor with almost perfect synchronicity, mine and Blaze's. "How did you know . . ." he began.

"Partly because it was what I would have done," said Warden, wearing the specific expressionless face I'd come to recognize as her smug one. "Mainly from how you reacted just now."

"You . . . still have the money?" I said, stomach churning. The knowledge that all the money had died with Carlos had left me with a little sorrow, but once I'd thought about it properly, a great deal of relief, as well. Now I felt like a dumbfounded hobbit watching his friend refusing to throw that plying ring into Mount Doom.

His smile became rather fixed and desperate. He clutched his temples with both hands, then stretched them toward me, jerking them in time with his words as he thought on the fly. "Well, it's just . . . you knew that . . . you weren't . . . actually . . . entitled to . . ."

"And you are?" I interrupted. "Actually, shall we call all those pilots back over before you answer that question?"

He made some kind of coughing noise as a reply, but it was drowned out by a considerably louder noise. A deep metallic rattling, like a rumble of nearby thunder, that startled everyone present into looking at the

Quantunnel gate that Blaze and his people had been constructing. *Had been* suddenly being the operative words.

"When the hell did you finish that thing?" I said, various predictions for the coming events running through my head as the shutters came down and crashed noisily into the floor.

"While you were on Cantrabargid," said Blaze distantly, eyes fixed upon the grand metal archway. "Who let the shutters down?"

He was met by clusters of blank, concerned looks. Any thought that they might have loosened accidentally disappeared when the shutters started shaking and making the telltale clangs of a Quantunnel being activated. Presumably the actual tunneling firmware wasn't installed, but only the origin gate required that, not the destination. That was how they'd been used to colonize distant space: just fly an unmanned gate as far as you can without needing to worry about keeping anything onboard alive, connect to it from back home, and pop through at your leisure.

The noises had caused a smaller version of the earlier crowd to reform, but when the gate fell silent, the entire room did likewise. The tension built up on our heads and shoulders like a cascade of unpleasant sleet, freezing us in place and slipping uncomfortably down our collars, before the shutters finally opened to reveal a rather generic military-grade transport bay that I didn't recognize.

Although I certainly recognized the platoon of soldiers in black armor, because they were dressed identically to the ones I'd encountered trying to truncheon their way into the *Jemima* back on Earth. The moment the shutter was up, there was a mass eruption of chaos. The soldiers poured into the station with a storm of thudding feet (I noticed at more or less this point that their boots were all wrapped in canvas sacks), screaming for everyone to display their hands. A number of the pilots, including that anxious-looking one who had spoken earlier, immediately attempted to flee the scene.

Those of us who were nearer the gate—including Blaze, Warden, and myself—were grabbed and pushed to the ground, with the cushioned end of a rifle held against our temples. The more outlying pilots were merely held at bay by an efficiently established perimeter, although the soldiers threw a few more individuals to the floor for displaying offensive behavior, such as looking at them funny. I saw Warden open her mouth to come up with some devastating legal threat, but she was screamed into silence by the owner of the gun pressed to her head.

And barely five seconds after they had entered the room, everything was still and silent again. I could only admire the efficiency of the United Republic's military as a gun barrel lodged in my cheek and ground my face into Salvation's brand-new floor. The cuts in my forehead were throbbing again.

I was in a perfect position to watch the president of the United Republic step through the gate onto the station, or at least her lower half, which was wearing what looked like men's formal shoes and a gray pinstriped suit. With slow, deliberate, measured steps, she approached the soldier pinning Robert Blaze and knelt cautiously beside them, as if regarding a turd the dog had left on the carpet.

Now that she had crouched into my visual range I could see that she was quite a small woman, not much more than five feet in height, with a helmet of tightly brushed brown hair and a complexion almost as orange as Henderson's. There must have been something up with the artificial sun at Cloud Castle, which Jemima and Daniel were spared from because they never left the house. "I only have one question," she said in a soft voice. "I am willing to ask it as many times as are necessary. Where is my daughter?"

"She's over there," said Blaze, trying to point through the use of eyeballs alone.

"I said, where is my—what?"

"I'm over here, Mum," said an unhappy Jemima from somewhere behind me, apparently having hidden herself among the onlookers.

She stepped forward, to a point just in front of my face, and her mother walked smartly over and hugged her, in a rather perfunctory manner I felt was more for the benefit of outside observers than either participant. When they parted, she was clutching both of Jemima's shoulders. "Where are you hurt?"

Her question turned a little uncertain toward the end as she saw that Jemima wasn't exactly sobbing with gratitude, but was directing an unhappy tight-lipped gaze downward. "I'm not hurt, Mum. I wasn't kidnapped."

The president of the United Republic shot looks of hatred all around. "Which one kidnapped you? I'll make sure they—"

"I WASN'T kidnapped, Mum!" Jemima finally looked her in the eye. "Dan got a new ship, and we decided to go exploring in it. It was my idea."

"Your . . ." She made several confused pseudo-words as she attempted to update the internal image she had of her daughter. "Why didn't you tell me where you were?"

Jemima's voice shook, growing in volume and confidence. "I didn't think you'd care that much!" She gestured vaguely at me and everyone else currently making out with floor tiles. "And I didn't think you'd, you know, completely flip out! At the people who saved me!"

"Saved you?"

I only realized that the little switch in my head had flipped on after I heard words coming out of my own mouth. "Yeah! You're lucky we found them when we did, ma'am. They flew straight into unpacified territory."

The president detached her hands from Jemima's shoulders, presumably because she would need them to get a proper grip on events. She made a meaningful jerk of the wrist, and my new soldier friend pulled me to my feet, his rifle's laser sight maintaining a lurid red pimple on my forehead.

"You are?" asked the president.

"Captain . . ." My eyes flicked to the side for less than a nanosecond. "Handsome. Of the Star Pilot Volunteer Peacekeeping Corps." I saluted, trying my best to not let it look sarcastic, like my salutes usually do.

"I've . . . never heard of such an organization," said the president. She seemed a lot less confident than she had been when she walked in: she was fidgeting with her elbows and her gaze was darting all over the place. I guessed that she was taking in the shiny new surroundings and drawing some conclusion along the lines of "this doesn't look much like a pirate ship."

"We're very new," I explained. Two seconds old, to be precise, I thought to myself. "Please accept my apologies for not rescuing your daughter sooner. There's a lot of space to patrol out here, and we don't have much funding."

The president scrutinized me through narrowed eyelids. "How, exactly, are you funded?"

Robert Blaze made an embarrassed little laugh into the piece of flooring against which his face was being held. "With difficulty."

The president took a few dazed steps backward. "Daniel's father told me that he and Jemima had been kidnapped by space pirates."

"Well, I don't know what to tell you," I said, scratching my head. "This guy who told you that, would you consider him trustworthy? Or has he ever done anything that might make you think he's a bit dishonest? Or a bit manipulative?"

Her face froze with the kind of embarrassment known mainly to people being informed moments after launching an elaborate surprise party that they got the recipient's birthdate wrong, but with the added spicy undercurrent of diplomatic faux pas. The pinkness to her features became vibrant enough to be detected even through her orange tan. She made that hand gesture again, several times, like an irritated conductor. "Let them up. Let them all up. And stand down."

The baffled soldiers followed her orders. Warden was the first back on her feet, straightening her clothing and brushing a couple of hairs back in place. Blaze stood slowly, making sure to keep up his winning, inoffensive smile throughout. With their guns lowered, the soldiers transformed immediately from an elite platoon securing a hostile area to a congregation of extremely embarrassed, overdressed men.

"Jemima, we're leaving," said the president, in a manner of speech that involved moving the mouth as little as possible, as she moved back toward the open gate.

Jemima stepped forward automatically, head bowed and hands gathered before her, as soon as the words registered. But then her conscious mind got in on the action, and her pace slowed and stopped. She met my gaze, then turned back to her mother. "Aren't you going to apologize?"

A weighty silence fell. The president seemed to have completely frozen stiff but for her eyes, whose gaze darted madly around the room, resting briefly on every face that stared at her expectantly. This, I realized, was a woman who had spent far too long in politics. I could almost hear the whirring of the gears in her head as she analyzed the possible outcomes. If she didn't apologize, she risked offending some kind of foreign authority. But an apology from the president herself would be considered an official one, and that raised all kinds of issues. Would it be politically unsavvy to make such a statement without the blessing of her advisers or cabinet? Would it be considered an endorsement of this group that could still be pirates, albeit well-scrubbed ones? Would other groups be offended that we had received an apology? Would the pundits accuse her of being improperly dressed for contrition?

Let's face it, she was only here in person in the name of some vote-winning show of personal strength and determination, I could tell. There were probably quite a few people back home who had already been sold the story that she was riding in, saber held high, to rescue her daughter from the oily clutches of subhuman off-worlders. Forget apologies, those people were going to froth at the mouth if she didn't come home with a necklace of testicles.

Jemima untensed with a sigh, then addressed Robert Blaze. "We're really sorry about, you know, all the soldier stuff."

Blaze said nothing, but he gave her an extra-special smile and nod that would have melted the heart of any woman of age like butter under napalm. Then Jemima turned to me again, and the next thing I knew, she was hugging me.

And this hug had a lot more warmth and friendship on her part than the one she had shared with her mother moments earlier. I met the president's gaze over Jemima's pink head and gave an apologetic grimace.

She broke off, not looking me in the eye, then saw Warden. There was a moment's hesitation, which Warden ended by extending a hand to shake. Jemima took it chastely. Warden had been the one to initiate the kidnapping, after all. I supposed it took saving her life from slime monsters to graduate from handshake to hug.

Jemima stepped past her still-unmoving mother, through the Quantunnel gate, and into the hangar beyond. The soldiers seemed to take this as their cue to leave, too, and the rifles came up again. They slowly backpedaled toward the gate, shouting for us to not move throughout, all in accordance with some no-doubt vitally important code of conduct. After they had formed a rectangle directly in front of the president, they swept her through the Quantunnel gate like a broom. I saw Jemima give one last wave before the shutters came down.

A minute of awkward silence passed before Blaze ordered the shutters reopened, and a sigh of relief was collectively released when there was nothing beyond but the far wall that was supposed to be there. This established, he rubbed his hands together happily and turned back to us. "Well, I think that wraps up our temporary crisis," he said, "unless there's anything I'm forgetting about?"

"Are you Jacques McKeown?" I asked.

The assembled star pilots that hadn't none-too-subtly legged it upon the appearance of the soldiers had mostly already drifted back to inspecting the station, it taking quite a lot to seriously rattle veteran star pilots, so it was near enough just Blaze and Warden left to hear my question. Blaze's neck and arms immediately went limp as if his puppet strings had been cut.

"Look, I'm really, really, really tired and my everything hurts and we just more or less saved your arse," I said, limping closer. "So I'd be grateful if you answered the plying question before I pass out."

He gave me a sorrowful half smile and touched me gingerly on the shoulder. "Come with me. Let's talk." Warden made the slightest movement to follow us, but I stopped her with a look that made it very clear how little trac I was going to put up with at this point. She hung back, conceding this particular wordless argument.

He led me to an isolated spot just behind one of the arms of the Quantunnel archway, then began to pace in a small, slow circle around me, thinking. I watched him with a varied mixture of feelings. The constant warm thrill I had from being around my idol clashed with my newer sense of betrayal, and they were joined by a quieter little nagging thought that I had just accompanied him alone to an ideal spot for concealed throat slitting.

"I'm not Jacques McKeown," he said eventually. "But."

He seemed to dry up there for a while, so I gave him the prompt. "But you know who he is."

He winced and wobbled a splayed hand noncommittally. "Ninety-nine-percent certain. And before you ask, I'm not going to tell you."

"Why not?"

"Because I don't hate Jacques McKeown. He and I have more or less the same goal." He looked up, as if he could see through the concourse ceiling to the stars beyond. "We want to keep the memory of star piloting alive."

"But the memories are wrong," I protested. "They're not real. And those kids bought into the myth and almost got themselves eaten by Zoobs."

Blaze clasped his hook with his good hand, face darkening. "Yes, all right. You've made your point. There's still a lot of work to be done. But there won't always be Zoobs. Or pirates."

"And what happens after they're all gone?"

He gave me an odd look. "Do you know what I realized when I left the Solar System? After Quantunneling put us all out of work, and I had to see all our peers debasing themselves in Ritsuko City Spaceport? I realized that the job of a hero is not to save the galaxy, or rescue princesses, or slay all the dragons. That may be part of it, but in the end, a hero only has one job, and that's to make himself unnecessary."

I looked at the floor. "If you say so."

"Quantunneling took that away from us. But out here, we make ourselves unnecessary on our own terms. That's how I see it."

I coughed. "Can I be honest?"

"Of course."

"I still think you might be Jacques McKeown."

He did the cut-puppet-strings gesture again. "Look, what can I possibly do to convince you?"

"You could give all of Jacques McKeown's money back," I said, expressionless. "Since you want me to believe that you have absolutely no claim to it."

For the first time in our personal acquaintance, I saw Robert Blaze show anger. A momentary twist of the corners of the mouth that he adeptly suppressed by pinching his eyes and taking a deep breath. "No. I am not entitled to the money. And neither are you. But the money is in my hands, and I have an important purpose in mind. So if you want it, you are going to have to fight me for it."

"I don't want to fight you for it. I want you to give it to me willingly after I tell you what I'm going to do with it."

He frowned. "What are you going to do with it?"

I told him.

Only one loose end remained, and a few minutes later, Warden and I were leading him back to the docking bay. Daniel was conscious enough to be walking by himself as long as we pulled him by the arm, but he still hadn't said anything, and his petrified gaze continued to be fixed on some invisible tormentor hanging permanently in front of his eyes.

"You want to do this right now?" I said.

"As long as Daniel is onboard, Mr. Henderson remains a threat to the station," said Warden. "And I cannot fly a shuttle by myself."

"Right, right. Just thought I might be entitled to at least a nanosecond of rest first, but there's me getting ideas above my station. Where are we taking him?"

"One of the outlying Solar System outposts. I can tip off one of my more reasonable contacts with the Henderson organization to pick him up."

"Are there reasonable people in Henderson's organization? 'Cos so far I've met him, and you, and from that sample it's not looking good."

She was glancing around distractedly, not paying attention. "What?"

"Never mind. Speaking of contacts, do you think you could get me a new

ID chip?" I waved my still-bandaged hand. "Nothing fancy. Just something that lets me use a bank account and park at Ritsuko spaceport."

Her eyes focused on the bloodstain in the center of the bandage, now long dried brown, and one eyebrow came up. "And this is something you feel that I owe you, is it?"

"Look, you're gonna have a go at working with Blaze, right? This is for a plan me and Blaze have for the McKeown money. Stop turning it into some psycho-div power play."

We entered the docking bay. It was still empty of people but crowded with badly parked ships, so making our way through the overlapping nacelles, wings, and landing gear to the shuttle was like exploring a haunted forest. "Fine," said Warden. "And will you be wanting one of your old names for it, or do you think it's time for another fresh start?"

Daniel's head banged musically on a low-hanging engine flap, since we were dragging him along without paying much attention, and Warden started at the noise, dropping into an alert crouch. Her hand slipped inside her suit jacket for a moment to grab the hilt of my blaster, which she was showing no sign of wanting to give back. "Keep it down!"

"Look, is there something on your mind?" I asked, carefully moving an unreactive Daniel's head around the obstacle.

Warden glared and very, very slowly rose from her combat position. "It occurred to me that there are very few explanations for how the United Republic knew that Salvation Station had a completed Quantunnel gate," she said, still looking around for threats.

We had reached the shuttle by this point, and she took up position by the airlock door as I fumbled with the lock. "What are you getting at?" I said.

"That Henderson may already have agents on or around the station."

I froze in the act of turning the handle. I took a few paranoid glances of my own around the docking bay, then spoke in a much quieter voice. "And you didn't think this was worth mentioning until now?"

"To be frank, McKeown, I thought it might have been you."

I pinched my eyes in exasperation, just as Blaze had done earlier, and took a deep breath. "Of course you did."

When I opened my eyes, Warden appeared to have grown two additional arms. Then I blinked, and realized that there was actually someone standing behind her. It was a man dressed in the uniform of the Interplanetary Security Service, and he had one hand on her forehead, pulling her head back. His other hand was holding a box cutter to her exposed neck.

I'd only just finished registering all of that when I heard the faintest of noises behind me, and a callused palm slapped against my own forehead, almost as a gesture of admonishment. A box cutter blade touched my Adam's apple as I was forced to take an interest in the ceiling.

"So what do you make of this?" I said, with difficulty.

"It invites deeper consideration," replied Warden.

CHAPTER 28

WITH SOME FIRM prodding in the small of the back, my captor made me walk. I let him steer me as I focused all my concentration on moving forward just slowly enough to not open my throat on his blade. With every step, a cold point pecked lightly at my jugular vein like an indecisive woodpecker. Out of the corner of my eye, I saw Warden being moved alongside me, and behind us, a third ISS officer was leading Daniel along.

As the mind seeks distractions in these moments, I wondered why they were using box cutters, rather than their standard-issue ISS blasters. Then I remembered that the ISS bureaucracy was strictly diligent about keeping track of issued ammunition and how it was used. The measures had been a response to the internal corruption that had arisen since the rise of Quan-tunneling, evidenced clearly enough by the fact that officers were doing side jobs for Henderson.

We turned a corner, and before us, squatting at the end of a tunnel of parked ships, the ISS ship lay in wait. The very same one that Henderson had commandeered to "rescue" us from Angelo, way back before our first trebuchet jump into the Black.

As we approached, the docking ramp began to lower, with what must have been deliberate slowness. Inch by inch, Henderson was revealed, partially silhouetted against the red warning light of the airlock.

He looked awful. His well-brushed hair was bedraggled, and from the darkening around his empty eyes, I doubted he had slept at all since we'd seen him last. His mouth smiled joylessly. He had discarded the reindeer sweater for a melancholy blue one with a single frowning snowman.

"I do hope we had a good vacation, boys and girls," he said, voice quivering a little as he descended the fully extended docking ramp with his hands behind his back. "Daniel. Over here."

I wasn't sure if it was a greeting to his son or an instruction to the officer holding him, but either way, the pair moved past us and took up position at Henderson's side. He gave his son's hair a tousle, holding his hand there a little longer than necessary, maintaining eye contact with Warden throughout. Assured that his son was safe, relief flowed through Henderson's body, untensing muscles as it went, although his face didn't change.

"You know," he said slowly, after a nice, long stare. "I respect a certain amount of independent spirit. I seem to attract a lot of yes men to my circle of subordinates. It makes it very hard to have a decent conversation. So, understand that I cherish these moments. And also understand that I'm really looking forward to seeing what kind of pressure I can get your blood spraying at."

I was trembling. The point of the box cutter tickled my throat as I did so. I couldn't see much of Warden with my head held in place, but I could tell that her lips were pressed defiantly closed.

Henderson chuckled hollowly at her expression. He took a step forward and put a hand to his chin, one finger tapping his cheek in mock contemplation. "But then again, that would be over so quickly, wouldn't it? I feel like really making a project out of this, you know? Seeing how much of you I could turn into a model train set while keeping you alive, that kind of thing. What do you think, Danny?"

When Daniel didn't immediately yell at him for being embarrassing, or indeed make any response at all, Henderson frowned, and looked him over properly for the first time since he'd arrived. His mood darkened again. "Warden, if you've hurt him in any way, I swear . . ."

He left it hanging, and she said nothing. Henderson knelt beside his son, placing his hands on his shoulders to shake them. His concern turned quickly to fear. "Danny? Dan? Speak to me! It's Dad!"

"D-ad?" said Daniel, his eyes focusing as Henderson held his face in both hands and pushed his cheeks forward.

"Danny! What happened?"

Daniel frowned, apparently confused by the question. Then his eyes grew wide and urgent and he spoke, his voice growing in volume along the way. "I had the BEST TIME!"

Henderson leaned back, stunned, as if Daniel had responded with a head butt he'd narrowly dodged. "What?"

"I went into space and we got attacked and we got kidnapped by pirates and then I stayed on their station and they fixed my ship and taught me how to fly it and then we got abducted by aliens and they tried to eat me but Jacques McKeown came and rescued me and . . ." He stopped to suck in a fresh lungful of air. "And it was the best holiday ever, Dad! Thanks!"

Henderson had been gradually leaning backward throughout the speech, and by the end of it he was sitting on the floor, staring open mouthed. Then he seemed to notice me watching him and quickly got to his feet, flustered. "Well. Uh. Didn't I tell you to trust your old dad? Get on the ship, now, time to go home."

"Sure, Dad," said Daniel, obeying without complaint.

Henderson watched him pick his way up the docking ramp, then pointed at each of his henchmen in turn. "You three. Go settle him into his cabin. Leave us."

"Sir?" asked the one holding me.

Henderson's expression froze, and then his cheerful persona returned in an instant. "Oh! I'm so sorry; I forgot you boys are new to working with me. Well, just for future reference, questioning my orders usually results in those orders getting carved into your scalp. Okay? So let's try that again. Leave us."

The box cutter blade came away from my throat rather hastily, leaving a light scratch, and the three ISS officers hurried for their ship. Henderson continued staring at them until they'd gone up the ramp, passed through an interior door, and vanished from sight, giving us one last fearful glance. They probably suspected that Henderson was about to do something so horrible to us that he needed maximum plausible deniability.

He kept his back to us for some time, tapping his foot. "That," he said, not turning around, "has left me kinda thrown. Sixteen years, nothing but yelling and 'I want this' and 'I want that' and 'you're so embarrassing.' I've never heard him say thanks. Not once. I never even realized that till now."

He fell back into silence for so long that I wondered if he was expecting one of us to reply, but then he shook himself and let his arms drop to his sides. "Oh well!"

Then he was on me. He spun around before I could blink and grabbed my shoulder in a vise-like grip. Then his other hand thrust forward, cassowary talon exposed.

My head reflexively shot back, but the claw stopped an inch in front of where my eye had been. Henderson's face was close enough that I could almost feel radiation coming off his orange skin, and his smile was pulled tight.

"Hm. No," he said. "Not you. Can't do that to him, not now. You get to live." He patted me companionably on the shoulder with his gripping hand, then spun off me and toward Warden.

Again, he grabbed her around the shoulder, and again, his talon stopped moments before it hit. Warden didn't recoil.

Henderson wasn't even looking at her. His smile was quivering oddly, like he was about to burst out laughing, but there was moisture in his eyes.

"Gah!" he exclaimed as he let her go, tottering back and grinning sheepishly. "Can't do it. Not feeling it anymore. I'm just too chuffed. Normally I'd cut out your finger bones and shove them up your noses until they hit brain just out of principle, but . . . Oh, I'm going to regret this by morning, I just know." His face unexpectedly went completely serious, and he gave us both a death glare. "If I ever see either of you again I'm going to start blowing your limbs off before a single word is uttered, but as of now, I'm gonna leave and let live. Say thank you, Mr. Henderson."

"Thank you, Mr. Henderson," I said. Warden remained silent.

The death glare immediately went away again. He clapped his hands—having retracted the talon—and rubbed them together, grinning happily at Warden's stony face. "Well then, I think I'll leave you big, bad pirates to pick fleas off each other or whatever else you do in this cesspit. I have to find a bathroom with a functioning bidet."

"Mr. Henderson?" said Warden as he reached the base of the ramp, finally breaking her silence.

He stopped and half turned, grin on full display. Then she blew his leg off.

She'd quietly drawn my pistol while his back was turned, and now fired all the remaining charge in one blast, deliberately aiming at the floor by Henderson's foot. It wasn't Solve All Immediate Problems level, but it was enough to warp the floor tiles and detach his right leg just below the knee.

The rest of him fell back against the docking ramp, his mouth wide open as his eyes boggled at the smoke rising from his new stump. Then the pain hit, and his silent scream transitioned into a very, very noisy one.

Henderson's leg, meanwhile, had landed just in front of us. Warden took two smart steps forward and picked it up by the ankle, keeping the gun trained on Henderson. "If I ever see you, or any of your agents, on this station or anywhere in the Black," she said, in a tone of voice like she was merely laying out conditions for a business deal, "then I, too, will start blowing off limbs. Or rather, resume."

"YOU'RE DEAD!" shrieked Henderson, clutching his knee. "YOU'RE DEAD YOU'RE DEAD YOU'RE DEAD!" The phrase appeared to be his equivalent of *ow*.

Warden hefted Henderson's leg like a stick grenade and threw it over his head, into the red-lit gloom of the ship's docking bay. He tried to follow it with his gaze, stunned. "I would move quickly, if I were you," she said. "This station lacks the facilities for limb reattachment, and you may still have time."

"YOU'RE DEAD!" Henderson shuffled his way up the ramp through a combination of hand plants, butt shuffles, and kicks of the remaining leg. Once he had established a rhythm, he screamed in time with it. "YOU'RE—DEAD—YOU'RE DEAD YOU'RE—DEAD!"

Warden jerked the gun once Henderson was in the cargo bay, and he started fearfully. He couldn't reach the ramp controls from the floor, so he picked up his disembodied leg and slapped at the Close button with it. Warden kept the sights on him right up until the ramp clunked into place and he disappeared from sight.

Moments later—exactly the amount of time it would take to yell an order down a corridor—the ISS ship's takeoff jets activated, and it gingerly extracted itself from the nest of badly-parked vessels. Then the horizontal thrusters kicked in with a burst like the yelping of a kicked dog, and it sped through the force field into space.

Warden relaxed. She let all the air out of her lungs in one long blast that seemed to go on for minutes, and when she was finished, she looked like she had lost a couple of inches of height. She offered me my gun, hilt first. "I think we are finally free of Henderson's influence."

Her little smile disappeared when she saw the look on my face. "Do you know what?" I said, carefully taking the gun with the tips of my thumb and forefinger as if I were picking it out of a patch of stinging nettles. "I don't agree."

CHAPTER 29

"**RITSUKO CITY SPACEPORT** welcomes visitors to Luna, the cradle of human spacegoing," droned the loudspeaker. "All visitors are reminded that they are under no obligation to charter unemployed star pilots."

The words were surprisingly clear, and becoming more so every day. The lines of star pilots at either side of the concourse had thinned out to the point that their combined voices could no longer match the loudspeaker's maximum volume. There was even enough room for everyone to have something to sit on, other than each other.

Most of the star pilots who were still here were getting old. They were stubborn, more set in their ways, or perhaps just resigned to having done all they needed to do in the universe. Most of the younger ones had gone to Salvation.

The pilot I was specifically keeping an eye on was an aging man with a goatee that had probably looked much cooler before his hair had receded to the top of his crown. He wore a weather-beaten flight jacket adorned with a large patch on the back depicting a red cylinder with a sparking fuse. Richard Deneuve, a.k.a. Dick Dynamite. He'd named himself unironically, as far as I knew; the Golden Age had been a more innocent time.

I cringed a little at his choice of location—right next to the potted plant, where he couldn't be seen from the gate—but not all of us had adjusted well to the new age. Dick certainly looked undernourished, but I was more concerned about whether or not the kid I'd temporarily employed was actually going to complete the task.

To my relief, I saw him then, moving across the concourse at right angles to the rest of the crowd. He was one of the Jacques McKeown fanboys that hung around the bookstore, so the hope that illuminated Dick's eyes when he saw someone approaching died the moment he took in the distressed flight jacket and self-conscious swagger.

But that disappointment shifted quickly to confusion as the kid held out a thick padded envelope. I couldn't hear their conversation, but presumably the kid's words were something along the lines of "Some guy told me to give this to you."

Dick asked the kid something—probably something like "Are you sure you have the right man?"—and the kid pointed to the envelope, which was very clearly printed with the words "Richard 'Dick Dynamite' Deneuve, Star Pilot." Then Dick asked who this was from, and if the kid could follow instructions properly, he'd reply, "Some guy. I didn't see his face."

Finally, Dick opened the envelope, and as he perused the contents, the kid melted back into the crowd, in full accordance with my instructions. I breathed a sigh of relief. This was the first time I'd used this method. Last time I'd left the envelope on the recipient's docking steps, and the time before that, snuck it into a load of freshly tumble-dried laundry at Frobisher's. I didn't want to start getting predictable.

Dick pulled out the topmost item in the envelope and stared at it, baffled. It was a copy of *Jacques McKeown and the Judgment of Juvon*.

Juvon was a planet on the direct opposite end of the Black to Cantrabargid, divided between two distinct cultures. The more bellicose one was constantly attempting to subjugate the other, and ground was being gained and lost on a daily basis. The conquest had come closest to succeeding in the last major war, but the aggressors had been foiled at the last moment by the intervention of a star pilot.

Dick was very familiar with the place, because he had been the star pilot in question, and his story had been ineptly fictionalized in the book that he now held. I could only imagine what he thought the intended message was, until he saw what else was in the envelope. His hands clenched tightly, scrunching the envelope closed, and he bit his lip so hard I thought he might draw blood.

Judgment of Juvon had been of middling popularity for a McKeown book, meaning that most publishers would have considered it a success worthy of immediate and lengthy retirement to their own personal cocaine farm. It had earned McKeown himself about eight hundred thousand euroyen, determined from the book sales figures on record, his contractual profit share, and one or two educated guesses. But the book itself was only there in the envelope to explain the rest of the contents.

Eight hundred thousand euroyen. In tightly bound stacks of untraceable cash.

Dick held his prize close to his chest, looking left and right to see if anyone else had seen. That was a fairly typical reaction. As was his next: he speed walked away, forgetting to take his cardboard sign with him.

"And what do you think he's going to do with that?"

I'd been watching Dick so intently that I hadn't noticed Warden arrive and sit opposite me. She was wearing a new suit, something with a slightly more daring dull-brown color scheme to reflect her new position as corporate adviser to the frontiers. I leaned back, sighed, and took a long sip on my coffee before I replied. "I don't know. Never work again?"

Warden leaned back as well, checking her nails for a moment, determined not to look less relaxed. "Or drink it away," she said. "Or get cheated out of it."

I rolled my eyes. "Or blow it on pimping out his ship. Or throw it straight in the bin. Lofty Doc did that; he was always one for the prideful gesture. I don't care what they do with it. The point is, the choice is in their hands."

"And more than one of them made the 'choice' to donate it all back to Salvation Station. It might have been quicker and more efficient just to leave it all with Blaze."

I wrinkled my nose. "What are you doing here, anyway? Ritsuko City is Henderson's turf. He's been building his power base since the moment he got back."

"I only just Quantunneled in and I'll be Quantunneled out by the time he hears about it." The corner of Warden's mouth curled up very slightly in her usual poor imitation of a smile. "Besides, he has shown me too many of his weaknesses. And we have eyes and ears wherever there are star pilots."

I exhaled angrily, through bared teeth. "I thought you were Henderson's victim. Not one of his protégés. I didn't help you get away from him so you could turn Salvation into some kind of rival crime family."

"Blaze is the one in charge, McKeown."

I showed her my scarred hand, where she'd implanted the bootleg ID chip. "It's Dashford Pierce now, remember? And Blaze is an old man. In a dangerous part of the galaxy. Don't think I haven't realized that you realize that."

Bit by bit, her expression changed. Just a millimeter's movement here and there to turn her smugness down half a notch and put a few emotional walls back up. "I take it there's no point in offering you a position again, then."

"Is that why you're here?"

She stared out at the concourse to where Dick Dynamite had stood. "Blaze asked me. Well, officially, he believes in your project and just wants to know how it's going and if you need anything. But I can tell what he really wants. We have also been contacted by the United Republic, wanting to set up a meeting to discuss what they can do to help 'the effort,' but they specifically want to talk to one Captain Handsome."

I gave a little smirk, which I unsuccessfully tried to remove before she saw it.

"You know, if you do have concerns about my intentions for Salvation Station," said Warden, meeting my gaze again, "your best course of action would be to join, and keep me under supervision."

I returned the look with tired, half-lidded eyes. "Cross the Black? Help create a place for star pilots in the universe? Hunt Zoobs and battle pirates?"

"It's a little Golden Age all over again. Isn't that what you wanted?"

I deflated in my seat. "I thought it was. When Quantunneling started, seemed like all I could think about was wanting things to go back to how they used to be. And back there, for a little while, it was. Just for a moment. And then a monster nearly bit my head off."

She raised an eyebrow. "Surely you don't expect me to believe that you're traumatized now."

"No," I said automatically. "But it brought back a few things. I came pretty close to getting my head bitten off a few times back in the war on Cantrabargid, too. And a hundred other places. What Blaze was trying with the new Cantrabargid, that might be fake, but no one's getting their head bitten off, either."

She nodded. "You've outgrown it."

"Maybe. Maybe there never was a Golden Age. Maybe some glorious delusion of one is the best we can hope for. Do you see what I mean?"

"Frankly, all I see is a thug who may finally have realized what he was all along."

I coughed. "Thug?"

"Maybe a little more than that," she said, glancing away in thought. "A mercenary. A thief. A con man, at best. But if it helps, being a thug is an improvement over being a delusional thug."

I glared at her over my new sunglasses. "If you're still trying to talk me into something, you're going the wrong way about it."

She sniffed. "So what will you do now?"

I produced my new datapad and called up the document that was on near-permanent display. I drew a little tick next to Dick Dynamite's name with my finger. "Keep going down the list. Keep sharing out the money."

"And then what?"

"I don't plan ahead, remember?" I glanced at the spaceport's Quantunnel gate as it opened again, disgorging a new horde of tourists that sent the star pilots into a fresh frenzy. "It's like Blaze said. A hero's only job is to make himself unnecessary."

She thought about that for a good five seconds. "An unnecessary man is also a man that nobody will miss."

I half smiled with incredulity. "Was that a threat? Are you serious?"

"No. I am merely pointing out that a threat exists."

"Henderson?"

She rolled her eyes and clasped her hands together in front of her, then spoke with a slow, condescending tone. "The money. That you are giving away. Belongs to someone."

"McKeown," I identified. "Funny, I came pretty close to forgetting that I'm not actually him. Why would he be a threat? He's never revealed himself before, not even to collect his plying pay. Why should he now?"

"Perhaps because he is believed to have died in the destruction of the *Jemima*."

"So why would he want to let anyone think otherwise? Everyone knows star pilots would crucify him."

That merest hint of a smile again. She'd definitely cranked the smugness back up. "You may be surprised. The beneficiaries of your campaign—I've heard a couple of them talking at Salvation. They have assumed that they have McKeown to thank for the gifts. They think it may be someone executing his will."

I felt pangs of disappointment. "I can see . . . why they would think that," I realized painfully.

"So if we are assuming that his reclusiveness was due to fear of reprisal from star pilots, you may be making it easier and easier for him to take action. As you mend his reputation in their eyes."

I considered the thought for a moment, biting my thumbnail, until a new thought sent it rocketing to the back of my mind. I met her gaze again. "You know who he is?"

"Blaze might have mentioned something."

I kept staring. In that moment, I thought my heart might have stopped. "So?"

"You've met him. McKeown, I mean. At least, I'm fairly certain you have. Any more, I see no reason to reveal."

My hands were at my brow. "Why would you plying tell me something like that and then leave me hanging?!"

She started gathering up her things. "That was merely a courtesy. I am not going to fully share such a valuable piece of intelligence with an *unaffiliated* party." She glanced up briefly to see if I'd caught the emphasis. "Well then, I think there's nothing more to discuss for now. You have my number if you ever change your mind."

I think she must have expected me to call her back, or at least throw out some kind of parting shot, because she slowed dramatically when she was a few steps away, but she didn't turn. I let her amble slowly across the café area until she sped her pace up again to join the outgoing spaceport crowd.

"Div," I called, a split second before she left earshot.

The old docking bay at Ritsuko spaceport was also becoming less and less crowded these days, to the point that the authorities were throwing around the idea of scrapping the booking system, but for the time being, I still had my own bay. I made my way toward it, passing by the ship of one of my beneficiaries. I took a moment to marvel at its new chrome-plated fins and spray artwork, depicting a wizard fighting a gorilla in a bra.

I could understand the thought behind it, to an extent. Since I'd gotten back to her, I'd been showering the *Neverdie* with affection like a cheating spouse trying to make amends. Nothing as flashy—just a new paint job and enough maintenance to put a comfortable distance between it and failing a rigorous safety check. Also, since *Jacques McKeown and the Malmind Menace* had been no slouch, saleswise, I'd treated her to a thorough inside-and-out seeing-to by the Lightspeed Cleaning Service (a Frobisher side venture).

Now, when I entered and saw her on the far side of the bay, she looked like a bride at the end of the church aisle. Not a young, virginal one, but maybe closer to the midthirties, one that had filled out nicely, who could challenge and surprise you in all the interesting ways. She stood proud and patient on her landing legs, as if standing with one hand on hip, her hull shining in the light and bearing its dents without shame.

I thought about Warden's warning as I crossed the docking bay's expansive floor, hands buried in jacket pockets. Maybe she was right. I was mending the reputation of the great betrayer Jacques McKeown in such a way that I remained the only person who still knew that he was a betrayer. Thus ensuring I would have no backup if he did come after me.

He'd have to find me first, and that was the point of the whole "anonymous drops of untraceable cash" thing. But even if he did, what could he do? Have me arrested for stealing his money, perhaps, but that would mean simultaneously revealing himself publicly and tanking his reputation with the pilots again. He could break my kneecaps with a crowbar, but then so could anyone else. I suppose he could always passive-aggressively base a character on me.

The point was, he didn't have any kind of power, because he didn't have any money. I'd taken it all. All that he made from the books, anyway. And that thought made me slow for a moment, because it occurred to me that there was one explanation for that. That he hadn't collected the money because he already had enough . . .

By then, I was at my ship's airlock, ready to get some shut-eye before making a plan for the next name on my list. But as I lowered the docking steps, a voice called out from nearby. It made me freeze, because it was calling out a name that I didn't go by anymore.

Two individuals stepped out from behind the cargo loader parked near my ship. On the left was someone I recognized from the spaceport's internal security staff, with whom I had a passing acquaintance. His mouth was tight and serious, although his eyes were apologetic. On the right was an older man in a shirt and tie, who seemed to have one eyebrow permanently raised in disbelief. He was wearing a shoulder holster with a gun, which the security officer didn't seem to have a problem with.

"Are you the registered owner of this vessel?" asked the second man.

My gaze flicked from one man to the other as I digested that. The gun and the official language pointed to him being a policeman. Or someone very convincingly disguised as a policeman trying to get close enough to knife me in the gut. "Yes?" I said, deciding there was no immediate danger in that, at least.

The cop produced an official document and a pair of handcuffs. "I have a warrant for your arrest."

"For what?" I attempted to sound incredulous.

"Contempt of court."

I leaned forward and inspected the text of the document without stepping any closer, but I'd already recalled the jabbering voices of that little doint Ronald and his horrible parents. That felt like years ago. I had a confusing sensation that came from wanting to cry with despair and laugh out loud at the same time.

He frowned, apparently picking up on my internal turmoil. "Are you the person named on this warrant or aren't you?"

I could already feel words assembling in my throat. Oh, that name? No, as you'll see from my chip ID, I am Mr. Dashford Pierce, man about town. The registered owner of this ship, you say? Well, I only bought it a week ago. I did think the guy seemed a bit eager to get rid of it. But at the time I was distracted by how uncannily he resembled me . . .

Maybe I could buy time. Just enough to pack up, get out, and get the *Neverdie* set up with a new paint job and registration number. Maybe a sex change and one of those cosmetic skin-tinting procedures for me. All I had to do was keep moving.

"Sir?" asked the security officer.

I could feel the imaginary finger resting on the imaginary switch in my head, ready to flip it. But as the moment drew on, all the words I'd prepared dried up and drifted away like autumn leaves.

I held out my wrists. "Let's go," I sighed.

All tension immediately left the two officials, and the policeman slapped the cuffs on. "Why'd you miss a court appearance, then?" asked the security guard conversationally. "Did you just forget?"

"No," I said, pulling my hands apart to test the strength of the chain. "But I stopped remembering."

I was escorted from the docking bay, walking ahead of the policeman, and the universe continued to turn.

ABOUT THE AUTHOR

Ben "Yahtzee" Croshaw is the sole creator of Zero Punctuation™, a popular weekly game review on the Webby Award–winning *Escapist* online magazine, for which he also earned the 2009 IT Journalism Award for Best Gaming Journalist. He was born and raised in the UK, emigrated to Australia, and then emigrated again to California. In his spare time he designs video games and emigrates.